The Last Sunset

The Last Sunset

Bob Atkinson

Greyhart Press

www.greyhartpress.com

The Last Sunset

Published by Greyhart Press
ISBN-13: 978-1478162155

Also available in
Kindle and ePUB eBook editions.

Beta Reader Team

The author and publisher wish to thank our beta reader team for *The Last Sunset*. We had invaluable comments and suggestions from:

Beth Barany

Angela Cottrell

Edwin D Ferretti III

Kellie Fry

Kristina Gehring

Elliot Halberg

Rosalyn Petroff

Thomas Rydder

Sasha Summers

Nicole Theobald

Thank you, all!

If you're interested in joining our beta reader teams, drop us a line at editors@greyhartpress.com or tweet @GreyhartPress

Prologue
Glen Laragain, Scotland — 1916

The old man gaped blankly around him. Only a moment ago he'd been in the mist of Glen Laragain with his son, searching for a lost ewe. Now, it was as if he'd stepped off the edge of the world. In an instant the mist had vanished to reveal a sky that was a tapestry of fire. Above the western horizon an angry halo curled around a blood-red sun. He'd seen halos before, but they were delicate, nebulous things, gently warning of Atlantic rain. This was different. Here was a warning of something infinitely more sinister.

Desperately he tried to make sense of what was happening. He had seen other visions in Glen Laragain. Images from the day long ago when the soldiers had brought death and destruction to the glen, as though those terrible events had taken root in the very land itself.

But this was no image from the past. A deep sense of foreboding told him this was a precursor to some terrifying event that was yet to occur.

His chest was becoming tighter and tighter now. It was so warm, so difficult to breathe... as if this hellish sky truly was—

A blinding flash lit up the sky above *Meall Banabhie*, to the south. Before he could take in this latest horror, a mountainous cauldron of fire began to climb into the heavens before his eyes, the gates of hell bursting open. The old man watched as the boiling inferno climbed higher and higher into the waiting sky. He was incapable of logical thought now. He was aware of nothing but the pounding terror in his chest.

As he watched, an arm of fire detached itself from the cauldron and began to curl towards the Glen Laragain pass.

He felt his chest explode moments before the fires engulfed him.

Chapter One

Glen Laragain — 1916

After two days of incessant rain, the skies were at last beginning to clear from the west. Glen Laragain slowly re-emerged in the watery light, like a newborn land rising from the sea.

The two brothers had trekked barely half a mile into the aquatic landscape, but their rough tweed clothing was already soaked through. Their khaki haversacks were also drenched. Only the hunting rifles slung over their shoulders remained impervious to the rain.

"In God's name, Colin, what were the two of you doing up the far end of the glen anyway?" the older man asked sharply.

"It was none of my doing," replied the other, his voice brittle and defensive. "One of the ewes had wandered off. Himself thought she might have strayed up yonder. You know what our father was like when he got an idea in his head."

"Where was it you found him?"

A faint shudder ran through the younger man. "Up near the old graveyard. I was on the far side when the mist came down and I lost sight of him." He looked forlornly towards the upper reaches of the glen, where the April sun had reappeared as a pale orb behind the softening layers of cloud. "It should have been yourself, Alistair, finding him like that. You would be used to it. You would have known what to do."

"It wouldn't have mattered whoever was there," murmured the older man.

Colin ran his fingers through the black mess of his hair. His young, weather beaten face was pale, his eyes red and swollen. "Is that what it's like, Alistair? Do they always look as... och, I don't know... Doctor MacIver said it was a heart attack, but when I saw his face... as if he'd seen something, away on up there..."

Alistair exhaled slowly and made a point of tightening the straps on his rucksack.

Colin went on, the words rushing from him like a river in spate. "He would never allow us up that part of the glen when we were wee laddies he always said the area was cursed he told me he saw things up there terrible things that no man should ever have to see... he said they were like images from the past..." The tumbling words suddenly turned to Gaelic: "*We should build a cairn for him, Alistair Mhor, like they did in the old days.*"

Alistair snorted in tired disapproval. "He always said you would be the last *tcheuchter* in Glen Laragain."

The ghost of a smile flitted across Colin's haunted face. "Do you remember the stories himself used to tell us, about the people who lived here before the massacre?"

Alistair glanced sharply at his brother. "Oh I remember his stories all right. They were always about the Glen Laragain men who went off to fight for their clan, or Scotland, or whatever. He never told us about the ones who stayed at home tending cattle, raising a family. It was as if men's lives only had meaning if they'd been to war." He looked to the west, where bright shafts of sunlight had begun to play on the desolate landscape. "Why are we like that? What is wrong with us?"

The younger man knew the question was rhetorical. "What's it like out there in France? You've been home three days and you've never mentioned it once."

Alistair continued to stare westwards, towards the heights of *Druim Fada*. Something in those rocky wastes was holding his interest, but when Colin followed his gaze, he could only see the bare elements of sky, rock and water.

"In his last letter, himself said you'd gone behind his back and signed up. He wanted me to talk you out of it. He told me Mr. Kitchener would surely understand if one of his sons was allowed to stay at home to run the croft."

Colin shrugged awkwardly. "It's all by the by now, isn't it? The croft can wait until after the war. We can run it together when we get home, like himself had always intended."

"...Aye, when we get home," the older man whispered. It was a while before he spoke again. "It's the sound of birds singing you miss more than anything out there. It's funny the wee things that come to you... you hear them sometimes, skylarks mostly, but it's not the same thing; not like here..."

He took a slow lungful of soft mountain air. To the west the sun had all but disappeared again behind another bank of low cloud. "We'd better get to the head of the glen and put up that cairn," he said quietly.

The best part of an hour had elapsed by the time the brothers had wound their way through the ruins of the eighteenth-century settlement, which stretched throughout the upper reaches of the glen. Long grey walls that had once separated cattle from corn meandered here and there, their patterns meaningless now that the cattle, and the corn, and the hands that laid the stones were gone. At intervals the remains of ancient dwellings appeared, their stark walls laid dry stone upon dry stone, all slowly crumbling under the onslaught of successive winters.

The uppermost ruin was wreathed in low cloud when they reached the western end of the glen. They entered a ghostly landscape, silent but for the gurgling of newborn streams.

Colin seemed unaffected by the hike. He watched his brother lean against the wall of the ruin as he tried to catch his breath.

"One year away from the Highlands, Alistair, and you've turned into a Lowlander."

"Wheesht, man, or there'll be two cairns up here," growled his brother.

Smiling faintly, Colin made his way over to the lone mountain ash that sprung from the ancient graveyard; its branches like skeletal limbs in the mist. Other than a scattering of low mounds, there was little to indicate this patch of ground had ever been a cemetery.

"This is where I found him," Colin said quietly. "The mist came down just as quickly that day too."

Alistair looked around at the grey, alien landscape fashioned by the mist. Without a word he threw off his rifle and haversack and began to gather the rocks that littered the area.

His brother stood for a while, contemplating the graveyard.

"Do you know what himself once told me? He said in the olden days the last person to be buried in a Highland graveyard was believed to guard the souls of everyone there, until the next burial."

Colin laid his weapon and haversack beside those of his brother. "When he told me that, I thought of the last soul that was buried here after the massacre. He said he had considered opening a family plot here instead of Kilmallie, after herself died three years ago. But, och, he couldn't bear the thought of one of our family being left to guard this place for all eternity. He's right, you know. Could you imagine such loneliness?"

As the monument took shape the mist grew more dense and overpowering. Alistair appeared oblivious to the conditions, but Colin looked nervously around him as he worked. More than once the mist seemed to come together, and take form, before dissolving again, like something conceived and then aborted.

Alistair pulled on his haversack as his brother manoeuvred the final stone into position.

"Was it as bad as this the day yourselves were up here?"

"This is much the same as it was that day. There's something about it... I felt it that day too... something unnatural..."

To his surprise Alistair was nodding. "You can see why himself would never let us up here."

Even the splashing of the burns had now ceased. All around them was deep, claustrophobic silence.

"Did you know today is the 21st of April; the anniversary of the massacre?" Colin asked in a nervous whisper.

The look on his brother's face made it obvious he did not. He suddenly shook his head. "Och, this is all nonsense. You're going to turn me into a simple-minded *tcheuchter* like yourself. We've done what we came to do, let's get out of this place before you have me seeing things as well."

Colin continued to glance fearfully around him as they set off down the mist-covered glen, with only the gradual sloping of the ground to show they were headed in the right direction. They'd passed more than a dozen ruins when Alistair suddenly went down on his haunches, silently commanding his brother to do likewise. Colin strained every sense before it came to him: An odour, faint at first, but stronger and more acrid once it was acknowledged by his senses.

"Do you smell it?" hissed Alistair.

"Aye. Something's on fire. Maybe something down the glen."

"Our house is two miles away. The next is three miles beyond that."

"Maybe someone is firing the grass."

Alistair glared at his brother as if he were an imbecile. "It's been raining for two days."

"Someone might be burning rubbish."

The older man snorted in disgust. The smell was now thick and pungent. Alistair would have expected to hear the crackling of flames, or see a fiery glow, but nothing accompanied the smell of smoke.

"Maybe one of those new-fangled aeroplanes has fallen out of the sky," Colin whispered behind him.

Alistair demanded silence with a wave of his hand. Sounds had begun to accompany the smell of burning. At first detached and fragmented, they quickly took the form of voices. Voices that had emerged all around them. Alistair's blood ran cold. His military ear recognised the barking of orders, and the shouts of excited men. He could hear women crying and pleading. But above it all, like a gathering of banshees, could be heard the screams of children.

One look at Colin's face told Alistair he was hearing this too.

At that moment the blanket of mist barely ten yards in front of them was torn apart. Two wraith-like forms materialised as completely as if they'd been raised from the dead. Rooted to the spot, Alistair felt a surge of fear that he was becoming a participant. His shocked mind took in some of the detail of the apparitions. The larger of the two was attempting to subdue the other. Alistair recognised a military uniform, more archaic than his own battle dress. The other figure was a young woman, clothed in a simple dress and tartan shawl. She was fighting with every fibre of her being against her attacker. The vision was colourless, like one of those new cinema films, but even amid the horror of the moment Alistair found himself struck by the wild beauty of the woman.

What would otherwise have been elegant arms and legs swung this way and that, trying to inflict damage on her attacker. Despite her struggles the soldier forced her to the ground. He thrust his frame between her flailing legs, briefly releasing his grip as he unbuckled his trousers. For a few moments she was able to claw frantically at his face, before her arms were again grabbed and pinned to the earth.

His victim now helpless, the soldier was able to savour the moment as he slowly entered her.

Like horrified voyeurs Colin and Alistair watched helplessly as the soldier's rhythmical thrusting grew more and more savage. What had begun as an act of lust had now become one of sheer brutality. The girl's mouth opened in a long, soundless scream.

The soldier was smiling now, triumph and contempt on his face.

At last he rose from her, adjusting his clothes. When he looked up, his gaze fell directly on Colin and Alistair. The two men had stood frozen from start to finish, and they remained transfixed as the soldier's eyes focused on them.

He began to walk towards them.

At that moment a violent wind exploded upon the glen. The thick blanket of mist was instantly blown westwards. As one, Colin and Alistair found their eyes drawn to the east, along the Great Glen, above which a huge ball of fire had appeared.

Neither man was able to digest its meaning before they were hit by a scorching shock wave.

Chapter Two

Glen Laragain — 1976

"This is beyond a joke here, by the way."

The soldier adjusted the collar of his combat jacket, but the rainwater continued to dribble down his neck. The ruined house he and his comrades occupied held little in the way of roof or walls to protect them from the elements.

Two of his fellow soldiers grumbled in support, their uniforms equally useless against the rain.

"Ah, stop whinin'," growled the corporal. "Count yerselves lucky ye're no' down there with those poor sods."

Eighty yards to the south, on the floor of the glen, a platoon of recruits formed a ragged semi-circle around their sergeant; their uniforms spattered with mud, their heads bowed in abject misery. Each man held a 7.62mm self-loading rifle — known universally as the S.L.R. — fitted with a yellow blank-firing attachment.

"I don't give a monkey's how cold and wet you are!" the sergeant bellowed. "If you wanted sunshine you should have joined the Foreign Legion!"

"Where do we sign up?" mumbled the soldier with the leaking uniform.

"Give it a break, Macsorley," growled the corporal.

The sergeant pointed to the assault course, which stretched like a black scar along the glen. "We will keep doing this until every one of you fairies gets it right! There are people in Ireland whose job is to get your horrible faces onto the evening news; and it's my job to make sure you remain the utter non-entities you are at present!"

"What a loada rubbish," grumbled the largest of the group; a well-fed individual whose uniform appeared to have shrunk against his huge frame. "Ah didnae join this man's army tae lie on a wet hillside in the back of nowhere, listening tae rubbish like that."

"Right enough, Rae," said the fourth soldier, "this is a criminal waste of a good psychopath."

The shrill ringing of the radio telephone drowned out Rae's answer. The four occupants sprang to life. Macsorley snatched up his rifle, while Rae and his comrade took up position behind the general purpose machine gun.

The corporal barked into the handset: "Bravo two three receiving. Over."

"Bravo two three, this is bravo one zero," the sergeant's voice boomed from the radiotelephone. "We go again in two minutes … and Corporal Macmillan, I want your pattern a lot tighter this time."

"Tighter, Sarge? We're already at ten feet—"

"You are not at ten feet," the radio snarled, "your shot is three or four feet above that elevation. Now give me a ten-foot pattern or I will have your section running the assault course and you will have me on the G.P.M.G. Do you understand?"

"Yes, Sergeant!" yelled Macmillan.

"What a creep," muttered Macsorley.

"Right!" Macmillan snapped. "Ye heard what Sergeant O'Brien said. Rae and Ferguson, adjust the sights on that jimpy. No more than ten feet above their heads. And get it right. Ah don't want any of these kids getting carried out of this place."

Rae adjusted his massive frame behind the machine gun, and for a few tempting moments allowed the sights to settle on the wrathful figure eighty yards away. To his right Ferguson cradled the ammunition belt, ready to feed the weapon's ravenous appetite. The G.P.M.G., or 'jimpy', could fire ten rounds per second. Today it would be fed a cocktail of one tracer to six ball, designed to add visual terror to its hellish din.

"Ah don't see the sense in all this," complained Ferguson. "They're only getting sent tae Northern Ireland."

"The principle is still the same," said the corporal. "Nothing else prepares ye for that first time ye come under fire."

"Ah was on foot patrol in Belfast," Macsorley put in. "Someone opened up on us with a Thompson. Man, Ah nearly wet maself. Ah thought, 'sod this for a game of soldiers', so Ah keeps ma head down. The noise was unbelievable. The last thing on yer mind was firing back."

"Ye get used tae it," said Rae. "Ye know what tae expect the next time."

"Right, save it," Macmillan snapped. "They're ready tae go again."

O'Brien and his entourage had returned to the starting point of the assault course. By now the rain had stopped, and a flicker of sunshine had appeared in the west. Between the soldiers and the remains of another house further up the glen lay two hundred yards of boulder, hollow and swamp, augmented by several wooden and barbed wire obstacles. O'Brien divided the recruits into three columns. With a last stream of oaths he tossed a thunder-flash into the air ahead of them. The explosion was like that of a hand grenade, but without the deadly shrapnel.

The front three stormed the first obstacle, a rudimentary six-foot wall. Instantly Rae's cocktail of ball and tracer cracked viciously over their heads. More thunder-flashes added to the bedlam as the next three recruits charged after their comrades. Regular bursts of tracer stitched the air, each round creating its own sonic crack as it flew past. Above the uproar raged the voice of the sergeant, snarling like a ravenous wolf, reminding them that of all the terrors they faced, his wrath was the most fearsome of all.

The leading recruits had negotiated the final obstacle, and were charging towards the grey ruin at the end of the course. As they ran they fired their rifles at imaginary targets; their blanks sounding like children's toys against the deafening crackle of the machine gun.

The G.P.M.G. suddenly fell silent.

"What's the problem?" Macmillan shouted.

"Bloody thing's jammed," Rae growled. "Piece of useless—"

"Follow the drill and clear it then!"

"…As much use as a bow and arrow…"

Rae opened the breech and levered out the jammed round. Quickly he checked the range and re-cocked the weapon. Two further bursts cracked over the heads of the tail enders before the machine gun jammed again.

"Aw for God's sake!" Rae yelled. "It must be this ammo."

"It's no' the bloody ammo!" cried Ferguson indignantly. "Ah checked it all maself."

"Whatever it is, get it sorted, pronto!" Macmillan bellowed.

At that moment a howl of outrage erupted from the floor of the glen. One of the recruits had lost his rifle in the quagmire of the assault course.

"Uh oh," murmured the corporal, "someone's in for it now."

The faulty machine gun was forgotten as everyone's attention turned to the hapless soldier. The sergeant was threatening all manner of horrible deaths, his face a mixture of rage and delight. The rest of his comrades backed away.

Macmillan and his group watched with professional detachment as the recruit was hounded back over the assault course, in a slithering search for his weapon. Eventually his plight lost its interest.

"That's not the first time the jimpy's done that tae me," grumbled Rae.

"Did ye clean and oil it properly?"

" 'Course Ah did. But these bitches've got minds of their own. D'ye know, the first time someone opened up on the sanger in Crossmaglen this useless piece of junk gets off two rounds... two rounds, for God's sake... before it jams. By the time we cleared it, yon I.R.A. git was back in Dundalk, drinking Guinness."

Macsorley lovingly caressed the stock of his rifle. "Ye cannae beat the S.L.R. It's a weapon that never lets ye down."

"It's an elephant gun," said Rae. "Fire that thing up the Falls Road and everyone in Ballymurphy has tae duck!"

"Aye, that's what Ah like about it," grinned Macsorley.

Macmillan cast an appraising eye over his little command. Rae and Ferguson, he decided, were a double act. In addition to teaming up on the G.P.M.G. they probably socialised together as well. Ferguson was fair haired and lanky, while Rae was built like an overweight boxer, and was obviously the dominant character of the two.

Macsorley was clearly out with this social circle, and probably preferred it that way. Macmillan guessed he was something of a loner; average height, average build, distinguished only by his crop of red hair. Macmillan had known so many like him; joining a peacetime army to escape a miserable home life, and never quite fitting in, somehow. They'd always been something of an enigma to him; these unhappy peacetime soldiers. Propelled into any conflict, they were usually as dependable and as courageous as any warrior born and bred.

How many tours have ye done in Northern Ireland?" the corporal asked, of no one in particular.

"The three of us were taken off our third tour for this lark," said Rae.

"What about you, Corp?" Ferguson asked.

"Ah joined up in sixty-seven, so Ah've been in the army nearly nine years." Macmillan took off his beret and scratched his head; his dark brown hair short and neatly trimmed, as per Queen's Regulations. He was tall and athletic, his face a curious mix of youth and world-weariness, as though his young features were already beginning to melt into middle age.

"Ah've done four tours in Ireland: After the last one Ah decided there was more tae life than getting shot at by a bunch of Micks, so Ah transferred tae the training centre."

Below them the mud-covered recruit had retrieved his rifle from the assault course. Already the sergeant's bellowing had dropped by a few decibels.

"What about Bilko?" Rae wanted to know.

Macmillan scowled. "Sergeant O'Brien's a career instructor. Been at the centre for as long as anyone can remember."

"What? Ye mean he's never been at the sharp end?"

"Right, that's enough," snapped the corporal. "Sergeant O'Brien's a top instructor."

"Aye, and them that cannae do, teach," Rae grumbled mutinously.

"What Ah don't understand," said Ferguson, "is why we have tae do this in the back-end of beyond."

"Glen Laragain is ideal training ground. The M.O.D. bought up the place over a year ago. Nobody had lived in the glen for ages."

"What happened tae the punters that used tae live here?"

It was Macsorley who answered: "21st of April, 1746; Redcoats from Fort William gave this place a helluva goin' over. It was reckoned more people died here than in the Glencoe massacre. None of the locals would ever live here again after that."

The others looked at him in surprise.

"Where the hell did that newsflash come from?" said Rae.

"Ma granddad was born near the mouth of this glen. Place called *Muirshearlach*. Before ma old man and old lady split up, they used tae bring us up here for our summer holidays. We were never allowed up Glen Laragain, though."

"Why would none of the locals live on in the glen?" the corporal wondered. "It's good, arable land."

Macsorley used his beret to wipe the rain from his face. "Because it's haunted."

"Haunted?"

"Ye're having a laugh, right?"

"Naw, Ah'm serious," said Macsorley. "Nobody knows how many were killed in the massacre and how many just drifted away in the months after. But within a couple of years there was only one house in the glen still inhabited. Nobody could bear tae live up here anymore…"

"Because it's supposed tae be haunted?"

Macsorley shrugged his shoulders. "So the story goes."

"Ah've heard it all now!" announced Ferguson.

"What d'ye expect? They're all inbred half-wits up this way," Rae explained.

"Lowland peasants." Macsorley retorted. "Ah'm telling ye, nobody from Lochaber would ever be found up here in the mist…"

"Why the mist?"

"The mist came down just before the massacre began. It helped tae conceal the redcoats as they worked their way up the glen. Animals raped the women; slaughtered every man they could lay their hands on. Some of them even killed lassies and weans. They say anyone caught here in the mist becomes swept up in the massacre; like it's all being replayed over and over."

"D'ye get tae see all the juicy bits?" asked Rae.

"Ye can take the mickey all ye like, but Ah'm telling ye this place is bad news. 'Way back in 1916 an old guy was found dead up here, frightened tae death, apparently. A week later his two sons vanished in the mist…" Macsorley realised everyone was looking at him as though he was the village idiot. "Ye'll no' be so cocky if that mist comes down," he ended defiantly.

Rae winked at Ferguson. "Ye mean like that mist coming down now?"

"Aye, very funny."

"Naw, it's dead gen," grinned Ferguson. "Look behind ye."

"Get lost."

"They're not joking," said the corporal.

Macsorley looked over his shoulder to the west, where a mass of low cloud was rolling down the glen like a tsunami.

"Aw shit."

"Oooo they're comin' tae get ye, Macsorley…"

"Look, sod off, eh?"

"All thae red bogey-men coming outtae the mist…"

"Look, just give it a break, eh?" grumbled Macsorley as the grey wall slowly drew closer, engulfing everything in its path.

In the glen below, the offending recruit had scuttled back to his comrades. All were now being punished for his mistake, their aching limbs being put through a circuit of brutal exercises.

As the little tableau disappeared into the mist, Macsorley's torment finally ended. All were enveloped in a blanket of cold air, which silenced the birdsong and the busy hum of the insects. Even the bellowing of the sergeant fell away to a series of low growls.

When Macsorley eventually broke the silence it was as if he'd been the first to blink in an unspoken battle of wills.

"Have ye ever seen it like this up here before, Corp?"

"This is the first time we've taken a squad over this course. Ah don't know how common this is, but it makes our job a helluva lot harder than it should be."

"So we're the first group that's operated in this glen?"

"As far as Ah know."

"Hey, wait a minute," announced Ferguson, "Ah've just thought; today's the 21st of April; the anniversary of yon massacre…"

"God Almighty, this just keeps getting better and better…" breathed Macsorley.

"This bitch shouldnae give us any more trouble now." Rae manoeuvred the heavy machine gun back into its firing position. "Ah cannae say the same about Fergie's ammo."

"Ah told ye, there's damn all wrong with the ammo!" Fergie cried.

Something like normality had also resumed in the glen below. Once again O'Brien lined up his troops in a semi-circle around him. All were clearly tired and demoralised, and for the first time that day his orders weren't accompanied by a stream of threats.

The mist was beginning to thicken now. The firing party could still identify individual shapes in the gloom, but they were like strange irregularities in a monotone landscape.

Macsorley was the first to notice the tang of smoke. He held his tongue, afraid of further ridicule.

"Is something on fire?" Rae asked.

"Have you been smelling it too?" Ferguson replied. "It's like somebody's burning the heather."

"It's peat smoke," said Macsorley quietly.

"Don't talk rubbish, Mac, the peat'll be too wet tae burn…"

"It's no' that kindae peat fire."

"Don't start that rubbish again," Rae growled.

"Mac's right," said Macmillan, "it's peat smoke from a house fire. Ah remember the smell from a croft house Ah used tae visit on Skye."

"There's something else Ah can smell," said Macsorley. "It's like dung. Ye know? Cow dung…"

"Your nose is too near yer backside, wee man," muttered Rae.

Ferguson suddenly pointed, wide-eyed, into the murk. He made faint gurgling sounds.

Macsorley let out a low moan of anguish. "Aw in the name of holy God, what the hell is happening here?"

Sixty yards in front of them, between their position and the assault course, a number of indistinct forms had begun to materialize, the mist appearing to be in the throes of giving birth. At first they were little more than shapes in the murk, but the shapes quickly began to take human form.

"What the hell is going on here, Mac?" breathed Rae.

"It's just like Ah told ye," Macsorley whispered accusingly, "ye wouldnae listen. But it's just like Ah said. Ah tried tae warn ye, but ye just took the mickey…"

The progeny of the mist had now materialised into a group of figures that seemed to be moving past their position, making their way towards the upper reaches of the glen. As some of the figures drew closer the shock of recognition hit them like a bombshell.

"They're Hanoverian soldiers," Macsorley groaned.

"Cumberland's army…" Macmillan breathed the words like an ancient curse.

The apparitions remained soundless and colourless, as if they truly were the children of the mist. The images, however, had now taken on a frightening clarity. The uniform, the musket and bayonet of each individual spectre, could be clearly seen.

"It's the massacre," Macsorley hissed. "We're watching the massacre of Glen Laragain…"

More apparitions were now appearing from the mist on their left, all moving westwards. None of the watching troops dared to breathe, terrified the slightest sound would attract attention.

The ringing of the field telephone broke the silence. The telephone rang again before Macmillan could grab the handset. The grey figures continued to stare ahead as they drifted past.

"Are you seeing this, Sarge?" the non-commissioned officer whispered hoarsely.

"Bravo two three?" the radio crackled in reply. "This is bravo one zero. Respond, over."

"Bravo… Can ye no' see them…? They're right in front of ye."

"Corporal Macmillan, what are you babbling about?"

"They're not seeing this," Macmillan hissed at the others. "Whatever's happening is only happening tae us!"

"Bravo two three. Get your head out of your backside and respond. Over."

As the corporal tried desperately to compose himself a number of spectral soldiers began to move directly towards Macmillan and his squad.

"They're heading this way! What do we do, Corp?"

Before Macmillan could respond the problem was taken out of his hands by Private Rae. The machine-gunner reacted in the way he was trained… The burst of tracer passed through the grey figures and crashed into Sergeant O'Brien and two of his recruits, standing directly behind. Even through the mist Macmillan could see the three soldiers collapse onto the moor, where a red tarn began to form around them.

He heard someone screaming; "*noooo!*" without realising it was his own voice.

The apparitions continued towards them, oblivious to everything else. They were now little more than twenty yards away. Rae squeezed the trigger again, but with no loader to feed the ammunition belt the weapon jammed. Now that they could see the faces of the spectres, they looked less like abominations and more like creatures of flesh and blood. They clearly had no sense of Macmillan and his group. Their attention was focused on something else. At that moment a number of shapes leapt from a point close to the firing position and began to run nimbly into the mist behind them.

At once the apparitions took up the chase.

"Where did they come from?" began Macsorley, before everything was lit up by a blinding flash to the east. It was as if the sun had erupted in a supernova explosion. At once the mist vanished, to be replaced by a cauldron of fire.

For a millisecond the four soldiers were caught like flies in a furnace.

Chapter Three
Glen Laragain — 2026

The automobile rattled its way along the old cattle track, its passage marked by a cloud of dust that hung in the still morning air. The track finally petered out beside a ruined cottage, bringing the car to an untidy halt.

The building had long ago lost its doors and windows to the passage of time, and it gaped in blank astonishment at the young couple who emerged from the car.

The man stretched to ease the stiffness in his muscles, a derisive smile on his face. "So, Shawnee, this is the old ancestral pile, huh? This is what y'brought us halfway round the world to see?"

"Oh, give it a rest, Sam," said Shawnee wearily. "Y'haven't stopped complaining since we landed in Scotland."

Sam laughed as he opened the boot of the car and began to fill two backpacks with food and water. Both were dressed in shorts, sweatshirts and walking boots. Although Sam was six inches taller than Shawnee, his skin bronzed, his long hair bleached by the sun, the apparel looked more natural on her than it did on him.

"Oh yes, I'm a direct descendent of the Camerons of Glen Laragain," he mimicked as he carried the packs over to the ruin. "We, like, totally have our own castle and everything…"

Shawnee had made her way through the gaping hole that once supported a front door. "Never said we lived in a castle," she yelled from inside the ruin.

Sam peered through one of the rotting window frames. The interior was choked with weeds and fallen masonry. "What I can't figure is why your people woulda wanted to leave all this to emigrate to the States."

She scowled as she stepped gingerly over the debris. "If you're gonna be such a pain why don't you just go back to the hotel?"

"Y'mean The Hotel Caledonia? *Mirrors on the ceiling, pink champagne on ice...*"

She swept her long, auburn hair from her face, her eyes narrow and threatening. "Being here means everything to me and I am *so* not gonna let you spoil it. Now, you can either be a part of this or you can... you can go screw yourself."

Sam took a moment to drink in her fiery beauty. She had such strength and determination for one so small and finely featured. He had learned the hard way that he could push Shawnee only so far. He offered his usual indulgent smile.

"Look, I'm sorry. Okay? I just feel I can't reach you when y'get all this... this totem pole stuff in your head. I can't see why you wanna carry all these dead guys around with yuh all the time, anyhow. It's *gotta* be unhealthy."

Her brow furrowed, but only for a moment. "You don't understand because y'don't have a single drop of Celtic blood in your body."

"You see, there y'go again! I don't even know what that's supposed to mean," Sam laughed. "The day old Gustav Kramer sailed past that lady with the torch he became an American. End of story. I'll never understand why you gotta have this... dual nationality."

"There's a lot you'll never understand..." she said quietly. She made her way to the rear of the old house, where an avenue of Caledonian pines led down to the nearby burn, which snaked out of Glen Laragain. Once, the stream would have overflowed with rainwater cascading from the hills on either side of the glen. Now its bed of rounded stones lay incongruously in a furrow of dust. On all sides the Highland hills stretched into the distance. Nothing disturbed the silence but the singing of skylarks, and the bumbling drone of an occasional insect.

"This is the spot my dad talked about," Shawnee said wistfully. "Way back in the nineteen nineties he vacationed in Europe. Spent a week in Scotland. This was the place he loved to tell me about."

She made a seat for herself on the bank of the dried-up stream and Sam flopped down beside her. From this angle the old cottage looked like a dried skull that was gaping in his direction.

"I don't suppose the reality ever matches up, huh?"

Shawnee's eyes widened in surprise, her hazel irises expanding in the rush of light. "Oh my God, no. It's exactly how I pictured it. Or at least how it used to be." She threw a pebble into the dusty bed of the stream. "What an idyllic spot this musta been before everything went all to hell. I wonder what this place was like before."

Sam tore his eyes away from the old house. "A guy in the hotel was telling me the winters here have averaged twenty degrees below zero since the North Atlantic Drift died. Hard to believe on a day like this."

She nodded sombrely. "*National Geographic* says there's only two seasons in Northern Europe now: Summer and Winter. They think it's only a matter of time before the ice wins out."

"Yet I read on the plane over that the rise in sea level is accelerating a lot faster than they'd anticipated."

"Have y'noticed how the news never carries stories about famine anymore?"

"Whole godforsaken world's finally gone biblical," said Sam. "There's torrential rain where there used to be drought. Countries that escape the floods are turning into dustbowls because there's no freakin rain! And as for China: hell, that's gotta be the ultimate nightmare. Now the army's taken over, they're spouting some paranoid shit about how the whole damn thing is a global conspiracy controlled by Uncle Sam."

He realised his voice had become a little too loud, a little high pitched. He grinned awkwardly. "War, famine, pestilence, death. Have I missed any of them out?"

"The four horsemen? No, y'got them all," Shawnee confirmed bleakly.

Sam grinned again. "And where are you and me while the rest of the world is heading for Armageddon? Hey, we're in the high-lands of Scotland, looking for the ruins of Brigadoon!"

Her feet dangling in a burn that had died of thirst a long time ago, Shawnee tried to smile at the absurdity of it all.

"Before my dad was killed he always said he was gonna bring me here on the anniversary of the Glen Laragain massacre, so we could climb to the head of the glen together."

"How long has it been?"

"One year ago today."

"That's why you wanted to be here today of all days."

She nodded her head. "Dad was killed on the two hundred and seventy-ninth anniversary."

"That is one shitty coincidence."

"The twenty-first of April has never been a good day in my family," she said ruefully as she rose to her feet. "It's like some kinda pilgrimage, I guess; making it up there to the top of the glen. It's just something I need to get out of my system, y'know?"

Sam glanced once again at the old ruin. "I sure hope so," he said quietly.

Chapter Four

In a perfect desert sky, high above a landscape carved by glaciers and scoured by rain, a lone buzzard made mournful accusations at anything that would listen.

Sam and Shawnee had hiked little more than a mile beyond Inverlaragain cottage, but already Sam's legs were aching and his body was bathed in sweat. Every flying insect in the area seemed to be buzzing around his face. At first the sight of Shawnee's fit and shapely rear end ahead of him had helped anaesthetise the pain, but eventually even this lost its appeal, and he was praying she would call a halt soon.

Unfortunately she was in her element. "Have you ever seen anywhere as beautiful in all the world?" she enthused, as she bounced along. "Wouldn't it be totally awesome to live someplace like this?"

Sam grunted in reply. He was wondering if he'd been a little charitable when he'd made up the backpacks earlier. He decided to compare weights when they stopped for a rest.

She was talking about water now; explaining how a running stream will re-oxygenate itself every twenty yards... or was it every twenty feet? Well... In any event, this explained how one small stream running through the glen could have supported scores of families in days gone by...

"Y'know," said Shawnee, "of the two hundred people who lived in Glen Laragain, nobody knows how many died in the massacre. All the young men had gone off to fight for Bonnie Prince Charlie, so nobody was left to defend the glen. Within five years only one family remained here; my great, great, great—"

"Hey! Maybe we could stop for a while, yeah?" There was a touch of desperation in Sam's voice. "Surely you could use a rest, or something?"

Shawnee turned to see Sam twenty yards behind, looking as if he'd trekked across the Serengeti. "Sure. Why not. I *was* getting kinda tired." She helped him remove his sweat-stained backpack. "Maybe you could use a little water?"

"Y'could say that. There should be plenty. I packed three two-litre bottles."

"Yes, I know," she said sweetly, "I changed two of them over to my pack before we left the cottage."

After a little food and a lot of fluid Sam felt a great deal more human.

"Didn't realize how much you were into this great-outdoors stuff."

"My dad used to take me camping when I was a kid."

"Figures."

Above them the buzzard had drifted beyond the southern lip of the glen, leaving the cloudless skies empty of life. Shawnee went off on her own to take in the view from the upper slopes. When she returned ten minutes later, Sam was huddled over his cell phone.

"There's something wrong with this piece of junk. They talk about putting men on Mars, but they can't even put a little circuit board together."

"Why d'you have to be such a news junkie?"

Sam obstinately searched for a live frequency. The crackle of static suddenly gave way to the strangely distant tones of a local newsreader. "...*Official sources in the Pentagon stated that the amount of food aid demanded by the Chinese is totally unrealistic, taking into account the poor harvests reported throughout much of the Northern Hemisphere...*"

"Same old same old." she said dismissively.

"Wait... This could be important."

"...*There has been no communication with Beijing or Washington since eight o' clock this morning; three hours after the deadline to General Chuo En Lee's ultimatum had passed. As you know, contact has also been lost with London and...*" Abruptly the transmission degenerated into a static hiss.

"Aw, hell." Sam twisted the cell phone this way and that, but the signal had gone. "These hills must be screwing up the reception."

"That sounds ominous," said Shawnee. "Everybody knows things are bad in China. Maybe it's worse than we thought. You don't think they're gonna do something stupid...?"

"Nah. It's all sabre-rattling and brinkmanship. There'll be the usual last-minute deal. Anyhow," Sam continued, with a burst of enthusiasm, "I can't stand around here yakking all day. If you've had a good enough rest maybe we can hit the trail again. And this time, *try* to keep up. Huh?"

She aimed a playful swipe at him, which he fended off with his backpack. Like two children playing tag they set off westwards. The game soon petered out, and before long Sam had fallen several yards behind. This time, however, he found it less of a struggle to keep up. There was no doubt the gradient had eased, but he also suspected Shawnee had slackened her pace.

He made a mental note to register with a gym when he got back to L.A.

The terrain around them began to change. The dry bracken, which had crunched satisfyingly under their feet, gave way to an expanse of grass, interspersed with patches of brown, lifeless ferns. Before long they encountered the first of the ruined houses. Shawnee paused to caress the cold stone slabs.

"After Inverlaragain cottage this woulda been the next house they hit. I know what happened here is nothing to the butchery that's gone on all around the world since. But what happened that day; it's more than just a piece of history. It's... I guess to me this place is what 'Wounded Knee' would be to the Native Americans. Y'know?"

"Uh huh, sure. Native Americans," mumbled Sam, turning his cell phone this way and that. "Freakin hills..."

As the afternoon wore on they made their way farther and farther into the upper reaches of the glen. En route they passed innumerable ruins, each like an ancient wreck sinking into a verdant sea. At last Shawnee calculated they'd arrived at the western end of the glen. The topmost ruin appeared less decayed than most of the remains they'd encountered. Nearby, a single mountain ash sprung from a patch of greenery, like a defiant symbol of life. A slight breeze had arisen from the west, gently ruffling the branches.

As soon as they'd taken off their backpacks Sam's attention returned to his cell phone. He switched wavebands, trying to find a way beyond the hiss of static.

Shawnee made a seat for herself beside him. "How can you even think of the outside world in a place like this?"

Sam gave up in disgust and threw the phone to one side. "Yeah. I guess."

Shawnee caught sight of a mound of stones lying close to the ash tree, and ran towards it like an excited child. "Oh my God, look at this!

It's an old cairn. This musta been erected to commemorate the massacre."

Sam made his way over to the monument. "A cairn?"

"They were erected in the old days to mark important sites. Dad said that before a battle each clansman would lay a stone on a mound just like this. When the battle was over the survivors would remove a stone from the pile…"

"…Oh, I get it; the stones that were left would represent the guys that died in the battle. Right?"

Shawnee nodded. "It's such a beautiful idea, don't you think?"

Sam idly lifted one of the stones from the little cairn, then with great care returned it to its position in the monument.

"This must be the site of the graveyard," she went on, apparently thinking aloud. "I wonder if any of the hauntings have taken place around here? More likely at the houses, I guess, where most of them were killed."

"Hauntings?" Sam echoed. "You never mentioned hauntings before."

"Didn't I?" Shawnee replied offhandedly. "Yeah, well, y'know what these kinda places are like. You always get stories… I know what most people nowadays think about that sorta thing."

Sam could see she was cautiously gauging his reaction.

"Don't think I ever told you about the time I camped out near the battlefield at Gettysburg," he said. "There was me, Tommy Phillips and Ralphie Schuster. We made a point of being there during the anniversary of the battle. I dunno where we camped exactly; somewhere to the south of the town. Anyhow, it was during the second night; I'll never forget it. It was as hot and humid as hell. Tommy said we just gotta have a campfire; it didn't matter that it was about ninety in the shade. He said you couldn't camp out without a campfire. Well, we had a few beers, and one thing and another, and in no time Tommy was asleep; out for the count. Ralphie and I, we just sat there, in this little clearing in the woods, not talking or anything, just sorta watching Tommy's campfire burn down."

Sam made a seat for himself beneath the tree. Shawnee sat down beside him.

"Anyhow," he went on, "it was way into the evening, but it wasn't so dark that we couldn't see around us, y'know? And, well, one moment Ralphie and I were just sitting there, staring into the glow of the fire, and the next moment we weren't the only ones sitting at that campfire."

"What d'you mean?" asked Shawnee warily.

"I don't know any other way of putting it. One moment there was two guys there, the next there was four."

"Don't you be making fun of me now. If this is some kinda stupid joke…"

"Give me a break, I'm telling yuh, these guys just materialized in front of us."

"Yeah… Who d'you think they were?"

"Oh, hell, you could see quite clearly who they were," said Sam. "They were Confederate soldiers."

"Waaw… That musta been so scary."

"Well, y'know, that was the really weird thing; it wasn't scary at all. It was like they belonged there as much as me and Ralphie."

She digested the image for a moment. "Go on. What happened next?"

"Well, y'know, I'd love to say we witnessed some scene from the battle. Like Pickett's charge, or something. But that was it. These two soldiers just sat at that campfire. You could see them talking to each other. We couldn't hear anything. But the weird thing was, they looked as if they were also carrying on a conversation with me and Ralphie."

"Jeez. I take it your friend was seeing all this as well…?"

"Oh sure. We didn't say a word to each other, but I could tell from Ralphie's face he was seeing everything I was seeing."

"How long did the whole thing last?"

"Thirty, forty minutes. As the light from the fire died down, they just sorta died down with it. It was the weirdest thing, and yet at the time it all seemed natural, somehow."

"God, you are so lucky," she breathed.

"I guess. Y'know, until this moment, I'd never spoken of it to a living soul. Ralphie and I never discussed it. We didn't even tell Tommy about it. Poor guy, it woulda broken his heart if he ever knew what he missed out on…"

"My God, Sam, how could you even begin to explain something like that?"

Sam was enjoying the novel sensation of having Shawnee eating out of the palm of his hand.

"Well, y'know, I thought about it afterwards, and I don't believe those soldiers were ghosts, or spirits; or whatever you wanna call them. I reckon they were in their own time. They weren't seeing Ralphie and me, they were seeing, maybe, another two Confederates occupying the space that me and Ralphie were occupying."

"Right. So you were seeing a fragment of the past?"

"Well, yeah, kinda. But I think we experienced what we did because we interacted with it. We were part of... how can I say this? A coincidence between two time spans..."

"...A coincidence between what?"

"Okay. Right. Take this area, for instance. You said this place is haunted. Yeah?"

"Big time; that's the main reason the survivors abandoned the place; couldn't bear to live on in the glen. One of my relatives was even found dead up here. They reckoned he died of fright."

"Not the kinda place you'd wanna be after dark, then."

She smiled. "I don't think we're likely to see anything today. It only ever happens in the mist..." Her eyes opened in sudden comprehension. "Oh, my God, is that what you mean?"

Sam nodded. "If you wanted to see something from that time, you'd know you'd have a better chance if the conditions were similar to what they were that day. Funny thing is; we all intuitively know this already. We all know if you create a link with that other time period—"

"Like being there on the anniversary..."

His eyes widened momentarily. "Yeah, exactly. See, we don't just witness these things, we help to create them. Given the right coincidences, different time periods can come together. Maybe time isn't as sequential as we like to believe."

Shawnee nodded. "I remember once, Dad and I came upon this old cabin in the woods. You could tell it hadn't been lived in for years. Even the fireplace was blocked up. Anyhow, we stopped over. During the night I woke up to the smell of burning wood."

"You mean, as though the cabin was on fire?"

"No, I don't think so. It was that distinctive scent you get when you burn birch logs."

"So, you were smelling a fire in the blocked up fireplace?"

"Yeah. Totally weird or what? And yet it's just the kinda thing you're talking about. I wonder why it doesn't happen more often."

"Yeah, I wondered about that too. I reckon some remote places remain undisturbed; y'know; left in their original condition. I guess there'd be a better chance of making a connection somewhere like that. Maybe it only happens in certain places." He smiled at Shawnee. "Y'know, before that camping trip I was just a regular college hard-ass. But that whole experience was like one of those defining periods in a guy's life. It's like; you come back not the same person, but you're not quite sure in what way you're different. D'you know what I mean?"

"Yes, I do," she said softly.

They sat together in comfortable silence, watching the idyllic scene below. From this distance little could be seen of the ancient ruins, or the waterless burn. It was a while before they became aware of the changes taking place above them. The time was barely 4 pm, but already the colours of sunset had begun to appear in the west. Before long a wide, nebulous halo materialised around the sun, its yellow-white glare turning a soft bronze, as if a saffron veil had been drawn across it.

As they watched, spellbound, a dull copper glow began to spread unevenly across the sky. Below them the vegetation appeared to wither in the reddening light, plunging the hillsides into ever-deepening shadows.

Sam said nothing to Shawnee. If he refused to acknowledge the phenomenon, it might seem less real. But even the meanest inhabitants of the glen sensed something was wrong. Not even the buzz of insects disturbed the deathly quiet.

The blue of the sky was now almost completely transformed into the colour of desert sands; the sun and its halo now a dull glowing red.

"This is not good," Sam murmured at last, "something has most definitely hit the fan somewhere."

Shawnee made no reply. She seemed mesmerised by the spectacle.

Sam retrieved his cell phone. The anxiety that had been gnawing at the back of his mind had now returned with a vengeance. For the third time that day he tried to establish a link with the outside world. Almost immediately he encountered the excited voice of an English newsreader:

"...spokesperson for the Chinese military government has stated that this action was taken as the only means of demonstrating to the United States

government, and to the world at large, the seriousness of China's resolve, and should not be interpreted as a declaration of hostilities between their two countries…"

"Aw, Jesus H Christ, what the hell is going on now?" Sam groaned. "We seem to go from one crisis to the next."

Shawnee tore her eyes away from the glowing inferno that was now the afternoon sky. "Whatever mess they've made of things can surely keep 'til we're outta here."

"Yeah, I guess…."

"…As yet there has been no official reaction either from the White House or from Downing Street. A statement due to be made by the Prime Minister was cancelled a few minutes ago. Earlier reports of major explosions in the vicinity of Beijing, Tianjin and Shanghai remain unconfirmed. The time is now 8 am, and we go over to our…"

At that point the broadcast erupted into a ferocious howl of static. Sam and Shawnee gaped blankly at each other. Moments later the voice of the newsreader blared from the phone:

"…The official Chinese news agency has confirmed the detonation of a nuclear warhead in what they describe as a thinly populated area of the United States of America. The attack took place at six o'clock this morning, Greenwich Mean Time. A spokesperson for the Chinese military government has stated that this action was taken as the only means of demonstrating to the United States government, and to the world at large, the seriousness of China's resolve, and should not be interpreted as a declaration of hostilities between their two countries…"

"Oh, Sweet Jesus," said Sam. "What've they done…?"

"As yet there has been no official reaction, either from the White House or from Downing Street. A statement due to be made by the Prime Minister was cancelled a few minutes ago. Earlier reports of major explosions in the vicinity of Beijing, Tianjin and Shanghai remain unconfirmed. The time is now 8 am and we go over to our…"

Once again the broadcast was drowned in a shriek of static. And once again after a few moments the newsreader's voice returned. Sam and Shawnee listened in horrified silence as the broadcast was repeated over and over, like a message being mechanically transmitted from the grave. Finally Sam sent the cell phone spinning into the distance.

For a long time both stood in shocked silence, beneath a sky that now appeared to be reflecting the fires of hell. Sam put his arms protectively around Shawnee.

"Don't suppose that was Orson Welles…?" he growled, in a wretched attempt at humour. His mind was filled with images of places… people… Los Angeles… San Francisco… Boiling clouds…

"How could we let it come to this…?" said Shawnee in an agonised whisper. "That up there. That's… That's what he was talking about, isn't it…?"

"It may not be as bad as it looks. It may just be some kinda localized—"

"Don't patronize me, Sam!" she yelled, pulling away from him. "I need to know how bad this is, and I don't want any fairy stories!"

"Okay, kid, you're right," Sam relented. "Look, I dunno, this stuff… It looks like it could be in the upper atmosphere. The way I figure… it's been carried from a long way off …" He sighed miserably, reluctant to continue.

"Go on."

"Aw hell, I dunno. I could be wrong, but I think this has been carried here on the jet stream from North America… I don't see how this could be the result of a single strike in a thinly populated area."

A moan of anguish left Shawnee's lips. She stood in tortured contemplation for a while, before suddenly pulling on her backpack.

"What're you doing?"

"What d'you think I'm doing?" she said calmly. "There's no point us standing here like hogs in a slaughterhouse. We need to get back to the car. We can decide our next move from there."

Without waiting for a reply she turned on her heel and strode off in the direction of the cottage. Sam lost no time in following her. There was no question now of stopping to savour the bittersweet draught of times past. They stumbled through a sinister and alien landscape, over which the gods appeared to be waging one last great war with each other.

After little more than an hour they were a mile from Inverlaragain Cottage. At this point Sam called a halt. Something was wrong. In a world that had been plunged into Armageddon *everything* was wrong. But this was different. Something was now *very* wrong. He barely had time to register this fact before his eyes were drawn to *Meall Banabhie*, the hill to the south of Glen Laragain, above which an enormous cauldron of smoke and flame was rising. It looked as if the hills of Lochaber had erupted in one colossal volcanic eruption. As the boiling inferno climbed higher and higher into the sky, comprehension seeped into Sam's paralysed mind. What had been abstract interpretation was now terrifying reality. The angels of the apocalypse had revealed themselves to the world this day. Now it was their turn to bear witness.

He thought of that little Highland town they'd passed through only the day before, which now lay beneath that biblical holocaust. Then his thoughts were of Shawnee... She was at his side now, her hand in his. He could see the searing cauldron of fire reflected in her eyes.

Meall Banabhie had absorbed the initial explosion, but as the gigantic fireball spread throughout the bowl formed by the Lochaber hills it found an outlet at the top of Glen Laragain. They watched as a huge fiery arm was channelled towards the upper pass, and then, by some perverse trick of gravity, forced down the glen, like a grotesque parody of a wall of mist, towards where Sam and Shawnee stood.

Sam's mind finally detached itself from reality. He turned to the tiny individual beside him. Devoid of all hope, her death only seconds away, her courage remained intact as she faced the onrushing wall of fire.

As Sam and Shawnee steeled themselves for their final moments, neither noticed a second colossal explosion lighting up the sky above Loch Ness, to the east. At the very moment the pyroclastic flow from Glen Laragain was about to engulf them, the shock wave from the second explosion blasted them both into oblivion.

Chapter Five
Glen Laragain — 1746

Achnacon stood on the grass-covered summit of *Meall Banabhie*, his red tartan plaid a defiant blaze of colour against the drab vegetation of early spring. Four miles to the west, where the Great Glen emerges from the salt swell of Loch Linnhe, his failing eyes searched out the star-shaped outline of *An Gearasdan*; the garrison of Fort William. Like a thorn in the flesh of the Highlands, the fort was manned by two regiments of King George of Hanover's hated redcoated soldiers.

Throughout the past two weeks, a Jacobite force of Camerons and Macdonalds had laid siege to the fort, their eventual aim to return the Stuart kings to the thrones of England and Scotland. His sons, Donald and James, both served with the Glen Laragain contingent of Locheil's Camerons. Both had been in the Highland army that had charged from the mists of Gladsmuir the previous September, to destroy the Hanoverian forces of General Cope. Both had been in the van of that army as it struck south, into the heart of their enemy's country. At their head rode a young prince, his mind filled with all the delusions of kingly grandeur.

And then the long, bitter retreat north, as the English Jacobite support failed to materialise. January had seen another victory for the clans, at Falkirk. But as winter turned to spring they had fallen back again, towards the sanctuary of their Highland hills, drawing the Duke of Cumberland's army behind them like a great plodding beast of prey.

The bulk of the Jacobite army remained at Inverness while elements carried the war to the Hanoverian garrisons scattered throughout the Highlands. Chief amongst these was *An Gearasdan Dubh*; the black garrison of Fort William.

Although the years had stiffened Achnacon's joints, and turned his hair and beard to silver, he had climbed the southern slopes of Glen Laragain every day to watch the momentous events unfold.

On each day he had made this climb, he had narrowed his eyes against the cold Atlantic wind, straining to catch a glimpse of colour; a hint of collective tartan that would indicate where the clansmen lay while they waited for the walls to be breached. However, all he could make out were great puffs of white smoke around the lower slopes overlooking the fort. Some days, if the wind blew from the south, he could hear the distant roar of cannon, like thunder in a far-off glen. The returning fire from the Hanoverian artillery in the fort, supported by the white-sailed warships on Loch Linnhe, seemed heavier than that of the Jacobites.

Achnacon's concern was more than a preference for one ruling dynasty over another; more even than a father's concern for his sons. He was aware of Glen Laragain's close proximity to the black garrison. He knew his green and fertile glen would bear the brunt of any Hanoverian reprisals if the fort was not taken and its garrison disarmed.

This morning all appeared unnaturally calm. For the first time in two weeks there was no billowing cannonade around the blurred outline of the fort. No telltale smoke. Near the mouth of the river two warships lay at anchor, their sails furled, their firepower redundant.

Even from this distance it was obvious the siege had been lifted.

For a long time he studied the scene, his plaid snapping in the wind. At last he turned and began the slow descent into Glen Laragain. He carried with him a deep sense of unease. A man did not need the second sight to realise that dangerous times lay ahead for the *Gael*. Even if they remained unmolested by the garrison, there was still Cumberland's army. From the tip of Kintyre to the straths of Sutherland all knew the contempt the king's son felt for Scots in general and Highlanders in particular.

Achnacon resisted the pull of gravity as he descended the steep hillside. Once upon a time he would have surrendered to the downward force in a wild headlong dash. But then, once upon a time he would have taken his place among the fighting men of the clan, instead of watching from a distant hilltop, like an old *bodach*.

His descent of *Meall Banabhie* ended at the western end of the glen. Here there were no ridges of cultivation, no straggling walls to protect hard won crops from deer or cattle. Only a lone circular wall of stone and turf, within which lay the Glen Laragain graveyard. No one knew how long this plot of land had been used as the final resting place for the folk of the glen. For as long as there had been people here, perhaps.

The number of families inhabiting the glen had changed little over the centuries; and so the years had seen little increase in the size of the graveyard. Instead, a collection of low green mounds had evolved, each marked with a simple wooden cross. The graveyard was surrounded on all sides by rushing burns. This was no accident since it was believed, for reasons Achnacon had never really understood, that evil spirits were forbidden to cross running water.

The Christian crosses and running water were symbols of the fusion of Christianity and Paganism that governed the lives of his people. When the Irish saints brought the holy word to these glens a thousand years before, they had encountered a people steeped in ancient beliefs. Here was a land inhabited by goblins and fairy folk; by water-bulls that lured the unwary into the black depths of the lochs; by dark spirits that walked the hillsides at night when disaster was imminent. In such a wild and brooding landscape it was little surprise the new faith had absorbed rather than replaced the old.

All continued to believe in the second sight; the ability to glimpse fragments of the future, which they had learnt to interpret according to the nature of the vision. To see a shroud about a person foretold their impending death. Some signs were linked to a specific area. The Callart light in Argyllshire, for example, was always seen to follow the same path from Callart House, across Loch Leven to the burial island of *Eilean Munde*. The light foretold the imminent death of one of the Camerons of Callart, and traced the route that would be taken by the burial party.

Glen Laragain too had its own specific sign that heralded death and destruction in the glen. *An adhar dearg*. The red sky.

An adhar dearg was said to bear no resemblance to the gentle hues of sunrise or sunset. Those who had seen the vision said it was as if the canopy of heaven had reflected the fires of hell. The vision had been known of in Glen Laragain for as long as there had been people here to witness it.

During long winter evenings when Lochaber was battered by Atlantic storms, or frozen beneath snow and ice, the people would gather for the winter *celeidh*. Here they would sing and dance, or huddle round the peat fire to hear age-old stories, such as the tales of *an adhar dearg*.

The red sky had appeared in the year 1513 before an old woman and her granddaughter, as they returned one afternoon from the graveyard. At that time twenty-five young warriors of Glen Laragain had taken their place within the ranks of King James' army, and it would be weeks before the people of the glen would learn that all of them had perished with their king on Flodden field the day after the apparition was seen.

The storytellers would also recount the last time *an adhar dearg* appeared above the glen. The vision had been seen by a redcoated soldier whose regiment was forcibly billeted upon the townships of the glen. This operation had been part of the government's response to the rising of 1715, and was intended to be no more than a sabre-rattling exercise. The people's response to the report of this vision was instant and dramatic. Mindful of the Glencoe massacre carried out under similar circumstances barely two decades before, houses were hastily abandoned as entire families made for the hilltop sanctuary of the summer shielings.

A wry smile creased Achnacon's grizzled features. As a warrior in his prime he had fought at Sheriffmuir during this fiasco. The battle had not brought victory to the clans, but nor had it brought defeat. Certainly the Cameron casualties had been light and were nothing to warrant the appearance of *an adhar dearg*.

As for the people of Glen Laragain, after a few days, when the soldiers were gone, they returned sheepishly from their hilltop dwellings. It was their good fortune the redcoats had been Highlanders like themselves. Loyal soldiers of King George they may have been, but first and foremost they were of the *Gaidhealtacht* and were bound by the laws of Highland hospitality. Not a stick of furniture had been broken, nor a single possession stolen. They had, however, suffered offence at the behaviour of their hosts, and before they left Glen Laragain had rounded up every domestic beast in the glen, and penned them all together in one great, wide-eyed mêlée of cattle, horses, sheep and goats. Months were to pass before the ownership of each animal was re-established.

Achnacon considered himself a rational man. Such tales instilled a necessary element of fear in the young and unruly. They had also enriched many a winter's *celeidh*. Beyond that, he had regarded the stories as no more than the bletherings of old women. But this day he felt something he had not felt since he put away childish things to become a man: He felt that anything was possible… Goblins. Fairies. Water-bulls. Anything…

It had been late in the afternoon of the previous day and he had completed his descent from *Meall Banabhie*. Near the graveyard his eyes had followed the flight of a distant eagle as it circled above *Druim Fada*. The great bird was no more than a tiny speck against a changing backcloth of mottled clouds and luminescent blues. Suddenly in the blink of an eye everything had vanished; clouds, eagle, the blue of the sky. All of it gone, to be replaced by a sky that seemed to be engulfed in flames. As far as the eye could see the heavens were ablaze. Above the western horizon hung a blood-red sun, around which glowed a halo of fire. The land below reflected this terrible transformation, appearing brown and decayed, the ground withered and dead. The cottages and steadings, even the circular wall around the graveyard had vanished; all signs of man had melted into the soil.

After the initial shock had passed, Achnacon tried to make sense of what he was seeing. He could make out patterns within the inferno, waves that were slowly moving from west to east, as though this holocaust was no more than another Atlantic weather system, spawned by that great western ocean. Only now the sea beyond the Hebrides seemed to be on fire, the flames reflected in the tortured skies above Glen Laragain.

And then as suddenly as it had appeared the vision was gone. The distant speck of the eagle had reappeared above *Druim Fada*, framed against the blue and white swirls of the afternoon sky. He had felt a sense of loss, a feeling of discontentment that nagged bewilderingly at his soul. But above all he felt a deep foreboding. He had told no one of his vision, anxious to avoid a panic such as that of thirty years before.

From his vantage point beside the graveyard, Achnacon could see every township in Glen Laragain, all the way down to Inverlaragain House at the mouth of the glen. Each clachan was separated from its neighbour by a patchwork of fields and ridges, all freshly planted with the coming season's oats and barley. On the lower slopes of the glen he could see the cattle that were the wealth of the clan. Soon the younger folk would lead the beasts into the higher pastures for the summer grazing. There they would remain until autumn, the little shielings of stone and turf their only protection from the elements. He felt a pang of nostalgia. Those months spent in the high summer shielings, when he had been more than a boy but not yet a man, had been the happiest of his life.

Above each cottage drifted a ribbon of grey-blue smoke. An indication that within each house lay warmth and welcome for any who came in friendship. Lately, however, he had become conscious of how vulnerable this community was to any who came in a spirit other than friendship.

Achnacon drew his plaid tighter around his shoulders. Something else nagged at him. At the very moment his vision had ended he had heard a voice, a woman's voice, emerge from no more than a few feet away, although he had been alone beneath that blazing sky. She had spoken in English; a language with which he was quite familiar. The dialect was strange but he had heard quite clearly what the woman had said to him.

She had said: "There's no point us standing here like hogs in a slaughterhouse…"

The message was obviously a warning, but of what? Was the glen about to become a slaughterhouse? Achnacon felt an agony of indecision. Should he risk humiliation and alert the clan? He thought of the old and infirm hiding out in the shielings, with no fires to warm their bones for fear of revealing themselves to an enemy. Perhaps if he held his tongue, thought about it some more, an answer would come to him.

Achnacon could hear the mournful cry of a distant buzzard as he made his way home.

Chapter Six

It was obvious now that the attack had failed. From the safety of the shell hole, Alistair had watched as waves of kilted infantry stormed forward, to founder on the undamaged barbed wire, yards from the enemy trenches. Flare after flare illuminated the entanglements as the attackers desperately searched for a passage through. Alistair watched in anguish as machine guns and rifles were turned upon every living thing trapped within those jagged nets.

Eventually the fury of the defending fire slackened. The tak tak tak of heavy machine guns gave way to the sporadic crack of single rifle shots.

Immobilised by fear, he wondered why he alone had been spared while all around him was useless sacrifice. He was no more than ten yards from the wire and could hear the screams and moans of those impaled Highlanders who were still alive.

Another flare was sent hissing into the air. As it floated back to earth Alistair could see the faces of friends and comrades enmeshed in their eviscerating prison.

"Alistair!" Somebody was calling his name now.

"Alistair! For the love of God, waken up." It was Colin's voice.

Alistair looked blankly at his brother.

"Don't make a sound, whatever you do," Colin whispered. "They haven't seen us yet."

"What; the Germans…?"

"SSShhhh! Keep your voice down or they'll hear you!"

Alistair was beginning to come to his senses. They were lying behind an embankment of the Laragain burn. He could hear the splashing roar of a waterfall to his left; its sound magnified by the mist.

"What are you blethering about?" he asked, in an agitated whisper.

"Them;" Colin hissed. "*Saigdearan dhearg!*"

Alistair gaped stupidly at his brother. "*Saigdearan dhearg?* Redcoats…?"

The terrible vision they'd seen earlier came back to him then. Those apparitions were gone. But other images from the past now filled the glen. Alistair smelt the sweet scent of peat smoke, and saw the dark bulk of cottages against the lighter grey of the mist. These were no pathetic ruins, but substantial dwellings topped by thatched roofs.

45

There was movement too amidst this archaic scene; with utter disbelief, Alistair caught his first glimpse of the red coats and white gaiters of the *saigdearan dearg*. He watched as a small group of soldiers emerged from a cottage beside the burn, driving an old woman and two children before them. A number of people were under military guard beside a second cottage. All seemed immobilised by shock.

Alistair could also see two figures lying prostrate on the ground. The vision was so clear he could make out their tartan plaids, and the pools of blood in which they lay.

Colin was whispering in his ear, his face flushed with excitement: "It's the massacre, Alistair! What should we do? We can't just sit here!"

"Himself was right. I thought it was all just some old *cailleach's* tales, but this is real…" Alistair's voice was a mixture of fear and wonder, as if he'd found himself in the halls of Valhalla.

A large group of soldiers appeared out of the mist. At their head was a thickset, brutal-looking individual. Alistair could see no badges of rank on the man's tunic, but guessed he was probably a sergeant. The bulk of the soldiers continued into the mist, heading west. The sergeant remained behind with a dozen of his men. He growled something at his troops, and one after another they plunged into the crowd and began to separate the men from the women and children. An old woman at the front of the group began to moan like a terrified animal.

"Alistair! We have to do something," Colin pleaded. "We can't just sit here and watch this."

"What can you and I do?" Alistair hissed in reply. "These are just images of the past… Turn away if you can't look…"

A soldier silenced the old woman with the butt of his musket. She was trampled in the mêlée as the soldiers struggled to tear the men away from their families. The sergeant waded into the crowd, using fists and boots to quell the rising hysteria. One by one, six old men and three youths were bundled into the nearest cottage and a water barrel was dragged in front of the door. Some of the soldiers looked uneasily at each other, as if not all had the stomach for this work. Some of the women were now wailing like lost souls.

The sergeant's intentions were becoming clear. Two of his men trotted over to the thatched roof of the prison. Moments later a wisp of smoke rose into the air. The women erupted into hysteria. Some of them breasted the hedge of bayonets, trying to force the blades to one side. Flames licked the bundles of yellow-grey straw, like a dog tentatively tasting a strange flavour. The sergeant stood twenty yards away, hands on his hips, like an evil deity, feeding on the horrors he'd sown.

"It's him!" Colin hissed through gritted teeth. "That's the one we saw!"

There was no mistaking that maniacal glow of pleasure. Here was the monster they'd watch rape that beautiful wraith in the mist. Alistair could hear Colin's breathing grow more and more shallow. Neither of them could endure much more of this nightmare.

A thick cloud of smoke billowed into the air as the flames began to overcome the dampness of the thatch. Alistair could hear a babble of voices coming from inside the cottage. The hands of the three youths stretched through the narrow windows. In their panic no longer young men, but terrified children.

Colin tore his haversack from his back and began to scrabble through its contents.

"What are you doing?"

"I can take no more of this!" the younger man cried. He located the box of shells and loaded the empty chamber of his rifle. The remainder of the shells were stuffed into his pocket.

Alistair grabbed hold of his arm. "Colin, none of this is real! You can't interfere; you don't know what you'll bring down upon us...."

A wild screech of excitement rang out as a dark-haired figure broke through the redcoat line. The brothers had a fleeting glimpse of bare feet and shapely legs beneath a red tartan shawl. The woman ran to the cottage, where she levered her body against the water barrel. Within seconds the barrel had been pushed over, the water draining away. Immediately the men poured out of the cottage, retching and coughing, black smoke belching out behind them.

Two of the soldiers ran over to round up the escapees. En route they were ambushed by the woman. She launched herself onto the back of one of the redcoats, clawing like a wildcat. The other soldier jabbed at her with his bayonet, nearly skewering his friend as he tried to rescue him.

The sergeant pried the wildcat off the soldier and carried her, spitting and snarling, away from the burning cottage... *What would otherwise have been elegant arms and legs swung this way and that, trying to inflict damage on her assailant...*

The sudden recognition brought Colin to a halt. His resolution vanished. At the cottage the soldiers were dragging two of the youths back towards the smoke-filled doorway. Already flames licked around the top of the door. Two children, aged about seven, ran off squealing in terror. They came to a halt beside the sergeant. Frozen in shock, they stood hand in hand as they watched him force his victim to the ground and unbuckle his trousers.

There was a deafening explosion to Colin's right. He turned to find Alistair at his side, smoke drifting from the barrel of his rifle. Colin almost wept with relief. Now, these nightmare images would surely return to hell where they belonged.

To his horror the images turned to face the brothers. Instantly the clansfolk were forgotten. The two soldiers at the cottage fired at the intruders. The shots were wildly off target; the lead balls whizzing over their heads. Alistair reloaded his rifle, responding to a threat that was at last tangible. He would try to make sense of it later. He saw the girl kick at the sergeant's groin as he desperately buttoned his trousers, and watched him hobble painfully back to his men.

The old men and the women, meanwhile, had seized the children and fled into the mist.

During this momentary lapse the remainder of the soldiers fired a ragged volley in their direction. Alistair felt a thump in his left arm, as though hit by a stick in a game of shinty. Colin let out a sharp cry and dropped to the ground.

"Where are you hit?" Alistair yelled.

"In the leg! But, I'm all right! I don't think it hit the bone! Alistair, I don't think these beggars are ghosts, at all…"

The older man smiled ruefully. He retained enough movement in his left arm to sight his rifle. He could see the cartridges of powder and ball being rammed into the barrels as the soldiers frantically reloaded. They were so densely packed he could hardly miss. As the weapon recoiled into his shoulder one of the soldiers was flung backwards, blood spraying from his mouth.

Alistair tried to reload. His left arm was stiffening rapidly, and the bullets spilled from his hands. As he steeled himself to receive the soldiers' second volley Colin levered himself onto one knee and fired at the two figures in front of the burning cottage. One of the redcoats took the round full in the chest and was flung backwards into the inferno.

Alistair hauled his brother to the ground as the second volley rang out. The smoothbore musket had no rifling that would spin the bullet and improve its accuracy, but the brothers were well within general volleying range. A hail of lead balls flew closely above their heads.

Colin loaded his rifle, handed it to Alistair, then levered a round into his brother's weapon.

Alistair jammed the rifle into his right shoulder. "When I say 'now' we get up and fire together, all right?"

Already, however, the initiative had been taken away from them. The sergeant sent his men forward in line abreast, determined to come to close quarters with these rebels, and their extraordinary weapons. Alistair rose to meet them, his brother one-legged by his side.

"Space out, don't give them an easy target. You take one on the right. I'll do the same on the left."

"You run for it, Alistair. I'll try to hold them off."

"Just take one on the right!" yelled Alistair.

He waited until his brother had fired at the oncoming redcoats. Alistair was no stranger to death but was still shocked to see Colin bring one of the soldiers down, in that familiar dreadful way. As Colin reloaded, Alistair squeezed the trigger, and another soldier crumpled. To his right another shot rang out from Colin, and another soldier ran on a few paces, before collapsing in a heap.

Alistair made no effort to reload. His left arm was now useless, and in a desperate bluff he pointed the empty weapon at the five remaining redcoats. From the side of his eye he could see his brother also standing his ground. As Alistair wondered if he'd had time to reload, the gallant little charge suddenly fizzled out. The soldiers halted, then began to draw back, defiantly at first, musket and bayonet to the front.

They continued to back away until eventually they were swallowed up by the mist.

The brothers surveyed the field. Two of the soldiers they'd shot were dead. The third was trying to crawl after his comrades, a red trail tracing his dying moments.

Colin hobbled painfully over to his brother.

"Alistair?"

As he drew closer he realised his brother was trembling uncontrollably, tears pouring down his chalk-white face. He saw the pool of blood in which his brother was standing.

"Och, Alistair, man. Your arm."

The blood was dribbling through the fingers of his left hand like juice from a fruit-press. The older man swayed, trying to remain on his feet, but he was unconscious even before he hit the ground.

In the distance Alistair could hear the incessant rumble of artillery. A smouldering glow illuminated the horizon, as if the door to some gigantic furnace had been left ajar. Everything was deathly still in his sector. He could see neither shape nor movement in the pitch-blackness before his trench. It was as if everything he knew to be out there: the barbed wire, the shell holes, the decaying remains... all had disappeared into a featureless vacuum.

He tried not to visualise the faces of comrades lost in that last assault. This stretch of ground had been fought over for weeks now. God alone knew how many lay out there, deprived even a Christian burial.

Something was moving in the darkness... He sensed a subtle change at first, as though some entity had been surreptitiously spawned in the night. He heard it then; a distinct sound coming from no man's land. Not the furtive chink of metal upon metal that told of an enemy raid, but something less... secretive, more like a heavy load being pulled along the ground. He heard it again, to his left, the same laboured dragging sound, now much nearer.

He held the flare pistol tightly in his hand, waiting for the right moment to flood the scene with light. The fear was like a dead weight on his chest. Absurdly he could hear singing, coming from... out there. It was an old Gaelic lullaby his mother had crooned at him when he was a child... He'd barely realised the singer was a woman, when the flare pistol was taken from his hands.

Immediately the scene was bathed in light.

Alistair opened his eyes, to see the face of an angel looking down at him. He recognised the little wraith who'd saved her people from the inferno.

"Her name is Mary," Colin explained brightly. "Herself has been singing to you this past half hour, man. I think myself somebody has a wee fancy for you."

He was lying in a bed of straw in one of the cottages. His arm had been dressed and bandaged and felt free of pain.

"Mary was able to get the ball out of your arm," his brother continued cheerfully. "We could have made enough black pudding to feed Lochaber with the blood you lost." He held up his leg to show his own war wound. "I was lucky, myself. The ball just skiffed my calf. Mind you, I'll be left with a scar."

Alistair tried to pull himself upright, but was restrained by two determined little hands.

"*No. You must lie still,*" his nurse said softly in Gaelic. "*You have lost too much blood.*"

Mary... Her name was Mary... He couldn't even begin to understand how this hauntingly beautiful fragment of the past could be with him here... now. As she fussed over his dressing her long dark hair fell carelessly over features that would normally have turned him to jelly. There was no awkwardness about her; Alistair guessed she'd grown comfortable in his presence while he'd been unconscious, and he found himself afraid to open his mouth in case he broke the spell.

Colin had no such inhibitions: "All the others have taken to the hills in case the soldiers come back. We could hear a lot of shooting away to the west a wee while ago. Mary said she would not leave us... but I think she meant yourself..."

"*Please,*" she interrupted then, "*if you have the Gaelic... please, spare my house the tongue of those men...*"

Colin apologised, but it was his brother's eyes that held her soft gaze.

She would not leave... yourself, he had said. Alistair knew then, amid the insanity of the moment, that somehow this beautiful Mary of the mists was about to become a part of his life. He began to lapse once more into unconsciousness. For the first time in a very long time he had no fear of the darkness. Perhaps this time he would be spared the dreams...

As he drifted off, however, he heard the distant crack of single, high-velocity rifle shots.

Chapter Seven

A rich, bovine smell drew all manner of strange associations in Macmillan's mind as he struggled back to consciousness. He opened his eyes to find the fearsome shape of a Highland cow peering back at him. Man and beast gaped at each for a few moments, before the animal resumed its rhythmical chewing.

Macmillan took stock of his surroundings. He was in a dank, foul-smelling byre, its earthen floor covered with straw. Beside him his comrades lay in a tangled sprawl, like a trio of newborn calves.

They had also begun to take stock of their surroundings.

"Get yer ass outtae ma face," growled Rae.

"Aw, Ah wondered where the draught was coming from." Ferguson rose gingerly to his feet. "What is the story here, by the way? Where are we?"

"Aw no…" Macsorley's voice was full of anguish. "There's dung on ma clothes. This floor is all covered with dung. What is going on here?"

"There's a horse in here with us!" Ferguson cried, his voice edged with panic.

"Look, sharrup the lot o' yez!" yelled the corporal. "It's no' a horse, it's a cow. Now gerra grip of yerselves 'til we find out what the score is."

"Aw naw, Ah'm all covered in cow dung."

"Where the hell are we…?" Macmillan murmured. The walls of the byre consisted of rough, dry-stone blocks, the low sloping ceiling of dried bracken. Its windows were little more than vertical slits.

"Looks like we're in some kindae prison," Ferguson observed, casting an experienced eye around him.

"And what's Morag been jailed for? Shitting without a permit?"

"Ah wouldnae be surprised," grumbled Macsorley.

Macmillan indicated the weapons and ammunition at their feet. "Well, we're definitely not in prison." He gave Rae a long withering look. "Not yet, anyway."

"Aw Gawd, that's right," Ferguson remembered. He backed away from his friend. "Aw hell, you've done some daft things in the past, but you've really screwed it up this time. You're gonnae get us all shot."

"It wasnae ma fault," the big man cried, "you saw what happened. Ah wasnae aiming at him, Ah was aiming at yon... yon..."

"And what about that explosion in the sky?" Macsorley put in, dabbing straw at his uniform. "What the hell was all that about?"

The images were coming back to them now in sporadic bursts.

As Macmillan retrieved his rifle he became aware of a faint glow edging a portion of the wall to his left. He realised he was looking at a doorway, concealed behind a shabby curtain. He snapped into action.

"Mac, put one up the spout, keep the safety on. Rae, Fergie, stay here 'til we recce this." He nodded at Macsorley, who'd moved to cover the exit. "Follow me through, okay?"

Cautiously the non-commissioned officer probed the makeshift curtain with the point of his rifle, before pushing the material to one side. The faint glow became a dull reddish light, and for the second time that day he smelt the aromatic tang of peat smoke.

The cow smelt it too and waddled towards the opening. Rae and Ferguson jumped out of its way as if they'd been ambushed by a predator. Macmillan allowed the cow to squeeze through the doorway and then followed on behind.

Man and beast emerged together into the smoky depths of what appeared to be another, larger cattle shed. To his left he could see daylight through a small window and around the edges of a badly-fitting door. In the middle of the floor a smouldering fire gave off equal amounts of smoke and flame. As Macmillan's eyes adjusted to the gloom he could make out pieces of rudimentary furniture. From the blackened rafters hung an assortment of fish and game, curing naturally in the sweet smoky air.

The building appeared to be uninhabited. The cow knew differently, however. Lowing softly, it lumbered towards a little recess at the far end of the building, where Macmillan could hear hushed voices shooing the animal away.

"On your feet, whoever's there!" he yelled.

Immediately the whispering ceased.

"Come on, out with ye!" Macmillan barked, his rifle at the ready.

Still there was no movement from the shadows, other than the contented swishing of the cow's tail. Macsorley added his voice then, in words that were lost on his corporal. Moments later four nervous figures began to emerge into the smouldering glow of the peat flame, clinging together like hinds cornered by wolves. The cow moved forward with them, as though it too were part of the family group.

Leading the little cluster was a man of about sixty. He was small, stocky, with long silver hair and flowing beard. He was dressed in the ancient Highland garb of tartan plaid, or *phillamhor*, the brightly checked patterns pleated above the knee to form a kilt, with the remainder of the material brought over his left shoulder and fastened at the breast.

The others were all women; the oldest in her mid-forties. Macmillan guessed the two younger women were aged about twenty and twelve respectively. All were dressed in shawls weaved in individual tartans, which hung attractively over dark, calf-length dresses. True to his profession, the corporal's eyes lingered over the shapely form of the older girl.

By now Rae and Ferguson had also made their way through the opening. Rae introduced himself, a smile of bright interest on his face.

"Hello there, darling, how's it goin'?"

The girl took one look at the latest intruders and shrank back into the shadows.

"What are they, Corp? Tinkers or what?" asked Ferguson.

"Of course they're not bloody tinkers!" Macsorley hissed.

"What the hell is going on here?" Macmillan breathed.

"Are they... you know... are they, like, real? Ah mean, they're no' like that other lot we saw?"

"They look real enough."

"What was it you said tae them Mac?" Macmillan asked.

"Ah got learnt a fair bit of the old Gaelic when Ah was a kid. Ah told them no' tae be scared. That you were only shouting like that because you were more afraid than they were."

"Ye said what?" Macmillan could see the girls looking fearfully in his direction, and decided not to pursue the issue.

"Don't they speak English, then?"

"Doesnae look like it."

"Can you translate for us?" Rae asked.

"Ah can try. Ah only remember bits and pieces, but."

"Good. Ask the doll if she's doing anything the night," said Rae with a suggestive leer.

"Right, give it a break!" barked Macmillan. "Mac. Get them tae talk if you can. Try tae find out who they are. See if you can... if you can..." He shook his head. "Just get them tae talk, okay?"

Macmillan and the others stood in redundant silence then, as the ancient tongue of Glen Laragain found its voice once more. Macsorley spoke softly to the little group, occasionally stopping to correct himself, as half-forgotten words and phrases came back to mind. At first his audience stared dumbly back at him, but eventually the soldier began to draw some response. Occasionally one or other of the women would offer a reply, but mostly the dialogue centred on the old Highlander.

At last Macsorley turned to his comrades, a stunned look on his face.

"What did they say, Mac?"

"You're not gonnae like this, Corp."

"Why doesn't that surprise me?"

Macsorley used his beret to wipe the sweat from his face. He took some time to compose himself, as if he was having difficulty translating his message into English.

"This place is *an tigh dubh*," he began, "a black house."

"Ye mean like a croft-house?"

Macsorley shook his head. "This house would be part of a township; like a farming community. Each family would've kept a cow, for milk and butter and that. During the winter, or when it was sick, it would've been housed in the *tigh dubh*."

"What about that lot?" The corporal indicated the inhabitants, who'd begun to recover some dignity now that the danger seemed to have passed.

"The *bodach*; the old guy; his name is *Domnhuill Beag Camshron*; Donald Cameron tae you and me. That's his wife; *Mhairi*, and his daughters *Ishbel* and *Shona*. He says he also has two boys, but he wanted to emphasise they're no' away with the army. They're away hunting venison."

"The army?"

Macsorley looked apprehensively at his N.C.O. "Prince Charlie's Jacobite army."

There was a long, horrified silence, which was eventually broken by Rae's studied response: "What a loada rubbish! Bonnie Prince Charlie? You've translated it all wrong, ya dumplin'!"

Macsorley shook his head. "It's like Ah said earlier; this isn't a croft-house; the old guy's never heard of the word. Crofts didn't appear until later in the eighteenth century."

Macmillan could see the old Highlander whispering at his family. Their expressions indicated they were having equal difficulty accepting events.

"So this is all real?" said Ferguson. "These people; they're no' ghosts or that? They think they're living in... in... seventeen sixty-four?"

"It's seventeen forty-six, and that's no' what Ah'm saying! It's no' them that's the problem, it's us! They *are* livin' in seventeen forty–six... This is it! This is the real thing! God alone knows what we're doing here!"

Rae shook his head angrily. "Aw, this is all rubbish! That's probably dope the old git's burning in yon fire! Ah've had enough of this. Ah'm getting tae hell outae here!" He pushed his way angrily out of the house, almost taking the door off its hinges. Immediately he came to a halt, moaning softly: "Aw, God Almighty."

Gone was the assault course that had been gouged out of the glen. Gone too were the ruins that studded the landscape. Before him, nestling in archaic splendour, lay a scattered hamlet of thatched cottages, each sending a little trail of peat smoke into the soft morning air. As far as the eye could see, the land showed every sign of habitation. Amid the pastoral clutter chickens, goats, cattle, sturdy little ponies grazed. Cultivated ridges snaked upwards into the cloud-covered hillsides.

"Have you ever seen anything so wonderful in all yer life?" said Macsorley, his eyes bright with excitement.

"This is no' happening," Rae mumbled.

"Did we do this?" whispered Ferguson. "We didnae do all this, did we?"

"Chentlemen, you will forgive my lack of hospitality," a soft, heavily accented voice interjected.

All four turned in surprise to find the old Highlander standing behind them. His womenfolk still hovered nervously on the threshold of their cottage.

"It is not ushual for visitors to be entering my house through the byre."

The soldiers gaped in mute astonishment. Encountering this phantom was one thing; discovering he could talk was like communicating with the dead.

"Yes, chentlemen, I have the English, myself," the old Highlander went on. " 'Tis a wise man who learns the tongue of his adversary, is it not?"

"Who... eh, who are you?" Macmillan mumbled.

"As your young friend informed you; I am *Domnhuill Beag Camshron* of *Achnacon*." He bowed elegantly. "And yourselfs, chentlemen? You wear the breeks of the Lowlander, but I am thinking you are not King Cheorge's men...?"

Macmillan shook his head, his eyes as wide as if he was confronted by Lazarus. "Corporal Andy Macmillan, from Stirling..." Mechanically he held out his hand, which the Highlander grasped.

"Macmillan, you say? From Stirling? An unshual home for such a fine name." His alert eyes took in every detail of his strange visitors. "Now there is a queer thing... And would yourself be kin to the Macmillans of Loch Arkaigside, at all?"

"Aaah don't think so..."

Their interpreter held out his hand. "Private James Macsorley, from... eh, from *Muirshearlach*..."

The old Highlander's face lit up. "Macsorley... from *Muirshearlach*? Och, but of course, yourself hass the red hair of *Muirshearlach*. You are welcome to my home, young *Muirshearlach*." He turned to the remaining soldiers, who stood like mute oxen, awaiting orders. "And your friends?"

"Private Archie Rae, frae Paisley..."

"Private William Ferguson, frae Irvine yer... er, yer Highness."

"Paisley... Irvine... Ach, well, never mind," the old man murmured disappointedly. "Och, but I am forgetting my manners. Yourselfs must be tired, and hungry, after your... ah, your chourney here?"

Food had been the last thing on their minds, although none of them could remember the last time they had eaten.

Macmillan smiled. "That would be very kind of you Mister... er, Mister Cameron. Ah'm afraid we've no way of paying you for food, but..."

The old Highlander was instantly offended. "Paying me... for my hospitality? Och, man, you do not pay for hospitality in the house of a

Highland chentleman." He looked accusingly at Macsorley. "You are of the *Gaidhealtacht*. You above all should know this."

The young man flushed and looked accusingly at his corporal.

"You should also know it is customary to address a chentleman according to his place of residence. To friends and foe alike I am known as *Achnacon*." A guarded smile replaced his expression of disapproval. "I trust *Achnacon* shares his bread with friends this day...?"

The soldiers were to learn that Achnacon of Glen Laragain was by no means a wealthy man. Almost everything he and his family owned, wore, or consumed was produced by their own hands. They lived well off their land, however, and according to the Highland code of hospitality the fruit of their labours was shared with all who entered their door. Their visitors were treated to a meal of cheese, oatcakes, bannocks, smoked venison and trout.

The lady of the house grew more at ease as her guests accepted the unspoken bonds of her hospitality. Like her daughters she was dark haired, her features strong and forceful. There was an air of simple dignity about her that had her young guests falling over themselves to show off their manners. All, that is, except Rae, who acted like an automaton, dumbly accepting everything he was offered.

The demure Ishbel remained in the background, ignoring every attempt at eye contact. Shona, the younger daughter, quickly ensconced herself amongst the company. She was ferociously inquisitive and tormented Macsorley with a barrage of unanswerable questions.

The master of the house chatted lightly to them about this and that, gently trying to cast some light on this mystery which had manifested itself within his *tigh dubh*. Ultimately Achnacon steered the conversation around to events taking place beyond Glen Laragain:

"A queer business this uprising, is it not? Many of the young men gone from the hills to fight for Prince Tchearlach... others to fight for King Cheorge..." His gaze flicked over the faces of his guests. "Many an honest man will lose all ere this business is finished, I am thinking, whichever royal backside sits on the throne of England..."

"Aye, that's right enough," Macmillan murmured noncommittally.

Shona had discovered the zip fastener on Macsorley's combat jacket, and was giggling with delight at this wonderful new toy.

"Some say Locheil and Keppoch will return to Lochaber to lay siege once more to the black garrison. Others say they have gone to Inverness to do battle with the Chuke's army..."

Macmillan looked to his troops in a silent appeal for help. They all sat by the smoky warmth of Achnacon's hearth, ensnared in the sweet trap of his debt, yet the N.C.O. had no idea what tack he should take.

Macsorley had no such problems: "It's like you said earlier, er, Achnacon, none of us here are King George's men. As far as Ah'm concerned the Hanoverians are a bunch of murdering animals. Pardon ma language and all that…"

The old Highlander nodded warily. "Aye, chust so, chust so." He looked at the N.C.O. "And yourself, Corporal Andy? Are you a Prince's man, or a Chuke's man? Or does yourself belong to no man whatever?"

Macmillan squirmed in his seat of heather and straw. "Ah don't know… Ah mean… What tae make of it all…"

Macsorley cut in, diplomacy thrown to the wind: "This cannae be an accident, Corp. We've all had time to think about it. Whatever happened to us has happened for a purpose."

Achnacon leaned forward in sudden interest. "And, ah, what might this purpose be?"

Macmillan glared at the young soldier. Ferguson looked as though he was about to offer his diplomatic skills, forcing the corporal to bite the bullet.

"Ah remember, er, years ago it was, reading how a lot of Macdonalds were saved during the Glencoe massacre by Campbell soldiers who'd been billeted with them. It seems a lot o' them passed on the warning of what was about tae happen. They say that's why only thirty-six people died, instead of the whole three hundred they'd intended tae kill."

Their host regarded the young corporal warily. "Aye, this is indeed so. But why speak of this now? Surely you do not think such a scheme has been hatched against ourselfs?"

Macmillan nodded, grateful he'd not had to labour the point.

"The Hanoverians are gonnae do tae Glen Laragain what the Campbell soldiers did tae Glencoe," he said, more bluntly than he had intended.

"What? But why would they do such a thing? In God's name to what end?" Without waiting for an answer Achnacon spoke urgently to his family. Instantly the mood changed. Shona was called away from her new friends and gathered into her mother's arms.

The Highlander was on his feet now, his eyes flashing wildly. "Achnacon's sword arm is as strong as ever it was, but I, myself, am but one man. All the young warriors is away with Locheil and the Prince. None is left but the old and infirm."

Macmillan and his troops sat like men who'd lit a candle and watched it turn to dynamite.

"And yourself, Corporal Andy. Have you come to betray the hospitality of Achnacon as the Campbells betrayed Glencoe?"

Macmillan was in desperate need of some higher authority to take control of the situation and return him to his rightful place within a clear chain of command.

Macsorley rose impassionedly to his feet. "No one here's gonnae betray you, Achnacon. We'll stand with you."

"Ah'm up for that," said Rae.

"We'll do *what*?" blustered Macmillan.

"...Ah've figured out what's going on here," Ferguson suddenly announced. "Ah think we were hand-picked for this. Ah think the army has us on some kindae special mission."

"What are you *on* about?" Macmillan growled irritably.

"Well, think about it. We all *just happen* tae be in the glen on a live-firing exercise, then we *just happen* tae be around when that mist with all thae things in it comes down, and then we *just happen* tae be in the area when there's yon big flash in the sky... Well...? Don't you see what Ah'm getting at?"

"Aw Gawd, Ah cannae wait...."

"The army's been experimenting with time travel. We've been specially selected and then sent back tae prevent the massacre. It's obvious when ye think about it." There was an expression of pure triumph on his face.

"Aw you great dumplin' that you are," Rae snarled. "The British Army has sent us back in time tae fight the British Army?"

A shadow of doubt ruffled the bliss on Ferguson's face. "Aye, Ah wasn't quite sure about that bit right enough."

Macmillan was relieved to see Achnacon's bewilderment. Not all of Private Ferguson's revelations were lost on the old clansman, however.

"You speak again of massacre, as if you have witnessed this terrible deed that is yet to be. You must say what you know, Corporal Andy..."

"It happens in the mist," Macsorley cut in before his corporal could reply. "Don't know the time o' day. A full company of infantry is deployed and when they come they move through the glen using just the bayonet, so there's no warning. None o' the men are to be left alive. Glen Laragain is to be laid waste from east to west..."

The blood drained from Achnacon's face. "And when is this... this crime to take place?" he whispered.

"The twenty-first of April."

A long sigh escaped the old Highlander's lips. "'Tis as I had feared... our warriors have proved too slippery for them, so they seek to punish the old and the helpless." He turned to Macmillan. "Our enemy seeks to extirpate the people of Glen Laragain. However we have eleven days grace. The lassies and bairns can be got to the shielings until the business is done. All who can will stand. And what of yourself, Corporal Andy? Will you stand with your men? With Achnacon?"

Macmillan shook his head in defeat. "Don't have much choice, do Ah?" He rounded on his jubilant troops. "But we don't replace one massacre with another. We do as little as it takes tae stop it happening, right?"

"Aye, sure, you're the boss," Rae murmured evasively.

"Yourselfs will all stand with me then?" The Highlander's eyes reflected the flicker of the peat flame. One by one he grasped the hands of his newfound comrades. "On the morrow we shall speak to all the people. You may tell them what you have told myself."

He spoke briefly to his wife, and moments later she reappeared with a large earthenware jug, which Achnacon lifted to his mouth with practised ease. Gasping with raw pleasure he passed the jar to Macmillan, who made the mistake of imitating his host. Immediately he felt a volcano erupt in his mouth, spewing lava throughout his digestive system.

"In the name of God," he wheezed, "what is that?"

"'Tis my own brew; the water of life, three-times distilled."

Achnacon's home-brewed whisky drew much the same reaction from the rest of the troops. None of them could have been more impressed if he'd turned water to wine before their eyes.

As the pyroclastic fires slowly subsided within him Macmillan decided to retain control of his wits and leave the drinking to the others. He'd become aware of the dark eyes of his hostess burning into his own. There was more than mistrust there; Macmillan had the impression he was being given a dark and terrible warning.

In that moment he discovered something about clan society that he'd never learnt from any history book.

Chapter Eight

"Corpohral! *Corpohral!*"

Macmillan did his best to focus on the two faces leaning over him.

"Corpohral Auntie!"

Someone was tugging at his sleeve. The faces were familiar... Isabel... No, Ishbel... Ishbel and Shona! The memory of Achnacon, his black house, and his deadly *uisge beatha* hit him like a rush of cold water.

Ishbel continued to pull at his sleeve as he sat upright. He had no idea if he'd been asleep for minutes or hours. He remembered allowing himself one more swallow of Achnacon's firewater, and then watching in drowsy detachment as his comrades degenerated into a drunken rabble.

In one corner Rae and Ferguson were sprawled together on one of the beds. Achnacon's wife was trying to rouse her husband from his chair by the hearth. He'd last seen Macsorley dressed in one of Achnacon's phillamhors.

Macmillan became aware of the fear on the faces of the two girls. Before he could utter a word one of Ishbel's fingers was pressed firmly against his lips.

"Sssshhh." She whispered so softly the sound was barely audible.

She waited until she was satisfied Macmillan understood, before leading him to the window of the cottage, her bare feet hardly touching the carpet of straw as she tip-toed before him. Young Shona brought up the rear, cradling Macmillan's rifle in her arms, a native accompanying a tiger shoot in the Punjab.

Ishbel crouched by the window, a flush of fear and excitement in her cheeks. Again she whispered at Macmillan; one of the few English words she'd learnt:

"Sholdiers..."

The corporal's eyes widened in alarm. He looked through the small square opening into the mist beyond, but could see nothing of any significance. No colour, no movement. Only the grey shapes of neighbouring cottages, like ships adrift in an ocean fog.

"Where? There's no one…"

"Sssshhh!" the sisters hissed together, both glaring at him as if he were an imbecile.

Macmillan withered under their gaze. Where was Macsorley when he needed him? "Macsorley?" he whispered. "Where is Macsorley?"

The girls made it clear this was no time for idle chitchat. Frantically Ishbel tugged at her ears and pointed to the west. Macmillan wondered if they'd been so terrified by all the talk of slaughter and massacre they'd panicked at the first sign of mist.

At that moment, far to the east, he heard what sounded like gunfire. Not the high-pitched crack of high-velocity weapons, but a series of thunderous reports, interspersed with sporadic single explosions. The firing continued for about thirty seconds, then died away into silence.

Macmillan shook his head in stunned disbelief. Achnacon had told them today was the tenth of April. He wondered if he'd emerged from an eleven-day coma. A glance at his watch confirmed the date was the tenth, the time seventeen-thirty.

Shona thrust the rifle into Macmillan's hands, as though she was handing a shovel to an idle workman. "Sholdiers," she whispered.

Macmillan tried to remember if he'd loaded with ten or twenty rounds. Either way he would need more ammo. The webbing with the spare mags was nowhere to be seen. He couldn't remember if they'd been left in the byre, or moved elsewhere. He held up the rifle and pointed to the byre.

There was a whispered conference between the sisters before Shona silently scuttled off. While he waited Macmillan listened intently for any warning of the soldier's approach. He could see Ishbel doing likewise.

He stole a glance at the girl. Like her mother she wasn't delicately featured in the classical sense, but her face was strong and well formed, her figure shapely and attractive. Like her mother, too, she was intensely feminine in a way that was natural and untamed.

He felt a rush of air behind him as Shona returned. Cradled in her arms, minus its ammunition belt, was the G.P.M.G. Without ammo it was as much use as a club. He smiled and nodded his head. Where the

66

hell was Macsorley? He considered leaving the girls on their own to search for the ammo pouches, but decided it wasn't worth the risk.

There was little he could do but settle down by the window and wait, the sisters crouched beside him like adopted waifs. He wondered about the inhabitants of the neighbouring cottages. None of the houses showed any sign of life. Even the livestock they'd seen earlier had vanished, dissolved in the mist.

Mhairi had given up trying to rouse her husband and was now slumped on the floor beside him. Only the shallow breathing of Ishbel and Shona disturbed the heavy silence.

Macmillan settled the cold, reassuring shape of the self-loading rifle. against the junction of his chest and arm. With the blanket of mist concealing all signs of life, and the air heavy with menace, he decided he could just as easily be occupying an observation post in Belfast.

The irony of this he would ponder another day.

Ishbel held up her hand. She turned her head to one side, trying to penetrate the blanket of mist. It was a while before Macmillan heard it too; the sound of faint cries and yells; the distant shouts of men caught up in the sudden excitement of the chase. With a shock he realised the sounds were coming from the west. If the attack had been launched from the east then the soldiers must have passed Achnacon's clachan already! Dear God, no wonder the girls had been so afraid. The sounds died away as quickly as they'd arisen.

Ishbel took her young sisters hand. "Sholdiers," she told Macmillan softly.

He nodded, aware of a sense of shame, feeling damned by association. He decided if they survived this day he would have Macsorley teach him the rudiments of Gaelic. He wanted to learn more about the world of Achnacon... and of Ishbel... especially of Ishbel.

She let out a little hiss of alarm. This time Macmillan heard it too; the murmur of voices coming from the far side of the hamlet, no more than a hundred yards away. The voices faded towards the west, and other voices took their place, until a line of invisible figures could be heard moving past. Macmillan guessed the shouting they'd heard earlier was the vanguard making contact with the next clachan.

Whether the mist began to thin, or whether the column drifted closer to the cottage, Macmillan couldn't tell. But gradually some of the figures began to emerge from the mist. Hardly daring to breathe he watched as the dreaded red-coated soldiers of King George of Hanover materialised before them. He could see individual infantrymen, their scarlet uniforms turned to sepia by the mist, their muskets barely visible in the gloom.

Macmillan was no stranger to active service and was familiar with that terrible fear that sends adrenalin surging through a man's veins, powering the urge to run or fight. He knew the most difficult thing of all was to do nothing. He pulled the S.L.R. into the crook of his shoulder and tried to keep his breathing as calm and regular as possible.

Neither of the girls had uttered a sound since the redcoats came into view. Ishbel had wrapped her arms around her sister, and was rocking her from side to side.

As the column of infantry trudged by, Macmillan realised the mist was indeed beginning to thin. He could clearly make out each individual infantryman. He could also see two motionless figures lying between the dry-stone buildings. They must have been taken so completely by surprise they barely made it beyond their front door. Achnacon's cottage lay apart from the rest, and was evidently overlooked in that first attack. Now that the mist was lifting they wouldn't remain overlooked for long.

Suddenly it dawned on Macmillan. These were the images the firing party had witnessed as that first terrible mist had descended upon them. He knew exactly what was about to happen, even before the group of soldiers caught sight of Achnacon's cottage, and began to move towards it.

Noiselessly Shona ran into the arms of her mother, while Ishbel remained beside Macmillan. Only then did he understand the origin of those final images they'd witnessed; the shapes that had sprung from nowhere and darted into the mist, to be pursued by the soldiers.

The Hanoverians were less than thirty yards away now. The corporal could make out the red stain on the bayonet of the lead figure. By Macmillan's simple criteria this signed his death warrant. With practised ease he cocked his rifle, allowed the scarlet tunic to fill his sights and squeezed the trigger. The single 7.62mm round lifted the soldier off his feet, spattering his comrades with bloody fragments of lung and bone.

Macmillan could have done the same to the others, but he held his fire. The soldiers returned a scattered volley before withdrawing to the nearest cottage, leaving a pall of grey smoke hanging in the air. Behind them he could hear a familiar cacophony of yells and screams as officers and N.C.O.s responded to this sudden resistance.

He knew it wouldn't be long before a second group was sent forward against him. Ishbel was tugging at his sleeve, trying to bring his attention to… what? She pointed to the barrel of his rifle. Of course; she was reminding him to reload with ball and powder. He shook his head and winked knowingly, hoping this meant the same to an eighteenth-century Gael as it did to a twentieth-century squaddie.

He saw only fear and despair in her eyes.

There was no time to explain. Already a force of nine or ten men had appeared around the side of the nearest cottage. As soon as they had formed up they began to trot clumsily forward. Macmillan could see the determination and apprehension on their faces. He blotted out any sense of kinship one soldier might feel for another, and aligned his sights on the three lead uniforms. One after another they were hurled back into their comrades as the rounds smashed through their chests.

The momentum of the charge was instantly lost. Two of the survivors turned and fled; the remaining five brought their muskets to their shoulders. Macmillan ducked down, but Ishbel remained at the window, her eyes wide with amazement. He hauled her out of the way as the little volley of musket balls peppered the stone blocks around the window.

"Stay down," he hissed. "D'ye understand? Down!"

She seemed oblivious to the danger. Her eyes remained fixed on Macmillan as if he was the great Ossian, come to save his people.

Outside, to his horror, the remaining soldiers were advancing once more. They were barely twenty yards from the door of the cottage, bayonets at the ready. Macmillan loosed off two rounds at the bobbing figures before they'd advanced beyond his line of fire. As he swung round to cover the entrance, the soldiers smashed through the door and spilled into the house. Macmillan stood before them like a psychopath, firing round after round into the screaming mob as they tried to fan out beyond the bottleneck of the doorway. Almost deafened by the crack of the S.L.R., half-crazed by the slaughter before him, he continued to jerk at the trigger long after the magazine was empty, and long after the only screams to be heard were those of Shona behind him.

At last even her screams fell away, until only the rhythmical creaking of Achnacon's ruined door disturbed the silence. Like the sole survivor of some terrible disaster Macmillan alone remained on his feet, facing a tangled mound of dead and dying men. The rifle slipped through his hands. He stood in the deafening silence, unable to tear his eyes away from the carnage before him.

"Aw man, whassgoin' on here, eh?"

Macmillan turned, as if in a dream, to find Macsorley at his side.

"Ah thought Ah heard a lottae shooting and stuff. Whass happening?" He still wore Achnacon's tartan plaid and looked, and smelt, as though he'd been sleeping in the cowshed. His voice was slurred, his eyes glazed from the effects of Achnacon's *uisge beatha*.

"Yer rifle," the corporal mumbled. "Where's yer rifle?"

Macsorley gaped stupidly at his N.C.O. for a moment, before his right arm appeared from beneath his plaid incongruously clutching his S.L.R. Macmillan's trembling hands took possession of the weapon. Its familiar, solid shape helped to calm him. He indicated the window, where Ishbel was kneeling, her hands still over her ears.

"Get her... get her tae find the rest of the ammo... mags, webbing... the ammo box for the jimpy."

Macsorley tried to focus on the strange mess at the doorway. "The lassies... did something with all that stuff earlier, so they did."

Macmillan was beginning to regain control of himself. He picked up his empty rifle and thrust it at Macsorley.

"Get her tae bring that stuff here. *Now!*"

For a moment Macmillan thought the young soldier was going to throw up over him. He belched noisily, and stood swaying for a moment before making his way unsteadily over to Ishbel.

Macmillan turned to the gaping doorway and the butchery that surrounded it. Four redcoats had made it into the house, and all had been shot down before they'd taken two steps beyond the door. They now lay tangled in a little lochan of blood, out of which a red burn trickled in bitter retreat.

Beyond the open doorway Macmillan could see the mist withdrawing up the hillside. He could make out fresh movements amongst the red uniforms on the other side of the cottages. The troops who'd trudged past them would have been recalled by now, but he was confident they would risk no more frontal assaults.

At the window Macsorley's slurred ramblings were drawing little response from Ishbel. She seemed unable to tear her eyes away from the entrance to her *tigh dubh*. Macmillan pulled the straw-filled mattress from beneath the unconscious shapes of Ferguson and Rae and threw it over the four corpses at the doorway. This seemed to break the spell under which Ishbel had fallen. The corporal could hear the soft lilt of her voice as she tried to respond to Macsorley's maunderings.

At last the young soldier reported back. "That is one… extremely nice wee bit of stuff… Ah reckon Ah'm in with a shout there…"

"Aw for God's sake!" Macmillan snarled. "Did ye find out where they stashed the webbing and the ammo?"

Macsorley smiled knowingly and tapped his nose, then pointed dramatically at the recess where they'd first encountered Achnacon and his family. Hidden beneath layers of plaid lay their magazines, pouches and khaki-coloured ammunition box for the G.P.M.G.

Macsorley leaned against the wall, grinning with idiotic pride, as Macmillan gathered up the hoard and carried it over to the window. By now Ishbel had joined her mother and sister near the hearth.

Outside everything remained quiet, but he knew it wouldn't be long before they made their next move. Macmillan discovered what had become of the fifth soldier who'd charged the cottage. Caught in his final fusillade before the doorway was stormed, the redcoat lay twenty feet from the window, bleeding heavily from a chest wound, but clearly still alive. Macmillan could see bubbles of pink froth rising and falling around the man's mouth as he clung stubbornly to life.

He forced himself to concentrate on the nearby cottages, lying deceptively at peace in the gathering twilight. As he waited he fastened his combat webbing around his waist, and checked the magazines in the front pouches.

Macsorley decided the corporal could use some company and flopped down beside him. He caught sight of the dying redcoat. "Hell's teeth, what happened tae him?"

Macmillan gave him a withering look, which failed to penetrate Macsorley's addled brain.

Macsorley decided things needed lightening up.

"Too much… tae drink, eh pal? You look like… like…" Slowly he became aware of Macmillan's other victims, lying spread-eagled in their own gore thirty yards from the cottage. He swallowed horribly a couple of times. "Aw Gawd… Gonnae be sick…"

He made it as far as the doorway, before emptying the contents of his stomach over the mattress. His moans of self-pity turned to horrified groans as he realised what lay beneath. Eventually he reappeared, looking grey and ill. He gaped at the corporal.

"Hell, Corp, if this is you trying tae avoid a massacre, Ah wouldn't like tae see you take the hump…"

"They didn't give me any choice," growled Macmillan. "It's all dead romantic, isn't it, but? Volunteering tae fight for the good guys, like you're one of the Magnificent Seven. See, next time you volunteer tae fight, try tae stay sober long enough tae actually do some fighting…"

"Aw, come on. How was Ah tae know the bastards would come today? This wasn't supposed tae happen until the twenty-first."

Macsorley still looked wretched, and smelt of stale whisky and cow-dung, but he seemed to be sobering up. Fast.

"How's the head?"

"Like Ah've been drinking two-hundred-year-old whisky."

"Aye? Serves ye right." The corporal indicated Macsorley's S.L.R. "That magazine's empty. Load with a fresh mag."

"D'you think Ah'll need it? D'you think they're gonnae come again?"

"Well, they haven't legged it, so Ah figure it's only a matter of time… Ah just wish Ah knew what the hell they were planning."

It wasn't long before his wish was granted. Macmillan saw a puff of smoke appear above the nearest thatched roof. A musket ball pinged off the outside wall. This was followed by a second shot, and then a third, as other carefully positioned infantrymen opened up a steady fire on the cottage. Before long some of the balls were whistling through the open window and door, ricocheting off the far wall.

"You've no' been making too many friends around here, have ye? Ah mean, these guys just haven't warmed tae you at all." Macsorley kept well away from the window. "Maybe we should get the women out of here."

Macmillan shook his head. "Don't be stupid, they're hardly gonnae be any safer out there. Go and talk tae them but, bring them over tae this near wall where they'll be out of the line of fire."

"What about Achnacon?"

"The old guy? Aye, bring him too. If ye cannae wake him, drag him over." He nodded towards Rae and Ferguson, who remained unconscious in the corner. "Get those two numpties on their feet as well, in case we have tae break out of here."

Outside, the flare of the muskets was becoming more and more prominent in the fading light. Even without the tell-tale flash, Macmillan could clearly make out each of their attackers. Soldiers who were trained to wage war in tightly packed ranks had no reason to conceal themselves, so long as they believed they'd cornered a group of rebels armed with smoothbore muskets.

He settled his sights on a soldier positioned on the roof of the nearest cottage. He was about to squeeze the trigger when the musket fire slackened, and then suddenly died away to nothing.

Macmillan peered into the gloom. "That's it now, just cut yer losses and sod off back to yer wee fort."

"Thank God for that," said Macsorley. "Ah didn't fancy the idea of…" He stopped in mid-sentence. "Uh oh."

"What's up?"

"We're on fire!"

"What?"

"We're on fire! They've set light tae the roof!"

Macmillan could see it for himself then. At either end of the cottage, smoke was billowing from the blackened thatch. As the musket fire broke out again he realised the sniping had only slackened off while the thatch was being fired.

Until that moment the women had been trying to tempt the master of the house back to consciousness. Now they hauled him to his feet and began to drag him towards the door.

"Mac! Stop them!" Macmillan yelled. "They're dead if they go out there."

Before the soldier could intervene the women encountered the mound of corpses. They veered away and came to a frightened standstill beside Macsorley.

"Mac, tell them we'll get them out of this. Tell them tae concentrate on wakening up Achnacon."

The corporal bounded over to Rae and Ferguson and dragged them both onto the floor.

"Aw, whassamatter here, eh?" Rae snarled like a disturbed grizzly. "Whatrafuck's goin' on?"

"Save it!" Macmillan snapped. "The place is on fire! The redcoats are outside!"

"Redcoats…?"

"Wur on fire…?"

Bloodshot eyes widened in horror as they took in the thick smoke billowing out of the thatch above their heads. Macsorley meanwhile had managed to calm the women down. All looked expectantly at Macmillan.

"Mac, we're gonnae have tae take on those guys out there, otherwise they'll slaughter us as we go out that door."

Macsorley swallowed horribly. "What d'you want me tae do?"

"Okay, Ah'm gonnae start from the window. You clear the bodies away from that doorway. Let me know when you're done!"

The shooting outside had died away now; Macmillan had no doubt they were waiting for the occupants to come spilling out of the cottage. He searched out the redcoats whose positions he'd marked earlier. They remained as he'd left them, muskets at the ready, like antique targets on a firing range. His sights settled on the face of the soldier he'd reprieved earlier; he gave the trigger a gentle squeeze and the familiar crack of the S.L.R. lifted the redcoat clear off the roof. Before his body had reached the ground Macmillan had marked his next target.

Like a deranged sniper he continued to mark and shoot, mark and shoot, firing round after round at the would-be execution squad. By the time he'd run out of targets the scale of his actions had removed any sense of guilt or accountability.

By now the roof beams were well ablaze. Rae and Ferguson had made their way into the middle of Achnacon's family group, drawn there by some blind herding instinct. Both looked as though they'd woken up in someone else's nightmare. Dumbly they stood and watched as Macsorley struggled to clear the corpses from the doorway, while flaming stalks of bracken rained down on them.

It was now that Achnacon's bovine resident decided that enough was enough. Bellowing with pent-up terror the animal charged out of the byre, towards its only exit from the inferno. With one sweep of its horns it knocked Macsorley out of the way, then bulldozed the corpses before it as it careered out of the cottage. Its appearance drew a ragged volley of musket fire, which only enraged it further. With horns swinging from side to side the animal charged towards the nearest group of soldiers, who immediately took to their heels. The others wavered, uncertain whether to reload or engage with the bayonet. In the end they did neither. The maddened animal swung this way and that, launching itself at anything it didn't like, and it did not like the redcoated soldiers with their strange-shaped hats and carrying those noisy sticks.

The women of Achnacon took advantage of the mayhem and followed their saviour out of the cottage, still supporting their unconscious chieftain. Rae and Ferguson were swept along with them, like sleepwalkers in a crowd.

In an instant all had melted into the gathering darkness.

As soon as Macsorley was clear of the inferno he dived to the ground, rifle at the ready. What remained of the enemy, however, was now in full retreat, pursued by Achnacon's deranged milk-cow.

Inside the cottage Macmillan threw the weapons and ammunition box through the window. The heat was so intense he could feel his hair smouldering. As he looked around to check nothing had been missed he heard the sound of wood cracking and knew the roof was about to give way.

Macsorley bellowed at his corporal to get out. Too late, the main timbers broke apart, collapsing into the building with a loud crash. Smoke and flame billowed out of the doorway. For one moment Macsorley considered battling through the flames, but he knew he'd be committing suicide.

At that moment something began to materialize from the wall of the cottage, like a moth emerging from its chrysalis. Macmillan had taken the only remaining exit from the inferno, and was struggling to pull himself free from the window. He was heaving with all his might but had become wedged in the narrow opening. Macsorley grabbed his N.C.O. by the collars of his combat jacket and added his weight to the struggle.

"Bloody pouches," Macmillan grunted. "Shoulda taken them off…"

"Breathe out! Empty yer lungs!" Macsorley hauled with all his strength, but his N.C.O. seemed to be cemented into the wall. He could see the first flicker of pain in Macmillan's face as the flames began to lick around his legs.

"Mac. Listen tae me," said the corporal, his eyes bright with fear, "Ah'm finished. Pick up yer S.L.R. Put one intae the head. There's no other way…"

Macsorley recoiled, his eyes widening in horror.

"Mac, ye cannae leave me like this…"

Macsorley picked up the rifle and levered a round into the firing chamber. He pointed the weapon at the corporal's head...

"Get it over with!"

Macsorley dropped the rifle. "No! This isn't right..."

With a roar of anger he grabbed hold of Macmillan's combat jacket and levered both his feet against the wall of the house. "Come — on — ye — fat — swine," he intoned fiercely. "Move — yer — horrible — carcass..."

Macsorley could hear Macmillan screaming, and then felt something give. He adjusted his footing, and slowly, steadily, as if he were easing a bung from a barrel, he pulled the soldier to safety.

As Macmillan fell on top of him Macsorley rolled his corporal over and over on the damp ground to smother any flames. Then he peeled off his burnt clothing and footwear. The soles of his boots were like melted liquorice.

Above them flames licked around the edges of the empty window, searching for their escaped prey.

"How are ye, Corp?" Macsorley asked.

Macmillan was trembling with shock, but he didn't seem too badly burnt. He held up his combat webbing, which Macsorley had torn in two as he'd pulled the corporal free.

"...Stubborn wee article," he muttered.

With a satisfied smile Macsorley took off his tartan phillamhor and laid it over Macmillan. His own uniform had gone up in flames but he could scrounge another plaid from Achnacon tomorrow.

Somewhere on the darkening hillside above he could hear Rae and Ferguson calling to each other, like two lost souls.

Chapter Nine

Sam awoke to a world shrouded in mist. This wasn't the mist with which he was familiar; the gentle salt-laden fog that drifts into San Francisco bay, like the sweet breath of the Pacific. Instead, this was something bleak and cold, that chilled him to the bone.

A few yards away, Shawnee lay face down on the wet heather. For one terrible moment he thought she was dead, but as he turned her over she twitched like a puppy in the midst of a bad dream. She woke with a last, frightened jerk, staring at Sam in wide-eyed panic, before the fear began to melt from her face.

"Where are we?" she whispered.

"I dunno. I know something... terrible happened, but..." Sam took in the grey moorland around them. "We were on vacation, in Europe... Scotland... but I don't recall anything like this."

Shawnee struggled to sit up. "Glen Laragain! We were in Glen Laragain! We were hurrying, trying to get away, from... from..."

It came back to them both then: That searing sky; the hellish explosion that had risen into the heavens before their eyes; the final horror as an arm of fire had reached down into Glen Laragain, as though Satan had resolved to incinerate the last shreds of humanity.

"Oh dear God, Sam..." The terror was back in her face. "It was like the end of the world!"

She shivered as he put his arms around her. She felt tiny and fragile.

"I don't understand. We're still in Glen Laragain, yet it's all different."

"None of it makes any sense. How come there's not even a scorch mark, for God-sakes? Where did all this mist come from? And why is it so freakin cold?"

Shawnee's trembling began to ease as she drew some warmth from Sam. He took off her backpack and pulled out a little quilted anorak, which he draped over her shoulders.

"I figured the nights might get cold in Scotland, so I packed these."
He dug out a similar anorak from his own backpack. "Shoulda got
matching pants as well, huh?"

"Sam, you don't think what we saw coulda been a vision of the
future? I mean, if a lotta people have seen images of the past here, then
maybe it works both ways."

He sighed and shook his head. "I dunno. It's possible, I guess. It's
just, what the guy said on the radio; everything that happened after; it
all kinda made sense, y'know? But there's something else been
bothering me. Listen, can you hear that sound?"

She turned her head to one side and listened intently for a few
moments. "Yes I hear it; running water." Her eyes widened. "Oh my
God! It's running water! In Glen Laragain!"

"Yeah. There doesn't seem to be a whole lotta global warming
around anymore, does there?"

They rose to their feet then, gazing fearfully around them, like two
children who'd woken up in the dead of night.

"Next year; what say we vacation somewhere nice and safe, like
Egypt, or Afghanistan."

Sam helped her on with her backpack. "We need to locate that
cottage we started off at; then get back to the car."

They set off hand in hand; following the contours of the land as it
gradually fell away towards the east. Ground that had been crisp
underfoot was now damp and boggy. Soon they encountered a path
that ran parallel with the burn. Here the water ran clear and pure as it
cascaded along well-worn channels.

They'd been following the path for less than ten minutes when a
dark mass of trees loomed out of the murk. Shawnee recognised the
avenue of Caledonian pines which led to Inverlaragain Cottage. Soon
they could make out the familiar shape of the house, a sentinel standing
in the mist. Both knew at once that something was wrong. This was
not the house they'd left only a matter of hours before. Gone was the
air of neglect and decay that had settled over the building like a shroud.
Its walls were no more than rough dry-stone construction, its roof of
homemade thatch, but the cottage was clearly inhabited.

"Tell me you're seeing this," Shawnee whispered hoarsely.

As Sam tried to respond the silence was shattered by a loud
commotion on the other side of the house. At first they could make

out only a high-pitched wailing, but after a few moments came the sound of male voices.

Sam bundled Shawnee into the cover of the trees, just as a number of figures materialised out of the mist. At first he was aware only that most of the group were dressed in red. It was a few moments before his brain acknowledged he was seeing not the scarlet anoraks of the outdoor elite, but the blood-red uniform of an ancient army.

His mind became strangely detached then. He was aware that Shawnee's breathing had grown fast and shallow, and that her fingernails were digging into his hand. He could hear her whispering; "Oh my God… Oh my God," over and over.

Five uniformed figures were half dragging, half carrying a young woman towards the cottage. She clawed and snarled at her captors, but this only seemed to add to their enjoyment. The soldiers dragged the woman into the cottage, then retraced their steps, their laughter rising and falling as each tried to outdo the coarse innuendo of the other. Within seconds the mist had swallowed them up again, leaving only the splashing of the stream to disturb the silence.

Long moments passed before Sam realised Shawnee was talking to him; "…what it was like for you the first time?"

"Huh? What… what're you saying?"

"That time you saw those Confederates at Gettysburg; was that what it was like for you?"

"I'm not altogether sure this is the same thing …"

"What d'you mean, Sam? My God, didn't you see them? Didn't you see the redcoat soldiers?"

"Oh yeah… I saw them. It's just that…"

"I totally cannot believe it," Shawnee went on blissfully. "We've seen the ghosts of Glen Laragain. Dad woulda given anything to be here today."

Sam tore his eyes away from the cottage. There was no trace of fear on Shawnee's face. She was like a little Sioux maiden who'd followed the braves on a war party.

"Listen, I'm not convinced we're seeing only fragments of the past here."

"What d'you mean?"

"I dunno; this is just so weird. That cottage looks nothing like the ruin we saw when we first got here."

Before Shawnee could reply, three of the soldiers reappeared out of the mist. All now carried muskets, their long bayonets stained from muzzle to point in scarlet. Shawnee gasped and put her hands over her mouth as she watched the soldiers re-enter the cottage.

Sam took Shawnee's arm to attract her attention and whispered urgently in her ear: "Listen, we should seriously think about getting the hell outta here."

"What? We're seeing history being re-enacted here. It doesn't get any better than this. You can't wanna leave now."

"Look, you just don't get it, do yuh? We are in real trouble here…"

Shawnee's answer was drowned out by the sound of gunfire reverberating down the glen. They listened as the crack of single shots was engulfed in a series of booming explosions. As a second burst of gunfire tore through the air the door to the cottage was flung open and a tall figure strutted into view.

To the concealed watchers, here was a man who commanded attention. He was resplendent in a uniform of scarlet and white, his wide-skirted coat edged with silver braid. Beneath his black tricorn hat he wore a grey wig, which hung over the scarlet collar of his uniform like the locks of a Greek hero. He stood a hundred yards from Sam and Shawnee, his outline blurred by the mist, but both could clearly make out the vivid red scar that extended from his right eye to the corner of his mouth.

Behind him came two of the soldiers they'd seen earlier. The tall figure listened as the gunfire echoed amongst the surrounding hills before it finally died away. What he had heard was not to his liking. He barked out a series of commands which sent his men trotting westwards.

He glared after them for a few moments, his right hand idly tracing the scar on his cheek. Suddenly he turned and stared directly at his two watchers, as if he sensed their presence amongst the trees.

At last his gaze fell away and he turned and withdrew into the cottage.

"Have you ever seen such a mean-looking son of a bitch?" Sam hissed.

Shawnee seemed distinctly unsettled. "I know that guy's face; there's a book my dad got me…" She glanced uneasily around her. "Maybe it is time we thought about getting outta here."

He nodded in sharp agreement. "We need to work our way round the back of the cottage, try to locate the car. If it's there, fine. If not, we go on foot and get the hell outta this godforsaken place."

Shawnee gave him a reassuring smile. "No one's gonna believe a word of this when we get back home."

Sam did his best to smile in reply.

Keeping low to the ground they circled around the back of the cottage. Sam regularly glanced over his shoulder to make sure Shawnee was behind him. Absurdly, he'd never seen her look so lovely. Her beautiful features were flushed with excitement; her long, auburn hair damp and untidy as though she'd just stepped out of the shower.

They reached the patch of scrub that marked the spot where they'd left the car. Sam worked his way through the undergrowth until he was on the edge of the clearing, then came to a halt.

Shawnee nudged him from behind.

"Is the car there?"

He turned and shook his head.

"What's wrong?" she hissed.

He shrugged evasively. "Car's not there. C'mon, we'll back off and try somewhere else."

"What is it, Sam? What are you seeing?"

She edged him out of the way, and looked beyond him, into the clearing. The spot where they had earlier parked the car was now occupied by a little stone-built outhouse. Along the near wall, face down on the ground, lay three figures; an elderly couple and a youth of about twelve. All were dressed in shades of red tartan, which appeared to be melting into the ground. Shawnee held her hands over her mouth as she realised each figure was lying in a pool of its own blood.

"Oh sweet Jesus, that girl we saw; oh Jesus, Sam… This is all for real, isn't it?"

Sam's eyes were wide with shock. "We need to get outta here. Need to get away from this place… Get as far's we can."

"Oh dear God, Sam, what've we got ourselves into?"

His face taut with fear Sam led the way back through the bushes, away from the clearing, keeping the enclosure wall to their right. At the opposite side of the wall they came upon a track, well-churned by footprints, which seemed to follow the same route as the road on which they'd earlier driven.

Sam was reluctant to lead Shawnee away from the undergrowth, but this seemed the only exit from the glen. Nervously they joined the path. As far as they could see in either direction the landscape was empty. The only sound to be heard was the gurgling of the burn to their left. As Inverlaragain Cottage began to disappear behind them there was a temptation to believe that all was normal in the world; that any abnormality had also vanished into the mist.

This illusion lasted all of two minutes. Ahead of them the path sloped gently for about fifty yards before disappearing into the gloom. Out of this grey blanket two scarlet shapes suddenly materialised. Sam had thought himself prepared for anything, but he stood frozen in horror as two of the redcoats they'd seen earlier emerged from the mist. Any hope that they were merely phantoms from the past disappeared when the soldiers began running towards them, barking out commands.

Shawnee grabbed Sam by the hand and led him scampering back along the path towards the undergrowth. The shouts of their pursuers grew more distant as they fell farther and farther behind. By the time Inverlaragain cottage loomed out of the mist the soldiers could barely be heard behind them.

As the couple came abreast of the cottage they stopped, uncertain whether to continue westwards, or risk being cornered amongst the undergrowth. During that moment's hesitation another burst of gunfire echoed down the glen. Before they could react the door of the cottage was angrily flung open and the tall officer reappeared barely ten yards away.

Instantly his attention was focused on Shawnee, even as he pulled a flintlock pistol from his waistband and pointed it at Sam.

"*Bonjour, Mademoiselle. Bonjour, Monsieur.*" He indicated the entrance to the cottage. "*Ici, s'il vous plait.*"

Like gazelle cornered by lions, the young couple stared wildly around them, searching for some avenue of escape. Sam considered their chances of making a run for it.

The officer seemed to read this in his eyes. He stepped closer and levelled the pistol directly at Sam's head. "Ah, ah," he said reproachfully.

Sam was aware of heavy footsteps approaching from behind. He caught a glimpse of the officer nodding in his direction. Moments later he felt as if he'd been hit by a sledgehammer.

Chapter Ten

Sam regained consciousness. Pain thumped his skull, far worse than any hangover. Before him stood a character from a colonial theme party.

"He wakes, sir," it yelled eagerly. "Shall I begin…?"

"All in good time, Corporal," said another, more cultured voice. "T'will avail us more if we hear what our mysterious visitor has to say while he yet has the tongue to say it."

Sam found himself strapped to a chair, unable to turn and locate the second speaker. He recognised the character standing before him as one of the redcoat soldiers they'd seen earlier. The expression on his coarse, rustic face indicated he was having a good day.

It was as though he'd awakened in a museum. By the light of a tiny window he could see bare stone walls, with here and there primitive-looking furniture scattered about a straw-covered floor. He realised he was under the thatched roof of Inverlaragain Cottage.

"Shawnee!" he yelled. "Shawnee! Where is she, you sons of bitches? If any of you scumbags… "

"I'm here, Sam," she called out from behind him.

"Are you okay?"

"I'm fine. Really, I'm okay" Her voice was clear and calm.

He strained against the bindings that held him to the chair. "Cut me loose, you bastards, or so help me God…"

"Enough!" the cultured voice interjected. "Such exquisite torturing of the King's English is but brief entertainment for a gentleman…"

"Aw screw all that horse shit!" Sam yelled. "Cut me loose, you sonofabitch!"

The soldier was given a sign by his master, and brought one of his fists crashing down on the side of Sam's head, knocking over both chair and occupant.

Sam took a few moments to absorb the crushing pain of the blow. He could hear Shawnee sobbing in the background as he and the chair were hauled upright, and decided a show of defiance was his best way of keeping up her spirits.

"That the best y'can do, ya pussy? Shawnee could hit harder'n that."

The soldier looked at his superior for his approval. This time his fist caught the side of Sam's face, splitting his mouth.

"Stop it, please!" cried Shawnee. "Sam, what're you doing? Don't antagonize them."

Sam could see the redcoat searching his master's face. The look of disappointment told him he was to be spared for the time being.

The cultured voice continued: "Monsieur, as one gentleman to another, let us establish an understanding. One of us has been charged, by God's grace, to serve and protect the interests of His Majesty throughout this kingdom. The other has been apprehended skulking in a valley infested by savages who are embarked in armed rebellion against our noble sovereign. An unusual occurrence in itself, you must own, but made doubly so by the fact that this gentleman has been apprehended without weapons, or horses. Most extraordinary of all, the gentleman and his good lady are attired in little more than undergarments." The speaker stepped into Sam's view. "Of the two gentlemen, Monsieur, upon whom would one consider it more incumbent to maintain a civil tongue?"

Even in the dingy light of the cottage the man cut an imposing figure. He was over six feet tall, his uniform an impressionist portrait of burning reds, delicate whites, fringes of blue and silver. The lurid scar that extended from his right eye to the corner of his mouth cut a savage swathe through an otherwise handsome face, complementing eyes that were the colour of ice beneath a cloudless sky.

"Or to pose the question afresh: One of the gentlemen in this room has been granted the power of pit and gallows over the other. Allow me to demonstrate…"

He nodded at his henchman, who brought another crunching blow down on top of Sam's head. This time the chair remained upright only because the blow was absorbed by the American's skull and vertebrae.

Sam was vaguely aware of Shawnee's pleading tones. "…Tell you anything you wanna know. Don't hit him again."

The officer moved beyond Sam's field of vision.

"There are few scenes more touching than a maiden's tears shed for her loved one. Most touching indeed…" Leisurely he paced the floor until his stroll brought him once again before Sam. "So then, what facts have been set before us? We have a gentleman — or not as the case may be — abroad with his good lady, in a country embarked in open rebellion against its rightful monarch. 'Tis plain to see that neither you nor your lady have been weaned in this barbarous climate, therefore what business have you here? Had you survived some calamity at sea you would most assuredly have presented yourselves to one of His Majesty's garrisons. Instead you choose to make your way into this nest of vermin, 'pon the very day chosen to stamp out the spirit of rebellion in this valley."

In the silence that followed, Sam could hear sobs breaking from more than one female breast. He realised another prisoner was being held with them.

The officer stood directly over the American, as if he was about to exchange roles with his henchman. The redcoat backed away, appalled at the prospect of occupying the same space as his master. The officer studied his prisoner for a few moments before he began to pace the floor again.

"Let us consider the question of your garments. When apprehended your attire consisted of these strange jerkins, the short boots 'pon your feet, your underclothing. Clearly you have divested yourselves of your outer garments. Given the cruel climate of these hills why would one do such a thing? What would one hope to conceal by this act? Is it possible that garments of an incriminating nature have been discarded? Garments such as the uniform of an enemy state perhaps? And yet, I perceive no sense there either. Clothed in French uniform, even to the point of taking up arms with these rebels, you would be assured of fair and honourable treatment by His Majesty's forces. One can only assume you have sought to conceal something else by this action... perhaps the involvement of a nation whose interest in this rebellion has been hitherto unsuspected...?"

Sam snorted in derision. "...Stupid, ignorant sonofabitch..."

For the first time the officer appeared ruffled. "I warn you, sir, 'tis naught but my forbearance keeps your life's blood in your veins. Make no mistake of it; should I grow weary of this sport you will most assuredly bid farewell to life this day."

"What is it y'wanna hear?" cried Sam. "Would it make any sense if I said that... that we sailed to Scotland on a ship from... from France? Is that it? Is that what y'want us to say?"

The officer regarded him with wary interest. "If that be the truth of it, then that is what I should hear, for I desire nothing less."

"The truth, huh? Right... Hell... How about this: The... uh... the ship sailed from Paris and landed us on a beach on the west coast of Scotland. Aah... the ship was carrying silver bullion, which was... ah buried somewhere near the beach..."

"Silver bullion?" the officer remarked, a faint spark of interest in his eyes. "And the purpose of this bullion?"

"To... ah... to pay the Scotch army..."

"The devil you say! And you would know the location of this treasure?"

"Yeah, it's buried on a beach near... ah... near Edinbourgh. Our job was to... uh... to get the location of the bullion to these... these Scotch soldiers fighting for... ah... for Robert Bruce..."

He thought he'd been doing reasonably well, until he heard Shawnee groan: "Oh, Sam..."

The officer reappeared before him. "By God you are insolent, sir! You think to take me for a damn fool..."

Angrily he nodded at his underling. With a growl of pleasure the redcoat rained a flurry of blows upon the American. As Sam struggled to understand his faux pas he felt his nose break with an agonising crack, and tasted the brackish flavour of his own blood. He heard Shawnee pleading on his behalf, but his torment only ended when chair and prisoner were knocked to the ground. The soldier hauled both upright, eager to continue, but his master stayed his hand.

Sam was dimly aware of Shawnee trying to intercede with her version of the bullion story, but the officer would have none of it. He realised then, battered and semi-conscious though he was, that he'd become a challenge to this man; that his subjugation was now an issue in itself.

Sam could hear the soldier cackling as he threw water over him. He could barely see out of his left eye. Blood was streaming from his broken nose, and from the battered lump of meat that was his mouth.

The officer was addressing him again: "You will have listened, as I have, to the discharge of muskets in the valley beyond. 'Tis a sound that pains me doubly. My men were under strict instructions to proceed from one end of this rebel nest to the other, dealing with them as befits such vermin, but without issuing the least noise. Well, you may judge for yourself what has become of that scheme. However, what further perplexes me are reports of strangely clad troops wielding what I am assured are devilish weapons against the King's forces."

The officer waited for some response. After a lengthy silence he continued: "No matter. We shall know soon enough who they were. The silence you now hear says more to me than any runner with a message. But what to make of it all... Two strange fish, in the same pool, 'pon the same day. Happenstance, perhaps? I think not. Now come. You will be so good as to furnish me with the truth of your presence in this valley, 'pon this day of all days..."

"The truth...?" Sam repeated, through bloated lips. "...Y'wanna hear the truth...? Here's the honest t'God truth... I left the city of angels 'n flew 'cross the ocean... 'cause the woman I love wanted... to walk in the sun... in the land of her father. Only... the sun went out... World came to an end 'n the freakin sun went out..." His voice fell away in bitter laughter, which collapsed into a fit of coughing.

The woman was now weeping uncontrollably. The officer could see that something in this gibberish had struck a lover's chord. He dismissed the face of his henchman and leaned over his prisoner.

"This city of angels; tell me more. Where does it lie? France, perhaps, or Spain...?"

The prisoner's eyes glared defiantly back at him out of a broken face. The officer shook his head in frustration. He was about to allow his bull mastiff off its lead once again when his question was unexpectedly answered.

"America... The city of Los Angeles is in America..." said the prisoner's woman, her voice trembling with emotion as she sought to intercede once more on his behalf.

"America...?" the officer repeated. "The city of Los Angeles in America..." He turned the words around in his mouth, as though savouring their flavour. "I am not altogether unfamiliar with the Spanish tongue... Los Angeles: The Angels... ergo, the city of angels."

He looked at his female prisoner.

"...I think, perhaps, somewhere here lies the key to this mystery. I think, moreover, the key may now be inserted into another lock altogether."

The officer's path had taken him out of Sam's sight. Desperately he tried to regain his attention:

"...Hey, fella, I'm the one y'want... I'll tell yuh what... y'wanna know. Leave the lady alone, y'hear?"

"Sir, you think me capable of mistreating a lady?" The voice carried genuine offence. "The whores and whelps of Jacobite rebels I would despatch without compunction, but a lady? By my oath, sir, may I be damned if I have ever mistreated a lady!"

He issued a sharp command at his underling and immediately Sam's chair was spun round, so that he might observe the officer's conduct.

Shawnee was seated at an old wooden table, as though waiting for a meal to be served. Beside her sat the young woman they'd seen earlier. She was barefoot and clothed in a red tartan shawl and saffron dress. Although similar to Shawnee in colour of hair and freshness of complexion, the Highland girl was much more earthy and robust than the American. Both were bedraggled and tear-stained. Strewn on the table before them lay Sam and Shawnee's backpacks; they seemed to have been discarded as uninteresting after a cursory inspection.

"Hi there." Sam managed a mangled grin. "Last time we come... to this restaurant... huh?"

"Oh, Sam..." The tears began to course down Shawnee's cheeks once again.

"Hey, c'mon... s'gonna be all right..."

"As you may judge for yourself, sir, no harm has befallen your good lady. As for her newfound friend: Mademoiselle, I urge you, do not concern yourself with this creature. She looks upon you as a stray puppy looks upon a kindly face. 'Tis no more than that. I am familiar with the vermin who infest these hills. They are a breed incapable of higher thinking. Few of them possess the wit even to understand common English."

He turned his stern gaze upon the woman, who shrank before him like a whipped cur.

"But, to business. You speak of this city of angels that lies within the Spanish colonies. 'Tis a long voyage from the new world to the old. Does King Philip think he can thus remain unnoticed while he meddles in His Majesty's affairs? By God, such treachery would be no great surprise. 'Tis but the span of one generation since Spanish forces landed on these shores to ferment the last rebellion. Much as any Englishman despises the French they at least are honest in their support for the Pretender."

This drew no response from his audience. On the contrary, the prisoner and his woman had taken to gazing into each other's eyes like lovelorn fools. He resolved to try a subtler route.

"Though modesty forbids that I should take pride in it, I must confess I am a gentleman of considerable learning. Yet you have me at a disadvantage, for nowhere have I learnt of a city of angels in the Spanish colonies. I have heard men speak of an El Dorado; a land of gold. But a city of angels... tell me, where lies this Los Angeles?"

Shawnee looked helplessly at Sam, clearly with no idea how to turn the situation to their advantage.

" 'Bout four hundred miles... south of San Francisco," Sam mumbled.

"San Francisco...?"

"S'right... Lies a hundred miles... west of Sacramento..."

"Sacramento...?"

"...State capital of California..."

Sam's pain and anger had got the better of him, and he'd given into the perverse pleasure of feeding his enemy's confusion.

"California? What stuff and nonsense is this...?"

"California's one of the fifty... states of the Union, pal." Sam's bloated lips spat out their staccato vengeance. "All part of the United States... of America. See, you don't know it yet... but you gotta whole mess... a trouble heading your way... in 'bout thirty years from now... you're gonna get... your Limey asses kicked... all the way from Concord... to Yorktown."

"Enough!" the officer barked, his face red with anger. "You think to play me like a damned fool with this... this... poppycock!" He pulled the flintlock pistol from his waistband and pointed it directly at Sam's head.

"No! Please," cried Shawnee, "he doesn't know what he's saying..."

"Don't beg him," said Sam. "He may be dumb... but he's not stupid... He knows he won't kill me."

"You think not, by God...?"

"S'right. Without me you're gonna learn nothing..."

"I have the woman. She will tell me all I need to know."

"Yeah, y'could try that," Sam replied with a coolness he did not feel, "But what do women know of the world? Huh? D'you wanna take the chance...?"

The officer lowered the pistol, then stood in silent contemplation for a moment, before levelling the weapon once again at the American's head.

"I think I may shoot you anyway, sir, for the pure pleasure of it..."

At that a slow smile spread across his face. Sam watched the smile die as it met the ice of his eyes, and suddenly, like a sleepwalker who has awoken on the edge of a cliff, he saw his own extinction yawning before him.

"...Lieutenant Giles Longholme was the, ah, the second in command of the garrison of... of Fort William." He heard Shawnee's voice in the background. "The garrison consisted of six hundred men, drawn from three different regiments. Lieutenant Longholme was instrumental in the successful defense of the fort during the Jacobite siege. After the siege had been lifted he led a force of one hundred and twenty men into Glen Laragain, with orders to carry fire and sword from one end of the glen to the other..."

The officer continued to point the pistol at Sam's head, but his attention was focused on the soft tones of the woman. She continued to quote from the book she held in her hands.

"...Lieutenant Longholme was specially chosen for this mission because of his abiding hatred of the Highlanders. At the battle of Prestonpans his face was so severely scarred by the cut of a Highland broadsword that his betrothal to the daughter of the Duke of Beaufort..."

"...Was ended four weeks before they were to wed." The officer's hoarse voice took up the tale. "Lieutenant Longholme's face being so ghastly to behold, his bride-to-be could not tolerate the very sight of it..." He turned to face the woman, the pistol still levelled at her companion. "My compliments, Madame; you ply your trade well. Truly you are the fairest spy that ever I laid eyes upon. Perhaps 'tis you should be staring down this barrel..."

Shawnee went on, seemingly devoid of fear.

"The massacre of Glen Laragain was one of many atrocities committed by the Hanoverian army at the end of the Jacobite rebellion, but it was considered the worst. Lieutenant Longholme's orders carried the signature of the King's third son; the Duke of Cumberland. However the Duke would deny ever having issued the order. The officer commanding the garrison at Fort William, Captain Scott, would also deny all knowledge of such an order. During a later enquiry it would be claimed that the royal signature had been forged by Lieutenant Longholme…"

The officer's eyes widened. "What treachery is this…?"

"…Within six months of the massacre, Lieutenant Longholme would be court-martialled, not for his part in the operation, but for daring to suggest that a son of the monarch could have issued such an order. He would be reduced to the ranks and transferred to garrison duty in the West Indies…"

The officer had now swung around, his pistol pointing at the woman. "You think to unnerve me by these foul lies, by God…"

"…It is believed by some that he died there, a broken man. Other sources claim he would reappear thirty years later, under a different name, as one of the prime movers in the events which led to the American war of independence…"

"…American war…?"

"…What is certain is that Lieutenant Longholme would never return to England again following his exile in November, seventeen forty-six."

Shawnee's voice died away into a deafening silence. Sam could see the officer's chest rise and fall as he struggled to absorb what he'd heard. He watched as the pistol dropped to the ground. When the silence was finally broken it was not by Lieutenant Longholme, nor by the American couple, but by the red-coated underling.

"Beggin' your pardon, sir, but the truth will be easy got at…"

"Leave us!" the officer snapped.

"Sir?"

"At once! Damn it!"

With a horrible scowl in Sam's direction the soldier picked up his musket and slunk towards the door.

As soon as he was gone Longholme turned to face his female prisoner.

"There are but three sets of eyes have witnessed the orders for this day's work. How could you possibly have known my orders carried the royal signature?"

"It's a matter of historical record."

"Historical record…? What is this meant to convey; that you have the power to perceive that which is yet to be?" He pointed contemptuously at the Highland woman. "These people claim to possess such power, but they are feeble-minded peasants who know no better…"

Shawnee could see the officer was beginning to recover some of his arrogance. "You asked what we were doing in Glen Laragain today, of all days? Well, you were correct. Our presence here on this particular day was no coincidence. We travelled halfway around the world specifically to visit the glen on the anniversary of your massacre…"

"The anniversary? What stuff and nonsense is this?"

"On the two-hundred-and-eightieth anniversary," Shawnee added softly.

"By God, Mademoiselle, you excel in your work," Longholme blustered. "You spin these dark webs, by which you think to trap honest soldiers in pursuit of their duty. Well, enough! While my mind is still my own I will hear no more of this madness. Not one more word, by God…"

Shawnee defiantly threw the book on the table. "Read it, if you got the courage. It's not every man gets to see what posterity thinks of him."

Longholme involuntarily stepped backwards. "T'will be something you have prepared to deceive my senses."

"Yeah?" The woman picked up the book and held it in the air, like a preacher delivering the word of God. "It's called 'The Massacre Of Glen Laragain.' Maybe I should get you to autograph the book. Hell, you're as much the author as the guy who wrote it."

The officer could hear mumbles of approval from the woman's accomplice: "Way to go, Shawnee… Give'm both barrels…"

Lieutenant Longholme strode forward and took the book from her. "Very well, I shall answer your deceit, for deceit I am sure it will prove to be."

His convictions remained intact only as long as it took him to examine the front cover. Incorporated there, in strange glossy colours, was an exceptionally life-like picture depicting a group of roofless dwellings. The legend 'The Massacre Of Glen Laragain' was emblazoned in garish letters over the vista. Inlaid within the scene was a tiny portrait, which his eyes initially passed over. It was only when he'd carried the book closer to the window that he realised he was looking at his own image.

Longholme recoiled as if he'd glimpsed the face of Satan. The book fell to the floor, and for a moment he seemed about to join it.

"This cannot be possible... A man of learning... prey to such black witchery..."

The officer's scar seemed to have sunk into the grey lines of his face. He gaped beyond the cottage window, into the mist, which was beginning to clear from the west.

"Shawnee!" Sam hissed. "C'mon over here and untie me, quick as y'can..."

Shawnee turned to her companion. "Knife?" she whispered, making a cutting motion with her hands. "D'you have a knife?"

The woman produced a small black dagger from inside her shawl. "*Skian dhu*," she explained.

Shawnee quickly discovered the Highlander's *skian dhu* was no ornamental weapon. In seconds Sam was free, the ropes falling from him like party streamers.

"Oh, Sam," she groaned, "what a God-awful mess they've made of your face."

Both his eyes were already beginning to turn black; his nose was angry and swollen; his mouth looked as though he'd encountered a psychotic dentist.

"'S alright," he mumbled, as she helped him to his feet, "y'shoulda seen the other guy..."

Shawnee smiled weakly. "Y'got nobody to blame but your own stupid self."

"I don' get it...Whaddid I say wrong?"

"Edinburgh is on the east coast of Scotland, not the west. But, worse than that, for Godsakes; Robert Bruce?"

"Yeah. You talked 'bout him once..."

"Robert Bruce had been dead more than four hundred years. These people were fighting for Prince Charles Edward Stuart, son of the exiled King James."

Sam nodded at Longholme. "Guess he'd've known that, huh?"

Shawnee shook her head in disgust. "Sam, there's plankton drifting off the Scottish coast knows more about this country than you do..."

Sam laughed raspingly, even as he began to look around, searching for some means of escape. The officer seemed to pose little threat now, but beyond the door of the cottage his underling would be close by.

"Whaddabout the pistol?"

With a shock both of them realised the Highland woman was standing barely ten feet from the officer, his own pistol pointed at the back of his head. Perhaps sensing her presence, he slowly turned around.

"It appears you might be doing me a service," Longholme said softly. He towered imperiously over the woman, like a magistrate over a ragamuffin.

"If it is myself that is ending your miserable life it is for my people, and not to ease your suffering," she hissed vengefully.

"You speak English!" Shawnee exclaimed. Surprise also appeared on the officer's face.

"*Oui. Je parle Français, aussi.* It is yourself is thinking we are no better than ignorant savages because the ancient tongue of the Gael is beyond your understanding. But tell me now, sir, of the two of us, who is it would be the most ignorant?"

"Very well, I stand corrected," said Longholme stiffly. "Clearly, you are neither ignorant nor a savage, but I will be damned if I own that you and your tribe are anything other than Jacobites and rebels."

"The young men of *Gleann Laragain*, my two brothers among them, was called to arms by Locheil to fight for our lawful prince…"

"Your lawful prince? You refer to the Jacobite pretender to the throne. Your true *lawful prince*, the Duke of Cumberland, approaches with an army to crush this damned rebellion in the name of your lawful monarch; His Majesty, King George!"

"Cherman Cheorge is no friend to the Gael, sir. We ask but to be left in peace. Instead we are surrounded by forts and garrisons, full of red-coated 'chentlemen' like yourself; who may fall upon us as they see fit, to murder and destroy."

"These are military operations," he replied rigidly. "We are but soldiers, answering our orders."

"And do your orders include the murder of children, and the violation of innocent women?"

"You, Madam? Molested? I think not."

"No, sir, not I. Perhaps your men thought me a tid-bit to be safed for yourself. But the others… like beasts… on my mother… my father forced to look on…" Tears poured down her cheeks. "You unleashed your hounds upon us, sir. Did you expect they would wag their tails at us?"

"Madam, I assure you, such behaviour was never intended…"

"You intended they should simply slaughter us like animals... As they did my father... my mother... my brother, Donald, barely more than a child...?" Her eyes sparkled with dark anger.

"My men were attacked. The youth possessed a hidden dagger..."

"His only crime was to defend his mother from your soldiers..."

"My orders, Madam... I was commanded to meet any resistance with the utmost force..."

"You have done more than obey orders this day, sir. It was said you was chosen because of your abiding hatred..."

The officer's hand traced the red weal on his face. "Clearly, Madam, I am damned whichever way I may turn, but beyond these hills all civilised men will benefit in the peace that is to follow, once the fever of rebellion is extinguished...."

The Highland woman moved closer to the officer, her hands now trembling with the weight of the pistol. "You dare speak of civilisation after what your people has done here this day?"

It was obvious the time for talking was over.

"C'mon, honey," Shawnee said softly to the other woman, "don't stoop to their level."

"I am Rhona Cameron, daughter of Ewen and Elsbeth Cameron of Inverlaragain. Until this day I thought I was without a care in the world. Now my only desire is to send you to your master in hell."

Helplessly Sam and Shawnee watched as her finger tightened on the trigger. The officer showed no surprise when the firing lock struck the pan with a dull metallic click.

"The weapon was not loaded," he explained. " 'Twas but a ploy, to loosen the gentleman's tongue."

For a moment, the woman seemed about to fling herself at the officer. Instead her strength evaporated, and she sank to her knees before him. Shawnee sprang to her side, her arms around her.

Sam turned to face Longholme's retribution. But instead of recalling his henchman the officer made his way to the table and began to empty the backpacks.

" 'Twas my mistake to leave the inspection of your haversacks to that oaf of a corporal. The man would starve to death were he not commanded to eat twice daily."

His eyes lit up as one wonder after another appeared on the table before him. He picked up Shawnee's digital camera, turning it this way and that. He shook it for a moment, before handing it to Sam.

"Tell me, sir, what function does this device perform?"

The American was in no mood to explain two hundred and seventy years of scientific progress to this man.

" 'S a camera," he growled tersely. "Takes pictures."

The officer shook his head in confusion. "Please demonstrate," he commanded.

Sam pointed the camera at the officer. " 'S gonna flash. Y'know? There's gonna be a bright light?"

"I warn you, sir, I am weary of trickery this day…"

"Yeah. Yeah. Yeah."

Sam pressed the shutter and Longholme recoiled in shock, his hands to his eyes. By the time his eyesight had returned to normal the camera had produced a perfect image of his face, frozen in mid-sentence.

" 'Tis I," Longholme breathed, his eyes wide open in wonder. " 'Tis my own face…"

"Yeah, bummer, or what?" murmured the American.

The officer held up one of Shawnee's unopened bottles of mineral water. "What manner of substance is this? 'Tis like glass, and yet it bends to the touch. Does this truly convey water?"

Sam nodded irritably.

"You use this soft glass to convey water in a land where water pours from the hillsides? What madness! With such a material I would convey the finest wines and brandies."

His excited gaze fell upon Shawnee's Ordnance Survey map of the area. He spread the sheet out across the table and began to pore over it. Even in the dim light he could make out the legend that recurred throughout much of the glen: 'Ancient Ruins'. Slowly he straightened up from the table.

"The words your lady spoke; that I am to be betrayed by His Royal Highness; they were uttered in anger…?"

"…Every word I said was true," came the icy tones of the woman. She was helping her new companion to her feet. "Of all the atrocities authorized by the Duke of Cumberland, only once did he put his signature to paper… The son of the reigning monarch couldn't be openly associated with murder. Somebody had to pay for that mistake."

"Looks like it's your ass, pal," Sam observed unsympathetically.

Longholme straightened his uniform. "Perhaps 'tis fitting that the field commander of this miserable affair should be its final victim. But the prime instigator… His Royal Highness?"

"As good as forgotten in England. Remembered to Scots throughout the world as 'Butcher Cumberland'."

"The devil you say! By my oath, there is much here to ponder on."

Before Longholme could ponder further an urgent knocking shook the door of the cottage.

"Sir, 'tis Corporal Sykes. An urgent dispatch from Ensign Shaw."

The officer sighed in exasperation. "I regret I am pressed by other matters. You will excuse me."

Outside they could hear the breathless voice of the runner as he poured out his report. From time to time he was interrupted by the clipped tones of Lieutenant Longholme.

"Anybody got any bright ideas 'bout how we get ourselves outta this?" Sam whispered.

"I still got the little dagger!" exclaimed Shawnee. "Maybe one of us could… y'know…"

"What: Jump him from behind? Slit his throat?"

"No. I meant if maybe if one of us, sorta threatened him, or something…"

"He thinks hisself a hunter; that one. A hunter of lowly vermin," Rhona put in darkly. "Only death will forestall him."

"Okay Let's think this through," Sam went on. "Shawnee, don't y'have one of those cute little pepper sprays you guys keep in your handbags?"

"Yeah, but for some reason I didn't think to bring it on our walk."

"I will do the deed," Rhona said softly. "If you will but return my *skian dhu*. 'Tis my family he has destroyed. It falls upon myself to avenge them."

Shawnee cupped the girl's face in her hands. There was such torment in those deep hazel eyes. She knew the girl's wounds would never heal if she tried to salve them with this man's blood.

"No, honey. He's booked his place in hell. Don't let him drag you there too."

Rhona's pain welled up once more from the depths of her soul. Sam could see the sparkle in Shawnee's eyes as she tried to soothe her suffering.

Outside, the tenor of the dialogue between Lieutenant Longholme and his underlings had changed. The soldiers appeared to be questioning their orders. The pitch of the officer's voice grew higher, on the brink of outrage.

As Sam looked out of the window he saw the corporal and one of his comrades trotting clumsily towards the west. "I don't like the looka this. The guy's up to something…"

Longholme opened the door to the cottage, and invited his guests to join him outdoors. "You may bring your haversacks. Tell the Highland wench to bring whatever clothing and food is easy obtained. You will have need of both."

Sam was the first to emerge, blinking, from the gloomy depths of the cottage. In each hand he held a hastily filled backpack. The mist had all but vanished now. Even in the fading light of early evening Sam recognised the landscape he'd first seen beneath that hot and cloudless sky.

"What's going on?" he wanted to know.

Longholme waited until the ladies had joined them, each cradling a tartan bundle in her arms. He looked directly at Shawnee. " 'Twould appear, madam, whatever force has deposited you in this valley, has done likewise with several others." He looked for some response, and caught the expressions of surprise that passed between the two strangers.

"What the hell is going on here?" Sam mumbled.

"Indeed," said Longholme. He turned to the bedraggled, tear-stained figure standing behind Shawnee. "Madam, 'twill be of scant comfort to learn that I have ordered the immediate end of all operations in this valley. My men will be gone by nightfall. Since I am to be made the sole architect of this day's work, His Royal Highness's orders no longer carry any authority." He bowed stiffly. "I wish you may know peace of mind, Madam. It may bring some comfort to know that I ne'er shall."

Rhona stared speechlessly at the officer, who then dramatically turned his back on them. "Begone now, all of you, as far from this blighted place as you can go. If I am any judge of His Royal Highness 'tis certain others will return to complete the work begun this day."

He remained staring at the distant hills, his hands clasped behind his back. When he turned around again the three figures had melted into the gathering twilight.

Inside the cottage he picked up the book from where he had dropped it on the floor. There was insufficient light to make out any of the text, but he flicked through the pages anyway.

Chapter Eleven

Andy Macmillan was no stranger to nights spent in cold bivouacs, but this night had been particularly uncomfortable. It was almost 4 am. He was cold and tired, but he'd found sleep impossible. He'd heard of men whose minds erased a traumatic incident as a means of coping with the horror of it. He was clearly not made that way. He could not shake off those terrible images from the siege of Achnacon's cottage, as if his mind was trying to lessen their impact by replaying them over and over again.

There was also the nagging pain in his legs. He doubted if the burns were anything more than superficial, but at this hour any discomfort tended to be magnified out of all proportion.

Macsorley had found a little out-building thirty yards from the burning cottage, where his injured corporal could shelter for the night. The building was like a miniature black house, with ubiquitous thatched roof and straw-covered floor. Having saved his corporal's life, Macsorley was like a child who'd made a special connection and was eager to maintain the bond. He'd fussed over Macmillan like a devoted nurse, until in the end he'd been sent into the night under the pretext of searching out the whereabouts of Rae and Ferguson.

The blazing inferno that had been Achnacon's cottage was now just a pile of glowing embers. Two hours earlier the front wall had collapsed inwards, sending a shower of sparks into the night sky. As the fire had died away so too had the stench of roasted flesh. It was odd how quickly a man became accustomed to the smell.

He couldn't recall how many redcoats had been left in the cottage and how many had been bulldozed out of the way by Achnacon's demented milk-cow. Yet he could vividly recall the features of each soldier he'd shot down during those few moments at the door. The shock and anguish on each face as his rifle had fired again and again into that scarlet mob was burned like a firebrand into his brain.

Equally vivid was the image of that other soldier he'd brought down near the front window. He hadn't given up life easily. Every pain-wracked breath could be seen in the pink froth that bubbled around his mouth. In his eyes Macmillan had seen an expression of… fear…? Hatred…? No, it was neither of those. It was defiance. The man had gone to his grave with the most intense look of defiance in his eyes.

With a start he looked towards the smouldering remains of the cottage. He'd taken it for granted the redcoat was dead, but he hadn't actually seen him die. He could see two bodies lying near the entrance, but with a growing sense of alarm he realised the soldier who'd fallen near the window was no longer there. Feverishly he peered into the shadows. Where the hell was Macsorley when he needed him? The fire obligingly flared up again and by its ghostly light Macmillan could make out the spread-eagled shapes of many of his victims. The dancing shadows lent all of them the illusion of movement, as if they continued to writhe in their death-throes.

He shielded his eyes, searching for a sign of life amongst the restless shadows. It was then he caught the tortuous movements of one particular shape as it crawled away from the fire. It could only be the redcoat he'd wounded in front of the window.

Macmillan rose to his feet. If he could do something for this individual it might salve his conscience. He was about to leave his hideout when he saw Rae and Ferguson appear from the darkness. Both made straight for the soldier. As Macmillan watched they forced him onto his back with their feet. Both were carrying muskets, the bayonets gleaming dull bronze in the firelight. He felt a deep unease. Something was wrong here.

"Rae! Fergie! Leave him alone. Ah'm on ma way down."

Neither paid him the slightest attention. Both began to toy with the wounded redcoat, jabbing at him with their bayonets; amusing themselves at the man's terror. Macmillan could hear him pleading for mercy. The corporal added his voice to the uproar, bellowing his disapproval.

Rae's response was instant and horrifying. He plunged his bayonet into the soldier's stomach, twisting the barrel as he withdrew the blade. Ferguson did likewise. The redcoat's hands scrabbled at each lunge, desperately trying to deflect the bayonets.

Above it all he could hear the high-pitched shrieking of a soul in torment.

Macsorley had now appeared on the scene.

"Corp! Hell, man, get a grip! You're gonnae have the whole army down on top of us!"

Macmillan tried to focus on the young soldier.

"You've been having a nightmare, Corp. Screaming like a banshee, ye were."

Macmillan stumbled to the door of the hideout. The first pale light of dawn had stained the eastern horizon, turning the cloudy skies a watery shade of grey. The fire in Achnacon's cottage had subsided to a dull glow, barely illuminating the burnt shell of the house. Everything beyond lay in deep shadow.

Macmillan slumped to the ground. "Ah saw Rae and Fergie... They were... God, it was so real."

The young man sat down beside him. "Those two are enough tae give anybody nightmares."

Macmillan ran a hand through his hair, trying to clear the dregs of sleep from his mind. "Don't suppose those redcoats were part of the nightmare..."

Macsorley shook his head. "Sorry, Corp. None of us have woken up from that one yet."

The younger man had acquired another tartan plaid. For all his pretensions the phillamor looked out of place on his slim frame, like a new skin within which he had yet to grow.

"Ah found this hanging up in one of the houses nearby," he explained. "Ah don't think the owner's gonnae be needing it again. Ah didn't go beyond the village, but Ah tell ye Corp, it's pure carnage out there."

"Aye, tell me about it."

"Ah wasn't taking about the redcoats. You want tae see what those animals had been up tae. Ah counted three dead in one cottage and two in another."

"Aye?" The non-commissioned officer looked up with pained interest.

"Aye. It's a pity ye didnae take out more of them." Macsorley rummaged in the folds of his phillamhor and produced something wrapped in a muslin cloth. "It's grub; at least Ah think it's grub."

"Where'd ye get this?"

"In one of the cottages. The soft stuff is like the cheese that Achnacon's wifie gave us. Ah think the wee hard things are oat biscuits."

Macmillan sniffed the objects suspiciously. "Ye sure these are biscuits? They look like something that's been scraped off a cow's backside." He took a cautious nibble of each. "Ah, hell, Ah've tasted worse."

"Ye know, Corp, maybe Fergie was right all along," said Macsorley. "Maybe we really are here for a reason."

"Aye? Well, if you figure it out you let me know. Ah cannae see what slaughtering a couple of dozen redcoats could achieve in the grand scheme of things."

"Listen, Corp. God knows how many died in the original massacre, but Ah can think of four that're alive because of you."

"Aye, Ah suppose."

Macsorley went on, imbued with the spirit of optimism: "You just don't know how many might've heard the gunfire and scarpered…"

Macmillan licked the last trace of flavour from the muslin cloth. "Aye. Maybe yer right at that," he murmured.

The skies were turning a paler shade of grey as the morning light penetrated the thick cloud. There had been little wind overnight, and here and there trails of smoke added their acrid breath to the gloom.

Macsorley looked edgily at his corporal. "That bright light we saw… at the end… above Loch Ness."

Macmillan nodded faintly. "We've seen it in training films often enough…"

Macsorley moaned softly. "Ah didn't even know we were at war with the Russians."

"Well, somebody was lobbing nukes at us."

"But how could things have got so bad…?"

Macmillan shook his head. He was too tired to debate the issue, and was relieved when Macsorley took the hint and lapsed into tortured silence. At some point sleep must have crept up on him again. He woke to find himself alone once more. He sat for a few moments, blinking in the light that flooded through the open doorway. The heavy blanket of cloud was breaking up, allowing bright shafts of sunlight to play upon the glen. A breeze had also sprung up, dispersing the haze of smoke that had gathered overnight.

It was 10.15 by his watch. He could see no sign of movement amongst the walls and fields of Achnacon's township. No soldiers. No clansfolk. No Rae, Ferguson or Macsorley. Even the bodies had disappeared. Bloodstained impressions in the grass showed where they had lain, but it was as if they'd been resurrected with the first rays of the morning sun.

Macmillan located his boots; the soles had more or less kept their shape as they'd solidified. He stepped gingerly beyond the doorway of his little sanctuary. He still wore his camouflaged combat jacket and shirt, but hanging below his uniform, like a shapeless ankle-length dress, was Achnacon's red phillamor.

He was greeted with an admiring wolf-whistle. Macsorley lay on the hillside beside the hut, clad in the blue tartan plaid he'd acquired overnight, a stalk of grass in his mouth.

Macmillan replied with a self-conscious twirl, which brought the entire tartan ensemble down around his ankles.

Macsorley howled with laughter.

"Ah sharrup," Macmillan growled. "How d'ye get this tae stay up anyway? Does it no' come with braces, or something?"

The younger man tutted in disgust, like a disapproving tailor: "Braces? With the phillamor? Aw, Corp."

He disappeared into the outhouse and reappeared a few moments later with the corporal's trouser belt.

"First of all ye spread the phillamhor out on the ground like a blanket. Then ye feed the belt under the material about two thirds of the way down." Macsorley carried out the instructions as he recited them. "Then ye gather up the material that lies above the belt intae pleats, so it's the same width as the belt..."

Macmillan awaited his involvement, Achnacon's plaid spread out before him like a collapsed tartan tent.

"Then ye lie down on top of it."

"See if you're taking the piss...?"

"Ah'm not," said Macsorley indignantly. "This is how they put on the phillamor. Ye lie on top of it, with the belt at yer waist."

Grumbling, Macmillan fastened the belt around his midriff and struggled to his feet. He looked like he was wearing a long dress that had been slashed to the waist. Clucking with disapproval, Macsorley made some adjustments around his midriff, then gathered up the excess material and pulled it over Macmillan's left shoulder. Finally he produced a brooch from his own phillamhor and fastened the remaining material to the front of the corporal's combat jacket.

"Perhaps, sir might wish to consider matching shoes and handbag...?"

"How do Ah look?" Macmillan wanted to know.

The younger man stepped back to admire his handiwork. "Well, no one's gonnae mistake you for Rob Roy, but ye look... no' bad. No' bad at all."

Macmillan took a few tentative steps in his new battle dress. "Man, ye could definitely see yerself charging through the heather in this..."

The other nodded sombrely. "Aye, well, you're no' gonnae be charging anywhere for a wee while."

Macmillan looked down at the blisters on his legs. This was the first chance he'd had to examine his injuries in daylight. As he'd guessed, the damage was only superficial.

"You look like you've had the vindaloo from hell," said Macsorley.

Macmillan traced the soft contours of the largest blister, which bulged from his right calf like a fungus. "Ah'll be all right so long as none of these things burst on me." He lowered himself to the ground. "Aw, man, what've we got ourselves intae here? This is a world that knows nothing about antibiotics, or anaesthetics. God help us if we develop appendicitis, or even a bloody toothache! There's no such thing as electricity. They haven't even invented the steam engine yet..."

Macsorley sat down beside him. "Now there's a job for a couple of enterprising ex-squaddies..."

"What d'ye mean; become inventors?" Macmillan laughed. "Ah don't suppose you know any better than Ah do how any of that stuff works. Even if we did, what's the point? We all saw where that technology's gonnae take the world. There's no point in speeding up the process."

"Ye know, Ah was thinking about that overnight," Macsorley replied. "What was happening in the world back in 1976?"

"Ireland... Strikes... That's about it."

"Exactly. There was nothing going on. At least nothing that would've led tae a nuclear war."

"Aye, Ah suppose."

"Ah think time is so messed up in this place what we saw may've been way in the future."

"Maybe. But, it might only've been five years later."

"Or five thousand."

Macmillan could see the sense in his argument, but was in no frame of mind to debate the issue.

"What did ye do with the bodies?"

"The what?"

"The bodies. Ah'm assuming it was you that cleared up that mess this morning."

"Aw, right. No. No, it wasnae me. Three young laddies appeared just after daybreak. Achnacon must've sent them down tae lay out their own people with some kind of dignity. Ah checked after they'd gone. There's eight of them laid out in one of the cottages."

"Three young lads?" Macmillan said thoughtfully. "Did you get talking tae any of them?"

"Naw, they kept their distance. Ah'm sure they knew we were here; they looked over a few times, but it didnae seem right tae disturb them, ye know?"

"What about the soldiers?"

"They've been piled intae one of the wee outhouses."

Macmillan breathed a long, slow sigh. "Ah wonder how many of Achnacon's people made it…"

"It's been some night, eh, Corp?"

"Aye, it's been some night, right enough. You can cut all that 'Corporal' rubbish, by the way. The name's Andy."

Macsorley nodded. "Jamie."

"Jamie."

They were interrupted by a storm of whistles and catcalls:

"…Ye see some ugly women in this job, but have ye ever clapped eyes on such hacket-looking bints in all yer life?"

"Ah know. Ah don't fancy yours much…"

"Naw, Ah don't either…"

Rae and Ferguson were crossing the nearby burn. Both had clearly spent a rough night in the hills.

"Morning ladies. Nice tae see there's still scope for self-expression in this man's army…"

"Where did you two get tae last night?" asked Macsorley.

"Escorting the civilians tae safety, of course," Rae explained brightly. "We figured we could leave you two tae look after the house." He turned around, appearing to notice the smouldering ruins for the first time.

"Oops," he added.

"So, where are they, then?" Macsorley asked.

"Who?"

"Achnacon and his family. Where are they?"

"God knows," Ferguson replied. "We lost track of them during the night. Last saw them up in the hills somewhere."

"So, what's the score then?" Rae asked. "Ah don't know about you lot but Ah could eat a scabby horse. Don't suppose there's anywhere we could get a curry around here…"

"There's a dead cow at the back of those cottages if ye're that hungry," said Jamie. He caught Andy's enquiring look. "They all look the same tae me, but Ah think it's Achnacon's cow."

"What a shame," said Ferguson "That thing should've got a medal."

"We need to locate Achnacon," said Macmillan. "But Ah've got a feeling he'll find us when he's ready. Meantime you lads check out the area. See what grub ye can find. Jamie, you show the others where the dead've been laid, tae avoid those buildings."

As they headed off Andy closed his eyes, consciously blotting out everything but the singing of the skylarks and the distant babbling of the burn. He could almost believe that everything was as it should be; that when he opened his eyes again the glen would be studded with mouldering ruins.

To his surprise he was not sure which reality he would prefer. As he pondered this extraordinary thought a shadow fell across his face. He opened his eyes to see Ferguson and Rae standing over him. Each cradled a musket in his arms, the sun reflecting brightly on the long fixed bayonets.

Andy jumped to his feet. "What the hell d'ye think yer doin'?"

"Eh?"

"Calm down, man, it's just a coupla muskets we found in the grass."

"Aye, they're just souvenirs, Corp," Ferguson explained. "These things are like valuable antiques, ye know?"

Macmillan cradled his face in his hands. "Aw God, stick a fork in me, Ah'm just about done."

"You all right, Corp?" asked Ferguson.

The N.C.O. shook his head wearily. "Aye, fine, just… just leave those bloody things here, lads. Okay?"

Macmillan could hear snatches of their conversation as they returned to their search for food:

"…time of the month…"

"…next thing ye know she'll be shaving her legs…"

Chapter Twelve

Other than the carcass of Achnacon's cow, none of Macmillan's foraging party found anything that resembled food. The youngsters Macsorley had seen earlier had apparently stripped the area bare.

As hunger began to take its toll, Rae became more and more belligerent.

"Ah don't see why we cannae just lop off one of its legs, or even take a whack out of its rump." He indicated the smouldering rubble of Achnacon's house. "We could chuck the meat in there for ten minutes. That should be enough tae cook it."

"Ye cannae just start hacking up the family cow, like it's a bloody chicken!" Macsorley exclaimed.

"How no'? The *tcheuchters* used tae bleed them during winter tae mix with their oatmeal. That's where yer black pudding comes from… Ah bet ye didnae know that!"

"Ah didnae know that," said Ferguson.

"It doesn't matter," insisted Macsorley. "It's no' the done thing, tae start eating the guy's cow. These things were part of the family."

Rae towered threateningly over his comrade. "How would it be if Ah pulled one of *your* legs off and chucked *that* in the fire instead?"

"Ach, get lost, ya big swine…"

Macmillan stepped in before things got out of hand. "Right, that's enough. Rae; you and Fergie take a wander down the glen tae the next township; see if there's any food there. Jamie, you do the same in the other direction."

Macsorley and Ferguson began to move off, but Rae stood his ground.

"That's another thing," he growled. "Me and Fergie were talking earlier; we reckon that we're no' on any parade ground any more. We reckon you've been demoted tae the rank of lost numpty, same as the rest of us."

Slowly Macmillan rose to his feet. He stood toe to toe with his mutinous soldier, glaring into his eyes.

"Ferguson?" he barked.

"Aye, well, it's like; we were just talking and that. Ah mean we were just, ye know, saying like," Fergie mumbled.

"Macsorley?"

"You're the boss, far as Ah'm concerned, Corporal," the young man yelled back.

When Macmillan spoke again his voice was low and full of menace. "Seems it's down tae just you and me then."

"Come on, big man. This is stupid," said Ferguson.

Rae shook his head. He stared unwaveringly at the N.C.O. "What are ye gonnae do? Put me on a charge? Report me tae the Company Sar'nt Major?"

"Chentlemen! Chentlemen! This is not the time to be warring among ourselfs..." said a familiar voice.

Achnacon had materialised barely ten yards away, accompanied by two youths. All were dressed in red tartan phillamors. On each head was perched a blue bonnet, adorned with a representation of a white rose. The hilts of broadsword and dirk extended from scabbards on either side of Achnacon's waistband.

"My apologies for leaving you so long to your own devices. There was other matters to which I was obliged to attend."

"It's good tae see you again," Andy declared, his own surly rebel still held in his gaze. "And yer family?"

"Better than many of their kinfolk," replied the Highlander. "They have took to the high shielings, with the others who escaped." He stepped closer to the two soldiers. "I have come to escort you to a house one half mile from this spot. There you will meet other strangers like yourselfs who have come to help. There you will find food..."

"Food?" Rae echoed, his attention instantly torn from his uprising. "Ye say there's food at this other place?"

Achnacon nodded.

"That's what Ah've been waiting tae hear!" Rae exclaimed. "Come on then. What are we hanging about here for?"

At last Andy was able to turn and face the old man. Achnacon looked tired and haggard, as if part of him had succumbed to his original destiny. The corporal found himself struggling for words.

"Ah couldn't stop it... what they did tae yer house... it wasn't supposed tae happen until the twenty-first..."

"Corpohral Andy," Achnacon interrupted, "I was told how you fought like a hero to safe us all, when others would have run to safe themselfs. How yourself would not leave a burning house until all had made their escape. 'Tis I should beg your forgiveness. I had seen the signs and still I allowed my wits to be stole away..." He indicated the blisters on Andy's legs. "I was told yourself was unhurt, but I see this is not the way of it."

"It's no' as bad as it looks." The corporal nodded towards Jamie. "Thanks to that wee man..."

A gruff smile touched Achnacon's grizzled features. "'Tis no more than I would expect from a Macsorley of *Muirshearlach*."

"Ye said something about food," recalled Rae, as subtly as his stomach would allow.

"Och, but of course. Fine words may nourish a man's soul, but they will never fill an empty belly." Achnacon spoke briefly to his two young followers, then with an expansive gesture he indicated eastwards. "Young Lachlan will lead the way. Those who... ah, whose bellies are more empty than others may dash on ahead with Lachlan."

As Rae and Ferguson were about to charge off, the corporal caught their attention.

"The jimpy and the ammo, yer webbing as well. Collect it and take it with ye."

Ferguson looked to Rae, who hesitated for a moment, before making for the out-building to gather his gear. Ferguson did likewise and in moments the three of them were disappearing over the nearest hill, Achnacon's young guide in the lead, like a hare in a greyhound race.

"The old and infirm must tread a softer path," said Achnacon. "Young Donald will march at our tail. Our good friend *Muirshearlach* may roam as himself sees fit."

"Ah'll bring up the rear with the young lad," said Jamie.

A shadow darkened Achnacon's face. "Be not offended if Donald declines conversation. 'Tis no easy matter to become the man of the house overnight."

Jamie nodded. "Ah'll get the rest of the gear."

Like two friends strolling in the park, Achnacon and Andy made their way slowly along the ancient path.

"Tell me, young Andy, what is the punishment for insubordination in your army? The Prince will not suffer flogging in the Highland army, on any account, whatever. But I am told the Chuke off Cumberland has no such scruples…"

Andy knew the old clansman was still trying to unravel the mystery of these strangers in his midst, but he was too tired for mind games.

"You said there were others like us; Ah take it they're soldiers too."

"Two of them was armed, like yourselfs. The other two? I think not. One is said to be as fair as any lass in Glen Laragain."

"One of them's a woman?"

"T'would appear they are as much a mystery to yourself as yourself is to them. All I have spoke to carry the same tale; that the attack upon my people has been ordained, but all have done what they can to forestall it."

"Ah don't know about the others, but a fat lot of good we were," Andy said miserably.

Achnacon came to a halt. He grasped the soldier by the arm. "Because of yourself, Achnacon and his family is safe. Because of your musket fire, others to the west made their escape before the soldiers came."

"How many?" Macmillan asked hoarsely.

"How many?"

"How many didn't get away?"

"We think two and thirty have been lost."

"…Aw Dear God…"

Achnacon searched out the soldier's eyes. "Five of every six of us is safe. Our losses was least to the west of Achnacon."

Andy turned away, trying to conceal his emotions, but Achnacon had seen the brightness in the soldier's eyes. His own grief trickled unashamedly down his face, but he allowed his friend the privacy of his tears. He had proved himself to be brave and resourceful, this young soldier, but it was clear his soul was more than that of a simple warrior.

The old Highlander looked over his shoulder. *Muirshearlach* had lost no time in befriending young Donald. The lad was being taught how to march in step, his blue bonnet already traded for the opportunity to carry one of the soldier's weapons.

Their destination was the clachan of *Meall An Fhraoich*, 'the hill of heather'. Here too one of the buildings was a burnt-out shell. They were taken to a cottage beside the Laragain burn. Outside, there was nothing to indicate the building was occupied, but as Andy's eyes adjusted to the gloom he could make out little groups clustered here and there. He felt as though he'd entered a mountain bothy, already occupied by bands of hikers, each claiming their own portion of space.

A group of women and youths, all bedecked in various shades of tartan, squatted by the cold ashes of the peat fire, perhaps drawn there by force of habit. A few of them gazed listlessly in the strangers' direction.

To their left two men were laid out on rudimentary beds, with a young woman in attendance. On the other side of the room a larger bed supported three figures, all apparently asleep. In the middle was a woman clothed in a tartan similar to Achnacon's. On either side of her lay a young couple. Both were dressed, ridiculously, in shorts, sweatshirts and hiking boots. In the centre of the room, Rae and Ferguson sat at a wooden table, gorging on the contents of a large communal bowl, like predators devouring a kill.

Jamie spoke in a hushed voice. "When Achnacon said there were others like us Ah wondered if we were gonnae meet some of those recruits. But Ah don't recognise any of this lot."

"Aye. It's like a refugee camp, isn't it?"

Achnacon spoke quietly to two of the women, and immediately one made herself busy preparing food while the other began to make up another bed of sorts.

"The lassies will attend to your needs," the old man said softly. "I regret there is other matters to which I, myself, must now attend."

"Is there anything we can do?" Macmillan asked.

"No, my friend. For the moment you must rest, safe your strength. I fear we will have need of yourselfs again before long." He summoned the four youths gathered around the ashes of the fire. "Achnacon must have keen eyes to guard the glen, and strong legs to warn him of danger. Until we meet again, chentlemen…"

As the old clansman led his troops away, gentle hands steered the two soldiers towards the table, where one of the women had already made room for them.

"How's the grub?" Macsorley asked brightly.

"No' bad, considering," Ferguson replied.

"Considering?"

"Considering ye don't know what yer eating," grumbled Rae.

"When ye think of what these people've been through, we can count ourselves lucky we're getting anything at all," Macmillan said scathingly.

"Aye, well, Ah didn't ask tae be here, so ye'll excuse me if Ah don't tip the waitress."

"None of us asked tae be here," hissed the corporal, "but we're all in the same mess taegether, and we're no' gonnae last five minutes unless we work as a team."

Rae's chair crashed to the ground as he rose to his feet. "Ye'll need tae excuse me too… Chentlemen," he snarled.

Ferguson grimaced apologetically as he too rose from the table. "The big man gets a bit moody at times. He'll be all right in a couple of days."

As Fergie followed his friend outside Jamie murmured: "Just what we needed. A headcase behind the G.P.M.G."

The N.C.O. managed a long-suffering smile. "Didn't ye know? It's part of the job description."

The food, Jamie informed his corporal, was cold brose; an oatmeal dish which clansmen carried with them on their forays. As they ate, one of the women knelt beside Macmillan and applied an ointment of sorts to his legs. She was young, perhaps no more than eighteen years old, with the type of mischievous face that might have been full of the joys of life under different circumstances. Not once did she make eye contact with either soldier, although at one point Jamie managed to bring a reluctant smile to her mouth.

"What did ye say?" Andy wanted to know.

An oblique grin appeared Jamie's face. "Ah told her she was doing a grand job, but no' tae forget the wee blister under yer sporran…"

The N.C.O. smiled. "She's a bonny wee thing, isn't she?"

"Aye; did ye get a look at that wee doll in the corner? What a honey."

The young woman had barely rejoined the others at the peat fire when the silence was broken by a series of loud moans. One of the figures in the corner had begun to thrash about in his sleep. His nurse dabbed his brow with a cloth, while his companion stood awkwardly to one side, embarrassed at the commotion.

"Time we were introduced," said Andy. The nurse had quieted her patient by the time the two men arrived at his bedside. He was staring intently at her; although his eyes were focused elsewhere.

His companion spoke in Gaelic to Macmillan.

"Sorry, pal, Ah don't speak the lingo."

The man gaped stupidly at him.

"No speak *tcheuchter*. Comprendez?"

"You speak English," the man gasped. "I thought, with the plaids..." His voice carried the distinctive lilt of the Gael, although English didn't appear to be a foreign language to him, the way it did with Achnacon.

"Naw, we're wearing this because we lost our uniforms in a fire last night." Andy glanced at Jamie, proudly sporting his blue bonnet. "Although some of us seem tae be going native faster than others."

The younger soldier held out his hand. "Name's Jamie Macsorley, by the way. This is Andy Macmillan."

Awkwardly the man shook their hands. "I'm very pleased to make your acquaintance. I am Colin Cameron, this is my brother, Alistair."

"Is he all right?" the corporal asked.

"Alistair was shot yesterday in a fight with the English redcoats. We both were." Colin stood on one leg to show the soldiers his bandages. His expression changed from pride to concern. "Himself lost a lot of blood, then he developed a fever overnight. Mary has not left his side since he was carried in here."

"Mary?" the two soldiers echoed in unison.

She remained oblivious to them, even though Alistair had lapsed once more into unconsciousness.

"I just don't know what to do. If anything were to happen to himself..."

Andy guessed the younger brother couldn't be much older than eighteen. He looked frightened, alone and utterly out of place.

His gaze flicked nervously from one soldier to the other. "The old gentleman...?"

"Achnacon."

"Achnacon. He said there were other... strangers like Alistair and myself who had appeared in the glen..."

"Aye, that would be us," Andy confirmed ruefully.

"That gunfire I heard to the west of here yesterday..."

"Aye, that would've been us as well."

At the far side of the room the two hikers had also stirred from their corner. As they made their way over to join the gathering a spirited discussion broke out between them.

"Mark ma words," Jamie whispered, "these two numpties will be bird-watchers from Cleethorpes. Ah've seen the type before."

The newcomers came to a halt while they were still a few yards away. The male bird-watcher scratched his head, then turned to the other.

"Don't suppose your dad ever taught y'any Scotch words, huh?"

"I told y'we shoulda waited 'til Rhona wakes up," the female replied. "Besides, it's not called Scotch, Sam, it's called Gaelic. These people spoke Gaelic."

"Yeah, well, whatever. Can y'speak it?"

She shook her head. "My dad was fourth generation; the language had died out in our family before he came along."

Andy and the others found their attention divided between the injuries on the man's face, and the striking attractiveness of the woman.

The man pointed to his companion, then to himself. "She — is — Shawnee. I — am — Sam. You understand? Sam?"

"Bird-watchers from Cleethorpes, eh?" Andy muttered at Jamie as he held out his hand.

A smile of relief appeared on the man's battered features. He pointed at the soldier's tartan plaid. "Hell, man, I thought you were, like, Scottish Highlanders, y'know?"

"That we are. Ah'm Corporal Andy Macmillan of the Royal Highland Fusiliers. This is Private Jamie Macsorley. We lost our uniforms in a fire yesterday. Another two of our lads are outside. This gentleman here is Colin Cameron, and that's his brother Alistair on the bed."

"We were both shot by redcoat soldiers," Colin put in, pointing to his upraised leg.

Sam took the soldiers to one side. "Look, I just wanna make sure of something. You guys are not, like, from these parts, are yuh?"

"Ye mean, do we belong tae this time period?"

Relief appeared once again on the American's face. "I take it you're in the same mess as me and Shawnee. We were told there were others. Look, d'you guys know what the hell's going on here? Is the British military behind this, or what?"

The corporal shook his head. "As far as we can make out we've all been slung intae this world as a result of some weird accident."

"One minute you're watching this fire in the sky, like it's the end of the world, and then pow! You waken up in the middle of this Hollywood epic?"

Andy nodded. He indicated the American's bruised features. "Ah see somebody took a dislike tae yer face…"

"Let's just say I had a difference of opinion with a British officer."

"Bastards the whole lot of them," said Jamie.

Alistair began to writhe in his bed once more, as if he were being attacked by an invisible force. Shawnee helped Mary restrain him.

"That guy needs a hospital," said Sam. He shook his head at the significance of these simple words.

"Aye, it hits ye at moments like this, doesn't it?" Andy remarked.

"Himself is a sergeant in the Cameron Highlanders," Colin declared. "It would take more than a single bullet to stop Alistair. Besides, he has Mary now; she won't let anything happen to him."

"Sure, honey, he's gonna be just fine," Shawnee murmured as she held his brother's hand.

Mary had taken to humming a Gaelic melody as she dampened her patient's forehead with a cloth. Everyone fell silent as the lovely air filled the cottage. The haunting strains seemed to overcome even Alistair's feverish struggles, and gradually he subsided into sleep.

The silence was broken by Colin, his eyes sparkling in the half-light. "Mary won't let anything happen to him."

"Way t'go, kid," Sam murmured. "Look, there's not a lot we can do here guys, whaddya say we get some fresh air? We gotta lot to talk about."

Outside, Rae and Ferguson were nowhere to be seen. The remnants of cloud had all but disappeared, leaving the hills basking in warm April sunshine. Sam's face looked even worse than it did in the gloom of the cottage.

"Might be an idea to have one of the lassies take a look at yer face," said Andy.

"Nah, it's fine. I've had worse'n this surfing back in L.A."

"You're a long way from home, aren't ye? What were the pair of ye doing in Glen Laragain, of all places?"

"Shawnee's folks came from this place originally. She wanted to visit the ancestral home."

"Och, of course," Colin interjected. "Did you not see the resemblance between herself and Mary?"

"No, can't really say I noticed. Now that I think about it though, she could be Shawnee's great, great, great, grandma, or something."

"Man, we should all have a great grannie that looks like that."

"How did yourselves manage to make it all the way from America to Glen Laragain?" asked Colin.

"Well, once we landed in Scotland we hired an automobile; drove up from Glasgow, stayed in one of the hotels in Fort William overnight."

"Och, man, you must have lots of money to afford all that..."

Sam looked quizzically at Colin. "No, not really," he murmured. "Anyhow, first thing in the morning we drove here; left the car where the road ends at the old ruined cottage."

"Aye, that's where we left the Land Rover and the three-tonner."

"Where the road ends?" said Colin sharply. "There's only one cottage where the road ends and that's where Alistair and myself live. I know it's a wee bit tumbledown, but it's hardly what you would call a ruin."

There was an awkward silence before Sam retorted: "Sorry fella, didn't mean to cause offence, y'know?" He turned uncomfortably to the others: "So, uh… tell me, guys, what's the, uh… what's the British Army doing up this neck of the woods, anyhow?"

"We were taking part in a live firing exercise. Training for Northern Ireland. My squad was the firing party."

"My God, has that all broken out in Ireland again? There's no mention of it in the news back home. Hardly surprising, I guess, the state the whole freakin world's in nowadays."

"I didn't know there was trouble in the north of Ireland," Colin mumbled unhappily.

"Maybe you're a wee bit isolated up here, eh?" said Jamie, glancing at the others.

The young man shook his head in bewilderment. "I didn't even know the British Army was training in Glen Laragain…" Like an outcast he slumped against the wall of the cottage.

"So, ah, you guys are British soldiers, huh?" Sam went on. "I take it from all that hullaballoo yesterday you brought some of your hardware with yuh?"

Andy nodded. "We have an M.G. and two self-loading rifles."

"Okay. Good. I take it your weapons are laser-guided, yeah?"

Macmillan and Macsorley looked blankly at each other.

"It's standard issue to all U.S. infantry personnel. I thought the British Army would be much the same."

"Sorry our gear's not up tae the standard of the U.S. Army," Jamie grumbled.

"Serviceman yerself, are ye?" asked the N.C.O. pleasantly.

The American flushed. "Easy, fellas, I'm just trying to take stock. I mean, you remember that British officer I told y'about?"

"The one that didn't like yer face?"

"The very one. Well, it seems the orders for this massacre of yours came from the Duke of, ah… Cumber…?"

"Cumberland. The Duke of Cumberland."

"That's the guy. Well, Shawnee and me — Shawnee really — persuaded the guy to put a stop to that shit yesterday."

"Oh aye? And how did she manage tae do that?" Jamie asked sceptically.

A twisted grin appeared on Sam's face. "That little lady can be pretty persuasive when she puts her mind to something."

"That might explain why the redcoats didn't reappear this morning."

"Yeah. Only we might have a slight problem here."

"Oh aye?"

Sam nodded sombrely. "Last thing that officer told us was to get away from this place, as far as we can go; that others are gonna return to complete the job."

"Did he say when?"

The American shook his head. "I reckon the time it's gonna take this Cumberland guy to kick a few asses, and send out the next buncha soldiers, is gonna buy us a coupla days, anyhow."

A long anguished sigh escaped Macmillan's lips.

"Andy gave them a doing yesterday," Jamie explained. "Against modern weapons they didn't stand a chance."

Colin seemed about to make a contribution, but then thought better of it.

"The only question now is what they're gonnae be more interested in," Andy said heavily, "finishing the job here…"

"…Or getting their hands on those weapons of yours," added Sam.

"Hell," said Jamie.

"Way I see it, fellas; either we take off, with or without these people. Although I gotta say; on our own we'd stand more of a chance…"

"Ah'm no' leaving," Jamie declared firmly. He saw the uncertainty in his corporal's eyes. "Ah can't believe you're even thinking about it. What about Ishbel, and wee Shona, and all the others… how can you even think about leaving them in the lurch?"

"I won't be leaving, either," Colin put in quietly. "Whatever yourselves decide to do, I'll be staying here with my brother."

All eyes turned to the American, who raised his hands defensively before him.

"Hey, I'm just laying out the options. The alternative is to make a stand here, and that means we gotta be prepared to fight this bad-assed Duke and his whole freakin Limey army, no offence intended."

"None taken," the corporal murmured.

Colin leapt to his feet, his face flushed with excitement. "What was your date of birth?" he asked the American.

"My what?"

"Your date of birth. When were you born?"

"The fifth of April. Why?"

"No, I mean what year?"

"Two thousand two. Why? What's that got to do with anything?"

Sam saw the shock in the soldiers' eyes and slowly the realisation dawned on him.

"Oh crap. You guys, you're, ah, you're not from my neck of the woods, are yuh?"

The soldiers backed away from the American, as though he was from another planet.

"I know my house is a wee bit ramshackle, but it was never a ruin," Colin whispered indignantly.

Jamie turned to his corporal. "Ye know what this means, don't ye?"

Dumbly Andy shook his head.

"It means that nuke we saw wasn't from our time. It must've been from the future…"

The last dregs of blood drained from Sam's face. "Oh dear God, you saw that… *thing* in the sky. You saw what Shawnee and me saw."

"Like the sun had exploded?" Colin mumbled. "We saw it too; Alistair and myself, just at the end…"

All four stared in astonishment at each other. The silence was broken by Colin's diffident tones:

"Did ourselves win the war against Germany?"

Nobody replied, as if all were afraid of betraying some terrible secret.

"Please, for Alistair's sake, I have to know if it was ourselves that won."

"Yeah, we won," said Sam. "It cost millions of lives and took the full might of the Americans, the British and the Russians, to finally defeat Germany."

"The Americans? When did the Americans join the war?"

"Nineteen forty-one."

"Nineteen forty-one?" Colin echoed. "The war went on all those years?"

Sam nodded. "Lasted another four years. Hitler wasn't finally defeated until nineteen forty-five."

Colin gazed at him, fascination and bewilderment on his face. "Who's Hitler?" he asked.

At that, words finally failed the American. He stared at the young man, as though he'd suddenly realised he was communicating with a ghost.

"When were you born, Colin?" Andy said softly.

"Eighteen hundred and ninety-eight."

"Oh fuck," said Jamie.

Chapter Thirteen

The late afternoon sun had begun its slow descent towards the cleft in the hills at the western end of the glen. The wind had died, and clouds of midges were swarming in the still of day. As yet they were no more than a multitude of tiny wings beating against the cool spring air. Only with the arrival of warmer weather would they become the detestable biting plague of the Highlands.

"D'ye follow the football at all, Sam?" asked Jamie.

"Y'mean soccer, don't yuh? Yeah, a little, I guess."

Jamie edged closer to the American. "D'ye ever watch the World Cup? Ye know, the competition that's held every four years?"

"When I was a kid I used to watch some of the games."

An expectant gleam appeared in the soldier's eyes. "Ye'd know, like, some of the teams in the competition then, wouldn't ye?"

"I guess."

Andy had also begun to pay attention. Jamie went on: "Ye couldn't tell us who's won the World Cup back tae nineteen seventy-eight, could ye?"

Laughter broke from the American's battered features. "That's some priority list y'got there, fella. I could tell ya who won the World Series no problem, but the soccer World Cup, Jeez that's a tough one." He scratched his head. "Let's see now; Brazil won the last World Cup eight years ago. The competitions before that?" He shrugged his shoulders.

Jamie asked the dreaded question: "How about England? They didn't win it again, did they?"

"I don't think so fellas…"

"And Scotland?"

The American shook his head, an amused smile on his face.

"Eight years ago?" asked Andy. "Why was the last World Cup eight years ago?"

The smile faded from Sam's face. "Y'gotta understand, guys, things were 'bout as bad as they could get. Since twenty twenty everything had started to go all to hell."

"The World Cup was cancelled," Jamie reflected in horror.

"That nuclear explosion we saw, right at the end," Andy said quietly. "We weren't seeing five thousand years into the future. We were seeing your world Sam, weren't we?"

The American saw the raw emotion in the soldier's face and decided the less he knew the better. "Hell, I dunno. There was famine throughout Africa and Asia. The U.S. was accused of hoarding food; maybe something escalated from there. Shawnee and me saw as much as you guys did."

"It doesn't really matter," Jamie put in. "Ah mean, there's no going back, is there? Even if there was something tae go back tae, it's never gonnae happen."

"Y'can't say that for sure. Whatever chain of events brought us all here could work in reverse."

Jamie nodded towards the fourth member of the group, who'd drifted off into a world of his own. His voice fell to a whisper:

"Ah used tae spend ma summers up here when Ah was a kid. This glen was out of bounds, big style. They used tae frighten us with the story of these two brothers who disappeared in nineteen sixteen, only a week after their old man was found dead in the glen."

Sam and Andy looked at Colin.

"Y'mean he's one of the brothers?"

"Aye, d'ye understand but; they were never seen again. And if *they* were never seen again…"

"…We're no' gonnae be seen again either."

Jamie continued softly: "Seeing that wee guy sitting there is like finding Glenn Miller in a dinghy in the middle of the English Channel…"

Colin became aware that all eyes were focused on him. "What's wrong? Why are you all staring at me?"

"Colin, what year is it?" Sam asked.

"Seventeen hundred and forty-six."

"No, I mean what year was it before y'came here?"

"You mean back in the real world? It was nineteen sixteen."

The American nodded. "Did y'leave any family behind?"

"Alistair and myself had walked to the head of the glen to build a cairn to our father." Colin sighed wretchedly. "It was only last week himself died up there. Now I'm told my house is a ruin and the world has been at war for over thirty years. I just don't understand what's going on at all."

"You 'n me both, buddy," Sam murmured softly.

In the far distance, on the southern slopes of the glen, three figures came into view as they descended *Meall Banabhie*. The sun's rays highlighted the tartan plaid worn by the middle figure.

"Achnacon," said Andy.

"Aye, with Laurel and Hardy," added Jamie.

"What the hell were those two bampots doing away up there?"

"Maybe your guys were trying to make a break for it?" suggested Sam.

"He should've let them go," Andy grumbled. "Best we don't mention this thing with the dates. We don't know how they'll react."

When they reached the cottage the two errant soldiers were in a high state of excitement.

"It's just amazing, man. Ye can see Fort William, and everything frae the top of that hill!" Rae exclaimed.

"Only, it isn't Fort William," Ferguson added, "it's like some kindae castle where Fort William used tae be."

"Aw you great tumchie that ye are," said Rae. "Ah've already told ye; that *is* Fort William. That's what the town was named after!"

"Aw, right. It's pure brilliant though. Ye can see these big boats, with sails and masts and everything, just like in the old pirate filums."

"T'would be best for now, young Andy, if your men stayed off the hills," said Achnacon.

"Sorry about that again, like," Rac mumbled. He glanced at his Corporal. "We wanted tae see if it's just the glen, or if everywhere has changed."

Andy glowered at his two runaways. "Well, now ye know."

Achnacon turned to the American. "The daughter of my cousin, Ewen of Inverlaragain, has told how the attack on my people was halted, because of yourself and your lady." He clasped Sam's hand. "Rhona said you was punished for your courage. Your wounds will fade in time, but your courage will never fade from the hearts of my people."

The American squirmed like a nocturnal creature caught in headlights. "It's okay, man. No problem, y'know?"

Andy smiled at the American's discomfort. He turned to the old Highlander. "What happens now? Is there anything we can do?"

The warmth faded from Achnacon's eyes. "I have posted lookouts at both ends of the glen, and on the top of *Meall Banabhie*. Young Ewen and Lachlan has been despatched to Locheil to advise him of developments. On the morrow those who survived the English attack must lay their kinfolk to rest. We dare not wait longer lest we have unwelcome guests at the funeral. I must carry this news to the shielings before nightfall so the people may return to their homes. One of your men may wish to accompany myself... *Muirshearlach*, perhaps?"

"If that's okay with you, Corp?" said Jamie.

Andy nodded. "Take yer rifle just in case."

The Highlander's eyes lit up as Macsorley reappeared, his webbing draped over his plaid, his rifle clutched in his right hand.

"Perhaps Achnacon may be permitted to carry the musket of Muirshearlach?" he asked lightly.

Jamie whispered at his N.C.O. "You know he's gonnae torment me, don't ye? Ah'm gonnae have tae tell him something."

Andy nodded. "Play it by ear. Let him know as little as ye have tae."

The young soldier removed the magazine before handing the rifle to Achnacon. The old clansman turned the weapon this way and that, an expression of bright wonder on his face.

Andy could hear the subtle start of the interrogation as the two men set off: "Tell me now, young *Muirshearlach*, how would myself go about inserting a musket ball in such a fine barrel...?"

Jamie's reply was lost in the splash of water as the pair began to cross the Laragain burn.

As soon as they were gone the American turned to the newcomers. "Y'haven't introduced me to the rest of your guys."

The N.C.O. glanced warily at Rae. "Aye, right. This is er, Archie Rae and Willie Ferguson. They usually answer tae Rae and Fergie."

"Pleased to meet yuh," smiled Sam.

"Aye, likewise," Fergie replied.

Rae grasped the American's hand with one of his fleshy paws. "So the Yanks are here, eh? Ah suppose that means we're all gonnae have tae duck when the shooting starts..."

Sam's smile didn't waver. "Only those with huge asses."

Rae nodded sharply. The pleasantries over, he turned to his friend.

"C'mon, Fergie, Ah'm starving. Let's see if there's any grub on offer."

As the pair were about to disappear into the cottage the door opened and Shawnee emerged, blinking in the daylight. The transformation in Rae was instantaneous. Once again he held out a huge paw, this time with an ingratiating smile.

"Hello there. Name's Archie Rae, Ah'm very pleased tae make yer acquaintance."

"Ah'm William Ferguson," his comrade mumbled behind him.

Shawnee swept the hair from her face, and smiled at both in turn. "Hi. I'm Shawnee. Nice to meet you guys."

"Shawnee?" Rae mused. "Is that no' an Injun name? You don't look anything like an Injun. Yer far too bonny for that."

She studied his overfed form, his great fleshy hand still wrapped around hers. "Rae, huh?" she replied, with a disarming smile. "Yeah, well, you don't look anything like a drop of golden sun…"

Shawnee retained her pleasant smile, while all around her hooted with laughter. Fergie hooted loudest of all.

"Drop of golden sun; that's a stoater. Ah must remember that one…"

"Ah sharrup, ya mutant," growled Rae. With a swipe of his paw he pushed Ferguson towards the cottage.

Shawnee made her way directly to Colin. "It looks like your brother's fever has broken."

The young man rose to his feet. "Does that mean himself is going to be all right?"

"Well, he's still kinda weak, but he's conscious now. He's asking for you."

As Colin followed the two soldiers into the cottage, Shawnee closed her eyes and took a long breath of mountain air. She was wearing the quilted anorak that Sam had secreted into her backpack; a little shiver nonetheless shook her body. Instinctively she made for Sam.

"Hello again," she smiled at Andy.

"Aye, er, how's it going?" the soldier replied awkwardly. "Listen, Ah'm, sorry about Darwin's missing link. If it's no' his stomach it's his loins."

Shawnee smiled dismissively. She shivered again, and burrowed into Sam's arms. "It's such a beautiful part of the world, isn't it? But it's gonna take some getting used to; the temperature, I mean."

"Aye, Ah suppose Scotland's a bit of a shock tae the system, compared tae America."

"Yeah, it is now, that's for sure. But back in, ah… well, back home I guess, things had changed terribly those last few years. You wouldn't have recognised the Scotland of our day. Didn't Sam tell you anything? I suppose all he's done is talk about The Dodgers."

Sam's eyebrows rose sharply. "Didn't get the chance; they only wanted to know about soccer. Anyway, how did y'know they weren't from our time?"

She shook her head in mock disgust. "How could y'not know? I mean, there's Colin's clothes, the way these guys speak; I figured straightaway we'd all been taken from different times. I knew for certain when Colin's brother began talking in his fever about the Western Front."

Sam nodded. "You remember that cairn we saw at the top of the glen?"

"The cairn that commemorated the massacre?"

"Yeah, seems it was erected by Colin and his brother the day they disappeared, as a memorial to their father."

Shawnee shook her head in wonder. "D'you remember how weather beaten that cairn was? It musta been more than a hundred years old. This whole thing is totally awesome."

"That's one word for it," murmured Sam.

"What about you, Andy?" she asked brightly. "What year was it when you were, y'know… taken?"

Andy glanced furtively at Shawnee, then directed his reply at Sam: "Nineteen seventy-six. The lads and me were training recruits for service in Northern Ireland."

"That gunfire we heard yesterday; that was you and your guys?"

"Aye, sorry about that," mumbled Andy.

Shawnee smiled. "Y'make it sound like you kept us awake, or something. Rhona, the girl we arrived with, she got talking to your friend; Ak na…"

"Achnacon?"

"*Aknak… Achnacon.* Seems the stand you took allowed a lotta people to get away. Seems Andy Macmillan is quite a hero around here."

Andy pulled at his nose. "Aye, well, he said much the same about you two."

"That's true," said Sam. He could see the soldier was uncomfortable in Shawnee's presence. He was used to the different ways in which men would respond to their attraction to her. She, as always, would sail serenely on; apparently unaware of the effect she had on the male gender.

"You met this guy: Achnacon?" she said to Sam.

"Yeah, he was here earlier. Took one of Andy's guys away with him. Said they were gonna get the people down from the hills for the funerals tomorrow."

"What's he like?"

"Well, y'know how it is; if you've seen one eighteenth-century Scottish Highlander then I guess you've seen 'em all."

Shawnee turned to Macmillan. "I'll get more sense outta you, Andy."

Macmillan picked at a piece of bracken that was stuck to his kilt. "Ah suppose he's no' what you'd expect a Highland clansman tae look like. Ah know he's old and everything, but Ah still expected all Highlanders tae be over six-feet tall; built like wrestlers. But this guy, Achnacon, cannae be much more than five feet four. But there's… something about him…"

"How d'you mean?" she asked.

Andy's kilt was finally free of all imperfections. He glanced briefly at Shawnee. "It's like, when we first met him he was just an old guy in a kilt; but now, he looks like he could handle anything."

Shawnee nodded proudly. "We could be related y'know."

"Yeah, well, your guy Colin reckoned he could see the resemblance between you and Mary," Sam put in.

"That's possible as well. After all, my dad was a direct descendant of the Camerons of Glen Laragain."

"You're a Cameron?" said Andy. "It didn't occur tae me that you were a Cameron."

A long-suffering expression appeared on Sam's face. "First thing y'learn about Shawnee; this Scottish thing. She's like this little Olympic runner that's been given this torch to carry…"

"Good for you, lassie," said Andy firmly. "And now ye've brought yer wee bit of flame home."

Shawnee smiled at the metaphor. "Yeah, but this isn't exactly what I had in mind. What was our plan, Sam? Two or three days in the Highlands, then Edinburgh... London... Paris...Guess now we're just gonna have to spend the whole vacation in Scotland, huh?"

"Yeah, well, whatever happened could still reverse itself," said Sam.

"That's true. We could all waken up tomorrow back in our own worlds," the soldier added with a reassuring smile. He seemed more comfortable with Shawnee, having learned of their common tribal ancestry.

"It's okay, fellas, y'don't have to protect me," she said calmly. "I'm sure we've all figured it out by now; whatever sequence of events took us from three different time periods is hardly gonna reverse itself. Besides, I'm not sure I'd wanna go back to our world..."

"That's if our world will ever exist now, after what's happened here," said Sam.

"That's what Ah was afraid of," groaned Andy. "Ah don't know about you two but Ah couldn't've caused more damage if Ah'd arrived with a bomb in ma hands."

"Maybe you've helped to right a wrong, Andy. Maybe all of us have come together to correct something that should never have happened."

"D'ye think so? Ah wish Ah could see how that slaughter could be tae the benefit of mankind."

Sam tried to offer encouragement. "Maybe one of those guys was the ancestor of Jack The Ripper, or some other evil son of a bitch."

"...Or Winston Churchill, or Abraham Lincoln. What if Ah turn out tae be like the guy that shot yon Archduke whatsisname away back in nineteen fourteen; he probably thought he'd done the right thing as well, instead he kicked off World War bloody One..."

"I am become death, the destroyer of worlds," Shawnee announced grandly.

Sam turned to look at her. "You've become a what?"

"I am become death, the destroyer of worlds. It's from the Hindu Scriptures. It's meant to convey how awesome and capricious fate can be. It's the kinda thing Andy's talking about."

"Ah only joined up for three square meals and a trade Ah could take intae civvy street," the soldier murmured wretchedly. "Maybe a uniform tae charm the lassies. That's all Ah joined up for..."

Inside the cottage, shutters were closed to allow a fire to be safely lit against the growing darkness. Before long smoke was drifting through the thatched roof, filling the air with the familiar scent of burning peat. Far to the east they could hear cattle lowing mournfully, their distant bellowing like the echo of some primeval beast. The sound died away as the sun disappeared behind *Druim Fada*.

"Y'know, if we have altered events to come," said Sam, picking up the threads of their discussion, "then how come we're still here? Or more to the point, Shawnee, how come you're still here?"

"Doesn't necessarily change my ancestry. I could still be descended from the same direct line."

"Yeah, that's possible, but it's unlikely if a lot more people survived the massacre. And what about Colin and Alistair? It's even less likely their ancestry would remain the same."

"What are you saying, Sam? In spite of everything that's happened these people are still destined tae be massacred?"

The American shrugged. "I remember reading about this theoretical time paradox. It goes something like this; a guy builds a time machine, goes back to when his grandpa was a boy and then shoots him…"

"Why would anyone wanna shoot their own grandpa?" Shawnee asked.

"It's just a hypothetical situation."

"Doesn't make any sense at all."

"Okay. Let's try something else. The guy was carrying a rare disease and infected his grandpa when he was a boy, and his grandpa died… horribly, and in a lotta pain…"

"The whole thing still sounds stupid to me."

"Whatever," Sam continued irritably. "The paradox is this; if the grandpa died when he was a boy then the guy with the time machine was never born…"

"…And could never have gone back and killed his granddad."

"That's it exactly. Y'see, the way I figure it; there must be boundaries that can't be crossed, laws that cannot be broken."

"Surely none of this is gonna affect us," said Shawnee. "I hardly think any one of us is gonna kill our own direct ancestor…"

"Let's hope none of us discovers the answer to that paradox," continued Sam. "But it doesn't just stop there though, does it? Say there's a second hypothesis; say two guys go back in a two-man time machine and one kills the other's grandpa. What's gonna be the knock-on effect?"

"In a two-man time machine? Well, assuming it takes two men to operate the machine, it's gotta be the same as the first hypothesis. It's gotta be the same kinda paradox, yeah?"

Sam nodded in agreement, then added; "not necessarily."

"He does this at times," she explained to Andy. "He comes at you from the front, then hits y'from behind. Go on, Stephen Hawking, enlighten us."

Sam sniffed imperiously: "It's possible, in such a situation, that past events could be adjusted to suit the new circumstances…"

"Meaning…?"

"…The grandpa dies, his grandson vanishes in a puffa smoke, and when the other guy goes back to the time machine it's become a one-man machine. There's no direct paradox, so past events are rearranged to suit the new reality."

Sam's audience took a few moments to absorb the concept.

"D'ye think this is what's happened tae us?" asked Andy. "Our pasts have been rearranged tae fit what's happened here?"

"Makes as much sense as anything. Us being here is an inescapable fact. That's gotta be the starting point for any changes that stem from us."

In the distance they could hear the frantic bleating of a ewe and her lost lamb as each tried to locate the other. Eventually mother and offspring were reunited, and only the soft rush of the burn disturbed the stillness. Venus had appeared, like a yellow lantern amid the fading glow of sunset, when the murmur of voices broke the silence that had descended upon them.

"That's Jamie and Achnacon," said Andy. "That'll be them down from the shielings."

They could hear other voices, to east and west of *Meall An Fhraoich*; the voices of men and women, chattering softly to each other, like geese on the wing.

Achnacon and Jamie emerged from the darkness.

"My friends, why do you not affail yourselfs of warmth and shelter?" the Highlander asked in dismay. "Why do you sit here in the chill of night like outcasts?"

"It's too beautiful a night to sit indoors," Shawnee whispered in reply.

The old clansman removed his bonnet and took the woman's hand.

"You will be the Lady Shawnee. An old *bodach*'s bones is denied many pleasures, but meeting one as fair as she is gallant is not one of them."

"And you will be Achnacon." She smiled. "I've heard so much about you. It's a real honour to finally meet you in person."

"My lady, the honour belongs to Achnacon." The Highlander kept hold of Shawnee's hand as he straightened up, gazing at her so intently her eyes fell away in embarrassment.

"Forgive me, please. T'was not my intention to stare, but your voice is familiar to me. A chentleman would never forget such a lady, and yet I feel as if ourselfs have met before..."

Shawnee smiled. "I've been told that before, but never so beautifully."

Achnacon looked reproachfully at Sam and Andy. "'Tis the pastime of fools and dreamers to sit beneath the cold stars when there is warmth and shelter indoors. For chentlemen to mistreat such a lady in this fashion..." He shook his head in disappointment.

Shawnee impishly added her expression of disappointment to his as Achnacon escorted her into the cottage.

Rhona and the other women of the clan sat in a semi-circle around the fire. Rhona's face was puffy, her eyes red-rimmed, but she smiled gamely at Shawnee and Sam. Rae and Ferguson were unconscious on a makeshift bed in the far corner. Diagonally opposite them Mary too lay asleep. Alistair and Colin were awake, however, both staring intently as the newcomers entered.

Achnacon spoke softly to the women, and the oldest of the group took a ladle to a blackened cauldron that was suspended over the fire. In the flickering shadows she looked like a sorceress stirring a witch's brew. The four newcomers were seated at the table, where the browned, steaming contents of the cauldron were served to them in wooden bowls.

As soon as Sam realised the dish was a stew he looked anxiously at Shawnee. "If y'can't eat that just leave it," he whispered. "We'll get something else."

Her reply was barely audible: "I don't think they do a veg burger here, Sam."

"Try it," urged Andy, "it's really nice."

Cautiously Shawnee lifted the tiniest fragment to her lips.

"Ah know what this is," Jamie announced. "Ma granny made this when Ah was a wean…"

"…I don't wanna know!" Shawnee hissed. "I'll eat it 'cause I'm hungry, and I don't wanna offend anybody, but I don't wanna know what it used to be, okay?"

"She's a vegetarian," explained Sam. "Doesn't like eating anything that used to have a pulse."

"*Was* a vegetarian," said Shawnee. Eyes tightly shut, she satisfied her hunger the way a shipwrecked sailor, dying of thirst, would sip his own urine.

While Shawnee's eyes were closed Jamie made the shape of antlers above his head.

"Anyway, Jamie, what did ye tell him?" Andy asked.

Macsorley looked at his N.C.O.

"Achnacon. What did ye tell him about us?"

Jamie shifted in his seat. "Well, Ah kindae thought it'd be better tae give him it straight; ye know, that we're from the future."

Andy looked at the Highlander, to study the effects of such an earth-shattering concept. The old man was deep in conversation with his ladies, oblivious to the little band of time travellers.

"He seems tae have taken it all right. What was his reaction?"

Jamie shook his head. "Ah thought these people were quite…eh, what's the word?"

"Primitive?" offered Sam.

Shawnee glared at him. "Spiritual?" she suggested.

"Aye, spiritual, that's the word Ah'm lookin' for. Ah thought their minds would be open tae that sort of stuff, but Ah just couldn't get through tae him. '*Tell me, young Muirshearlach, how can a man exist before he has been conceived?*' And ye know, how can ye explain something ye don't even understand yerself?"

"So what did y'tell the old guy?" Sam asked.

"Well, ye see, these people believe in what they call the second sight; the ability tae see intae the future. He thought Ah was talking in riddles, and Ah think he might've got the impression, like, that we can see intae the future. Or at least that one of us can…"

"Which one?" asked Shawnee.

The young soldier glanced uneasily at his corporal. "Ah think he might've sortae got the impression that it's you, like…"

Andy groaned. "Aw for God sake; so now on top of everything else Ah'm a bloody fortune teller."

"It just sortae came out that way," murmured Jamie.

"What did y'tell him about Shawnee and me?"

"Oh, he knows you two are from America. He also knows that Shawnee's people came from Glen Laragain originally. From what Ah can gather, a number of clansmen from the Glen were captured after the battle of Worcester in sixteen fifty-one, and sold tae plantation owners in Virginia. So just pick a Donald Cameron as yer ancestor; you can guarantee there was a Donald there, somewhere."

"Donald?" she echoed pensively. "That was my dad's name."

"Right then, in that case, you're the great granddaughter of *Domhnuill Beag Camshron* of *Gleann Laragain*."

"What does that mean?"

"Wee Donald Cameron of Glen Laragain."

"Wee Donald Cameron. He'd have liked that."

"What about all our weapons and suchlike? How the hell do we explain all that?" Andy scowled.

"Well, he kindae thinks that you're really good at this looking intae the future lark."

"What? He thinks Ah made all this maself?"

"No, not yerself, but he thinks you picked up the designs in your visions."

Andy groaned horribly.

"Look at it from the bright side," Jamie went on. "You're gonnae be quite a catch around here. Ah mean, he seemed really chuffed that you were interested in Ishbel."

"Aw naw, tell me ye didn't…"

"Aye, sorry, that just kind of slipped out as well."

Macmillan unleashed a stream of oaths under his breath.

"Who's Ishbel?" laughed Shawnee.

"Achnacon's older daughter. She's really bonny. Ah think Andy has a wee thing for her, if ye know what Ah mean…"

Macmillan glowered evilly at his comrade. Before he could translate this into words, Achnacon was at the table.

"I trust the food was to everybody's satisfaction?"

"Yeah, really nice, thank you," said Shawnee.

"Good. Good." The Highlander turned to the despondent figure of Macmillan. "Young Andy; if ourselfs could have a moment together?"

The corporal glared at Macsorley before following the old clansman outside, like a condemned man on his way to the gallows.

Shawnee looked worriedly at Jamie. "What d'you think? Is he gonna be mad at poor Andy, or what?"

Jamie appeared totally untroubled. "No way. Ah knew what Ah was doing. People like Andy just need a wee push."

Shawnee's face held the faintest of smiles. "I dunno, Jamie, maybe there's a certain etiquette that shoulda been observed here…"

"That's true," Sam agreed. "God only knows what the correct protocol is for this kinda thing."

Jamie glanced anxiously at the door. "Ye don't think Achnacon's giving him a hard time?"

"Well, we are talking about the guy's daughter," Sam winked at Shawnee. "For all y'know your buddy might be in the middle of a duel right now."

Jamie was appearing less and less confident by the minute.

"Maybe Ah should go outside and see if everything's all right."

At that moment the door opened and Andy re-entered the cottage on his own. Jamie stared wide-eyed as the corporal stood over him, clasped his head with both hands, and planted a kiss on the top of his skull.

Shawnee clapped her hands with delight.

"See? Ah told ye," beamed the young cupid. "Some people just need a wee push."

"What did the old guy say?" asked Sam.

Andy lowered himself gingerly into his seat. "He wanted tae know if Ah wished tae pay court tae his daughter. Ah asked him what Ishbel thought of this, and it seems an approach from Corporal Andy would not be looked upon unfavourably. So it looks like Ah've got a date."

"Where's Achnacon now?"

"He's away tae make arrangements for the funerals tomorrow." Andy turned to his friend. "Gonnae check with me first the next time ye fix me up with a lassie?"

"Aye." Jamie condescendingly gave the idea some consideration. "Ah'll think about it."

Chapter Fourteen

Andy was woken shortly after daybreak by a succession of moans, which were stifled before they reached a crescendo. The ensuing silence was fringed by the soft whisperings of the lassies as they prepared breakfast. The girl who'd applied the ointment to Andy's legs sat before the fire with the Americans' friend, Rhona. Both were busy tending the cauldron, which hung suspended over the smouldering peat.

He could hear Colin and Alistair chattering quietly to each other in Gaelic, and decided now was as good a time as any to meet Alistair. Colin sat on the edge of his brother's mattress and gaped blankly at Andy as he approached.

"Hi, how's it going? Name's Andy Macmillan. Lately of the Highland Fusiliers; now part of the Jacobite army, apparently."

The older brother nodded impassively as he took Andy's hand. "I'm Alistair Cameron; you've met my brother, Colin."

Alistair looked pale and tired, but his voice was clear and his grip reasonably firm. "I'm sorry if it was myself that woke you. Colin tells me I've become a terrible noisy sleeper."

Andy shook his head dismissively. "Ah don't know how much Colin has told ye…"

Alistair glanced at his brother, who seemed intimidated by Andy's presence. "Colin has told me about yourself and your friends; that none of you belong to our… time. He says our cottage at Inverlaragain is a ruin in your world."

Andy rubbed the back of his neck, massaging away the overnight stiffness. "Ah'm sorry that came out as it did. Ye have tae understand; in nineteen seventy-six you guys had been missing for sixty years."

Alistair took a moment to absorb this confirmation of his brother's ravings. "Ourselves never made it home, then?"

Andy shook his head.

"Alistair, maybe this is God's will," Colin put in. "Maybe you were never meant to return to France."

"Och wheesht, man," said his brother scathingly. "I'll have been posted as a deserter; everyone will be thinking I'm a coward, and you're blethering about God's will…"

"Ah don't know about any of this being the will of God," Andy intervened. "But we're up tae our necks now in a different kind of war. Ah heard the gunfire yesterday coming from this direction. What d'ye have: a Lee Enfield?"

Colin shook his head. His brother's anger had brought a pink flush to his cheeks. "We both have hunting rifles. When you're in the hills there's always a chance of taking a beast for the pot. Anyway, with these new-fangled underwater submarines the Germans have got, you never know who might have been landed off the west coast."

"Aye, well, at least that's one thing we won't have to worry about."

Alistair nodded. "Himself has been telling me about the war; he says it doesn't end until nineteen hundred and forty-five."

Andy scratched his head awkwardly. "Right, sorry; somebody should've clarified that. The First World War armistice was declared in November nineteen eighteen…"

"The *first* world war? God in heaven, how many has there been?"

Andy glanced uneasily at the sleeping figures of Sam and Shawnee. "There'll be time enough tae answer yer questions. It's probably best you rest up for now." He wanted to leave Alistair with a last encouraging thought, soldier to soldier, but something in those dark tormented eyes prevented him from even trying. "Anyway, look, we'll, we'll talk again later, eh? Okay?"

He couldn't get out of the cottage quickly enough. Outside, the clear skies of the previous night had given way to a grey cloak of cloud and drizzle. He leaned against the wall of the cottage and closed his eyes, to find the after-image of that haunted face imprinted on his retinas. To his surprise he was soon joined by Colin, a bowl of porridge in each hand.

"Alistair says no soldier should be left to break his fast alone."

Andy took the food with a nod of appreciation.

"Alistair never talks about France. I think he feels guilty that he has survived while most of his friends were killed. I hear him sometimes calling their names in his sleep."

Andy nodded. "Highlanders were an endangered species by the time that bloody war was over."

"These hills have always given birth to soldiers," Colin explained. "How could any man who does not enlist look those people in the eye; the ones who have lost sons or brothers? I was also about to enlist, to fight alongside Alistair."

"Aye? Well, Ah think ye'll get the chance before too long."

A proud smile spread across Colin's face. "We fought together yesterday, Mister Macmillan, when the redcoats were here."

"Andy."

Colin nodded. "I thought they were going to keep coming until they had all been shot down, but I think some of them enjoyed life more than others. But, och, man, you should have seen Alistair. The blood was pouring from his arm like a red burn; he couldn't even reload his rifle, but he wouldn't fall, not until they had turned and ran. Being so brave and everything, that must be why himself has survived so long in France."

Colin's naivety brought a grin to Andy's face.

"What's this thing between your brother and Mary? She's like something ye'd rub from a genie's lamp."

Instead of the bashful smile Andy expected, a dark shudder ran through the young man.

"Just before… it all happened, Alistair and myself saw Mary appear out of the mist. A soldier was with her; a redcoat soldier. They were like something that belonged to the mist; but what that brute did to her was terrible… Andy."

"Ye think this is still tae happen?"

"It started to happen just before the fight yesterday, the same soldier, with Mary. We were able to stop him; Alistair mostly. That's why she has eyes for no other. The American, Sam, said the redcoats will be back. Perhaps Mary is still destined to fall beneath that beast."

"There's people around her now who'll make sure it'll never happen."

Colin looked uncertainly at the soldier. "Your friend, Jamie, said he would stand and fight, but yourself and the others…?"

"Rae and Ferguson are a law untae themselves. But Ah won't be going anywhere; ye have ma word on it. Far as Sam and Shawnee are concerned, when push comes tae shove, Ah think he'll do whatever Shawnee tells him."

Colin smiled shyly. "I like the way you say things; it's like you're speaking another language. Does everybody talk like yourself in nineteen hundred and seventy-six?"

Andy grinned at the young man's candour. "See Mary? She's what we would call a pure doll."

"A pure doll."

"That's right. A wee cracker."

"A wee cracker..."

"Ye know Ah'm surprised ye haven't thought about moving in there yerself."

"Moving in there myself?"

"Ye know? Making a move. Chancing yer arm. Ah mean, the redcoats didn't just run from yer brother yesterday."

Colin's cheeks became tinged with scarlet. "Och no, I'm not very good with the lassies; I never know what to say. Besides, I thought the wee cracker who tended to your legs yesterday was awfully nice."

Andy laughed. "Ah tell ye what, Colin; you take these bowls inside and get us another helping of that porridge, and while ye're in there why don't ye try chatting up yer wee cracker?"

"Chatting up?"

"Talk tae the lassie; get her interested in ye; use a wee bit of the old charm, ye know?" Andy wiggled his hips, to demonstrate the required body language.

"Och, I don't think that would work very well for myself. I would probably knock the lassie into the fire."

"Aye, maybe yer right at that, wee man," grinned the soldier. "Tae tell ye the truth, Ah've never been all that good at chatting them up either."

Left on his own, the smile faded from Andy's face. The ointment that Colin's wee cracker had applied to his legs had been so effective he hadn't even thought to check them before now. Most of the blisters had subsided, leaving little more than discoloured patches on his calves and thighs. He drew another breath of West Highland mist into his lungs. The surrounding hills were no more than invisible sensations in the murk. It would be so easy to believe that beyond there lay his own familiar world. But this probably had as much to do with the timelessness of the Highland landscape, as the struggle of his mind to accept the new reality.

"…Here's your porridge," Colin announced, a fresh bowl in each hand. "The wee cracker; her name is Catriona Macphail. The other girl, Rhona, says that Catriona lost her father yesterday. I don't think she'll want to be bothered with anybody chatting up her for a wee while to come."

"Aye," said Andy. "Best tae leave it for a wee while, right enough."

The young man looked brightly at his new friend. "You said something earlier about a second great war…?"

"Aye," said the soldier heavily. "Ah did, didn't Ah?"

As soon as all the strangers had breakfasted Rhona passed on the message left with her by Achnacon:

'If young Andy, and Muirshearlach, and the other chentlemen could find it in themselfs to offer their assistance, perhaps they would care to make their way to the cemetery. Achnacon understood the Lady Shawnee must follow the customs of her own land, and do as herself thinks best.'

Shawnee insisted on accompanying the men, but not before Rhona had found her a calf-length dress to protect her from the elements. Colin elected to remain behind with his brother, but the prospect of the legendary Highland funeral feast enticed Rae and Ferguson along.

It was well after 10am by the time they left *Meall An Fhraoich*. As they followed the old track westward a clachan would occasionally appear out of the mist and they would catch the faint echo of peat smoke where a meal had been cooked that morning. Otherwise they encountered few signs of life. Drained of colour and warmth, the land itself was like a corpse awaiting internment.

They had walked perhaps two miles when Andy suddenly stopped in his tracks.

"Did anyone hear that?" he hissed.

The group came to a disjointed halt. Everybody inclined their heads to the west, trying to penetrate the wall of mist.

"What did ye hear?" whispered Jamie.

"Ah don't know. Away ahead of us; like an animal crying."

"It's this freakin fog," Sam put in. "It's enough to spook anybody."

They were about to continue when a distant wailing sound echoed through the mist. Before the noise died away it was accompanied by a second cry.

"What in God's name is that?" Shawnee whispered, edging towards Sam.

Andy and Jamie cocked their rifles.

"Everyone get behind me and Jamie."

The unearthly howls continued as the group bunched together into a protective phalanx. Before long a third creature added its voice; its mournful wail clearly coming from the direction of the graveyard. There was something melancholy and heart-rending about the cries, as if the dead of Glen Laragain were mourning their lost lives.

"They sound like banshees," Shawnee murmured.

"I thought the banshees came from Ireland," said Sam.

"D'you wanna go and tell them they're on the wrong side of the Irish Sea? Anyhow, there's probably a Scottish equivalent."

Andy was reluctant to continue until he knew what lay ahead. The smell of fear in the air was so tangible it would have taken little to trigger a stampede.

"Wait a minute!" exclaimed Jamie. "Ah know what that is; Ah remember ma granny talking about it; that's the *coronach*."

"Is it dangerous this coronak?" Sam asked, his arms wrapped around Shawnee. "Some kinda weird animal, or what?"

Jamie's anxious expression had given way to a condescending smile. "It's no animal, ye great pudding. What ye're hearing is the funeral wail of the clans. This is how the Highlanders mourned their dead. Every township had a woman that would cry like this. They called it the *coronach*."

"Ye mean that's just a bunchae old wifies greeting and howling?"

"Are ye sure about this?" said Andy, as the anguished keening reverberated down the glen. "Ye'd hardly believe that was human."

"It's the *coronach*," Jamie reiterated. "Ma granny told me this used tae be heard at every funeral in the old days. Usually there was just the one, but then usually they only buried one person at a time."

Now that the mystery had been solved, the defensive phalanx disintegrated. Even Shawnee lost no time in re-establishing her own personal space. Uneasily they continued along the track. However, as a fourth *coronach* arose from behind them the group began to bunch together once more.

As they approached the graveyard the tone and pitch of the voices ahead of them became more uniform. The lament that had struck up from the east had now been joined by a second, more distant cry.

A number of dark shapes suddenly appeared out of the gloom, huddled in a motionless clump, like so many scarecrows. Behind them the drystone wall of the burial ground curved away to left and right, before disappearing into the murk. A woman in the group spotted the strangers and immediately the scarecrows sprang to life. The females were hustled to the rear, while an elderly Highlander in dull green tartan stepped forward, broadsword in hand.

Andy and the others came to a halt; even the Gaelic-speaking Macsorley was lost for words. As the effect of their arrival spread around the graveyard, like ripples on a lochan, the wailing cries fell away into silence.

The old warrior bellowed something. Behind him three other *bodachs* fingered the handles of their dirks.

"They think we're redcoats," said Jamie.

"Drop that old git," urged Rae, "before he skewers somebody with that bloody sword."

At that moment Achnacon appeared out of the mist, rushing towards his fellow warriors. There was a heated spat between him and the old swordsman, before Andy and his group were waved forward.

Achnacon's eyes were red and swollen. "Please, young Andy, all of you, you are welcome here. My gallant cousin, *Larachmor*, was angry you did not announce yourselfs, but 'twas my fault for thinking our ways was known to you."

The clansfolk slowly returned to their vigil, and the wail of the *coronach* echoed once again around the mist-shrouded cemetery. Achnacon brought Larachmor over to meet his newfound friends. He was similar in stature to Achnacon, but several years younger. He was clean-shaven, his dark, coarse-featured face inclined suspiciously to one side. He nodded curtly at each of the group as he was introduced, his hand still on the hilt of his broadsword. Only when he was introduced to their leader did he break his silence. Macmillan had no idea what the old clansman said to him, but his tone was clear enough.

Jamie interpreted the message: "The old guy, Larachmor, he doesnae like ye and he doesnae trust ye. He says he'll be watching every move ye make, and the moment ye give him just cause he's gonnae have ye, so he is."

The Highlander continued his tirade, even as Achnacon angrily took him to task.

"...And the same goes for all the restae us... He says something about weasels warning rabbits about a fox... whatever the hell that means."

Having vented his wrath, Larachmor pulled himself free of his cousin and strode off to rejoin his fellow mourners. Achnacon turned to the newcomers, an angry flush in his face.

"I had hoped this would not happen; I had hoped they would think otherwise when they had seen yourselfs in the flesh."

"There's others like him, then?" Macmillan asked.

Achnacon nodded bleakly. "Where once there was hospitality now there is chust fear and mistrust. All who have met yourselfs know otherwise; they know you as our friends."

"Is it gonna be safe for us 'round here now?" Sam wanted to know.

"You all enchoy the protection of Achnacon," the old man said stiffly. "None would dare abuse that protection. However perhaps 'twould be best if yourselfs returned to *Meall An Fhraoich*." He caught sight of the dismay on Shawnee's face. "My lady, they only know that the worst calamity ever to have visited Glen Laragain has descended upon their heads. T'would be a fool's mission to try to persuade them they have been blessed by your arrival..."

Chapter Fifteen

Since their return from the graveyard the newcomers had been left to their own devices while the women of *Meall An Fhraoich* prepared the burial feast. As the afternoon wore on, smoke streamed through the thatch of each cottage in the settlement, the gentle reek of burning peat blending with other smells, as every cauldron and pot was pressed into service.

As the setting sun began to spread an eerie stain across the western horizon, the clachan filled with mourners who had made their various ways back from the cemetery. Eventually the entire population of the glen seemed to be milling around the surviving cottages of the township. The mood of the people had grown a little lighter, some of their grief perhaps buried with their loved ones.

"Don't recognise too many of this lot," Andy whispered from the doorway of the barn they occupied.

"Yeah. We'd all feel a little safer if Achnacon was here."

"It's no' Achnacon he's looking out for," grinned Jamie.

"I'm looking forward to meeting this Ishbel," Shawnee put in. "I'm sure she's really pretty."

"Y'know she could be one of your ancestors, don't yuh?" said Sam.

"Yeah. Hey, Andy, I could turn out to be your great, great, great, granddaughter."

"Was your old man one of us, then?" asked Fergie.

"My dad? No... His grandpa was though; old Donald Cameron. Came from Glen Laragain originally. Emigrated to the States 'way back in nineteen twelve. Apparently he had what they called 'the sight'. The story was he'd originally booked passage on The Titanic, but cancelled two days before he was due to leave. It's the usual story; he had a dream, people drowning, the ship going under... y'know?"

Rae had taken to sniffing the air like a scavenger searching out a rotting carcass. "Ah'm starving tae death here. Ah wonder when we're gonnae get some grub."

As the last shreds of daylight disappeared from the sky the little clachan faded into deepening shadows. The glow from the open doors and windows grew correspondingly brighter and more precious against the immensity of darkness that surrounded them. As the first stars appeared two of the women prepared fires between the cottages. Fuelled by the ubiquitous peat, they too began to pierce the darkness, like beacons lit in response to those distant points of light.

Wooden frames were erected over two of the fires, and soon the carcasses of a sheep and a calf were rotating slowly on hand-operated spits. Before long the odour of barbecued meat was added to the array of smells drifting from each of the cottages.

Rae was drawn to the larger of the two spits, where he stood like a salivating dog. The attendant *cailleach* kept him at bay with a stream of warnings and oaths, clearly enjoying the power she had over the stranger. Only when she'd tired of the game did she let him off the leash. Rae snatched the lump of roasted meat he was offered and slunk off into the shadows before the old harridan changed her mind.

Sam, Shawnee and the three soldiers claimed one of the little campfires as their own, using slabs of stone as seats. They stared wordlessly into the dull orange glow until finally Andy voiced what was in all their minds:

"Right now the Duke of Cumberland is setting up camp about thirty miles from here. In the weeks tae come he's gonnae let loose the worst army of occupation this country has ever seen. Nobody knows how many people were slaughtered, or how many glens were laid waste. We might've stopped them the first time, but they're gonnae be back. These people aren't safe yet, and each one of us is gonnae have tae decide whether we stand with them, or what..."

One of the burning lumps of peat collapsed into the fire, sending a shower of sparks into the night sky. All gazed longingly at the sudden flare of light, like moths drawn from the darkness.

"Ah say sod it," said Rae around the slab of veal he'd manoeuvred into his mouth. "Tonight we've got grub, maybe a wee touch of the old guy's firewater later. Tomorrow we can worry about fighting. For now Ah say sod it."

His companions looked at each other, their faces redrawn in shades of orange and black by the flickering firelight.

"He's right," said Shawnee. "Sod it."

Andy nodded, a wry smile on his face. For once his oversized rebel had captured perfectly the mood of the moment.

As Rae licked his fingers one of the women approached the group and made an eating motion with her hands. Behind her stood a large wooden table laden with all manner of delights. Jamie pointed out oatcakes, bannocks, cheese, butter, eggs, fish, mutton, and beef.

Only Rae was still eating when another of the lassies brought a small wooden barrel to the campfire. Moments later she returned with a number of wooden goblets.

"Is this what Ah think it is?" breathed Fergie.

Jamie felt around the top of the barrel until he encountered a bung. "Swally," he whispered, as if he'd discovered the fountain of youth.

"Swally?" echoed Sam

The bung came away from the barrel with a hiss of escaping gas. Andy sniffed the opening.

"Swally," he confirmed.

"Ya beauty!" exclaimed Fergie.

"Is somebody gonna tell me what the hell 'swally' is?" growled Sam.

"Beer," said Andy. "These people only make their own beer…"

The American's face lit up. "Well, I'll be damned. Maybe things are beginning to look up at last."

The barrel was passed from one waiting goblet to another. Sam swirled the frothy mixture around his mouth.

"Well, it's not Miller Lite," he decided, before emptying the goblet in one long draught. "…But dammit, that's not bad."

The smacks of contentment from his companions told him that their world had also become a happier place.

"If ye think this is nice, wait till ye taste their whisky," said Fergie. "Man, it'll blow the top o' yer heid off."

Rae stifled a belch. "All Ah remember the other night is putting this jug tae ma mouth, next thing Ah know Ah'm wakening up on the top of a mountain with yon bloody eejit in ma arms."

"So it *was* just the drink then?" retorted Fergie, a hurt expression on his face. "Does this mean we're no' really engaged?"

"Lady present," said Andy, mindful too that Colin was now timidly approaching their campfire.

"Good evening. I hope nobody minds if myself joins your company."

"C'mon, Colin," said Shawnee, "you come sit between me and Sam."

"How's yer brother?" asked Andy.

"Och, Alistair's with Mary. When she's around I don't think himself even knows anyone else is there."

"That's young love for ye," pronounced Jamie.

Colin went on. "I was hearing, myself, what happened at the funeral. The women thought it was terrible that *Achnacon*'s guests were mistreated in such a way."

"Izzat a fact?" replied Rae. "How come they're still treating us like a bunch of lepers, then?"

"Och, that's just their way. They keep their distance because they believe it's what yourselves want. I think perhaps they're also a wee bit frightened of you."

Rae sucked the dregs of beer from the barrel as another of the women approached the campfire.

Andy and Jamie recognised the lassie who'd tended to Andy's burns the previous evening. Her eyes remained lowered as she collected the empty barrel from Rae.

"She doesnae seem too friendly," complained Jamie, the ruins of a smile on his face.

"They buried her father today," said Andy. "Little wonder they're a wee bit reserved."

"If only we'd arrived one day earlier," sighed Shawnee. "Together, all of us, we coulda stopped it from happening."

"Ah tell ye what Ah don't understand; when was the massacre supposed tae have taken place?"

"The twenty-first of April, seventeen hundred and forty-six."

"...And yet Achnacon reckoned the date was the tenth of April that first day we met him, and that was... God, was it only two days ago?"

"Well, Mary seems to think that today is only the twelfth of April," remarked Colin. "I know it sounds a wee bit daft, but I remember thinking; this would mean, for the second time in two weeks, the night after tomorrow would see the anniversary of the sinking of The Titanic..."

"The Titanic?" echoed Shawnee.

"Yes. I don't suppose it's remembered in your world, but the Titanic was a ship that sunk in the Atlantic Ocean with the loss of over one thousand and five hundred souls. My own uncle was due to sail to America on her, but he cancelled his booking and took passage on another ship instead, after himself had seen the ship sinking in a dream."

"Your uncle," gasped Shawnee.

"Yes, my Uncle Donald; he had the second sight. Och, I know it sounds daft but…"

With a squeal of delight, Shawnee threw her arms around Colin. The young man stiffened and gaped at Sam, as if the woman's uncontrollable passion was no fault of his.

"He was my great grandpa," Shawnee explained, her voice muffled by Colin's jacket. "He was the younger of two brothers; left Scotland when he was thirty to make a new life for himself in America…"

Realisation was beginning to dawn on Colin. "Oh my goodness… then I must be…"

"A jammy wee swine," complained Fergie.

"…The son of my great, great uncle," beamed Shawnee.

"Oh my goodness," said Colin again. He forced one of his limp hands to caress his beautiful relative.

"Well, I'll be damned. If that don't beat all…" Sam sounded relaxed and amused by the strange turn of events, but Andy, sitting beside him, could see the narrowing of his eyes and the tension in his face.

Realisation of a different kind was dawning on Rae. "There's something screwy going on here."

"How d'ye mean?" said Fergie.

"Well, look at them, for God's sake; does he look a hundred years older than she is?"

"No," replied Fergie, still none the wiser. "Why? Is he over a hundred years old, like?"

Rae groaned. "No, ye great balloon, he isnae. That's the whole point." He turned appealingly to Sam, Shawnee and Colin. "Gonnae put this numptie out of ma misery and tell us what year it was when yez were wheeched here?"

"Nineteen hundred and sixteen," answered Colin, awkwardly holding Shawnee's hand.

"Twenty twenty-six," said Shawnee.

"Bloody hell," groaned Rae and Fergie together. Both sat in silence for a while before Rae asked the only obvious question:

"Ah don't suppose either of yez watch football?"

Sam's hollow laughter was the only answer he was likely to receive.

149

Andy's young nurse returned with another barrel of beer, which she laid at Macmillan's feet. All around them the earlier bustle had fragmented into disjointed murmurings as each township gravitated towards its separate campfire.

As the goblets were refilled Fergie turned to Sam. "So you're from the future, then? Man, that must be pure brilliant. What's it like then, tae live in the future?"

As the American searched for a sensible answer Rae howled with delight.

"Aw ye great pudding that ye are! What's it like tae live in the future? Ye great numptie…"

Fergie glanced at Shawnee and flushed with embarrassment.

"Aye, well, if Ah'm such a numptie answer me this; how come Ah'm the only one that knows why yez got the dates wrong? Eh? Answer me that, fat boy."

The smile vanished from Rae's face. "Ah told ye no' tae call me that."

"What d'ye mean 'got the dates wrong'?" Andy cut in.

"What yez were saying earlier," glowered Fergie. "How nobody could figure out how ye thought it was the twenty-first and the *tcheuchters* thought it was the tenth."

"This should be good," said Rae.

"Go on Fergie," urged Macmillan, "let's hear what ye have tae say."

Ferguson glared defiantly at Rae's sneering face. "Well, it's like this, before Ah joined up Ah used tae be in one o' them kick the pope bands…"

"A Protestant marching band," Andy translated.

"…We used tae travel all over tae march in these parades. The biggest day of the year was the twelfth o' July; when we went over tae Belfast tae march with the Irish bands. This was before the troubles, like; we used tae stay on the Shankhill Road. Man, they were rare days; those boys from the Shankhill really knew how tae knock back the swally…"

"Ye were gonnae tell us about the change of dates?"

"Oh aye, right. Well, it was one year we were over in Belfast and Ah got talking tae this guy and he was saying that the battle of The Boyne was fought in sixteen hundred and something, but it wasnae fought on the twelfth of July, it was fought on the first of July."

"Why the change of dates?"

"Well, ye see, the guy said it was because they brought in a different calendar back in the seventeen hundreds. For some reason the old calendar was behind what it shouldae been by eleven days. The guy explained the reason for it, like, but this wee Shankhill bird was giving me the eye at the time, so Ah wasn't paying much attention."

"Oh my God, he's right," breathed Shawnee. "They changed from the Julian to the Gregorian calendar in the second part of the eighteenth century. When they'd calculated what the date shoulda been since the birth of Christ, they figured they were slow by eleven days. My dad told me in some parts of Scotland they continued to celebrate New Years on the twelfth of January…"

"Ah remember now!" exclaimed Fergie. "That's what the guy said! They wouldn't accept the new dates…"

"…And why the date of the massacre went intae folk lore as the twenty-first of April instead of the tenth," said Andy.

"My family used to observe Hogmanay on the eleventh of January," Colin admitted, "but ourselves always believed the massacre took place on the twenty-first."

"Ye know what this means, don't ye?" Jamie said breathlessly. "If this is only the twelfth of April then Culloden hasn't been fought yet…"

Andy's eyes began to widen. "Come on tae hell, Jamie; don't even think about it…"

"How no'? Half an hour ago ye thought the Hanoverian army was gonnae descend on us. Now we've got the chance tae stop them getting intae the Highlands in the first place."

The flickering glow of the fire seemed to emphasise the deathly pallor of Andy's face.

"Fighting for these people is one thing, but taking on Cumberland's army… that's no' our fight…"

"Seems tae me the choice here is simple," put in Rae. "Either we sit here while our guys get wiped out, or we side with the good guys while they're still around."

"It's just like Ah told ye," said Fergie. "They've sent us back in time tae sort everything out."

"In the name of God will ye listen tae yerselves!" Andy yelled. "We're no' talking about a game of football, we're talking about an army of ten thousand men."

"There'll be a lot less when Ah've finished with them," Rae smiled evilly.

All four soldiers were on their feet now, their argument stilling the other voices around them. Macmillan turned to his friend.

"Jamie, for God's sake, think about this. How many are ye gonnae have tae kill tae stop Cumberland's army? A thousand? Ten thousand?"

"Ah only need one clear shot at that fat bastard, Cumberland."

"What happened tae us all being in the same mess taegether?" yelled Rae. "All that bilge about us getting through it as a team."

Andy ran a despairing hand through his hair. "In the name of God, man, Ah wasn't talking about declaring war on the British Army."

"Macmillan; ye're all mouth," shouted Rae. "As soon as the chips are down ye turn intae a bloody pacifist."

Andy's patience snapped. Savagely he grabbed Rae by the throat, his fist held like a club above the big man's head. Jamie and Fergie came between them, before blows could be traded.

Rae continued relentlessly, the corporal barely visible in the melee: "Difference between you and me is, Ah got no problem dropping anyone that gets in ma way... You included."

"Is this what ye want, Jamie?" Andy's lip curled in distaste. "Tae throw in yer lot with this moron?"

"For God's sake, Andy, this isn't about you or him. This is about Culloden. We've got the chance tae stop it happening; all the murder and rape and destruction these animals carried intae the Highlands. What d'ye think's gonnae happen tae Achnacon and Ishbel and all the others once those bastards reach Lochaber?"

Andy realised he and Jamie were clutching each other's combat jacket, as if they were about to come to blows.

"If Sam's right then what dae *you* think's gonnae happen if we go swanning off tae Inverness?"

"Those redcoats got a tanking the other day. There's a chance they won't show their faces again, but we all *know* what's gonnae happen after Culloden. We don't have a choice here, Andy, and if you weren't so wrapped up in yer own guilt ye'd see that."

Desperately Andy turned to Shawnee, Sam and Colin. "Surely you can see the sense in what Ah'm saying...?"

Colin seemed to have been awaiting his opportunity: "At night, from Inverlaragain cottage, the stars are the only lights you can see. You feel like you're the last person alive on Earth. That is what

Cumberland and his kind brought to the Highlands. I am sorry, Andy, but you are wrong about this. If I had to, I would walk to Culloden Moor on my own."

"Nice one, wee man," grunted Jamie.

Colin flushed, aware he'd made himself the centre of attention. "I have to away and tell Alistair the news…"

The last ounce of Andy's resistance crumbled then. Miserably he returned to his seat beside the campfire. The murmur of nearby voices began to fill the darkness once more.

"What about you, Shawnee?" Jamie asked. "Whatever's decided here is gonnae affect you and Sam. It's only right you guys should have your say."

Sam made a point of answering first. "I remember watching a soccer match on T.V. between your Rangers and your Celtics. I don't recall who won, or anything, I just remember the hatred between the fans. I thought it really sucked. It was so stupid and parochial. I thought; why the hell are they showing this Scottish crap on American T.V.? This isn't our war, none of this matters to us…"

"Ah'm sorry tae have tae tell ye, Sam, but you're in the same mess as the rest of us now," said Jamie indignantly. "Ye cannae switch this one off."

The American shrugged his shoulders. "The bottom line is this fellas; whether Shawnee heads off to the other side of the country, or whether she stays here to fight these freakin soldiers, that's where you'll find me too." He stared intently at her. "Fact is, if Shawnee decided to settle down and raise a family with some inbred Scottish relative in this craphole, that's where I'll be, hanging around like some sad-assed piece of work, 'cause I got no other reason for being here, and nowhere else to go…"

Shawnee rose from her seat by the campfire, the back of her hand against her mouth. "Excuse me, please," she mumbled, the sobs breaking from her as she disappeared into the darkness.

All eyes turned accusingly towards Sam.

"What the hell was all that about?" said Jamie.

"She's all right, is wee Shawnee," Rae added, shifting his attention from Andy to Sam. "She's a wee stunner, but she's got more balls than anyone else here…"

"Ah, what the hell would you know, y'big ape?" Sam growled.

Rae took a step towards the American, looking about to fight Shawnee's corner. "Ach, ye're no' worth the bother," he decided. "Where Ah come from you're still swimming around in yer grandda's scrotum."

Sam seemed to find the remark hugely amusing, although there was a harsh edge to his laughter.

"Yeah, whatever you say, pal."

In the strained atmosphere that followed, Rae decided he'd never been at a more boring funeral in his life. With a last challenging glare at Andy he picked up the beer barrel, and with Fergie in tow went off to see if things were livelier elsewhere.

Jamie suffered the deadening silence for a few minutes, before deciding he had arrangements to make for the journey ahead.

"You gonnae be all right?" he asked Andy.

Andy's sense of betrayal was visible on his face.

"Just help us get there," Jamie pleaded. "You don't have tae put yer finger tae any trigger. You can leave that tae those of us that don't have a conscience."

Andy snorted in disgust. "Here is where we'll make a difference, no' wandering off intae the swamps like the lost legions o' Rome."

Jamie shook his head. "Ach suit yerself. Ah've got things tae do…"

Left on their own, Sam and Andy stared morosely into the fire, each lost in his own misery. Eventually one of the lassies brought over another keg of ale.

Andy looked at the American. "Ah don't know about you but Ah'm in the mood tae get totally wasted."

Sam drained the first goblet of beer in one swallow, and only looked at Andy when he'd half drunk the second.

"Seems we've both been dealt a shitty hand, huh?"

"Life's not about holding good cards, but playing a poor hand well. That's what ma grannie used tae say."

"Yeah? Just once I'd like to know how it feels to hit the jackpot."

Andy looked dubiously at the American. "You don't think ye've hit the jackpot already then?"

"Shawnee y'mean? Lemme tell you something about beautiful women, my friend. Most beautiful women don't know how dangerous their world is. The lucky ones have schmucks like me riding shotgun for them."

"Ye make yerself sound like a hired gun."

"Yeah? I guess that's how it feels sometimes."

"Ah take it you guys arenae married or anything?"

"Hell no, anybody that's not blood is only allowed so close." A poignant smile appeared on Sam's face. "First time I saw her she was laying flowers at this little statue in San Francisco. I thought she had the saddest, most beautiful face I'd ever seen; she was like something fragile and wounded that y'just wanted to protect, y'know? I think I fell for her the moment I laid eyes on her..." Sam swivelled round to face the soldier, and realised Shawnee was standing only a few yards behind him, her tear-stained face reflecting the faint glow of the fire.

"Andy, would y'mind if Sam and I had a few words in private," she said softly.

Andy looked round in surprise, and scrambled to his feet. "Aye, Ah'll, eh, Ah'll have a wander round, see what's happening."

Sam waited until the soldier was out of earshot. "How long you been standing there?"

"His name was John Mclaren," she said quietly. "It was the first thing y'said to me; 'who's the little guy, is he a relative or what?' I told you his name was John Mclaren, and he helped to create Golden Gate Park. I told y'my dad used to go there a lot. Don't y'ever listen to anything I say?"

"Not usually, no," Sam automatically replied. "But I remember the Bay area was shrouded in fog that day, and you were wearing a little white fur coat and hat. You looked like a little Eskimo. And I remember how pale y'were, and how y'tried to hide the fact that you'd been crying."

"Yeah, I seem to do that a lot," she murmured.

Sam made a faint gesture with his hands, as if a part of him was trying to apologise. "I don't know what y'want from me, Shawnee. I'll do anything y'say. Go anywhere y'want me to go... hell, I'll fight the British, I'll even wear one of those goddamned skirts if that's what y'want... But I can't make myself into something I'm not. I can't be one of these guys. I wouldn't wanna even if I could. And I can't be your father. God knows I've tried, but I'm tired of trying to compete with the guy."

"Is that what y'think?" She shook her head despairingly. "That I want you to be some kinda substitute for my dad?"

Sam grimaced awkwardly. "It just feels like there's only ever been one guy in your life. That the only thing that ever matters to you is what woulda mattered to him, if he was still alive."

Sam could see the tears rolling down Shawnee's cheeks, and he fought the familiar powerful urge to hold and protect her.

"He was everything to me for such a huge part of my life," she said, her voice racked by sobs. "I still miss him, Sam, and it hurts that I never got the chance to say goodbye. But I love you in a totally different way, and I just don't see why there should have to be any kinda conflict…"

"…One helluva time to finally tell me that," Sam interrupted softly.

Shawnee dabbed at her eyes with the sleeve of her jacket. "Tell y'what?"

"Y'know; what y'just said…"

Her lips began to tremble once more, and it was a while before she was able to answer him. "I didn't think I needed to spell it out. Besides," she added, with a wretched attempt at a smile, "when did y'ever listen to anything I say?"

Andy had drifted aimlessly around the clachan, looking for familiar faces amongst the groups of mourners. All who caught his eye smiled pleasantly or nodded in his direction, but everyone seemed a little reserved with him, and the experience only heightened his sense of isolation. Before long he found himself wandering back towards the campfire.

The little peat fires cast a surprising amount of light when seen from the darkness, and long before Andy had reached the campfire he could see Shawnee and Sam, framed together in the shifting glow of the flames. They were kissing with such tenderness that he found himself captivated by the scene. At last, feeling like a voyeur, he turned away, a bleak smile on his face.

"Way tae go, Sam," he murmured into the cold darkness.

Chapter Sixteen

Andy edged his way through the crowded cottage to where Alistair lay, surrounded by a little group that included Mary, Rhona and Colin.

Alistair's frame of mind had improved since Andy had spoken to him earlier that day. He greeted the soldier warmly, insisting Colin pour him a large dram. Mary smiled shyly at Andy as she took his hand, able to acknowledge the existence of others, now that her patient was on the mend. The other ladies also took his hand, before retreating behind that familiar air of reserve. There were some thirty people crammed into the cottage, many clutching bowls of food or tumblers of *uisge beatha.*

"Ah take it ye're feeling better this evening?" the corporal asked.

"Och, a man on his deathbed would be thinking all's well if he had an angel such as this for his nurse," Alistair replied.

Colin translated this into Gaelic for the ladies. Mary's friends reacted with shocked delight, as though the bold *Alasdair Mhor* had stolen his first kiss. Mary studied the floor, a self-conscious smile on her face.

"…Thanks to Mary I should be up and about in a day or two," continued Alistair, "but tell me this and tell me no more, Andy Macmillan; is it true what himself has been saying; that today is only the twelfth day of April?"

"Aye, it seems we got the dates wrong by eleven days. Ah take it Colin has told ye what they're planning?"

Alistair looked proudly at his brother. "Indeed he has; I pray to God they reach Drummossie Moor before the sixteenth. They have given themselves no more than three days to travel sixty miles."

"Drummossie?"

"It was the old name for Culloden," Colin explained.

Alistair went on: "My brother has also said you have volunteered to remain behind with ourselves in case the English come back…"

Andy nodded. "Sam and Shawnee think it's only a matter of time before they return tae finish the job they started."

To Andy's surprise Rhona echoed his anxiety.

"The devil's servant may have repented his sins but the devil's work continues," she said darkly. "Even as that creature sought forgiveness for his crimes he warned us others would return to complete the business."

Rhona saw the surprise on Andy's face and added disapprovingly: "He looked chust as yourself is now. As if one of the beasts of the field had spoke to him in his own tongue."

Andy realised he was staring and smiled apologetically. "Most of the beasts Ah've met in Glen Laragain have been in uniform. Maybe when this is over you could help me learn some Gaelic."

The little touch of diplomacy seemed to satisfy Rhona. " 'Twill be my pleasure, sir; and perhaps I should also help my cousin Ishbel learn some of the English tongue?"

"Does everybody know about that?"

"All know the Lady Ishbel has accepted your suit, sir. All know yourself has been spoke for."

Only then did Macmillan understand why the women had been so reserved with him. He took a gulp of whisky, and felt the fiery liquid burn a path into his stomach. As the warmth spread into his bloodstream he took another gulp, draining the glass. The whisky wasn't as volcanic as Achnacon's brew, and Andy guessed it had been watered down for Alistair's benefit. Colin offered a refill but Andy shook his head. He turned to Rhona:

"What was he like, this officer in charge of the redcoats?"

Her lip curled as though she'd smelt something putrefying. "He carried the devil's own brand on his face. He has nursed a hatred of The Gael since he was marked by a claymore at Gladsmuir."

"Gladsmuir?"

"Prestonpans," explained Colin. "It was the first battle of the forty-five, when the English were driven from the field like sheep."

" 'Twas a pity yon claymore did not split his skull; perhaps *Gleann Laragain* might have been spared this terrible day."

Andy decided not to disturb Rhona's illusions; coming to terms with what had happened might be easier if she carried the image of a face she could hate and revile.

"It must have been Lieutenant Longholme," said Alistair.

"You know of this man?" Rhona asked sharply.

"I've read about him; Cumberland gave the original order, but it was Longholme who carried the can for the massacre..."

"Carried the can?"

"Took the blame. Cumberland later denied issuing the order so Longholme was made the scapegoat." Alistair grimaced, aware he'd made extravagant use of the past tense.

The faux pas had not been lost on Rhona. "Your manner of speech is most curious, sir. The Lady Shaw-nee, spoke in similar fashion, as if..." She shook her head. "...She possessed a book so terrible to behold even that devil himself almost swooned at the sight of it. 'Twas the contents of that book that made him call off his hounds."

Macmillan's eyebrows rose in sudden interest. "D'ye know if she still has this book?"

"I know not; perhaps it was left behind with him..."

"Och, I think the English will have learnt their lesson," Colin interjected. "I see no reason why they would risk another defeat in Glen Laragain. Especially now the main battle will be fought on Drummossie Moor."

Macmillan's scepticism was plain for all to see.

"You think those who set out for Drummossie tomorrow embark on a fool's errand?" observed Alistair.

"Ah think they're playing at being God; toying with history."

"You think our history is worth preserving? You think, given another chance, ourselves would not benefit from some of the terrible mistakes we have made?"

Andy shrugged his shoulders. "Maybe. Or maybe we'd always mess things up, no matter how many chances we had. But that's not why they're off tae Culloden tomorrow, is it?"

"Alistair and myself grew up in a land that was emptied by Cumberland's army," Colin put in, "and by a hundred years of dispossession and eviction. If the world benefits from righting these wrongs so much the better."

Alistair nodded approvingly. "Some would argue that the benefits might have been felt far beyond these shores if the dice had fallen differently in this land. I only know that in the world that grew from this one I, myself, have seen hell on Earth. And now Colin tells me it was all for nothing; that there would be a second great war, where cities would be destroyed by bombs falling like rain from the sky, where camps would be created for the sole purpose of putting innocent people to death… women, tiny babes… in their thousands and millions…" Alistair was almost upright in his bed now, his face contorted in pain. "What an awful low opinion you have of the human race, Andy Macmillan, if you think that is the best ourselves are capable of…"

Mary gently stroked Alistair's head as he sank back into the mattress. Andy was conscious of the looks of disapproval he was receiving from the others gathered round the bed.

"When d'ye plan tae set off?" he asked Colin gruffly.

"At first light. We need to travel at least twenty miles a day to arrive at Drummossie before the sixteenth."

"Do Jamie and the others know this?"

Colin shrugged. "Och, I have seen neither hide nor hair of them since I came in here. I had hoped to ask your friend, Achnacon, if he could spare some of his people. I had thought, perhaps, yourself might have had second thoughts…"

Andy shook his head. "Jamie seemed determined tae make the journey and he'll no' let ye down. As for those other two; Ah'm not sure Ah'd even want them on ma side, but if you're serious you'll need their firepower."

"…Yourselfs will be needing someone who is familiar with the road to Inverness," Rhona interrupted softly.

Andy looked at her in dismay, uncertain how much she'd gathered. "Ah don't think it would be a good idea for a lassie tae go along; it's gonnae be dangerous enough for the men…"

"…I was not asking your permission, sir," she said sharply. " 'Tis the foolish adventures of men which has brought the wrath of the English down upon our heads. All I have left in the world is two brothers who face the English at Inverness and I will not chust sit here, like an old *cailleach*, while the last of my family is took from me."

Andy looked helplessly at Colin, whose responsibilities were growing by the hour.

"It would be an honour if yourself was to come with us," he told her, his cheeks aflame.

Rhona nodded sharply and quickly composed herself. She spoke to the other women grouped around Alistair's bed, and with a soft rustle of skirts all except Mary glided towards the door.

"Surely they're not all going with ye tae Culloden," said Andy in disbelief.

Colin shook his head, the colour fading from his cheeks. "Rhona is the only one travelling with us. Herself and the others are away to prepare food, blankets and horses. Trust the lassies to take over and start organising everything…"

Andy groaned, his soldierly senses outraged at such unmilitary goings on. He appealed to Alistair: "The idea was daft enough before, but now it's just a disaster waiting tae happen; ye know that, don't ye?"

"If I could I too would be going with them," Alistair said firmly.

Beside the smoking peat-fire an old worthy was recalling some epic adventure that was probably as old as the language itself. Before the story was complete Andy noticed Sam guiding Shawnee around the rear of the crowd towards them.

"Hey guys, what's going on?" Sam whispered as they reached Alistair's bed. "We saw Rhona and some of her girls; where are they off to in such a hurry?"

Andy looked to Colin, as the keeper of the dread secret.

"They are away to make preparations for our journey tomorrow," the young man explained.

"What are you guys gonnae do?" asked Andy. "Nobody would blame the pair o' ye if ye just took off. As you said earlier, this isn't your war."

Sam looked to Shawnee, murmuring; "yeah, I say a lotta stuff, but y'don't wanna listen to anything I tell yuh."

Shawnee listened for a moment to the toneless voice of the old bodach. His audience had probably heard the story many times before, but they sat spellbound before him, like disciples before the Messiah. She smiled wistfully and turned to Sam. "I think if these people would allow us I'd like to stay here. If that's okay with you…?"

Sam smiled gruffly and kissed Shawnee on the lips.

Something was definitely different here, Andy decided. Gone was the usual prickly repartee. It was only when he noticed a wisp of straw tangled in Shawnee's hair that it struck him in what sense things had changed. Shawnee must have seen the comprehension in Andy's face because a faint flush rose into her cheeks, as if a little part of her soul had been left bare. Andy smiled back, unable to tear his eyes away, helplessly basking in the warmth of another's fire.

Colin, meanwhile, was trying to explain to an irate Sam that he had no control over every daft lassie in Glen Laragain.

"...She is a law unto herself, that one. If it's yourself that thinks she should not go, then you may speak to her yourself, for she will pay no heed to me!"

"It's a crazy idea; at least while Rhona's here we can try to protect her, but out there..." Sam turned to Shawnee. "You've seen what those sons of bitches are capable of..."

"Rhona wants to go to Culloden with the guys?" Shawnee said, horrified. "Oh my God, no! Andy's guys are trained soldiers, they can defend themselves... But Rhona? I was even hoping we'd be able to talk Colin out of going."

The young man stiffened indignantly. "I am not skulking around here while the men go off to fight."

"You're my kin, for Godsakes. I don't wanna find you and then lose y'again in the same week."

Colin looked to his brother for help. "Alistair says he would also go if he had the chance. Himself is your kin as well."

Shawnee looked at Alistair as if noticing him for the first time.

"I was wondering when somebody was going to introduce us." The older brother held out his hand. "Colin has told me we are related, in the queerest of ways."

Shawnee's response was a lot more muted with Alistair than it had been with his brother. She held his hand, a poignant smile on her face.

"You have my dad's eyes. Colin has too, but it's more pronounced in you. I'm glad to see you're a lot better. We were all worried about y'there for a while. Mary wouldn't leave your side 'til your fever had broken. I'd say any man who's earned devotion like that is a very lucky man indeed."

Alistair nodded in agreement and translated for Mary's benefit. Unexpectedly she responded in her native tongue, her voice soft and deferential. Even before she'd finished Alistair had begun to reply.

"Mary says she can never repay the debt she owes Alistair," Colin translated. "Had ourselves not intervened when we did she would have fallen beneath the most evil of brutes. She says that since Alistair almost lost his life saving Mary, her life belongs to him now. She knows he is a good and brave man and will devote herself to him, and no other."

Before Colin had finished translating Alistair's tone of voice had changed. He took hold of Mary's hand and began to address her sharply. She looked him full in the face and withdrew her hand from his.

"That's good, isn't it?" said Shawnee. "He's gotta be happy about that, surely?"

Colin went on, dismay in his voice: "My brother has told Mary she should leave this instant if herself remains beside him only out of duty. He says he would rather be freely offered a single kiss by an old *cailleach*, than a life given under obligation, even by the fairest lass in all of Lochaber."

"What has Mary said to that?" whispered Shawnee.

"She has made no reply yet." The young man's voice was barely audible. "Whatever has come over Alistair?"

"The guy knows what he's doing," murmured Sam. "He's trying his best to play a poor hand well."

The wake moved from prose to song. A lassie barely in her teens held her audience spellbound with a melancholy piece which could only have arisen from a people steeped in hardship and loss.

As soon as her song was finished, Mary rose from beside Alistair's bed, and took her place amongst her clansfolk. She began to sing the same haunting lament she'd sung when Alistair's fever was at its worst. As the melody once again filled the old cottage, Achnacon appeared by the door, held in the same spell that enchanted everyone else, unable to tear his eyes away from the lovely enchantress.

When the last note had died away Achnacon held Mary's face in his rough, calloused hands and kissed each cheek, paying an old man's homage to a young woman's gift.

"Now I recognise that song," Colin told the others. "It's a love-song from the Isle of Barra, about a man who recalls the summer shieling he shared with the one true love of his life, before he lost her to another." He looked at his brother. "Her name was Mary too."

"I want to win the lassie, not own her," Alistair snapped.

The old storyteller led the others in a brighter, communal song as Achnacon made his way towards the newcomers.

"Is such a voice not a gift from the anchels?" he said. "And will yourselfs be singing for us later perhaps?"

Nobody said they would, and nobody said they wouldn't. All made evasive noises, glancing hopefully at each other.

"Muirshearlach and the two Lowlanders have given grand entertainment in the next-door cottage with the singing and the dancing."

Andy groaned as he visualised Rae and Fergie treating everyone to the dance of the seven veils.

"Perhaps 'tis well few of my people have the English," Achnacon added subtly. The smile faded from his face as he took Andy to one side. "Muirshearlach has spoke of the great battle to be fought at Drummossie four days hence." He searched Macmillan's face for confirmation of the prediction. "Himself says the battle will spell disaster for the *Gaidhealtacht*."

Andy nodded, afraid his eyes would betray the full extent of the coming catastrophe.

"This vision yourself has had; is it a vision of what must be, or what may only be?"

Andy shrugged evasively. "If Jamie and the others can reach there in time, perhaps with the weapons they have…"

"Muirshearlach thinks yourself will have a change of heart and will lead them to battle."

"No!" Andy said firmly. "Ah'll be staying here, no matter what the others decide tae do."

The troubled expression remained on Achnacon's face. "Muirshearlach has said Lochaber will be laid waste from saltwater to fresh if Cumberland is victorious. He has said the few warriors who return home will return to a blackened land."

Muirshearlach has been saying far too much for his own bloody good, Andy thought bitterly.

"Your men look to yourself to lead them into battle, young Andy, and yet you propose to remain behind with the old and the feeble."

Something in the Highlander's tone brought the blood rising into Andy's face. "Even if we destroyed Cumberland's army, what would it matter if Ah returned tae find all this in ruins?"

Achnacon nodded slowly, his eyes searching the face of his friend. "I also fear Cumberland. I know his heart is filled with hatred for the Gael, but I know 'tis the soldiers of *An Gearasdan* who cast a darker shadow over this glen. I am happy yourself is to stay. There is one other who will also be happy, one who sees yourself as her protector."

Andy looked stupidly at the old Highlander.

"The Lady Ishbel," Achnacon explained. He watched a smile appear on his friend's face and then disappear just as quickly.

"My friend seems less enamoured now at the prospect of meeting the daughter of Achnacon. Surely he does not wish to withdraw his suit?" The old man's voice carried the threat of outrage.

"Aw God, no," Andy replied hastily. "Any man would be honoured. It's how Ishbel feels towards me that might be the problem."

"Your turn of thought carries no sense," Achnacon said coolly.

"Earlier, Alistair told Mary he didn't want tae take advantage of her just because he'd saved her life. He felt it wouldnae be right tae base a courtship on some kindae sense of duty. Ah know what he means, because that's how Ah feel about Ishbel."

A slow smile spread across Achnacon's face.

"Never before had Mary sung that song so well; 'tis now I see why. Lassies listen to their hearts. Perhaps men should do likewise; nothing makes bigger fools of us than our own heads."

Andy looked blankly at the old Highlander.

"What the lassies know of you they have took to their hearts," sighed Achnacon. "They are like flowers that have opened themselfs to you and your foolish friend; how you conduct yourselfs will decide how much else they take to their hearts."

He took the soldier by the arm and began to guide him towards the door. "Come, we have kept the good lady waiting long enough…"

"What d'ye mean; Ishbel's here now?" Andy looked to his friends for help, his eyes wide with fear; but this time he was definitely on his own.

Moments later he was in the cold night air. From the adjoining cottage came the sounds of riotous celebration. Andy guessed his troops would be in the middle of that obscene stramash. To his relief this wasn't their destination. Instead he was led to a nearby cottage, from which flickered the dull glow of the ever-present peat fire. The door to the building was gone. In its place was a rough curtain of sacking material. Achnacon guided the soldier through, then left him on his own.

Andy narrowed his eyes in the smoky air, trying to peer into the gloom. He had a strong sense of déjà vu, remembering how he'd first laid eyes on Achnacon's family. He'd had a rifle in his hand then, something cold and solid to counterbalance the fear in his stomach.

Like some creature of the night he inched his way nervously into the cottage, the tang of burning peat giving the room the air of an opium den. He caught sight of her standing beside the fire, squinting into the smoky darkness. She looked slim and elegant in a red calf-length tartan dress, overlaid with a white lace shawl. Tresses of long dark hair hung over her shoulders, framing a face that was flushed with anxiety and expectation.

When Andy had first laid eyes on Ishbel he'd been drawn to her, as he would have been to any good-looking female. Thereafter, it had been the usual game that men play; stealing furtive looks at a beautiful woman, trying to conceal his gluttony as he feasted his eyes upon her. On that first occasion he had thought Ishbel effortlessly attractive. Now... arrayed in the finest her people had to offer... Now she was simply stunning.

His stomach was in knots. He shouldn't even be here; a scruffy mongrel trying to win the affections of a beautiful pedigree. He wanted to flee back to Alistair's bedside and pour the remains of Alistair's *uisge beatha* down his throat.

Ishbel was speaking to him, her voice soft and barely audible. At first he thought she was talking in Gaelic, but as he drew closer he realised she was delivering a speech in English.

"...Sister Shona thank yourself for safing our lifes. Yourself iss a very prafe man..." She rubbed her hands nervously together. After a few moments she tried again: "My family iss forever in your debt, Corpohral Auntie; my father and my mother and myself and my sister Shona thank yourself for safing our lifes. Yourself iss a very prafe man."

As she looked hopefully at him, Andy did his best to deliver a suitably heroic response.

"Aye, eh, Ah mean, anytime ye need help just give us a shout and that, ye know?"

Her smile was a mixture of bewilderment and grace. Andy broke out in a cold sweat. He stood as close to her now as he had done at any point during the horror of that first night, and he recalled how he'd sensed there was something pure and untamed in this woman. Now, as he took in her luxuriant mane of hair, her strong, well-formed features, he had the impression of a free spirit straining against the tartan finery of the occasion. He fought back another surge of panic, and in a moment of desperation knelt on the straw-covered floor before her.

"You probably don't understand a word Ah'm saying, but Ah'll tell ye this anyway; you are so far outtae ma league it scares the hell outtae me just being in the same room with ye. The best Ah can hope for is Ah don't make too big a clown of maself before Ah get found out. But whatever happens Ah promise ye this; Ah'll no' let ye down." He began to struggle to his feet, and then added: "Oh aye, and no red-coated bastard is gonnae lay a hand tae ye as long as Ah'm around."

When he rose to his feet Ishbel's hazel eyes were wide with surprise. In a strange way, however, Andy now felt he could meet this woman on equal terms.

"Have ye no' got somewhere we can sit down?" he grinned, making an exaggerated sitting motion with his backside.

This drew a little laugh from Ishbel. It was the first time he'd seen her smile, and the warmth of it added to her face a wild beauty that was all its own. She pointed to a semi-circular seat that lay before the fire. They sat down together and looked awkwardly at each other. The dancing shadows cast by the fire made the room seem inhabited by strange Gothic creatures.

"Corpohral Auntie, yourself iss a very prafe man," she said, filling the silence.

He shook his head and pointed at himself. "Not Corporal Andy. Just Andy. Ye understand; Andy?"

"Auntie," she replied. She levelled an elegant finger at her own breast. "*Ishbeal.*"

"Aye, Ah know. Ishbel. That's a bonnie name; Ishbel."

"Auntie," she repeated, a maidenly smile on her lips.

Macmillan took a gulp of air as if he was knocking back a stiff dram. "The thing is, ye see, Ishbel, Ah usually go tae pieces if Ah'm anywhere near a gorgeous wee thing like you and you are the most gorgeous wee thing Ah've ever laid eyes on and the only reason Ah'm able tae tell ye this is because ye don't understand a word Ah'm saying."

She looked confused that he should expect her to comprehend such a long speech.

"You are absolutely gorgeous," he told her. "D'ye understand? Gorgeous?"

"Gorcheous," she mimicked, savouring the strange texture of the word.

"Aye, that's it!" Andy tapped his heart, then drew a circle in the air around her face. "Gorgeous," he told her again.

A faint blush coloured Ishbel's cheeks. She touched her own heart and drew a circle around Andy's face. "Gorcheous," she responded, with a smile that started his stomach churning all over again.

It was clear she wasn't here under duress, but of her own accord, willing to open her heart to this young stranger. Andy was warming to the occasion. In many ways it was easier to create a bond without being encumbered by language. Here, he was spared the pointless prattle of chat-up lines; the soft lies that men believe are part of the art of seduction, and which often have the opposite effect.

She spoke to him again in Gaelic, pointing to his bare legs. Andy recognised the word 'phillamhor', and realised she was commenting on the tartan plaid he now wore. He rose to his feet and responded with a low bow.

"Formerly Corporal Andy Macmillan of the Royal Highland Fusiliers. Now apprentice clansman Andy Macmillan, at your service, m'lady."

Ishbel replied with a genteel curtsy. "*Ishbeal Camshron, de Achnacon, deth Gleann Laragain.*" She daintily held out her hand, which her young suitor kissed.

Laughing together, the couple returned to their courting couch. Andy had no idea where the limits of correct behaviour lay, but she made no attempt to withdraw her hand. Her skin was as delicate and as soft as that of a child, and was almost swallowed up by his own scarred shovel of flesh.

"Hand," he told her.

Ishbel nodded. "*Lamh.*"

"Hand."

"*Lamh,*" she insisted, with a mischievous grin.

Andy laughed at the spirit of the girl. "*Lamh,*" he conceded.

She smiled at the way he'd allowed her to win the game, and began to chatter softly at him, filling the silence with her gentle maunderings. She made little popping noises with her mouth, and let go of his hand to point an imaginary weapon at the doorway:

"Pchoow... Pchoow... Pchoow."

He realised she was reliving the events of the night they'd met. In her eyes Andy could see something of the terror she had felt. He took her hand in his once more, and as he did, Ishbel moved closer and nestled herself under his left arm, her head resting on his chest. Andy wondered if she could hear the frantic racing of his heart, or smell his primitive male fear.

For a long time she seemed content to remain in this half-embrace, her face hidden from view. Next door her people were singing another slow, mournful song, the melody faintly familiar to Andy. Before it was over, Ishbel was humming along, dreamily swinging one tartan-clad leg after the other.

With his free hand Andy gently traced her thick, dark hair. His touch was so light he barely made contact with her. He could detect a faint odour from Ishbel's hair, and indeed from Ishbel herself. The odour was far from unpleasant and was like something natural and unsullied, like the raw scent of a dog or cat. The unfamiliar form that had found its way into Andy's personal space was becoming less unfamiliar by the minute, and he wondered if he should dare to hope that she felt the same sense of intimacy he felt.

Her fingers discovered the edges of a scar that extended from one side of Andy's palm to the other. She pulled away so she could swing around and face him again.

"*Cleadh mhor?*" she asked.

Andy nodded stoically. He'd actually cut himself with a kitchen knife during a drunken escapade. But he'd bled like a stuck pig, and it couldn't have hurt any more if he *had* been slashed by a claymore.

She lifted the scarred flesh to her lips and applied the balm of a maiden's kiss.

"*Poch,*" she told him.

Andy felt her breath on his skin, as if a butterfly had risen into the air.

"Kiss."

"Kiss," she echoed, her eyes now fixed expectantly on his. After a few moments she tutted impatiently and leaned forward to kiss her dilatory suitor. Her lips barely made contact with his. He decided that convention demanded he make the all-important move. Only then did he finally allow himself to taste the sweet, natural flavour of her. And as his heart began to race once more, and his sense of self became strangely blurred, he wondered how he could feel so much a part of someone he knew almost nothing about.

Andy had no idea how long he held her like this, drawing the warmth of her being into his soul, aware of the familiar and oddly intrusive stirring in his loins, before he became aware of a coughing sound coming from the far corner. For a moment he thought they were being watched by a Peeping Tom, but when he saw Ishbel's annoyance he realised they were being attended by a chaperone. The fit of bronchitis ended as soon as the couple broke off their embrace.

Outside, Andy could hear the wake following its traditional pattern. Having begun as a memorial to the dead, it had then moved on to being a celebration of their lives. Now it had entered its final stages where it was simply an obscene celebration. He could hear the wild screech of the Highland fiddle as it led the festivities.

Ishbel suddenly grabbed him by the hand and rushed him out of the doorway and towards Alistair's cottage. The building was heaving with bodies, most of them caught up in a strange, primitive dance. Andy began to make for the sanctuary of Alistair's corner, and almost had his shoulder dislocated as Ishbel dragged him into the swirling mob. This was like no Highland dance that Andy knew. Their steps were wild and extravagant, their arms held rigidly by their sides.

Ishbel was like a wild, untamed creature celebrating the culture that had produced her, drawing as much from the dance as from Andy's efforts to imitate her. Amid the tumult he recognised faces that had been raw and tear-stained the last time he'd seen them, and for the first time he began to see beyond the apparent obscenity of the Gaelic wake.

The last screech was dragged from the fiddle and the spell that had driven the people into such frenzy was broken. Ishbel hugged her partner excitedly before pulling him through the crowd towards a little knot of people at the far end of the room. Andy recognised Achnacon's wife, Mhairi, and their other daughter, Shona. Achnacon was there too, a glass of amber fluid in his hand. Ishbel chattered breathlessly at them, her hand clasped in his. Andy watched their eyes flick from their daughter to him and then back again. Where the hell was Macsorley when he needed him?

Achnacon handed his whisky glass to his wife with such care that it might as well have contained nitroglycerine. Then he grasped the soldier with both arms and lifted him off his feet in a bear hug.

" 'Twas a grand day for Achnacon when yourself entered our lifes, even if yourself did see fit to enter by the byre."

A glass of the dreaded *uisge beatha* was thrust into Andy's hand. He looked to Ishbel for help, but she seemed delighted by her father's reaction, and waited for him to accept the offering. He emptied the glass in one suicidal swallow and felt the nitroglycerine detonate in his stomach.

"Aw Gawd…" He gasped for air, trying to extinguish the flames. "Aw Gawd Almighty…"

Achnacon clapped the soldier's back. "Enjoy the pain, my friend, manys a one in the cold earth would be grateful for such pain."

Andy waited until the fires began to subside. Already he could feel the raw alcohol surging into his brain.

" 'Tis the brew of Larachmor. Himself alone dares distil the *uisge beatha* four times."

Andy laughed as if he'd been the victim of a practical joke. "Ah should've known. Larachmor said he was gonnae nail me, right enough."

Achnacon seemed to understand the irony. "You will have another, of course."

Andy shook his head. Already he could feel that first numbing of his tongue, and knew what would follow: The slurred speech; the need to be everybody's pal; crashing into tables; unconsciousness. Oh God, no, not tonight of all nights.

The Highlander was insulted. "Yourself would not be one of those queer creatures who turn their noses up at the *uisge beatha*?"

Achnacon's wife interceded then, and the Highlander nodded and drew back. For the first time Andy saw a look of approval on her face. He wondered if the chaperone had still to submit a report.

The wild squeal of the fiddle reanimated the crowd. They formed themselves into parallel lines, ready to launch into the next dance. Ishbel tugged at Andy's hand, but as he prepared to be led off Achnacon took him by the arm. Andy thought he was about to have a shot fired across his bow, but the expression on the old man's face was one of concern rather than menace.

"You will allow some advice from an old head, my friend; 'tis unwise to be giving a lassie free rein. My Ishbel is a grand lass, but herself is like her mother, she is wilful and headstrong. Women is like horses, young Andy; a man must show who is master from the very first day."

Perhaps to emphasise the point, his daughter hauled the soldier away from her father and into the sea of bodies. Andy laughed at the spirit of Achnacon's unbroken filly. He decided he'd leave the horse breaking to others. Besides, he might have been more impressed if her father hadn't lowered his voice to prevent his wife from overhearing.

The dance was a predecessor of the notorious 'strip the willow'. The Highlanders' version, however, was a more graceful affair than the coarse mêlée Andy knew. He was only dimly aware of the museum of long-ago faces and ancient costumes that swirled before him, like images from a Burns poem. His eyes never left the wild and untamed daughter of Achnacon as she whirled and pirouetted around him, her face alight with the simple joy of living.

It was only when the music finished that Andy realised Shawnee and Sam had been drawn into the dance beside them. Shawnee was jumping up and down with unexpended energy. Excitedly she threw her arms around the soldier.

"Isn't it just fantastic? I had no idea it could be as exhilarating as this."

Shawnee looked beyond Andy to the dishevelled beauty standing behind him, her breasts still heaving from the dance.

"Oh my God, Andy, she is so pretty." She stretched out her hand as though trying to touch some timid creature. Ishbel's eyes flashed menacingly. She stepped towards Andy and linked her arms in his.

"Oh, honey, I'm no threat to you," said Shawnee. She put her arms around Sam and kissed him on the mouth. "See? This is Sam; y'understand? Sam? He's a little sweaty and he's not too bright at times, but he's mine, same as Andy is yours." She looked at Macmillan. "Oh, Andy, she's absolutely gorgeous."

Here was a word Ishbel understood. She touched her heart and traced a circle around her partner's face. "Gorcheous," she said firmly.

"Ah taught her that," said Andy.

Ishbel then performed a little curtsy before Shawnee, walked over to Sam and threw her arms around him.

The American was taken by surprise, but he quickly recovered his wits. "Sorry about this, big guy. Either y'got it, or y'don't."

Ishbel returned to Andy's side with a retaliatory sniff.

Shawnee laughed delightedly. "I guess that puts me in my place." She returned Ishbel's curtsy. "I hope we're gonna be friends, honey; apart from anything else, I'm gonna be needing a coupla bridesmaids soon."

Andy resisted the temptation to give Shawnee a congratulatory hug.

Chapter Seventeen

Andy woke to the whispers of the women preparing breakfast, and the ever-present tang of peat smoke. He knew at once where he was. Such impressions were imprinted so powerfully upon his mind he had difficulty remembering any other reality.

His head hurt like hell. He should never have accepted all those drams after Ishbel had left with her family; but he'd had to help Sam and Shawnee celebrate their engagement.

He opened one bleary eye, and decided his enflamed optic nerves weren't ready for daylight yet. He wondered if the Highlanders had a cure for a hangover, some herbs or plants perhaps. Maybe they reverted to the dark alchemy of their pagan ancestors: *'Tis like this, first you kiss the head of a life toad, then you bury the creature in the centre of a dung heap.*

Perhaps their insides were so well preserved by the raw spirit they poured down their throats they were immune to hangovers.

God, his head hurt.

He'd dreamed of Ishbel during the night.

Ishbel.

Ishbel Cameron of Glen Laragain.

Ishbel Macmillan of Glen Laragain?

In his dream Ishbel spoke English, but with an American accent. He'd taken her home to Stirling to meet his mother. He hadn't seen his mother for years, and she was sitting outside the family home, wearing a bright red coat.

Sort that one out, Sigmund Freud.

Ishbel. He tried to remember at what point he'd stopped being Andy Macmillan, and had become part of this new individual called Andy and Ishbel. When they'd kissed? When he'd first held her? Could it even have been the first moment he'd set eyes on her? She'd been so taciturn then, keeping herself secret and hidden; but beneath Ishbel's attractive exterior had lain a complex character; elegant and fiery, assured and childlike. She could be overbearing, *and* she had the irritating habit of insisting he learn the Gaelic equivalent of every word he taught her. But, oh God, how he'd come to love her little secret smile, and the way she held his gaze at every opportunity.

Long before the end of the wake Ishbel's mother insisted the family leave while the master of the house remained on his feet. Andy had helped load Achnacon onto one of the makeshift hearses, and had stood listening to the clip clop of the little garron's hooves until they'd disappeared into the night. Then he'd gone back into the cottage and joined the two Americans.

Rhona had returned to the cottage as most of the mourners were making their way home. She made it clear she had no interest in merrymaking. She'd spoken at length to Colin before approaching Shawnee, Sam and Andy.

"You sure you're doing the right thing, honey?" Shawnee had asked her.

"There is nothing here for myself now," Rhona replied bleakly. "All that remains of my family is at Drummossie preparing for a battle Muirshearlach says will destroy the clans. Perhaps if ourselfs are fortunate we may forestall this disaster."

He could hear Rhona's voice outside the cottage now. He also recognised Jamie's nervous laughter. Dammit! He'd hoped his own guys would still be unconscious this morning, and the whole idiotic idea would have come to nothing.

Groggily Andy rose to his feet. He looked around for his combat jacket, then remembered he'd given it to Ishbel to keep her warm on her way home. His head hurt even more when he moved, but he managed to make his way outside without serious embarrassment.

Tethered to a post was a train of six Highland ponies. One was laden with packs, another carried the G.P.M.G. and ammunition box. Rhona looked grim faced as she tightened the girth on one of the saddles. She was dressed in dark green tartan trews and green tartan jacket that didn't quite match one another. Colin stood to one side, rifle in hand, looking lost and out of place. Jamie, Rae and Fergie were making last-minute adjustments to their webbing.

"Ye're still gonnae go through with it, then?" he said, narrowing his eyes in the early morning sunshine.

A surprised grin appeared on Jamie's face. "Didnae think we'd see ye up this early." He looked at his N.C.O. the way an evangelist would look at one of the unconverted. "It's still no' too late. We're gonnae be gone six days at most. Even if the redcoats do come again it'll no' be within the week. You're gonnae be sitting here twiddling your thumbs while ye could be out there with us."

"Jamie, we've been over this…"

"Ah, sod 'im," Rae put in sourly. "He's got more important things on his mind."

The remark drew a coarse laugh from Fergie. Andy was too tired to rise to the bait.

"We have but three days to reach Inverness." Rhona interrupted. "We may say our farewells now for we must leave this instant."

Jamie drew a deep breath and slung his rifle over his shoulder. His pouches bulged with spare magazines.

Andy searched for something meaningful to say: "Listen, if ye make it tae Culloden in time, ye'll be arriving from the west, the Highlander's right wing, where the battle's gonnae be decided. Take out the artillerymen. If ye get the chance take out some of the dragoons as well. That'll even up the odds a bit."

Jamie nodded. He would have known all this already, of course.

Colin came over to shake Macmillan's hand. "If anything should happen to ourselves will you tell Alistair that… that…"

Andy nodded. "You two keep yer heads down, ye hear me?" He lowered his voice. "Any chances tae be taken let those two morons take them. And keep an eye on that lassie. She's no' as strong as she likes tae make out."

Already Rhona was on the path heading east, the train of ponies strung out in single file behind her. Rae and Fergie followed, both with their hands in their pockets, emphasising their ex-military status. Colin and Jamie fell in behind, the soldier taking up the rear as if he was on patrol. They were nearly four hundred yards away when Jamie turned and yelled something at his corporal. Andy caught only brief snatches:

"…Mags… twenty rounds… spare ammo…"

With a last wave Jamie disappeared from view. Andy was left with a nagging sense of failure. Then he thought of the soldiers from the fort licking their wounds only a few miles away, and he thought of Ishbel, and his sense of failure vanished.

It was barely 6.30 am. The fresh air was beginning to ease his headache, and the thought of returning to the smoky depths of the cottage held little appeal.

A layer of frost had gathered overnight; Andy could see the white hoar in the north-facing hollows. Vapour rose from vegetation and thatched roof alike as the morning sun began to warm the glen.

He scratched at the three-day growth on his chin. A tentative sniff told him he was overdue a scrub down. He made his way to the burn and followed the downstream flow until he came to a point where the water cascaded over a waterfall into a pool about five feet deep. He decided this must be where the people bathed and washed their clothes. In the distance he could hear cattle lowing, otherwise there was no sign of life.

Andy stripped off and plunged into the water. He clawed handfuls of sand and gravel from the bottom of the pool and scraped wildly at his body until he could stand the cold no longer. He dried himself as best he could with his army shirt before putting on his phillamhor. He spent another ten minutes washing socks, shirt and underwear before tiptoeing barefoot back to the cottage, teeth chattering from the cold. Between him and Mother Nature lay nothing but a tartan plaid, belted around his waist.

All seemed quiet inside the house. Andy draped his wet clothes on the overhang of the roof and padded into the cottage, looking for dry clothing. The lassies had returned to their beds. In one corner somebody was snoring rhythmically. Nearby a young woman was murmuring in her sleep. He squatted beside the fire, trying to force heat into his shivering limbs. He wondered how these people survived such a lifestyle. Yet they seemed to maintain a reasonable standard of hygiene; any odours he'd detected were natural and not unpleasant. Perhaps they rubbed some plant extract over themselves; perhaps the secret lay in their dark past: ...*First you rub a life toad under your oxters*...

Warmth was returning to his hands and feet. The contents of the cooking pot had begun to look appealing. He helped himself to a bowlful. It was the same porridge he'd eaten the previous day, the texture grainier than he was accustomed to, but he marvelled at the flavour of such a simple dish.

He scrabbled about in semi-darkness until he found a pair of woollen stockings and a thick hand-woven blanket, then stumbled outdoors once again. The stockings were of different shades of tartan, and one barely reached his calf while the other stretched to his knee. But at least he was able to put on his boots. Andy stretched out on the blanket, his back against the wall of the cottage. His headache was now gone, and for the first time in days he felt clean and refreshed. He decided he would rest his eyes, for a few moments perhaps. Maybe go for a wee wander later.

Andy felt the sudden loss of heat on his face as the sun was blotted out. He looked up to see a woman standing over him. At first he thought it was Ishbel, but as he scrambled to his feet he realised it was Shawnee.

"Sorry, Andy, I didn't mean to waken you. Y'were so still, for a moment there I thought..."

Andy ran a hand through his hair, and was surprised to find it dry.

"Ah must've dozed off," he mumbled. He looked at his watch. "God Almighty, it cannae be ten-thirty already..."

Shawnee nodded. "Most of us have been awake for a while; some poor girl's been crying out in her sleep. Poor kid; it's awful what these people have been through."

The soldier was beginning to gather his senses. The sun had climbed well above the southern ridge of hills, melting the last remnants of frost. It was a beautiful spring day, with barely a cloud in the sky.

"Have ye had any breakfast? The lassies did a lovely drop o' porridge earlier."

Shawnee shook her head. She was casually dressed in the shorts and sweatshirt she'd been wearing the day they'd first met. "Y'know I would give anything for a nice warm shower. Sam can be quite useful with his hands, maybe when things settle down he could put something together for me."

Andy had an image of the house that Shawnee would demand from her husband to be, with sturdy chimney and wooden floorboards, and half a hundred other improvements on the black houses of Glen Laragain, and he realised it was probably women like Shawnee who'd been the driving force that had taken the species from caves to suburbia.

"There's a decent-sized pool about four hundred yards downstream," he told her. "The water might be warmer now. It was freezing earlier."

Andy could see Shawnee taking note of the washing hanging from the roof, and he suddenly became conscious of his nakedness beneath the bolt of cloth that covered his waist.

"Wha Ahndy Macmillan," she said, like a shocked Southern Belle, "Ah do believe yawl's bin skinny dippin'."

The soldier laughed at the ease with which this lovely American handled such awkward moments. Not for the first time he found himself confused by the effect she had on him. She and Sam were as good as walking down the aisle, while Andy's world had begun to revolve around Ishbel; yet he still found it important to make a good impression on Shawnee.

"Let's just say nature in the raw is no' all it's cracked up tae be."

She smiled and made a half-hearted attempt to pull some of the tangle out of her hair. "Ishbel was so pretty last night, and did y'notice how clean she looked and how shiny her hair was? One thing's for sure, she didn't get to look like that by jumping into ice-cold water. Whatever it is they do, I need some of it and I need it soon."

They could hear the sounds of movement and the murmur of voices from inside the cottage.

"It's no' gonnae be easy, ye know," he said suddenly, "trying tae make a life for ourselves here."

"Yeah, I guess," she murmured. "Sometimes it scares the hell outta me when I think of what we haven't got here, and then I think are people from the future any happier than these folks? D'you think our lives are richer, more purposeful, with our automobiles and refrigerators, and television sets? I think it's in our nature to wanna make our lives as comfortable as possible, yet without adversity we become stale and bored."

"Aye, Ah saw that maself. Most o' the lads preferred tae take their chances in Ireland rather than vegetate in Germany."

"Germany?" she echoed. "Of course, you guys were part of N.A.T.O., weren't you? Before the fall of communism."

Andy looked stunned. "Before the fall of communism? Ye mean in Russia? God Almighty, when did that happen?"

"Back in the nineteen nineties."

"Ah cannae believe this. What happened? Was there a war, or what?"

"No, not really, there was a series of popular uprisings throughout Eastern Europe. The whole Soviet empire just sorta crumbled away."

"Jeezus," he breathed. "Of all the things we reckoned were gonnae come at us from Eastern Europe, Ah don't think too many saw that coming. What about China? Did they get rid o' the communists as well?"

It was a logical question, but immediately Andy knew he'd touched a nerve.

"In a way they did," she said, trying to avoid his eyes, "but the old guard clung on in China, like a dead hand at the wheel…"

Realisation hit Andy like a fist in the face. "That nuclear explosion we saw; it *was* from your time, wasn't it? It was the Chinese… It wasn't the Russians, it was the bloody Chinese…"

Shawnee nodded faintly. "China was gripped by famine, appealing for international aid. When no aid came they musta resorted to force."

The blood drained from Andy's face. He felt as if his mind was about to implode. He turned his back on Shawnee, his hands swiping at the sides of his eyes. Sam emerged from the cottage before he could collect his thoughts.

"Hi, guys, how's it going?"

Sam's attention was taken up by Shawnee, uncertain of her reaction this morning after the momentous events of the night before. She gave him a reassuring peck on the cheek.

"Hi, honey, how y'feeling today?"

"Not too bad I guess. Head's a little sore."

"Good," she said. "The way you were downing that stuff last night, anybody'd think prohibition was coming back."

He smiled conspiratorially and nodded at Andy. "I didn't wanna offend the old guy that made the stuff, so I tipped a lotta the moonshine I was given into Andy's glass."

Sam's voice had been loud enough for Andy to share the joke, but the soldier was lost in his own world.

"What's wrong?"

Shawnee took Sam by the arm and led him out of earshot. "He knows about some of the stuff that happened, about the Chinese and all. He's gonna wanna know more…"

She stood on tiptoes and kissed him again. "Go easy on him, huh?"

"Me? Y'want *me* to tell him?"

She looked over her shoulder as she was about to re-enter the cottage. "I'm gonna see about getting a bath, or something. I feel kinda dirty, y'know?"

Andy turned around as Sam approached him. The soldier had the eyes of a man who has seen the fires of hell.

"Okay, big guy. Let's get this over with," the American said bluntly.

Andy had to clear his throat before he could respond. "None of us really believed they were gonnae be used. They were only meant tae be a deterrent. What the hell went wrong?"

"What didn't go wrong? Everything had been going to hell long before there was any talk of ultimatums, or war."

"Right, things got a wee bit tough so out came the nuclear missiles," said Andy scornfully.

"Y'ever hear of something called global climate change; G.C.C. for short?"

Andy shook his head.

"Okay then, whaddabout C.R.O.C.: changing regime in ocean currents? Or, G.E.E.; global extinction event? No? Then how about the destruction of the ozone layer? The greenhouse effect? Global warming?"

"What the hell has this gibberish got tae do with a bunch o' trigger-happy cowboys kicking off a nuclear war?"

"That's the world Shawnee and me inherited," Sam replied scathingly, "thanks to all those generations before us that treated the planet like a garbage dump."

"What are ye sayin'; your lot went tae war with the Chinese because we didnae keep the bloody place tidy?"

Sam took a deep breath to compose himself.

"The people of this world are still living in some kinda harmony with nature. The population would be, I dunno, probably less than one billion. By the end of the twentieth century the population of the world is gonna pass the six billion figure. Six billion people, all wanting the same thing; apartments and automobiles and refrigerators and television sets, and so on, and so on."

"What's yer point, Sam?" Andy asked sharply.

"I'll tell y'what my point is, buddy: while all those scientists and engineers were finding new ways to grow and to build bigger, better, faster, the dumb-assed mothers had taken the human race 'way beyond the planet's ability to support the species. That's my freakin point! The planet couldn't take any more poison being pumped into the atmosphere, couldn't take any more forests being cleared, or pollution being dumped into the oceans. At the end the average temperature was rising by one degree centigrade every year. The polar ice caps were melting, sea levels were rising all over the world. Weather patterns were changing, even the ocean currents had begun to change direction, nothing was where it was supposed to be anymore."

Andy could see something of the anger and despair that Sam must have known; Sam and Shawnee and all the rest of that last damned generation.

"How did it start? The war, Ah mean." His voice had lost its accusing edge.

"The world couldn't adjust," Sam replied hoarsely. "North America, most of Europe, was able to cope with the changes in climate; different farming methods, different crops. But Asia and a lot of Africa was turning into one huge desert. God only knows how many millions were dying of hunger and disease. China musta figured the West was holding out on them. Maybe they thought a nuclear war was a gamble worth taking."

"How bad was it?" Andy wanted to know. "Ah mean; could it maybe have been just a localised thing?"

"I don't think it was any kinda localised war. It all happened real sudden while Shawnee and me were in Scotland. We were able to piece together what musta taken place from what we heard on the cell phone; what we saw appear in the skies here."

"That explosion above Loch Ness?"

Sam nodded his head, and then looked at the soldier. "Hold on, Shawnee said Loch Ness lies to the east of here."

"That's right."

"What exactly did you guys see, Andy?"

"Just a bright flash, like something colossal had exploded in the air way above the loch. Why, isn't that what you saw?"

"Aw hell," Sam said quietly. He stared at the distant hilltop as if he'd been lulled into confessing some terrible crime.

"Have y'ever heard of Krakatoa?" he murmured at last.

"It's a volcano, isn't it?"

"That's right. For a long time after it erupted people around the world saw spectacular sunsets. Something to do with all the stuff that was blown into the upper atmosphere. Well, it was the same kinda effect we saw."

"What d'ye mean; like a red sunset?"

Sam snorted faintly. "Krakatoa woulda been like a smokestack compared to what Shawnee and me saw. Everything that woulda hit North America; all that... stuff rising into the air... like the sky was on fire. It was coming from the west, from the Atlantic, and it looked like the sky was on fire and the world was being swallowed up by the sun."

"It mightae been another volcano, or something," Andy put in, desperation straining his voice. "Maybe out in the Atlantic; Iceland, or somewhere…"

"There was something else," Sam said quietly. "Right at the end we saw something explode on the other side of those hills. It musta been a ground burst; nothing too big, I guess, but then it didn't need to be, the size of that little town…"

"Fort William?" Andy gasped in horror. "Ye saw something hit Fort William? It doesnae make sense! Why would they want tae hit a town as wee as Fort William…?"

Sam's eyes were closed now, his body rigid, as if he were once again facing that avalanche of fire that had roared down the glen towards him.

"Same reason they detonated one to the east of here; to poison the land and the water; to prevent your government, your military, any survivors from the south, from finding sanctuary anywhere in the U.K."

Andy felt sick, as though his body was trying to reject the poison this man was feeding into his soul. He stared at the ridge, above which Sam and Shawnee had seen the fires of hell, and he found he was clenching his teeth so tightly his jaw ached. He had to get away from this unborn harbinger from the future, away from the nightmare seeds he was planting in his mind.

"Ah'm gonnae… go for a wander," he mumbled. "Ah'll… see ye later."

Andy had heard of soldiers sleeping on the march; so exhausted or so traumatised they'd trudged along with their comrades, completely unconscious. When he began to take in his surroundings once more he found he was halfway up the southern slopes of Glen Laragain, the uppermost part of his phillamhor trailing behind him like a wedding gown. His automotive functions had drawn him towards the obvious escape route, into the hills.

He slumped to the ground. He'd wept when Shawnee had first told him. He wasn't sure why. He had no siblings, his father was long dead, his mother a stranger. Perhaps he'd wept for all that wasted potential; all that nobility and generosity and self-sacrifice that lay in the human spirit. Perhaps he'd wept because the darker side of human nature would triumph in the end.

He rose to his feet, gathering the plaid over his left shoulder. He was about five hundred feet above Glen Laragain. From here he could see the entire length of the glen, from Inverlaragain Cottage in the east to the cemetery in the west. Here and there he could make out blackened ruins, where the soldiers had done their work. He could see the little out-house where he'd spent the night following the massacre. He could see the thatched cottage where he and Ishbel had held hands and kissed. He'd known more contentment during those few minutes than he'd ever known with any woman he'd managed to charm or fumble his way into bed with.

Ishbel.

He visualised the boiling inferno rising out of Glen Laragain, turning every living thing into charred atoms. He saw that strong, mischievous, innocent face melting before his eyes. She had come to personify humanity, and the terrible end humanity would create for itself.

He continued to climb towards the southern ridge of hills, trying to escape from Glen Laragain and the terrible things that Sam and Shawnee had seen there.

Chapter Eighteen

It was early evening before Shawnee and Sam located the soldier. He was squatting on an outcrop of heather high on the southern slopes of *Meall Banabhie.*

"It's amazing, isn't it?" he said, his back to the advancing figures. "Ah know we've had three days tae get used tae the idea, but it hits ye over again when ye see this."

He could hear Sam struggling to catch his breath as he and Shawnee came to a halt beside him.

Andy pointed to a distant sprawl of grey walls and grey buildings some miles to the south. "That's Fort William over there; where the River Nevis flows intae the loch. It's no' the Fort William Ah knew. This here's the real thing, where those soldiers came from."

In front of the fort lay the elbow of sun-dappled water where Loch Linnhe gives birth to Loch Eil. A motley collection of sailing ships was dotted about the loch; from small, single-mast fishing boats to large ocean-going vessels. Tiny wherries shuttled between the fort and one of the larger ships anchored nearby.

"That's been going on all day. They're unloading supplies for the garrison. The bigger boats are probably Royal Navy warships."

"It's incredible," breathed Shawnee. "We haven't just landed in some enchanted little corner. We really are here."

"About an hour ago Ah watched a long column of troops marching towards the fort from the south. Ye could clearly see the scarlet of their tunics."

"Y'think they're building up to something?" asked Sam.

"Aye," Macmillan replied succinctly. He turned to look at the Americans. Shawnee was flushed with excitement and looked very much in her element, as if she'd been born into this primitive and dangerous world. It was the appearance of Sam, however, that captured Andy's attention. True to his word, he had allowed himself to be dressed in the native garb of the Highlands, his phillamhor extravagantly colourful, with elements of blue and scarlet in its pattern.

He looked prickly and defensive, the victim of an elaborate practical joke.

"Not one freakin word, okay?" he growled.

Shawnee giggled at the transformation in her fiancé. "Andy, tell him, for Godsakes, he looks real handsome in it. He won't listen to me."

Andy looked at the contrast of Californian tan and Highland plaid and told the American what Jamie had said to *him* the first day he'd gone native: "No one's gonnae mistake ye for Rob Roy, but ye look no' bad."

Sam grunted in reply, and Andy decided a change of subject might be a good idea. He returned his attention to that distant hive of activity.

"It's only a matter of time before they come at us again; ye can smell it in the air."

"Well, at least from here somebody should be able to see them coming," Shawnee reasoned.

"Aye, Ah suppose. It's a wee bit worrying that Ah havenae seen any of Achnacon's laddies, but. Ah would've thought this ridge would be the perfect viewpoint for them."

A knowing smile rippled over Sam's dark scowl. "Who d'y'think sent us up here; told us where to come?"

"Achnacon?"

"One of his kids reported back to the old guy. Seems he was a bit concerned about you; thought y'looked kinda upset. Achnacon was gonna come up to check things out personally, but we..." He glanced at his fiancée, "...and by that, of course, I mean Shawnee, volunteered to come up instead..."

Andy smiled sheepishly. "Ah had a few things tae sort out. Ah didnae mean tae worry anybody."

The Americans had remained standing, waiting for the soldier to rise to his feet and descend with them into Glen Laragain. Andy, however, showed no desire to leave, and Sam and Shawnee eventually sat down beside him.

"This is where ye saw that explosion," Andy said quietly. "All this wouldae been melted, turned tae ashes in an instant. What was it ye said, Sam; ye reckoned they sent a few missiles intae the north of Scotland tae make sure there was no sanctuary anywhere in the country? Ah've been trying tae work out how many missiles they must have had for them tae attack such a low-priority target. Ah mean, what was the state of the planet by the time they turned their attention tae here?"

Sam sat motionless, his face a mask. To his side Shawnee had discovered a little clump of primroses, which she carefully traced with her fingers without touching the flowers.

The soldier continued, his voice soft and reflective: "Ah read somewhere that a butterfly can flap its wings in the Brazilian rain forest and the wee breath of wind it creates can grow intae a tropical storm."

Sam looked at the soldier but said nothing.

"Ah was thinking earlier about all those millions of butterflies fluttering about the jungle, having no effect on the world around them. Ah think it's the same with us. Ah think most of us go through life without the slightest effect on the passage of history. But every now and then there's times when the tiniest change in events could've sent human history off in a different direction altaegether."

Shawnee smiled as she considered the idea. "Y'think that's what we're doing, Andy? Flapping our wings; beating up a storm?"

The soldier's eyes remained fixed on that distant outpost. The sun was now low on the horizon, painting the walls of the fort a ridiculous shade of pink.

"Ah hope so," Andy said, rising to his feet. There was a damp patch on his kilt, where he'd been sitting on the moist ground. "What was decided here was the dynasty that would rule Britain, just as Britain was creating the greatest empire the world had ever seen. The world that we all inherited was shaped by the British Empire. At first Ah was horrified at the idea of changing history, altering events tae come. But now...? Maybe Jamie and the others were right. Maybe the more damage we do in this world the better."

The glen was almost consumed by shadows when they arrived back at *Meall An Fhraoich*. Achnacon was waiting for Andy outside the cottage, anger and concern on his face.

"What if the soldiers had chosen this day to return? How could you have been any help to us, to Ishbel, if you was away yourself wandering the hills?"

Andy returned the old man's gaze, but he accepted the rebuke.

"And your friends away looking for you; you have seen what those Hanoverians will do to all of us, given the chance. Whatever was yourself thinking?"

"Ah'm sorry if ye feel Ah've let ye down, Ah had things on ma mind."

Achnacon's tone softened. "You have made yourself one of us now. All of you have. This is your home, if yourselfs choose to make it so. But you must understand, to be part of a clan means we have a chuty each to the other. None of us stands alone."

"Ah promise it won't happen again."

Achnacon didn't pursue the point. Something in the soldier's eyes had stirred an uneasy memory.

"Did yourself see something when you was in the hills?" he whispered. "Was it *an adhar dearg* you saw, up there, when you was on your own?"

Andy looked tiredly at his friend. "Ah don't follow…"

"The red sky," the old clansman replied, as if he was recounting an ancient spell. "You have the eyes of a man who has seen the red sky."

Andy looked at the darkening sky where once he had seen fire. Shawnee spoke up before he could reply:

"What is it; this red sky? What is it meant to signify?"

Achnacon hadn't missed the look that passed between the Americans. "It has been witnessed as long as there has been people in Glen Laragain. The red sky is taken as a sign that death and destruction is soon to visit the glen."

Shawnee suddenly became incapable of speech, as though her soul had been torn from her body.

"Where… ah, where is this red sky usually seen?" said Sam hoarsely.

"Time and again it has been seen at the graveyard," Achnacon replied, his attention still drawn to Shawnee's horrified face.

"D'you know of anybody who's seen it? Anybody we can talk to?"

The old clansman looked intently from one to the other. " 'Twas but ten days ago the vision was shown to myself, as I stood by the graveyard."

"That's what ye were talking about the other day," Andy recalled, "when ye said ye were shown the signs."

Achnacon nodded unhappily. "Who could have known it wass more than chust a legend? But I told no one. I was afraid people would take to the hills in fear. I was afraid of what might befall the older folk, up there, at this time of year…"

He stared at the young faces before him; at his friend, Andy, who appeared to have seen a vision of hell. To the strange couple from the Americas, who knew more than they were willing to admit.

"Yourselfs will not say to any of my people;" he told them anxiously, "that I had been shown the vision and did not tell. None would understand. All would think Achnacon had betrayed them…"

"Can y'describe what it was y'saw?" Sam asked.

Achnacon shook his head. "I have said too much already. I think myself 'tis best these things be left alone."

"Was it like the sky was on fire; as if the flames were coming from the west?" Shawnee had found her voice again. "Like the earth had turned brown and dead; and there was like a circle of blood around the sun?"

Achnacon stared intently at the young woman. "You have seen it," he whispered.

Shawnee eyes were as wide as a possum's. "An ajar jerag; you guys have even gotta name for it…"

"When? When did yourselfs see the red sky?"

"Three days ago, at the top of the glen, near the graveyard. Just before… the massacre began."

"Two times in the space of chust two weeks," Achnacon reflected in awe. "It has been thirty years and more since the vision was last seen, and now two times in as many weeks. It was a warning of what the Hanoverians planned against ourselfs; a warning which a foolish *bodach* chose not to heed."

In the fading light the old man looked grey and ill. Shawnee took hold of one of his calloused hands, the shock still visible on her own face.

"They're the ones responsible for what took place; those bastards down there in that fort. God only knows how these people woulda got through this if it hadn't been for you. Hell, you're like a father to them, to all of us."

Achnacon blinked in surprise at the passion and the language of the woman. "The Lady Shawnee is too chenerous," he mumbled.

The clachan of cottages was fading into darkness, the glow of peat fires shining faintly through the tiny windows of each house.

"Yourselfs will be tired and hungry," Achnacon remembered. He ushered his guests towards the cottage. "Come, the lassies prepared enough food for the wake to feed the whole of Lochaber."

Andy hesitated at the entrance to the cottage, recalling what he had seen from the ridge.

"There's a lot of activity at the fort; ye know that don't ye? Fresh troops arriving. Supplies being unloaded by boat."

Achnacon nodded sombrely. "Young Donald has the same tale. I fear 'twill not be long before Glen Laragain again feels the displeasure of his Royal Highness."

"It's gonnae be different this time. This time we'll be waiting for them." Andy's voice was calm and reassuring. Gone was any trace of self-doubt.

"Way t'go, Andy," Shawnee added. "I reckon we're gonna have one or two nasty shocks waiting for those guys if they're stupid enough to come back."

"Whaddya mean 'we'?" Sam wanted to know. "Listen, lady; long before the shit hits the fan I want you outta harm's way. The women and kids will need to be got to safety. Wherever they're gonna be put, I want you along with them."

"Y'can want whatever the hell y'like, Kramer," she replied firmly. "I'm gonna be where I can do the most good. And there's no point us standing here arguing about it."

Andy had considered intervening on Sam's behalf, but the tone of Shawnee's voice persuaded him otherwise. As he made his way into the cottage he heard Sam grumbling behind him:

"We'll see, lady. We'll see..."

Achnacon remained outside, staring fixedly at the spot where the American woman had stood only moments before. He could not have been more shocked if *an adhar dearg* had reappeared before him. It was foolish of him not to have realised it before; but he knew now, it had been the Lady Shawnee's voice he had heard moments before the vision had disappeared.

'There's no point us standing here like hogs in a slaughterhouse,' she had said.

The message had long since become clear. He'd had a premonition delivered through the voice of a woman he had yet to meet; the voice had tried to warn him about the terrible plans that had been laid against his people. It was a warning he had chosen to ignore. Achnacon had intended to dine with his new friends, but in that instant he lost all appetite. He closed the door to the cottage and walked off into the night.

As Shawnee, Sam and Andy sat down at the table they noticed Alistair's corner was empty.

"I hope everything's okay," said Shawnee. "He looked kinda upset after his bust-up with Mary."

"Did anybody see if Mary came back?"

Sam shook his head. "Last I saw of Alistair he was downing the old guy's firewater. I don't think I saw Mary again after she sang that sweet little song."

"Ah'm sure it'll all sort itself out," Andy murmured. He glanced at the door, surprised Achnacon hadn't followed them into the cottage. Perhaps he had other matters to attend to.

"What the old guy was saying about the red sky; that's what you two saw, isn't it?"

Shawnee stole a glance at her partner. "I take it Sam told y'all about the things we saw during that hour or so before everything went all to hell?"

Andy nodded.

"What Sam and me saw that day; these people have been seeing visions of the same thing, down through the centuries. It's just so amazing, y'know? *An ajar jerag*, that's what they call it. Is that not the weirdest thing?"

"Ye don't think what you saw was just a vision as well; a glimpse of the future?"

Sam shook his head. "What we saw was no vision; it didn't just appear and then disappear again. We watched it grow and develop like some kinda weather system."

One of their hosts coughed gently to announce her presence, and began to lay plates of food at the table. There was cheese and butter, as well as bannocks and oatcakes, hot from the griddle. There was also a stew, made from the remains of the barbecued calf. She returned with three sizeable bowls, which were placed in front of her guests.

Daintily Shawnee filled her bowl with cheese and butter, and a selection of griddled hotcakes. "Y'know, Sam, it's a weird coincidence that this vision of theirs is seen near the old graveyard, where we first saw that red sky."

"I don't think it's a coincidence." Sam spoke around a mouthful of veal stew. "Other than you and me, who else was in Glen Laragain that day?"

"Nobody, I guess. Why?"

"Then other than you and me, who else stood by that graveyard and watched that nightmare unfold?"

"I gotta feeling we're gonna be treated to one of the revelations according to Sam," Shawnee said, trying to maintain some dignity through a mouthful of buttered oatcake.

Her partner snorted. "Remember that story I told y'about Gettysburg?"

"Sam camped out on Gettysburg battlefield with two of his buddies," Shawnee explained. "Sam and one of the other guys watched two Confederate soldiers materialize around their campfire."

"It sounds dumb when it's just blurted out like that," Sam frowned, "but I guess that's about the size of it."

"What's this gotta do with the red sky?"

Sam shovelled another spoonful of veal into his mouth. "I told y'at the time those soldiers we saw were looking in our direction, like they were talking to me and Ralphie."

"Yeah, you reckoned you and Ralphie had created some kinda coincidence between two time periods."

"That's it exactly. I figured we saw what we did because we sat in the exact spot occupied by two other Confederate soldiers, so we were able to look through their eyes and see what they saw."

"Are you saying the same sorta thing has happened here?" asked Shawnee. "That everybody that's ever seen an ajar jerag has made some kinda connection with you and me?"

"We were the only ones who watched that sky developing for real. It seems obvious all those people that have seen this vision of the red sky have been looking through our eyes, seeing what we saw that day…"

"Oh my God, that is so disgusting," she mumbled. "Dead people, looking through your eyes; it's like being possessed."

"It only seems to happen in certain places…" Sam came to an abrupt halt. He began to gag, his face turning a violent shade of red. He gagged again, noisily, before coughing something onto the table. The object rolled towards Andy, who caught it and held it between thumb and forefinger.

"It's a musket ball."

Sam cleared his throat, his face beginning to regain its normal colour. "It's a what?" he wheezed.

"A musket ball. Ah wondered why they'd butchered a calf for the wake. Their cattle were the only currency these people had; they didn't usually eat them. This one mustae been shot by the soldiers."

He rolled the ball across the table to Sam, who picked it up and examined it.

"Whaddya make of that, huh?" He studied the musket ball for a few moments, and then with a philosophical shrug popped it into his sporran and continued eating. Shawnee looked at her compatriot, a wedge of buttered bannock perched daintily in her hand.

"*Bon appetit*," she told Sam as he manoeuvred another spoonful of veal into his mouth.

Chapter Nineteen

Andy had been awake for some time, listening to the wind sighing around the old house, like something alive that was drawn to the souls within. Occasional gusts would make their way under the door, or through the thatch, drawing swirling patterns in the smoky interior.

It was strange Ishbel hadn't shown up yesterday. Perhaps her father had sent the family to the shielings until the crisis was over. Perhaps she *had* been here, while he'd been wandering the wilderness like the doomed Messiah, confronting his demons. If so, he would need to grovel to more than Achnacon today.

Andy had begun to drift off to sleep once more when the sound of raised voices dragged him back to consciousness. Two lassies beside the peat fire were talking excitedly to one of Achnacon's young scouts. The boy was highly agitated, and had clearly not called in for breakfast.

As Andy struggled to put on his phillamhor the boy ran to his bedside.

"*Saigdearen! Saigdearen!* Auntie, to come pleas; *saigdearen dearg!*"

Andy could hear Alistair's voice in the background.

"Achnacon is three miles away and has sent young Donald to let ourselves know the redcoats are approaching." Alistair's voice remained calm, even as he scrambled for his clothes.

"Does he know how many? How far away they are?"

Alistair spoke to Donald in his own tongue and the boy looked from one to the other, taken aback that one of these strangers had the Gaelic. He shouted his reply at Andy.

"No more than a dozen have been spotted," Alistair translated, now dressed and on his feet. "They are approaching from the west; from the shores of Loch Eil."

"From the west? Ah didn't know there was any way intae the glen from the west."

"It's a rougher track, and a longer way in. Perhaps they thought they would take us by surprise."

Alistair brought over Macmillan's webbing and self-loading rifle, the weight and complexity of the weapon attracting his interest.

"Perhaps you could teach me how to operate your weapon… in case anything should happen to yourself."

Andy nodded. "First chance we get Ah'll go over the drill with ye."

"Yeah, count me in on that," added Sam. He was floundering about in bed, trying to locate his clothes. Beside him Shawnee sleepily opened her eyes, her face hidden beneath a tangle of hair.

"Whassup? Whassgoin on?"

"It's okay. You go on back to sleep. The guys are just gonna check something out."

She sat up, sweeping the hair from her face. "What d'you mean 'check something out'? What're you guys up to? What's going on?"

Andy could see what was about to develop between the two Americans. Beside him young Donald seemed ready to pounce on the soldier and drag him towards the door.

"Alistair, you're still no' a hundred percent, you make yer own way there. Ah'll send the wee lad back tae meet ye. Sam, you come along with Alistair. Ah can move faster than the pair of you, so Ah'll get going now with the laddie here, okay?"

Without waiting for a reply he strapped on his webbing and nodded towards Donald. The boy bolted for the door, like a greyhound being sprung from its trap.

He was relieved to find that no rain had fallen, although heavy clouds were sweeping inland on a hard, westerly wind. Donald adjusted his pace so that he stayed ten yards ahead of the soldier. The boy's running was so free and effortless Andy wondered what speed he would need to achieve if he was ever to bridge that gap.

It wasn't long before they reached the settlement of *Achnacon*. There was no sign of life; evidently the people had been dispatched to their mountain hideaway. It was to be the same story with the other settlements they passed through: *Dail Na Bruthach, Larachmor, Ceann Laragain*. Andy recalled the lilting music of their names when he'd first heard them flow from the tongue of Achnacon. Now they were all cold and deserted, as if a terrible plague had passed this way. By the time they reached the cemetery, Andy was dry-mouthed and sweating, the rifle stock slipping in his greasy hands.

Without warning, Donald abandoned the path and began to run up the hillside to his left. The gap between them quickly grew as Andy stumbled on the slanting ground. By the time he'd struggled to the brow of the hill Donald was out of sight. He was about to charge through a thicket of gorse when his legs were pulled from under him. As he scrabbled for the butt-end of his rifle he heard Achnacon's whispered voice:

"Wheesht, man! They are on the other side of this hill."

Now that he was at ground level Andy could make out young Donald, as well as Larachmor and three other *bodachs* he'd seen at the wake. All were lying motionless beneath the gorse bushes, their faces turned to the west. Beside each *bodach* lay a captured army musket.

Below them stretched the wild, uninhabited western reaches of Glen Laragain. Andy's eyes followed the course of a burn as it tumbled from the wastes of *Druim Fada* towards the distant shores of Loch Eil. The drab browns and greens of early spring threw into sharp relief the scarlet uniforms of a group of men resting by the burn some four hundred yards away.

Andy felt a wild tangle of emotions: excitement… fear… anger… Jamie's predictions had been no more than wishful thinking; the redcoats had come back, exactly as he'd feared.

He could only make out nine figures. His eyes followed the sweep of the landscape until the glen curved out of sight miles to the southwest. Where were the others?

"The other laddies; they're still watching the hills, in case this is a diversion?"

The Highlander snorted disdainfully. "Not even the Hanoverians would think us so easy deceived."

Some of the redcoats had peeled off their outer uniforms and were washing themselves in the burn. Two of the hardier souls had stripped off altogether and were splashing about in the water, like children at play.

"There is something else which makes no sense whatever," Achnacon whispered. "They may have pistols or dirks concealed about themselfs, but not a one of them carries sword or musket."

"This has got tae be some kindae trick."

Achnacon shook his head doubtfully. "After what has taken place these men must know they are being spied upon. To divest themselfs of clothing in their enemy's land; they have either taken leave of their senses…"

"…Or they're tryin' tae send us a message."

Larachmor crawled over to Achnacon and whispered excitedly at him. Achnacon's reply was sharp and succinct, and clearly not to Larachmor's liking. He scowled horribly at Achnacon, then scowled at Andy for good measure, before dragging himself back through the bushes.

"What was yer friend so upset about?" asked Andy.

Achnacon shielded his eyes as he studied the distant redcoats. "Och, himself was always a terrible man for the claymore. 'Twas never his way to skulk in the heather. Larachmor always enchoyed the wild charge."

Andy smiled. "For what it's worth, Ah think it's best we wait tae see what their intentions are."

"Achnacon is of the same mind," said the other with quiet authority.

The sky was now leaden, the clouds whipped along on a stinging wind, speckling the ground with pellets of rain. The distant soldiers hurried to put on their uniforms. In some ways Andy sympathised with Larachmor. There was a strong temptation to eliminate this problem before it became a threat to the glen. He began to prepare himself for the worst. His ammunition pouches contained four magazines, of twenty rounds apiece judging by their weight. Jamie's last shouted message came back to him as he encountered two muslin bags full of single 7.62mm rounds. The lad must have plundered Fergie's G.P.M.G. ammo. Andy felt a little better as he settled his sights on that faraway clump of scarlet. Even from this distance he could take out each one of them should he so choose.

He remembered his arrangement with the others. "Perhaps ye could send the young lad back along the path tae guide Sam and Alistair here."

Achnacon spoke briefly to Donald, and the boy melted out of sight, the gorse remaining undisturbed as though a ghost had passed through it.

The redcoats were on the move again, following the burn towards its watershed. A sharp exchange broke out between Achnacon and Larachmor. At once Andy saw the problem; if they stayed put they would be bypassed by the soldiers. Should they intercept now or fall back?

"We shall withdraw from here and continue to observe as best we may," Achnacon said quietly.

Andy could hear Larachmor muttering dark oaths as he retired through the bushes.

Away from the cover of the gorse there was nothing but bare hillside between them and the approaching soldiers. Achnacon pulled his force further and further back until he found a suitable hollow, twenty yards south of the path, and a little to the east of the graveyard. Here they could remain concealed while they continued to watch the redcoats. From such a position, however, there could be no further withdrawals.

The rain was becoming heavier now, stinging any exposed flesh as it drove inland. To the east there was still no sign of Alistair or Sam. It wasn't long however before the redcoats came into view. When they were two hundred yards away they were halted by their leader; a tall, striking-looking individual, who seemed to command instant obedience from his fellows. He scanned the horizon before him, as though expecting to be intercepted.

Soon they were on the move again. As they drew closer Andy found his attention drawn to the scarred face of their leader.

"Longholme!"

The name meant nothing to his companions, although their eyes too were drawn to the incongruous image of disfigured face and highbred bearing.

"You know this man?" Andy could hear surprise and alarm in Achnacon's voice.

"Alistair read about him in a book."

"Himself must be important if someone thought to write of him in a book."

"Aye. Ye could say that…"

"Whatever could a chentleman like that want with folk like ourselfs?"

Achnacon seemed cowed by the very demeanour of the man. The redcoats were barely a hundred yards to the west and would soon be abreast of their position. Andy took hold of his rifle.

"There's only one way tae find out," he murmured, as he rose to his feet.

At once the redcoats came to a halt. Macmillan could feel their leader taking stock of him as he crossed the few yards of heather to the path. The wind and rain were now full in Andy's face, bringing tears to his eyes.

"What is it yez want here?" he bellowed.

One of Longholme's comrades murmured something into his master's ear.

"We have come here to offer the good people of this valley our assistance," the officer replied.

"What makes ye think we need yer help?" Andy yelled back.

Longholme inclined his head once again as he took advice from his subordinate.

"You should know that each and every one of you is in mortal danger…"

"…'Tis chentlemen such as yourselfs that pose the only danger to Glen Laragain!" Achnacon interjected.

Andy turned to find the five old clansmen standing to his right, their muskets held awkwardly before them.

This time Longholme needed no translation. "My companions and I remain in these uniforms to protect us from the worst of your climate, not to dismay the good people of this valley."

He began to approach, his men shuffling uneasily behind him. At once five muskets were pointed in their direction, aging hands trembling with the weight of the weapon.

"Hold your fire, gentlemen, I implore you!" Longholme pulled open his wide-skirted coat to show he was unarmed. He ordered his men to stand still, and approached Achnacon and his ragged little band on his own. As he drew near his piercing blue eyes flicked from one face to another.

"You are in the gravest danger, all of you. Even the safety of your women and children is not assured. As we speak, the destruction of this valley is being planned to the smallest detail. My men and I have come to you this day to offer our help."

"And why would a fine chentleman like yourself be offering to help the likes of us?" Face to face with the tall redcoat Achnacon seemed to have recovered some of his self-confidence.

Longholme towered loftily over the little group of *bodachs*. He tried to smile at them as one comrade to another, but the expression sat uneasily with those cold, searching eyes.

"The men you see before you have incurred the wrath of His Royal Highness. In the space of but three short days the life of every wretch here has become worth as little as that of any man who has taken to the field with your prince."

"And how would a chentleman like yourself have come to such a pass?" Achnacon asked dubiously.

"How many of your people no longer draw breath this morn?"

"Three and thirty." Achnacon had replied before Andy could urge caution.

Longholme nodded solemnly. "I am heartened so many have survived. As loyal soldiers of the crown my men and I came to this valley in pursuance of the orders of His Royal Highness, the Duke of Cumberland. These same wretches left that very day, their orders unanswered; aye, even though it should mean they have forfeited their own lives. We were to be taken by ship to London, there to stand trial as an example to other men of principle who do not share His Highness's taste for blood."

The doubt remained in Achnacon's eyes. "A Chuke's man who speaks of principles. 'Tis a notion that means as much to my ears as to the dead ears of my kinfolk."

Longholme drew a long breath. "Whether or no you choose to believe the facts of our miserable fate, you must at least hear what we have to…"

"…And how should ourselfs know truth from fancy?" Achnacon interrupted sharply. "You may tell ourselfs any story that pleases you. How shall we know you are not a part of this wickedness that is planned against us?"

Indignation coloured Longholme's face, painting his scar a vivid purple. "Sir, as an officer and a gentleman I give you my word of honour…"

Achnacon handed his musket to the nearest *bodach*, and drew a long, wicked-looking dirk from its scabbard. He pointed the blade at the officer's chest, then spun it around to offer him the handle. Uneasily Longholme took the weapon.

Achnacon spoke as if he was preaching fire and brimstone to a sinner: "In this land men of honour swear upon the holy iron of the dirk, that they be cursed to suffer a coward's death, alone and without friends, should their word be broke."

Longholme forced the cold metal to his lips. "All that I have told you is true, 'pon my sworn oath as an English gentleman," he announced stiffly.

Achnacon stared into the officer's eyes as he retrieved his dirk. At last he nodded and looked beyond Longholme to his bedraggled companions.

"How long since yourself and your men have eaten?"

The officer's brow furrowed as he counted back the lost meals. "The breakfast before yesterday. A last ration of bread and cheese before we were transferred from Fort William."

"Yourselfs will be hungry then."

Longholme nodded, rigid and formal. "Whom do I have the honour of addressing?"

The old clansman bowed, as elegantly as any well-bred gentleman.

"I am Donald Cameron of Glen Laragain, known to friend and foe alike as Achnacon."

"Achnacon," repeated the other. "Achnacon of Glen Laragain."

"And yourself, sir?" Achnacon enquired lightly.

The officer directed a sharp bow at the Highlander. "Giles Fawkener Longholme… formerly lieutenant of a grenadier company, now a wretched bandit skulking in a land at war with itself. We meet under extraordinary circumstances, sir, but I am no less honoured to make your acquaintance."

The two men shook hands briefly, aged clansman and elegant gentleman, before Longholme motioned his men to join him. As the redcoats came forward two of them addressed the Highlanders in their own tongue. Achnacon saw the surprise on Andy's face.

"Soldiering is an honourable profession, is it not? Many a canny chieftain has sons in both armies, as an inshurance, you understand."

They were to learn that two of Longholme's men were clansmen of Macleod of Raasay, who'd found themselves in the wrong uniform when the rebellion broke out. They'd refused to take part in the Glen Laragain operation and had been arrested on their return to Fort William. The remaining redcoats came from the northern shires of England. Four of them had also grounded their weapons rather than take part in the slaughter. All claimed there were many others of like mind who'd been too afraid, or too prudent, to do likewise.

The two other redcoats had been arrested on charges of cowardice in the face of the enemy. Both had been ostracised by their fellows. One was a pale, nervous-looking boy of sixteen. Andy took an instant dislike to the other man; a stocky, brutish-looking individual who glanced slyly around him without making eye contact with anyone.

Andy recognised the type: coarse, primitive, drawn to the military, not by patriotism, or the promise of regular meals, but by murderous instinct.

He made up his mind to keep them all at arms length, advising Achnacon not to reveal him as anything other than a common clansman.

Achnacon began to lead the motley group along the path, his aged comrades holding the flanks, Macmillan bringing up the rear. Andy smiled at the image of that half-naked old warrior subtly interrogating the elegant individual who strode beside him.

"However did yourselfs manage to escape the clutches of your gaolers?" he enquired casually.

Longholme's face darkened. " 'Pon my arrest my commanding officer saw fit to transport his former second in command in a damned supply ship, as though he were a common criminal, by God."

"The chentleman shows as much regard for his own people as he has shown for mine."

"Captain Caroline Frederick Scott is no gentleman, sir. The man is as crude and ill-mannered a villain as ever it has been my singular misfortune to serve under. I daresay it flattered the creature's vanity to have been granted power over one such as I."

"And how did yourselfs manage to escape?" Achnacon enquired again.

"The fools transported us from Fort William to our ship in a single wherry, with no more than two fellows to guard us. That damned idiot Scott must have supposed us disinclined to hazard an escape in such a dangerous country. My men overpowered the escort in a trice."

Achnacon came to a halt. "But why came you here, to the blighted lands of Glen Laragain? Why do you not flee to your homes in Raasay Isle, or in faraway England?"

"I announced my intention to return to this valley the instant we came ashore. The others elected among themselves to remain together as a body. I cannot answer what lies in their souls, any more than I may claim to be responsible for their conduct. Once they have fed and rested they may elect to go elsewhere."

Achnacon continued along the path, drawing the disparate group along with him.

"…And yourself, sir, what lies in your own soul?"

Longholme considered the question. "In our different ways, Achnacon of Glen Laragain, we are not unalike. The mark of a soldier's life is upon you, clear as day. You too would have sworn to bear true allegiance to a royal master. Perhaps you too came to learn that allegiance and conscience sometimes make uneasy bedfellows."

"Yourself has found your conscience amid the ruins of Glen Laragain, sir?" The Highlander's voice was edged with outrage.

"Whatever may have been in my heart, sir, my hands are free of blood," Longholme said briskly. "That's the God's truth of it. I answered my orders, I directed my men, as any officer must. There alone lies my guilt."

Achnacon nodded, the red anger fading from his cheeks.

"Yourself has said that each and every one of us is in mortal danger. Are we to be attacked again, like wounded deer that have survived the hunt?"

"Your resistance three days past has made your enemy all the more determined, sir. Since the original order came from none other than the Duke of Cumberland, the matter has become an issue unto itself. Captain Scott has sworn to carry fire and sword from one end of this valley to the other. He has vowed that the least resistance will incur the severest penalty, irrespective of age or sex. Privately he has sworn vengeance for the losses suffered on the previous occasion. I have endeavoured to inform the good captain that His Royal Highness will deny any part in the madness as soon as other men see the insanity of it. The fool believes his craven obedience to the royal command can only lead to his own advancement."

"And yourself, sir; you have chose to forsake your oath of allegiance, to risk the gallows for a people you thought your enemy... 'tis a queer tale."

Longholme's face tightened, but his voice remained impassive. "How fickle is human fate, Achnacon of Glen Laragain. It has occurred to me that men are as leaves borne on the wind, to be carried where e'er the winds may please. As you say, sir, mine is a queer tale indeed. Three days past I was the King's man and proud of it. But my mind was turned in the most extraordinary fashion. I scarce still believe the facts of it myself."

Achnacon looked questioningly at the officer.

"Suffice it to say that formerly my conscience belonged to my royal master, but my conscience is now my own again."

The Highlander nodded. "...And what would your conscience have to say about The Chuke of Cumberland's unfinished business?"

Longholme looked directly at the old clansman. "My conscience would cry out to all in this valley; leave here now, this very day. Take as much as you may carry, and flee from this place. Harbour no thoughts of returning until this damnable business is over, or until the Duke's wrath has been satisfied elsewhere. Then and only then should you turn your face to your native heath once more."

Achnacon paled. "But where would we go? Who would dare giff us food and shelter in defiance of the king's son? Our neighbours in Glen Loy? Glen Mallie? They are Locheil's people like ourselfs, but who among them would risk such terrible retribution? And what would we return to? With our homes burnt, our crops destroyed, our cattle took, we would return to a slow death in a country ravaged by war. No, sir, every one of my people will tell yourself what I am telling you now; if we must die, then better we die here in our own land."

Longholme nodded impassively. "In truth, sir, your response is no less than I had expected, and no more than I had feared. Before your mind is set, however, you should know they plan to attack you tomorrow, shortly after noon..."

"...Tomorrow?" echoed Achnacon. "Your Captain Scott is anxious to see an end to the business."

"Indeed, sir, that he is. Three companies, with the bold captain at their head, will approach from the east. A further three companies will approach from the west, travelling the same route my men and I followed this very day. Six hundred men, drawn from three regiments, will take the field against you. Captain Scott's forces have the easier route, and with them will come two pieces of field artillery."

"Artillery?" Achnacon repeated, dismay written across his face.

"Coehorn mortars. Small, and easy carried over rough ground, effective up to eight hundred yards. With these he may demolish any resistance, with small risk to himself. I must own, the man is boorish and coarse, but he is a methodical soldier."

Achnacon blanched at the prospect of what they were about to face. He stole a glance at his comrades, young and old, who trudged along behind him, each man soaked to the skin. His feisty old friend, Larachmor, grinned back at him, defying the elements to do their worst.

The rain was now coming down in torrents. Achnacon could see the clachan of *Ceann Laragain* three or four hundred yards ahead, and hurried the rain-soaked men towards the nearest cottage. Once inside they threw off their outer clothing, while one of the old warriors hurried to light a fire. Before long the smoky warmth from the burning peat began to penetrate the circle of damp, shivering men.

Larachmor displayed another of his talents by preparing a large pot of cooked oatmeal. He glowered evilly at the redcoats as they devoured his food, but he was bound by the laws of Highland hospitality to deny no starving man shelter or sustenance.

At the first opportunity Achnacon took Longholme to one side. "Why do your former masters despise us so?" he asked darkly. "In what way have we made ourselfs unworthy to breathe even the same air as the beasts of the field?"

"You have defied them, sir," Longholme explained. "You would not die when it was ordered that you should. Your very existence has become an affront to them."

Achnacon shook his head bleakly. "...At least there is comfort in knowing the lassies and children will be safe. The shielings will be a refuge to those who cannot fight."

"If you refer to your hilltop summer dwellings; alas, your enemies are aware of their existence. They have foreseen that this would be your response and plan to deploy a portion of their forces along the ridges above the valley."

Across the room Andy saw Achnacon's face turn grey, his hands trembling as if the rain had brought on a fever. He hurried over.

His voice barely more than a whisper, Achnacon repeated all that the officer had said. Andy wondered aloud if they could trust the word of a man who had turned his back on his comrades. Longholme's ear had grown accustomed to Andy's vernacular, and he was outraged at the insult. Instinctively he reached for the sword that had been taken from him at Fort William. Achnacon stepped in to smooth ruffled feathers, drawing his friend to one side and insisting he withdraw the slur.

"Ah'm more concerned about the safety of you, and Ishbel, and all the others, than in yon big eejit's hurt pride," Macmillan hissed defiantly.

"No more than I, my friend, but himself has give his word of honour, and what would our world be coming to if one chentleman was to dispute the sworn word of another?"

Andy held his tongue. He had come to love so much about this archaic world he was reluctant to disturb such noble ideals. In the end he apologised to the redcoat only to oblige his friend. Honour barely satisfied, Longholme stiffly rejoined his men.

Andy was still trading disdainful looks with the officer when Achnacon's young messenger entered the cottage. The water poured from the boy's clothing as he delivered his report. Achnacon questioned the lad for a few minutes before he ruffled his hair like a proud father, and directed him towards the fire.

"Donald has returned with a queer tale," the old Highlander told Andy, a faint smile fringing the dark lines around his eyes. "The Lady Shawnee would not stay where herself was bid, and your friend Sam would not allow her to accompany him, so they remain at *Meall An Fhraoich* still, each loath to accommodate the other. *Alasdair Mhor* has more sense than both. Himself remains with them, reluctant to choin one battle while another may break out behind him."

The smiles of the two men quickly faded.

"The women and children are at the shielings now?" said Andy.

"We thought them safe in the hills, where they have always fled when danger threatens. Who would have believed men capable of such wickedness?" The Highlander grabbed Andy by the arm. "Yourself will take Ishbel this very night and you will flee from this place. Perhaps you could find it in your heart to take Shona as well. Herself is young but she is spirited and will complain little."

Andy shook his head. "We're wasting time here. We need tae find somewhere large enough tae hold us all taegether, but small enough tae defend."

Achnacon's hand dug into the soldier's arm as he tried to force his attention. "If enough off us stay and suffer their vengeance perhaps they will be satisfied." He grasped one of Macmillan's hands. "I could not have chose better for my Ishbel, had herself allowed it. Take her and her sister, keep them both safe. I pray Achnacon's grandchildren will be born to a better world than this."

Andy finally acknowledged the old man's pleas. "Nobody's leaving anyone behind. Our best chance is tae stand taegether. If we hurt them badly enough they'll lose the stomach for a fight."

Achnacon groaned in frustration. "Och, man, how can ourselfs hurt an enemy who stands one half mile off while their cannon does the business for them? Even our stoutest walls will crumble under cannon fire."

Andy held up his rifle, the magazine still attached as insurance against Longholme. "You havenae seen what ma wee cannon can do, have ye?"

Achnacon was beginning to suspect the strain had become too much for the young man. He tried to explain the problem, as patiently as he could.

"Andy, my friend, 'tis clear yourself is a brave and noble soul, but 'tis also clear you have no sense of what modern weapons can do to flesh and bone. Too many times I have seen what remains of men who have smelt the terrible breath of the cannon. 'Tis an end I would spare yourself. Aye, and my own lassies, 'tis an end I would spare them most of all…"

Andy considered taking Achnacon outside to demonstrate the power and accuracy of the innocuous-looking weapon in his hands, but too many eyes would be watching. He decided to try a different approach.

"Ah had another dream last night," he remarked casually.

The Highlander looked at his friend as if his mind had begun to wander.

"Of all the visions Ah've had, this vision was the most vivid of all," said Andy. "It was so clear, it was in colour, with sound and everything."

Achnacon looked obliquely at the soldier. "A vision, you say? And what might this vision haff told you?"

"…It was summer in Glen Laragain. The sun was shining, the wee birds were singing high above the glen, and the cattle were up by the shielings. Everyone in the glen had come tae see Ishbel in this lovely dress she was wearing. She had a veil over her face, and flowers in her hair, and she looked really happy…"

"…'Tis a wedding…" The old man took the bait, his eyes wide. "…The wedding of my own Ishbel."

Andy went on, inspired. "Mhairi, the wife of Achnacon was there, and wee Shona, and Achnacon himself, and Larachmor, and all the people from the glen. Sam and Shawnee were there too. Everyone had gathered tae see the wedding."

"And the sons of Achnacon, Donald and Chames, were themselfs home, safe from the war?"

For a moment Andy was caught off guard, but he quickly recovered. "Aye, well, there was a couple of young guys with yerself that Ah hadn't seen before."

"And yourself? Was it yourself Ishbel was about to wed?"

A mischievous shadow of doubt clouded Andy's face. "Well, now, ye cannae always tell with these things. Ah mean, ye don't get tae see yerself in these visions, ye know?"

The old Highlander looked concerned. "Did yourself see another who might have been the groom?"

Andy considered the question for a moment, then shook his head. "No. There was no one else there who might've been the groom."

Chapter Twenty

Achnacon lost no time in sharing Andy's vision with the other elders. It caused such a sensation that even the two Gaelic-speaking redcoats tore themselves away from the fire to ask if they'd appeared in the dream. The Highlanders' faith in the second-sight was so unshakeable that all who'd featured in the vision felt impregnable.

When the excitement died down Andy tried to focus Achnacon's attention on more pressing issues.

"As soon as this weather passes we'll need tae get everybody down from the shielings and concentrate them in an area we can defend."

Achnacon's spirits had moved so rapidly from one extreme to the other it seemed he had yet to re-encounter reality.

"Och, man, you trouble yourself too much with this or that detail. We shall triumph, never fear. The die is cast, whatever ourselfs may try to make of the game."

Andy sighed heavily. "Look, it doesnae work like that. We have tae make it happen. God won't be intervening on our behalf."

Achnacon's faith remained undimmed. "Och, man, I know all that. I just meant whatever yourself decides to do will surely be the right thing."

Andy grunted sourly. "Aye, right, if you say so. Look, the first thing we have tae work out is how tae get word tae all the shielings."

"As soon as young Donald is fed and rested, himself may carry the message into the hills."

Andy nodded his head. "Right, that's a start. Next we have tae figure out where we can defend ourselves against an army of redcoats. One of yer townships would be best. We'll need at least two adjacent cottages tae shelter yer people, and somewhere we can defend from all sides."

"The walls of *Meall An Fhraoich* are as stout as any in the glen. No man may approach but he is seen a long way off. If ourselfs can hold them anywhere, t'will be there."

Andy nodded. *"Meall An Fhraoich* it is then. What about muskets? How many do we have?"

"We took three-and-twenty Brown Bess from the men yourself, *Alasdair* and *Cailean* killed. 'Twould be a fitting irony if they was to be used on their own comrades."

"What about ammunition?"

"Each soldier had been issued a pouch of four-and-twenty cartridges of ball and powder. Those who stood and fought had less."

Andy nodded towards the group of redcoats. "What do we do with them if they decide tae stay? Do we trust them with weapons?"

Achnacon shrugged. "I will speak to the lefftenant when himself has rested, but perhaps 'twould be best if they chose to flee. Better to haff a sworn enemy at our front than a doubtful friend at our back."

"My sentiments exactly," murmured the soldier.

The wind was now howling around the cottage, threatening to separate the thatched roof from the walls and send it tumbling down the glen like a huge straw hat. Torrential rain battered against the building, creating puddles of muddy water where it forced an entrance. This was clearly no passing weather system, but a full-blooded Atlantic storm.

Achnacon's aged warriors laid claim to the available beds, while Longholme's men staked out their sleeping spaces around the fire, the soldiers radiating outwards like spokes on a wheel.

Achnacon decided to bring the people down from the hills immediately, before the fury of the elements did their enemy's business for them. Young Donald was sent out to spread the word to the shielings, his phillamhor still steaming from the last soaking he'd received. Achnacon and his comrades would remain at *Ceann Laragain* for now, while Andy returned to *Meall An Fhraoich* to warn the others.

The soldier was soaked to the skin long before he reached the village. At first the atmosphere inside the cottage was as chilly as it had been outside, but as soon as Andy passed on the grim news the American cold war came to an end.

"So Longholme's back, huh? I wouldn't trust that guy as far as I could spit. For all we know he's back to finish the job he started."

Andy squatted before the fire, his wet phillamhor replaced by a blanket. "Achnacon seems tae be taking him at his word. And, ye know, if Ah was trying tae catch somebody by surprise Ah'd want tae put them at their ease, make them complacent..."

"The last thing you would do is put them on their guard," said Alistair.

"Exactly. We may have tae take what Longholme said as genuine."

The soldiers' eyes met then, only briefly, but long enough for each to see the dark apprehension in the other. Two men separated by sixty years of technological achievement, and united by sixty years of human failure. Both looked to the Americans, as condemned men would look to those who are offered a reprieve.

Shawnee instantly understood. She shook her head determinedly. "Forget it, fellas. This is as much my fight now as it is anybody's."

Sam groaned like a long-suffering martyr. "For Godsakes, lady, can y'not even give an inch? Come tomorrow this place is gonna be like the Alamo. We should get the hell outta here while we can. Maybe lie low somewhere till it all dies down."

She drew herself up to her full height, like a diminutive gunfighter. "If you think for one moment I'm gonna turn my back on these people, then you don't know me. You've made it clear this isn't your fight, so nobody's asking you to stay."

"Dammit, Shawnee, you are way outta line," Sam growled, "I was thinking about you; getting you the hell outta here till it's over."

"It's something tae consider," Andy said quietly. "Alistair and I are pretty much the only hope these people have, so we have no choice. But you two could get away if ye leave now."

The outrage melted from Shawnee's face, giving way to a pale smile. "Where are we gonna be safer, guys? Here, with all you big strong men to protect us, or out there? Think about it, for Godsakes. Where are we gonna go? Apart from anything else, have y'any idea what rain like that can do to a girl's hair?"

"Shawnee, for the love of God, y'don't have to be a rocket scientist to work it out..."

"...I've done the math, Sam, same as you have," she said sharply. "I know what we're up against."

Sam groaned wearily. He had spent a long, hard day playing push and shove with Shawnee and had little energy left to pursue the point.

As soon as Macmillan had dried off and found another plaid, Sam insisted the two soldiers give him a crash course on their respective weapons. Alistair was introduced to the S.L.R., while the American quickly learnt how to strip and assemble both rifles. Ammunition was too precious for the loading and firing drill to culminate in anything more than the hollow click of a firing pin on an empty chamber.

"How many buildings do we have here at *Meall An Fhraoich*?" Andy wanted to know.

"There's the main house here," replied Alistair, "then there's three other sizeable cottages, as well the wee house where yourself was wenching yon lassie. Then there's two other buildings; a wee storehouse kind of affair, and a wee barn where they keep their hay…"

"Seven in total," Andy reflected. "Right, we need tae choose the one that'll give us the best all round field of fire."

Shawnee had found a coarse brush and had begun to remove the tangled knots from her hair. She seemed to have lost all interest in the proceedings.

"The wee storehouse would be best," Alistair decided. "It's on the fringe of the settlement, and would present a smaller target than most of the other buildings. We'll need to create a few more windows in the walls, though, to give ourselves a complete field of fire."

"Aye, we cannae leave any blind spots," said Andy.

"We're gonna need at least two windows in each of the walls to give us all-round visibility."

"That's gonnae take us a while. We'll need tae get working on it as soon as the rain goes over."

"Why don't y'just take off the roof?" asked Shawnee. "Then y'got three hundred and sixty degrees visibility, and y'still got the walls for protection."

The three men looked at each other, sheepish grins spreading across their faces.

"Or we could always take off the roof," murmured Andy.

Shawnee dragged the brush through the tangled mess of her hair. "Like I say, so long as I got you big strong men to protect me what've I got to worry about?"

By mid-afternoon the people of the glen had begun to make their way down once again from the high shielings. Under the ceaseless rain they looked like survivors of a shipwreck. Soon huge peat fires glowed in the five cottages of *Meall An Fhraoich,* sending equal amounts of smoke and steam into the howling skies.

Some thirty of the clansfolk crowded into the cottage occupied by the newcomers, where they huddled around the fire like penguins on an ice floe. Neither Ishbel nor Mary was amongst them. Food and warmth did little to raise their spirits, and it was hard to believe these were the same people who had filled the night of the wake with such fire and passion, hurling the wild joy of their culture into the surrounding darkness.

Two hours after sunset Achnacon appeared in the cottage, his limbs red with cold. Like the last survivor plucked from the sea he was ushered to the fire and given newly dried clothes. Andy waited until the old clansman had been warmed and fed before approaching him.

"Everyone make it safely down from the shielings?"

Achnacon nodded. "At least we may be assured our enemy will keep to his dry barracks so long as ourselfs remain in the bosom of the storm."

"What about Longholme and the others?"

A worried frown creased the old man's face. "The good chentleman and his men remain at *Ceann Laragain* in the care of Larachmor and two others. He has swore to help us defend ourselfs against the soldiers. All of his men have elected to stand with him."

"Ah don't trust him," Andy said bluntly. "What kindae man can order a massacre one week, then offer tae defend the same people the next?"

To Andy's surprise the old Highlander nodded in agreement.

"Who can say what lies in the soul of a man such as he? However, the two Raasay men declare the lefftenant to be a changed man since the day he blighted Glen Laragain. On more than one occasion he has spoke of a book given to himself that day."

"A book?"

"An almanac," said Achnacon, his voice dropping to a whisper. "An almanac of things yet to be, that he holds close to himself as if it was the Holy Scriptures. It is said the book was give to himself by a beautiful lady from the Americas."

"Shawnee's book," Andy recalled.

The old Highlander searched out the eyes of his friend. "The Lady Shawnee has spoke to yourself of this book?"

Andy chose his words carefully. "Rhona, the daughter of your cousin, Inverlaragain, told me that Longholme halted the attack on Glen Laragain after Shawnee showed him the book."

"Whatever could this book contain?" Achnacon whispered in awe. "Is herself an enchantress, come to us in our time of need?"

"Aye, she's a wee enchantress, right enough," said Andy, smiling. From the far side of the room Shawnee caught the soldier's eye and lifted her eyebrows enquiringly. Andy responded with a reassuring smile, letting her know all was well with Achnacon.

"Ah'll tell ye something else too," he told the Highlander, "Ah'm glad she's on our side."

Andy lay awake listening to the rain drumming against the walls of the cottage. The peat fire flared into life whenever a gust of wind found its way under the door. Sam and Shawnee's periodic whispers had given way to deep, regular breathing. The refugees from the shielings were also stealing what rest they could. Even Alistair seemed to have fallen into a peaceful sleep.

He sensed the presence, even before he saw the lithe shape emerge from the shadows. At first he thought he was dreaming, but when he felt the little hand cover his mouth, and heard the voice whispering; "…ssshhh, not to speak, Auntie," he realised Ishbel had come to him like a ghost in the night.

Silently she slipped into bed beside him, burrowing under his left arm until her shape moulded perfectly with his. Andy stared into the darkness above his head, hardly daring to breathe. If she was conscious of the frantic hammering in his chest, or the rigor mortis that had gripped his body, she didn't show it. She seemed to be wearing no more than a long nightshirt, and her body was trembling with the cold. He held her close with his left arm, feeling the soft promise of her female form, waiting for her to take the initiative. She seemed content merely to lie beside him, however, and gradually Andy realised she had come simply to lie with him and share the warmth of his body.

He couldn't tell how long they lay together like this, no words passing between them. It was the most sensuous experience of his life. At some point he must have fallen asleep, for in the early flush of dawn he turned with a start to find he was on his own again.

Alistair was murmuring in one corner, his ramblings finding a response at the far end of the cottage as some young lassie moaned in her sleep. Andy closed his eyes, trying to recall the soft rhythm of Ishbel's breath against his chest.

Outside the wind howled around the cottage, warning those, who had ears to listen, of the dark shadows of death that were gathering once more in the glen.

§

The storm raged all that night and into the following day. After breakfast Achnacon held a council of war. He agreed the little storehouse would make a strong defensive position, and laughed when he learned it was Shawnee's idea to remove the roof. He also proposed to turn one of the adjoining cottages into a second strongpoint, both connected to the other buildings by a series of protective walls, so that anybody could move from one to another in relative safety.

Long before the storm had blown itself out Achnacon had set his clansfolk to work, fortifying the cottages where the people were to shelter, linking the buildings to each other by walled passageways. He had every wall and enclosure within a half-mile radius levelled to the ground to ensure the soldiers would have no cover when they took up their positions around *Meall An Fhraoich*.

His own family was made to labour as hard as any. Andy worked his way over to where Ishbel was laying stones for one of the walls. Her clothes were wet, her face and hair streaked with grime, but she still managed to look pert and attractive. If he had any suspicions that the night's tryst had been only a dream, they were soon dispelled by her conspiratorial smile. Achnacon pretended not to notice the furtive kisses and caresses that passed between his daughter and his friend. Eventually, however, his wife was sent over to find other work for Ishbel.

It was late afternoon before the racing clouds began to withdraw up the hillsides, and the rain finally eased off. By now the settlement looked more like a military fort than a country hamlet. The five cottages and the little storehouse had all been linked to each other by passageways worthy of an Orcadian tomb. The stones of the burnt-out cottage had also been incorporated into the fortifications, leaving only a rectangular scorch mark where the house had stood.

When the rain had finally stopped, the two soldiers accompanied Sam and Shawnee on a tour of the fortress. They made their way to a point east of *Meall An Fhraoich*, where it was expected their enemy would position his cannon.

"Everything we see here will be severely tested by the iron shot of those coehorn mortars," said Alistair.

Andy turned to the Americans. "It's still no' too late for you guys. The pair o' yez could be long gone before tomorrow."

Sam looked to Shawnee, who'd been gazing eastwards, to where the scarlet column would approach. She turned and smiled teasingly at Andy.

"And miss the society event of the year? Achnacon told us about your latest vision. He was quite definite about who was gonna be dancing at this wedding of yours, and what would he think if Sam and me weren't even gonna be here?"

The soldier grimaced. "It was the only way Ah could think of tae give him a wee bit o' hope."

Shawnee looked at the little citadel that a hundred pairs of hands had toiled over. "Yeah, well, one way and another, I reckon you've sure done that, Andy. But whaddya think our hightailing it outta here would do to that little bit of hope you've given them?"

Sam managed a phlegmatic shrug of the shoulders as Shawnee began to lead him back towards the fortified settlement.

Now that the rain had passed Achnacon turned his attention to the storehouse. The supplies were transferred to a nearby cottage, and the weighted ropes that helped to secure the roof removed. As the thatch was lifted from the timber framework the building was instantly transformed into a skeletal ruin. A buzz of excitement and apprehension swept through the onlookers. To see one of their buildings being de-roofed brought home to them the seriousness of the situation as nothing else could. It was as if the cover had been removed from the first of the Titanic's lifeboats.

As darkness began to descend the thatch was also removed from the cottage diagonally opposite the storehouse. In the gathering gloom the flickering light of fires began to appear through the windows and open doors of the remaining cottages. The clansfolk drifted away to eat and rest, but for Achnacon there would be no rest yet. With Andy and Alistair in tow he anxiously examined every angle of the sprawling fortress, searching in the last shreds of daylight for some weakness in their defences. Even when it was apparent they had done all they could, he continued to fret over the connecting walls, removing stones and replacing them again. Ultimately he took to staring out into the darkness.

" 'Tis times like this," he remarked at last, "that a man looks for something he can bargain with. Something that will merit the Lord's favour over his enemy."

"Ah suppose the Lord helps them that help themselves," murmured Andy.

"Aye, chust so," murmured the old Highlander. "And yourself, Alasdair Mhor? Is it your practice to look on high for assistance on the eve of battle?"

Alistair's expression was invisible in the gathering twilight. "I have never known a field of battle where the believer was favoured over the heathen, or the Christian over the Muslim. So I think, myself, it makes little difference either way. We all walk in darkness. Why look for light where none exists?"

Andy expected Achnacon to recoil in horror, to search for faggots to pile at the heretic's feet, but the old Highlander looked at Alistair with pained concern.

" 'Tis a terrible thing, *Alasdair Mhor*, for a man to lose his faith. Whatever could have made yourself feel so alone you would prefer to walk in such darkness?"

Achnacon laid a fatherly arm on his young kinsman and began to lead him back to the main cottage of *Meall An Fhraoich*, with Andy quietly taking up the rear. Around them the smell of cooking and the occasional burst of laughter was already beginning to fill the evening.

Long after everyone else had fallen asleep, Andy lay awake, his ears straining for that soft rustle that would tell him Ishbel had returned. He felt like a child on Christmas Eve, waiting for that illicit sight of white beard and red coat... an ironic combination under the circumstances.

His mind had drifted away, exploring the contrasting associations of this image, when he felt a gentle rush of air. Moments later Ishbel was stealing into bed beside him, nestling under his left arm. As she drew warmth from him, he felt he'd re-entered a familiar dream world.

Even before she'd fully warmed herself, it became obvious that this night she would not be content merely to lie beside him. He could feel her soft hands gently tracing his upper torso, his arms and neck, exploring the fearful wonder of his body. Andy was desperate to reciprocate, to discover the secret places of this lovely woman, but he knew she was exploring more than just the shape of her lover to be.

Unfortunately he'd become aware that something else was different this night, something that was also beyond his control. He could feel the little warrior stirring in his loins, dutifully rising to attention, until ultimately Andy felt as if three individuals were sharing the bed.

She had now drawn his face towards her own, exploring his mouth with hers. To Andy it was torture, made worse now that he could feel the stirrings of excitement in Ishbel's body. He wondered if she wanted him to take the initiative. Perhaps it would be the only opportunity they would ever have… After all, Sam and Shawnee…

She let out a little moan and pulled away, as though recoiling from a precipice. He felt an impending sense of loss as she disentangled her body from his. He knew she was preparing to rush back to her own bed. At the last moment she stretched over for one final kiss, and as she did so he felt the gossamer touch of her fingers as her hand stole down to his groin and briefly stroked that eager little warrior, assuring Andy she'd known he was there all along. Then she was gone, like a spirit in the night, barely opening the door as she ghosted out of the cottage.

Andy's bed remained inhabited by two occupants long after Ishbel had returned to her own bed.

Chapter Twenty-One

Shortly after dawn a cold draught swept through the cottage. Andy peered expectantly into the shadows, but it wasn't Ishbel he saw, framed against the pale glow of morning, but the elegant silhouette of Mary. She'd been tiptoeing out of the cottage when a gust of wind had blown through the opened door. Andy realised she must have come to Alistair in the dead of night, as Ishbel had come to him. He lay awake for some time, wondering if the gentle Mary had been able to apply any balm to Alistair's soul.

It seemed he'd only closed his eyes again for a moment, when he awoke to find pandemonium breaking out around him. People were crowding into the cottage, some carrying children, others bundles of possessions. In the distance he could hear Achnacon yelling in Gaelic. Alistair was at the cottage door, rifle in hand.

"Andy, are you awake, man? They're on their way!"

These words were like a shot of adrenalin to his heart.

"How far away? Which direction?" Andy's hands trembled as he pulled on his boots.

"From both east and west, just as Longholme predicted. Achnacon's young laddie has just arrived from Inverlaragain. One column was spotted half a mile to the east. Longholme and the others arrived from Kinlaragain five minutes ago. They report a second column three miles west of the graveyard."

Andy's mind worked feverishly: "One lot's gonnae reach us long before the other. They must've tried tae coordinate their movements, but instead they're gonnae arrive piecemeal."

Alistair shook his head. "They won't know we're planning to make a stand here. More likely the eastern column intends to drive ourselves westwards, like a herd of deer, into their trap."

"Aye, that makes more sense, right enough," Andy had to admit.

By the time he'd pulled on his webbing and checked his rifle, the furore had begun to die down. As many as sixty women and children had crowded into the cottage. Some Andy recognised; others were unfamiliar to him. He joined Alistair outside, to find the day bright and clear.

The other non-combatants had already been moved into an adjoining cottage. The only people now braving the open air were old men and striplings… and Longholme's redcoats. Like outcasts they stood at the western perimeter of the clachan, their heads and shoulders showing above one of the walls. Andy wondered if the sight of these uniforms had helped spark the commotion, the way the scent of a lion would panic a herd of gazelle.

Near one of the cottages he could see Achnacon handing out muskets and ammunition pouches to young and old alike. Some of the *bodachs* turned the weapons over in their hands, their eyes wide with interest. Two of the youths were lunging at each other, expending nervous energy in a macabre game. A shout from Achnacon put a stop to the fun.

There was no sign of Shawnee and Sam. Andy had seen neither of them since the previous evening.

The two soldiers made their way over to Achnacon. The Highlander was dressed for battle in a blue phillamhor, his bonnet topped with an eagle's feather, as befitted his rank. The handles of broadsword and dirk projected from his waistband.

"Well, my young friends," he declared heartily, "what better morning to give our Hanoverian neighbours a true Highland welcome."

Andy found his enthusiasm a little disconcerting. "Ah see that none of Longholme's men decided tae leave."

Achnacon nodded. "Himself has told Larachmor they have elected to fight beside us this day and will deem it a great insult if they are not treated as any other man here."

Aware that he had become the topic of conversation, Longholme made his way over. He looked pale and tired, his scar less vivid than usual. He bowed stiffly before Achnacon.

"You have made good use of the time you were given, sir. Nonetheless you will need every musket at your disposal. You must arm my men and I at once." Longholme saw the uncertainty in the clansman. "By my honour, sir, Captain Scott seeks the destruction of my men and I as much as he seeks the destruction of your people. If we must die this day then at least let us die as soldiers."

To the east, they could hear the distant tap of a drum; the slow, regular beat that accompanied men on the march. Larachmor came running along an adjoining passageway. He was dressed much the same as Achnacon, the sun glinting off a pair of claw-handled pistols in his waistband. He spoke excitedly to his friend, nodding as he did at Longholme. The two old comrades embraced each other, before Larachmor ran on towards the sound of the drumbeat. Alistair followed behind, eager to catch a glimpse of what they were about to face.

Achnacon turned to the English officer. "Trust does not come easy to one such as himself. But he has spoke at length to your two Gaels, and is certain no deception has been hatched against us."

"Have I not already given my word to this very effect?" Longholme replied sharply. "In the name of God, sir, my men and I could have left you to your fate. Instead, as men of honour we chose to share your fate rather than seek our own safety."

"But why, sir?" Achnacon at last put voice to his worries. " 'Tis a worm that eats at my brain. I can make no sense of it whatever; that... that a chentleman like yourself would give his life for a people he considered savages."

"Yeah, that's what I'd like to know as well," a female voice added.

Longholme spun round to find the American couple standing behind him. Shawnee was dressed in a red tartan shawl and the same calf-length skirt she'd worn on the day of the funerals. Wisps of straw clung like confetti to her hair. Her companion was also dressed in Highland garb, although the tone of his skin set him apart from the natives.

"I see you have recovered well from your injuries, sir," the officer observed.

"No thanks to you, fella."

"So, why didn't y'leave when y'had the chance?" Shawnee asked pointedly.

The officer reached inside his uniform and took out an object bound in a leather pouch. "I wished to reunite a lady with her property."

Shawnee's eyebrows rose sharply as she remembered the book she'd left at Inverlaragain. Without a word she accepted the offering.

"I have also come to reunite a gentleman with his conscience," added Longholme, his eyes on the dishevelled beauty before him. " 'Tis not every man is so fortunate as to learn what posterity thinks of him. Those were your words, as I recall."

"I hate to break up this reunion," Sam put in, "but we got people coming today, remember?"

In the distance they could hear the noise of wheels grinding over the rough path. Without wasting any more time the old Highlander handed the officer a musket and ammunition pouch.

"And my men?" Longholme asked.

Achnacon nodded sharply. "By your honour, sir," he reminded him.

Andy felt distinctly uneasy as he watched the redcoats being re-armed. The brutish-looking soldier was the last to come forward. He grabbed the weapon like a Neanderthal reclaiming his club. Andy and Sam were both aware of the sly interest he took in Shawnee. She also became conscious of the attention she was attracting, and instinctively pulled her shawl tightly around her.

All were glad to see Longholme lead his troops away. The officer had marked out the roofless cottage as the main defensive strongpoint and lost no time in positioning his men there. The sound of their approaching enemy was growing louder.

Achnacon turned to his young warriors. "Well, chentlemen, the time has come to choin our comrades."

Sam turned to Shawnee. "I gotta go with the resta the guys now. You get yourself into one of those cottages and keep your head down 'til it's over, and don't worry about me, I'll be fine." He leaned over to kiss her and recoiled as he saw a familiar glint in her eye. "No," he said firmly. "Definitely, absolutely not."

Sam watched the glint turn to steel. "Aw for God's sake, Shawnee, what are y'trying to do to me? Why d'y'have to act like G.I. Jane all the time? Huh? I mean, y'don't see Ishbel out here with Andy, do yuh? And why d'y'think that is? Because she's with the other women taking shelter, that's why!"

"Ach, man, if only this was so." Achnacon looked accusingly at Macmillan. "I have done the best a father can do, but young Andy failed to heed the warnings he wass give. Now she thinks herself equal to her chosen man, and will not be bid in any matter whatever. Even now she waits for himself by the storehouse, determined to stand beside him, as she did before."

Andy's sympathetic grin vanished. "What? Ye've let Ishbel out there, with those animals about tae descend on us?"

A look of righteous indignation came over the Highlander. " 'Tis not my doing. I had expected the young man she chose for herself would tame her spirit, but 'tis plain I was mistaken."

"Now d'yuh see what you've done?" Sam growled at Shawnee, as Andy stormed off.

The storehouse lay fifty yards from the cottage occupied by Longholme and Larachmor. Inside the roofless building Ishbel was sitting on a flat stone that projected from the wall. She was dressed similarly to Shawnee, her face bright and expectant, her hair as beautifully preened as if her courtship was about to resume. She rose to her feet as the soldier approached, an anxious smile on her face. Immediately Andy's anger evaporated. He held her tightly against him, aware her trembling now had nothing to do with the cold.

"What are you doing here?" he whispered.

"*Ishbeal agus Auntie*," she told him. "*Ishbeal agus Auntie gu brath.*"

He didn't need an interpreter to know what she was saying.

"Give it up, buddy, this is one fight we can't win," grumbled Sam.

Shawnee, meanwhile, had found a toehold in the wall and gazed excitedly over the top as the first red uniforms appeared on the horizon. As she watched, a long column of men, marching two abreast, came into view. Behind them rumbled two horse-drawn wagons. The front ranks halted six hundred yards away and formed into an extended line. Soon a mass of red uniforms stretched across the breadth of the glen, the morning sun reflecting off the polished steel of their bayonets.

The drumbeat had now become more insistent.

"I didn't think there'd be so many of them," breathed Shawnee.

" 'Tis their scarlet coats," Achnacon explained. "They mislead a man into thinking he faces an enemy greater than he truly is. Every clansman knows to select one man in the line, and to look upon him alone as his mortal enemy."

"Like the little guy with the drum?" said Sam. "Say, Andy, d'you reckon y'could put one into the little son of a bitch from here?"

Andy realised he and Ishbel were still clinging to each other. "Aye, if nothing else it'll let them know tae keep their distance."

He loaded and cocked the S.L.R., and rested the barrel on the wall. His hands shook as he searched out that frenetic little figure. At this range he decided not to risk ammunition on such a small target, and instead shifted his sights to a nearby line of soldiers.

Suddenly he could hear Alistair's voice: "Andy, no! Hold your fire!"

He looked up to see the young Highlander rushing along the passageway that separated the two strongpoints.

"Don't fire on them yet... whatever you do!"

"D'ye wantae shout a wee bit louder," Andy said dryly, "just in case any o' the redcoats didnae hear ye?"

Alistair waited a few moments until he'd caught his breath. "At this range, if they discover what's waiting here for them, they'll stay where they are and not risk an advance..."

Andy closed his eyes. "Aw Jeezus, Macmillan, waken up you idiot."

"What's the problem?" asked Sam. "If you guys can take out a few of those sons of bitches at this range there'll be less to hurt us later."

"If we do that, they'll keep their distance and pound us with their cannon. We need to let them think it's safe to move their cannon closer so Andy and myself can have a clear shot at the artillerymen."

Sam scratched his head for a few moments. "Yeah, I guess that makes more sense. Hey, good thinking, fella."

Andy breathed a heavy sigh. "Thank God someone's on the ball today."

Alistair nodded. "They'll have seen our barricades. It's only a matter of time before they launch an attack."

Even as he spoke the line of troops began to move slowly forward. Behind the advancing soldiers the two wagons continued to follow the path through the glen, the iron clang of their wheels contrasting with the silent tread of the infantry. A small party of horsemen had now come into view, bringing up the rear.

"How many muskets do we have here?" Alistair wanted to know.

"The lefftenant and Larachmor have eighteen. The other five is here with ourselfs," Achnacon replied.

"I don't suppose anybody other than Achnacon knows how to load and fire a musket?"

"There's no point," said Sam. "Not while we got Andy's elephant gun."

"Yes, but if they launch an infantry attack first we can't let them know we have anything out of the ordinary here, not until Andy and myself have disabled their artillery."

"Now, hold on there just one minute, fella," Sam protested. "If you're saying what I think you're saying…"

"For God's sake, Sam, listen to the guy!" exclaimed Shawnee. "What Alistair's saying makes perfect sense to me…"

"…Goddamnit, Shawnee, you don't even know what this is all about!"

"I do too!" she yelled back. "Alistair's saying we're gonna have to fire muskets…"

"Alistair's saying we're gonna have to fire muskets? Goddamn it to hell, lady, you shouldn't even be here…"

"Ishbel was taught from an early age how to load and fire a musket," Achnacon put in. "What kind of soldiers are yourselfs, that you must take lessons from an old man, or a slip of a lassie?"

Andy treated the question as rhetorical.

"Alistair's right. We have tae use muskets, at least until they're so close nobody'll know the difference. Perhaps Ishbel could show the restae us how to load and fire, while Achnacon keeps watch."

The old Highlander nodded, and translated the message. Ishbel's eyebrows rose in surprise. She smiled coyly as she replied to her father.

"Herself will do as you ask," he told them. "In return she asks that young Andy teach herself how to load and fire *his* musket."

The line of infantry was no more than four hundred yards away now. Andy could see no movement in the other strongpoint. He wondered what they thought of the noisy chaos coming from his location.

He nodded at Ishbel. "Tell her she drives a hard bargain."

She was certainly the prettiest weapons instructor Andy had ever known. She showed them how to tear open the cartridges of powder and ball with her teeth. How to sprinkle a few grains of the black dust onto the pan, before ramming the remainder of the cartridge into the barrel of the weapon.

An experienced soldier could load and fire his musket four times a minute. After sixty seconds Andy's ramrod was jammed in the barrel, and Shawnee was still coughing up the black powder she'd inhaled after tearing open her first cartridge. Andy kept his side of the bargain, and briefly showed Ishbel how to load and fire the S.L.R. Her face lit up as she peered down the sights of the weapon.

There was no time for any more lessons. The wagons and horsemen had halted, but the infantry were no more than two hundred yards away now. While Achnacon freed the trapped ramrod, the remaining muskets were made ready. As they waited, hidden behind the wall, Andy caught Ishbel's eye and winked at her, recalling the last time they'd crouched together like this. She smiled back, her mouth smeared with black powder, her face flushed with excitement.

The soldiers were so close now that Andy could hear them talking to each other. His blood froze as he recognised the accent; they were Lowland Scots like himself. In that instant he understood yet another tragic aspect of Prince Charlie's rebellion. He also understood it could make no difference to the business in hand. He longed for Alistair or Achnacon to end this torment and give the word to open fire. Maybe they were waiting until Longholme's men fired first. He could hear N.C.O.s growling at their men:

"Close up! Keep in line there, damn yer hides!"

His hands were trembling. What the hell was going on? The soldiers were surely so close they'd be climbing over the wall any moment. His mind began to race: Longholme had no intention of turning his coat, he'd simply been waiting for the chance to spring his trap... Another five seconds and he'd let them have it with the S.L.R. The first shot would be for that devious...

Andy was deafened by the blast of eighteen muskets being fired simultaneously. An instant later Achnacon, Ishbel and Alistair leapt up and added their fire to Longholme's. Andy and Sam sat stupefied for a moment before they jumped to their feet. Andy was amazed to find the redcoats still a hundred yards away. Two men were down, the rest rooted to the spot. Sam and Andy pointed their muskets and yanked on the triggers. More noisy clouds of smoke added to the uproar.

"Freakin useless piece of crap." Sam struggled to reload the weapon. "I told you we shoulda used those rifles when we had the chance!"

Now that battle had been joined the N.C.O.s began to bellow out the drill:

"Company... present... fire! Load..."

The returning fusillade was terrifying. Some of the balls whizzed overhead, others crashed against the protective wall. Unable to help, Shawnee crouched against the wall, her hands over her ears. Andy heard a second booming volley from Longholme's position. Someone was screaming in the distance. Achnacon leapt to his feet again, braving the fusillade. The ramrod jammed again in Andy's musket. He saw

Ishbel rise to her feet, and grabbed her weapon. He thrust his own useless musket at her, then bobbed up to send his second shot at the massed ranks. Dimly Andy realised the screaming was coming from the other fortress.

Ishbel had freed the barrel of Andy's weapon by the time he'd ducked down. Once again he wrenched the loaded musket from her, and saw outrage in her eyes. Her father shouted something, and she glowered at him instead. Andy took aim at the nearest soldier and squeezed the trigger. The soldier was still there when the smoke cleared. Achnacon was now on his feet again. Sam and Alistair leapt up to join him. The three men fired together. A roar from Achnacon indicated a shot had found its target.

Suddenly Sam tumbled to the ground, clutching his face. Blood oozed through his fingers.

"Oh dear God, Sam, not you..." yelled Shawnee.

He seemed to be in shock. "I'm okay I'm not hit! The sonofabitch missed!"

She tried to stem the flow of blood. "I know, honey. Everything's gonna be all right... Aw Jesus, Sam..."

The redcoat fire was incessant now. Lead balls peppered the walls of the cottage or whispered viciously overhead. From Longholme's position regular volleys thundered in reply. The screaming from over there had stopped. Alistair, Achnacon and Andy did their best to maintain a running fire on the troops facing them. All the while Ishbel scowled at her father as she loaded the muskets.

Sam pulled himself free of Shawnee and struggled to his feet. She rose with him, her face smeared with blood and tears. Sam took his hand away from his face. The blood was seeping from a number of lacerations in his left cheek.

"...Trying to tell yuh! Just splinters. Freakin bullet hit the top of the wall!"

Shawnee threw a couple of wild punches at Sam, and then buried her face in his chest.

"You idiot! You scared the hell outta me..."

Alistair pointed at the soldiers facing Longholme's cottage. "Look! Some of them are pulling back! We have them on the run!"

Everyone peered over the barricade. Redcoats were withdrawing from Longholme's sector. But far from retreating they were moving to their left, reinforcing the troops in front of Achnacon's position.

"Oh hell," said Alistair, the first time anyone had heard him swear.

"They are concentrating themselfs here, at our weakest point," Achnacon realised. He hurried to help his daughter load the muskets. "I fear we are about to be stormed. Those in front will occupy ourselfs while others turn our flank. We must alert Larachmor."

"I'll go!" yelled Shawnee. "I'm doing nothing here!"

Before anyone could stop her she was off, head bobbing precariously up and down above the wall as she ran towards the other fortress.

The red-coated soldiers were on the move again. A large group advanced towards the storehouse, while others peeled away to their right. Achnacon made everybody wait until the enemy was less than fifty yards away, before allowing them to open fire. Smoke and flame roared from five barrels, instantly dropping two men and drawing a return fire from the others. N.C.O.s bellowed at their men. In the confusion some stopped to reload, others advanced, bayonets at the ready.

Andy left the reloading of the muskets to the others. He picked up his rifle and pulled it into his shoulder. It had the feel of a prosthetic limb being reattached to his body. His trembling had now vanished. He felt calm and detached, as if something artificial had taken over from his sense of self. The ferocious crack of the first 7.62mm round lifted the nearest redcoat off his feet. Before he'd hit the ground Andy's second shot had felled his comrade. The van of the attack was so close now he could hardly miss. Again and again the rifle butt recoiled savagely against his shoulder as high-velocity bullets smashed into anything in red. N.C.O.s screamed at their men, apparently incensed that so many were dropping. Andy searched them out. One grotesquely large individual seemed to explode as the bullet impacted his breastbone.

Suddenly the fury of the charge was spent. The survivors began pulling back, like waves receding from a cliff. Through his rifle sights Andy swept the area. At last he lowered the weapon and turned his back on the carnage, unable to face what he'd done.

To his amazement he was completely alone. Achnacon, Ishbel, Alistair and Sam had all disappeared. He was still trying to fathom this out when he found himself sitting on the ground, his rifle lying three feet away. He tried to retrieve the weapon, but for some reason he had no control over his right arm. It was only when he saw the blood seeping through his phillamhor that he realised he'd been shot.

He felt adrenalin surge through his veins, followed by a wave of panic.

"Easy easy easy easy…. Remember yer training. Don't panic… Don't let yerself go intae shock… easy now, easy…"

Where were the others? Oh God, maybe they'd all legged it and left him here on his own. He could feel no pain, just a heavy, numb sensation on the right side of his chest. What is it they say? You don't feel the bad ones, not the really bad ones. He felt another surge of panic. He didn't want to die here, not like this, not on his own…

People were running along the passageway, approaching from behind. In an instant they were past him and away.

Someone else was approaching.

"Hey! Gonnae help here?"

He heard a muffled scream, then two small arms were flung around his neck. He recognised Shawnee's tiny hands, even before he heard her voice.

"Oh God, Andy no, don't do this to us…"

"Sorry about this," he mumbled.

Shawnee did her best to take control of the situation. "Oh God, Andy, don't try to talk, just lie back… Everything's gonna be okay"

Gently she helped lower him to the ground. For the first time her face came into view. Andy felt curiously gratified to see fresh tears flowing down her cheeks.

"Where does it hurt, Andy? Tell me where it hurts."

Now that he was no longer on his own he felt strangely light headed.

"Doesnae hurt," he heard himself say. "Right chest feels funny, but."

She pulled back his blood-soaked phillamhor. Whatever she saw drew a sharp intake of breath from her.

"You're gonna be fine, Andy, you're gonna be just fine… but listen now, I gotta get some help. You lie still, I'll be back before y'know it."

"No!" He grabbed hold of her arm. "Don't leave me alone, please…"

Shawnee knelt beside him and applied pressure to his chest, where the blood was welling up into his plaid.

"Okay Andy I'm not going anywhere. You just lie still now, the others'll be back in a minute."

He tried to thank her, but it was becoming harder to talk. He just wanted to lie here and rest for a wee while. His chest was beginning to hurt now. He couldn't remember if that was a good or a bad sign. He'd think about it later. Perhaps if he just closed his eyes for a few seconds…

"Don't you go to sleep on me!" Shawnee yelled. "Y'hear me now? You stay awake, somebody'll be along soon."

She made him sit up, then knelt behind him to support his weight. It was only then she discovered that Andy was bleeding from his back as well as his chest.

"Oh God, where is everybody?" For the first time the situation began to get the better of her. "Hey! We need help here! Sam! Alistair! Heeeelp!"

She could feel Andy sagging heavily against her.

"You stay awake, soldier. D'y'hear me? Don't you die on me, Andy Macmillan. We can't do this without you. Please, Andy, don't do this to me…"

But she knew by the way he'd slumped against her he was no longer listening.

Chapter Twenty-Two

It was the sheer ferocity of the pain that dragged Andy back to consciousness. He felt as if molten lead was being poured over his chest. He was held in a sitting position between Alistair and Mary. Alistair had one of Larachmor's whisky jugs in his hand.

"I'm sorry, I had to cauterize your wound."

Andy tried to stand up, but was held firmly in place by Mary. She spoke softly to Alistair as she wound a long strip of cloth around Andy's chest.

"She says you must sit still until she has bandaged the wound, otherwise the bleeding will start again."

Andy tried to concentrate on Mary's face to take his mind off the pain. Under his stare a faint flush rose into her cheeks. The fiery heat of the whisky was giving way to a relentless ache in the right side of his body as though he'd been trampled in a stampede.

"You were very fortunate," Alistair went on. "The ball passed clean through. I'm sorry ourselves weren't here. The redcoats were probing our flank. They got into one of the empty cottages, but Longholme's men arrived in time. Anyway, you didn't seem to need help."

At last Mary finished bandaging her patient.

"As soon as one of the men comes back we'll lift you out of here. We're using one of the buildings as a field hospital."

"No!" Andy gritted his teeth against the pain of talking. "Ah'm staying!"

Alistair nodded. He spoke briefly to Mary, and together they manoeuvred him against the back wall. His rifle lay where it had fallen, in a little tarn of blood.

Alistair offered him the whisky jug. "Here, it will help the pain."

Andy took a quick gulp of the raw spirit, coughed painfully a few times then took another swallow.

"The others okay?" he whispered hoarsely.

"We've lost three of Longholme's men. One was shot like yourself, but wasn't as fortunate. Another lost his head completely, poor wee laddie. The third ran off as soon as the shooting started. Two of Achnacon's young laddies have musket balls in their limbs."

"How about our guys?"

"Och everyone's fine, apart from yourself. There's a wee bit of a lull just now, so Sam and Shawnee are away getting his wound dressed. It was Shawnee who called Mary and myself. I don't think Achnacon and Ishbel know about yourself yet."

By now the shooting had died away completely. Alistair peered over the top of the wall.

"They've pulled themselves back about four hundred yards. They must have lost a quarter of their men in that attack, so I don't think they'll try any more frontal assaults. I can see a lot of activity around the wagons. They must be starting to unload their cannon." He looked worriedly at Andy. "I'd hoped they would move their cannon a lot closer first."

"Sorry about that," grunted Andy.

Alistair shrugged. He caught sight of Sam and Shawnee scampering along the passageway towards them.

Shawnee made straight for Andy and took hold of his hand. "I stayed with you like y'said, right up until they told me you were gonna be all right."

A pale smile appeared on the soldier's face. "Thanks for everything, pet."

"I didn't do anything."

"Aye ye did," murmured Andy.

Sam grinned sardonically at the soldier, his own wounds now cleaned and dressed. "Way to hide what y'got, huh? I guess this kinda blows it for Plan A."

"Help me tae the wall," Andy grunted. "Ah can still hit them at four hundred yards."

"You're not going anywhere," Shawnee said emphatically. Mary, too, moved to restrain him.

"We need tae stop their cannon," the soldier growled.

"You couldn't stand on your feet, far less aim a rifle," Alistair told him.

Sam picked up Andy's rifle and began to wipe it clean of blood. "Guess that training session's gonna come in useful after all…"

Alistair had continued to observe their distant enemy. "They're up to something," he said quietly.

Sam joined him at the wall. "What are y'seeing?"

Alistair pointed out a knot of blue-uniformed men to the right of the main body.

"They've lit a fire in that large metal thing. Do you see it? It's like a brazier."

"Maybe they're having a cup of tea…"

Alistair grunted sourly. "I don't like the idea of ourselves just sitting here, waiting for them to take the initiative."

"Did you say a brazier?" Andy hissed. He forced himself to his feet, and reached the wall before his legs buckled. Alistair and Sam caught him as he crumpled to the ground.

As the two men hauled him upright a plume of white smoke belched from the redcoat lines. Something like a fiery meteorite rose out of the smoke and arced towards *Meall An Fhraoich*. Moments later the object crashed to the ground a hundred yards away.

"What the hell…?"

"Cannon," Andy grunted painfully. "Braziers heat the cannon balls."

Moments later a second missile followed. This one landed twenty yards short of the roofless storehouse. A third projectile overshot Longholme's stronghold and crashed through the roof of an empty cottage. The thatch collapsed into the building, sending a shower of sparks through the window and doorway. Smoke billowed from the shattered remains.

Another cloud of smoke erupted from the Hanoverian lines. The red-hot cannonball smashed into one of the passageway walls, sending debris flying in all directions. Shawnee and Mary clung to each other, as if sheltering from an air raid. The two riflemen hurried to make ready their weapons.

"Who'n hell are we supposed to be shooting at?" Sam yelled.

"Guys in blue," Andy grunted. "Gunners…"

Alistair waited until the American had settled himself behind the sights of Andy's rifle, before giving the word. The two weapons fired together. Alistair stepped back to reload, while Sam blasted off a further six shots.

"Hell, Andy, y'got some recoil here. Freakin thing could bring down a T. Rex!"

"Did ye hit anythin'?"

"How 'n hell should I know? Too busy trying to keep the son of a bitch under control!"

Andy groaned. "This isnae Vietnam… cannae just blast away… gottae fire single shots…"

Another cannonball appeared out of a plume of smoke. The missile ricocheted off a huge rock embedded in one of the walls, before sailing spectacularly over the village.

Alistair was now firing as though he were on a practice range. Almost every shot found a target. Andy watched in horrified wonder as one distant figure after another crumpled in a heap.

Sam lined up the rifle once more, aligning his sights on a group of blue-uniformed shapes to the left of the brazier. He settled his breathing and squeezed the trigger. Instantly one of the shapes was flung backwards.

"Got one! Lime-sucking sons of bitches…"

"Again," growled Andy, " 'fore they scatter."

The gunners, however, were made of sterner stuff than the infantry and doggedly stood their ground as death cracked and whistled around them. Only after they'd lost half their number were they finally driven back, hauling two sleds behind them.

A stunning silence descended on the glen, broken by Sam's version of a rebel yell.

"Y'can take that as a declaration of independence, you sons of bitches!"

Cautiously the two women rose to their feet.

"Is that it?" Shawnee asked. "Is it over?"

"It's over for now," said Alistair, wiping the sweat from his forehead, "but they won't give up that easily. There's too much at stake here now."

Now that the danger had passed Andy began to lose his grip on the wall. The others grabbed him as he fell, blood seeping from his chest and back.

Mary gave him a sharp lecture as she adjusted his dressings. Achnacon appeared in the middle of her tirade. His weary smile vanished as soon as he saw Andy. He rushed to his side, anxiously addressing him in Gaelic. Mary's reply seemed to reassure the old man. At last the English came back to him.

"It pains myself that you have been brought to this. But Mary hass said you have been touched by fortune. Your wounds will heal, if yourself is sensible of them."

Andy had no time for such minor issues. "Where's Ishbel?"

Achnacon shook his head despairingly. "Och, Ishbel is fine. I bid her stay with yourself when we rushed to guard the flank, but 'twas a waste of breath. She was most displeased you would not allow her to stand with yourself, and even now sits in high dudgeon watching to the west."

Even in his pain Andy smiled at Ishbel's spirit.

Achnacon lost no time in turning to other matters. He eyed the two rifles with sharp interest. "With such a musket a man need never live in fear again. 'Tis truly wondrous weapons yourselfs have brought to Glen Laragain."

To Andy's dismay Sam handed the rifle to the old clansman. Achnacon examined the strange shape of the gun, his eyes bright with wonder. He asked the same question he'd put to Muirshearlach:

"And how might a man insert a ball into such a fine barrel?"

Sam unclipped the magazine and showed him the uppermost bullet.

"These little babies do the same job as ball and powder, except y'feed 'em into the bottom of the rifle... right here."

Andy drifted off into unconsciousness, missing the rest of Sam's training session. When he awoke again his head was cradled in Ishbel's lap. She was stroking his hair, humming a plaintive melody over him. His chest hurt like hell, and his mouth was sour with the taste of blood.

"Hi," he smiled up at her, "how's it goin'?"

Ishbel's beautifully groomed hair had been reduced to an untidy mess, concealing her face from Andy's view. Her only reply was a snuffling sound.

"As y'can see your girl got the news," said Sam. "How y'doing? Y'musta been out for nearly a half hour."

"No' bad... only hurts when Ah breathe."

Andy could see Alistair and Mary standing with the two Americans at the rampart. From somewhere in the background came the murmured voices of Achnacon and Longholme. They seemed to be convening a council of war.

"What's happening? Any more attacks?"

Alistair looked worriedly to the east. "Everything's been quiet since they pulled their cannon back. But a lot of their infantry have been withdrawn out of sight. Whatever they're up to they're taking great pains to conceal it from ourselves."

Ishbel swept her hair back and gently kissed Andy on the mouth. He smiled wanly at her, and with his left hand tapped his heart and drew a little circle in the air. She replied with a watery smile that dissolved into another trickle of tears.

Andy wasn't sure if he closed his eyes for a moment or an hour, but with a sudden start he was fully conscious.

"Incoming!" yelled Sam, as a red-hot cannonball sailed lazily overhead. The missile crashed against one of the rear walls. Instantly Shawnee and Mary disappeared out of sight, while Longholme hurried back to his own position.

"I can't see them!" Alistair yelled. "They've moved their cannon out of sight!"

Andy met no resistance from Ishbel as he struggled to his feet. He could see a distant cloud of smoke rising into the air. Ishbel did her best to support Andy, but the pain of standing upright showed on his face.

"...Must have someone spotting for them," he grunted.

Achnacon joined them at the rampart. "Not even your fast muskets can strike a concealed enemy," he said grimly. "Perhaps if some of us sallied out we may silence their cannon."

"That would be suicide!" exclaimed Alistair. "They will have infantry close by to protect the guns."

Another balloon of white smoke appeared above the eastern horizon. The boom of the cannon reached them as the projectile smashed into a wall yards from Longholme's position. Splinters of rocky shrapnel felled one of the *bodachs*. They watched as redcoat and tartaned youth alike carried him to the rear, using his own plaid as a stretcher.

"Somebody's gotta come up with something," said Sam, "before we all get turned to hamburger."

"We need elevation... Need tae get above them..."

"The northern slopes of the glen," said Alistair. "If somebody can get far enough up the hillside they might have a clear shot."

"Hell, man, you'd be adding a coupla hundred yards to the target. You'd need to be a marksman to make a shot like that."

"Indeed you would," said Alistair.

Another cannonball crashed against the fortified wall of one of the occupied cottages. The wall held, but the impact created fault lines in the drystone construction. Another direct hit would bring the building down on top of everyone inside. Achnacon rushed off to evacuate the cottage. From the cries within it was clear some of the people were close to panic.

"Unless anyone has a better idea," Alistair shouted above the din, "I would suggest Sam and myself get moving straightaway."

Shawnee stood to one side, her face a mess of conflicting emotions, her eyes large and tear-filled. Mary was more tactile, clinging to Alistair for long moments before she was gently eased aside.

The two men splashed across the burn and began to ascend the northern slopes. Before they'd climbed more than a hundred feet they heard a thunderous roar. They turned to see a long trail of smoke smashing into the burning cottage. The two men gazed frantically to the east, searching for the gun position, but could see only scarlet infantry idly watching the drama unfold. The smoke indicated where the cannon stood, but gun and gunners remained invisible.

"From the rate of fire they can only be using one cannon!" shouted Alistair.

"Guess we left 'em short-handed."

Alistair pointed to the plume of smoke, now drifting towards the east. "There's a wee hillock beside the path. They've positioned themselves behind it."

"Does that mean we can't get at the sons of bitches?"

"Not from this angle. Not unless we climb the ridge, and the range would be too great then."

"Well we gotta come up with something."

Alistair studied the slopes above them. "We might have a chance if we head east as we climb. With any luck they won't see us until it's too late."

Sam's eyes widened. This would take them closer to the infantry and further away from *Meall An Fhraoich*. In the village below smoke billowed from the stricken cottage. A woman was screaming like a wounded animal.

"Guess we don't have much choice."

As they ran obliquely up the hillside, red-hot missiles continued to rain down on the village, helping to mark the position of the artillery.

The blue uniforms of the gunners finally came into view when Sam and Alistair were six hundred yards east of *Meall An Fhraoich*, and four hundred feet above the floor of the glen. They moved more cautiously now, hugging the hillside, like stalkers trailing deer. The infantry filled the dead ground between them and the guns, all eyes drawn to the bombardment of the village.

Alistair came to a halt. "There are seven or eight of them serving the cannon," he said softly. "You can make out another one lying just this side of the hillock. He must be the spotter."

Sam gulped oxygen into his heaving lungs. "What range... y'reckon?"

Alistair squinted into the bright sunlight. "Six hundred yards. Maybe six hundred and fifty."

The American half sat, half collapsed on to the hillside. "Gonna take some shot... give me a minute... catch my breath."

The Highlander made himself busy preparing his rifle.

"Some shooting back there... I take it that's what y'were... out there in France...?"

Alistair looked at the American.

"...Y'were a sniper?"

Another projectile appeared from the far side of the glen, sailing westwards in a slow, looping trajectory. The noise of its impact was lost in the roar of the cannon.

Alistair brought his rifle up to his shoulder. "Whenever yourself is ready."

Sam cocked his rifle and adjusted the sights to six hundred yards. The blue-coated artillerymen looked like so many exotic ants. He watched as Alistair squeezed off his first shot, and heard him grunt with satisfaction as one of the ants fell to the ground.

As Alistair reloaded, Sam fired off three shots in rapid succession, the crude recoil of the weapon driving the butt hard into his shoulder. The rounds fell short, and to the left. He adjusted the sights to seven hundred yards and squeezed off another four rounds. When he looked again one of the gunners was down, and the others were frantically searching around them. The surrounding hills had thrown the harsh bark of the rifles from one to the other, disorientating those in the glen below. Some of the gunners made for the safety of the infantry, directly towards the two riflemen.

Sam blazed wildly at those who ran into the open, while Alistair calmly loaded and fired, dispatching any who remained by the cannon.

The nearest redcoats had spotted the men, and were lumbering towards them. Alistair scanned the area, making sure nothing in blue was left standing. Some of the infantry stopped to fire a volley, sending musket balls whizzing past their ears.

"Time we weren't here!" Alistair yelled.

Already Sam was scampering back along the hillside. He ran in a straight line, sweat streaming down his face. Musket fire suddenly broke out from the slopes to their right. His eyes stinging with salt, Sam saw a line of red uniforms spring from the heather six hundred feet above. A party of redcoats must have been sent to fire down upon the village. Musket balls now whistled past the two men from above as well as below. Sam kept his head low as he ran, presenting as small a target as possible. The settlement was only two hundred yards away now. Volley fire broke out from behind the walls as the defenders tried to cover their retreat. The noise on all sides was deafening.

Sam had no idea how he made the settlement in one piece. He knew Alistair was close behind as he dived over the wall. The Highlander hit the ground beside him, bringing rocks down on top of both men. The storm of musket fire didn't die down at once. The clamour subsided only gradually, finally dwindling away to a sporadic exchange of pot shots.

Bruised, and half out of his mind with fear, Sam was shaking with laughter when Shawnee, Mary and Achnacon found him.

It was only when he saw the blood on the ground, and the red trail that led out beyond the safety of the wall. Only when he realised Alistair was lying motionless beside him, that Sam's terrible laughter died away.

Chapter Twenty-Three

Alistair was carried to the drystone barn, where his blood-soaked clothing was peeled away. The dark arterial haemorrhage, which had sprung from two circular wounds in his back, had already subsided to a trickle. Neither ball had found an exit.

Mary sat by his side, gaunt and drained of emotion, as if she was fulfilling some melancholy destiny. There were tears in Achnacon's eyes. Shawnee, too, wept as she clung to Sam.

"I didn't know," he whispered. "He was behind me all the way. I swear to God, I didn't know."

Shawnee looked to the old Highlander. "Surely there's something we can do for him?"

Achnacon was lost for words. Unable to look Shawnee in the face he turned and made his way out of the barn.

Mary smoothed Alistair's hair, making soothing noises as she worked. His dark hair contrasted vividly with the waxen pallor of his face. The Americans looked helplessly at each other. Sam nodded towards the door, and without a word they left the girl on her own.

Outside, two of the cottages were ablaze, the flames devouring the accumulated soot of countless peat fires.

Achnacon had already passed on the news to Andy and Ishbel. Macmillan remained on his feet by the rampart, an array of muskets propped against the wall beside him. He tried to smile at the two Americans, but managed only a grimace.

"Cannae believe either of yez... made it back."

Sam shrugged, his face pale and drawn. He knelt on the ground and busied himself filling the empty magazines.

"Alistair had only five rounds left. Y'got about sixty for your buffalo gun. Don't suppose you're up to using either of them?"

Andy shook his head. "...Right arm's useless... couldnae hit a barn door... Ah can fire a musket wi' the left... Ishbel has tae load..."

The musket fire had now died away. Only the crackling of flames and the sound of weeping from one of the cottages broke the silence.

Andy peered over the wall, looking for signs that the enemy was abandoning the surrounding hills, but the scarlet uniforms remained in position. The soldiers seemed to be resting on their arms.

"Maybe they're waiting 'til darkness..." Andy began.

Ishbel made a little hissing noise and turned her head to the west. It was a few moments before the others heard it; carried on the westerly breeze, the distant tap of a drumbeat.

"Aw sweet Jesus," Sam groaned. "It must be that other buncha soldiers Longholme warned us about."

Achnacon, Longholme and Larachmor had also heard the approaching drumbeat, and sprinted along the adjoining passageway. Longholme shaded his eyes with his right hand, his face stained black by gunpowder. As they watched, the foremost ranks of the second column came into view. Their comrades on the hillsides cheered and waved their hats in salute.

" 'Tis most unjust that such gallantry should receive so cruel a reward," said Longholme. He bowed stiffly before his eclectic band of comrades. "I had prayed the second column might be intercepted, or dissuaded from its task. 'Twas but a faint hope. Gentlemen. My Ladies. It has been the most singular honour to have shared this day with you. Alas, I fear not even your extraordinary weapons will be sufficient to turn back the tide that now approaches."

"No, I won't believe it's all gonna be for nothing," Shawnee retorted. "We can't just stand here like... like..."

"...Hogs in a slaughterhouse?" Achnacon suggested with an ironic smile.

"How many muskets we got in total?" Sam asked.

"We have sixty now, with ammunition for all," replied Achnacon. "Sufficient for a small army, but the lefftenant has lost a full third of his force, and ourselfs are little better. We are in sore need of help from whatever quarter..."

From one of the cottages came the sound of women singing, their voices faint and hoarse, barely rising above the crackle of flames. Achnacon looked uncertainly at the others.

"Why not?" said Shawnee. "I know I'd rather be out here where I can see the shit coming than in there waiting for it to hit!"

Longholme studied the young woman, a smile on his face. It was the first time she had seen anything like warmth touch the ice of his eyes.

"Madame, 'tis my fervent wish that I may one day set eyes upon this city of angels." He turned to her fiancé. "Sir, I have known many a noble lady for whom a gentleman would draw blood, but I have known few for whom a gentleman would gladly shed his blood. I implore you, keep your sword arm free and your lady close at all times, she is a most extraordinary creature."

Sam would have been happier with Longholme's advice but for Shawnee's maidenly blush.

Achnacon spoke briefly to Larachmor. The old clansman looked dubiously at the two cottages, and then at the mass of scarlet assembling on the western horizon. He nodded in sharp agreement, and ran towards the nearest cottage, shouting at those inside. Old men and fair maidens alike clutched one another as they were assembled outdoors, the distant throb of the drum doing nothing to ease tattered nerves.

Achnacon and Larachmor arranged them inside the two fortified strongholds, and in a straggling line along the west-facing passageways. Most grew in confidence once they were given muskets.

"This is crazy," Sam grumbled. "I'm not sure what side of the wall I'd wanna be on when this bunch start firing."

"Way to be positive, Sam," replied Shawnee.

"Only thing I'm positive of; I wish to hell we'd gone to Vegas for our vacation."

She picked up one of the muskets, straining to bring the weapon up to her shoulder. "And miss all this? No sense of adventure, Kramer, that's your problem."

The Hanoverian reinforcements had come to a halt half a mile from *Meall An Fhraoich*. The drums fell silent as a little party of horsemen galloped to the front, where they were joined by a detachment from the southern slopes of the glen. Behind the battered walls people held their breath.

"That's right, it's not gonna be as easy as y'thought," Sam murmured. "Just turn around..."

The drum began beating again. To left and right, lines of scarlet figures peeled away from the main body and began to climb the slopes above the glen, joining their comrades already there.

"Dammit!" hissed Sam. "What is it with these guys? Are they too dumb to know when they've had their asses kicked?"

"They are brave soldiers, answering their orders," said Longholme with quiet pride.

Detachments of redcoats from east and west converged along both flanks of the glen, three hundred feet above *Meall An Fhraoich*. The remaining troops guarded the low ground on either side of the settlement.

Ishbel spoke hastily to her father, pointing at the narrow passageways they'd erected the previous day.

"Herself is right!" shouted Achnacon. "The lanes will afford protection from a crossfire!"

Clutching muskets and ammunition pouches, soldiers and clansmen, ancient warriors and young women alike, withdrew into the lanes that ran parallel with the glen. Those remaining in the cottages filled the nooks and crannies as best they could.

Sam lay on top of Shawnee, using his body as a shield. Easing himself down, Andy tried to do the same with Ishbel, and drew a stream of Gaelic indignation for his trouble. The soldier looked ruefully at her as she lay beside him.

"Ssshhh, *Ishbeal*, not to speak," he whispered.

The irony of the moment drew a poignant smile from her.

The roars of the N.C.O.s barking out the firing drill rang out from the slopes above. Moments later plunging volleys of musket fire fell upon the cottages and stoneworks of the settlement. Lead balls ricocheted this way and that. The screams of the women and children inside the cottages rose above the clamour. Longholme's force tried to return fire, but did little more than add to the din.

Andy yelled at Sam: "Northern side's the nearest... doing most damage... need tae hit them... get us outtae this crossfire..."

Sam twisted around so his mouth came up to Andy's ear. The soldier could barely hear him above the continuous volleying.

"I've taken a hit... Gonna have to do it on your own..."

The American pushed the rifle towards the soldier. Andy could see the wound in the back of Sam's upper thigh. The blood was trickling down either side of his leg. He looked up to reassure the American, but already Sam had crawled back on top of Shawnee.

Andy manoeuvred himself in short, painful jerks until he was squatting with his back against one wall, the barrel of the S.L.R. resting on the other. He felt as if a knife was embedded in his ribs.

The infantry were in two lines on the sloping hillside, one line twenty feet above the other. Holding the rifle between his knees, Andy cocked the weapon with his left hand, and adjusted the sights to one hundred yards. He should have been left with an easy shot, but he couldn't align and fire the rifle with one arm. He blasted off two rounds but his aim was so wild he may as well have used a musket.

Ishbel leaned over and removed the rifle from his grasp, pulling the butt into the crook of her shoulder, just as she'd been taught. Those gentle hands, which had wrought such beautiful torment only a few hours before, now held sudden death in their grasp. As she squeezed the trigger the nearest soldier was hurled violently back against the hillside. Ishbel, too, was jolted backwards by the recoil, the rifle clattering to the ground. She picked it up and fired again, but the shot was wildly off target. Her next shot went the same way. She now held the weapon as if it was about to explode in her hands.

Before she could fire again Andy grabbed the rifle and returned the butt to his right shoulder. He held the stock with his left hand and sighted along the barrel.

"Shoot!" he yelled at Ishbel.

Her eyes flashed in fierce indignation.

"Ah'll hold the thing… you pull the trigger!"

Above the din of the musketry he could hear Achnacon shouting at his daughter. At last she understood. Her finger curled around the trigger, squeezing gently. Instantly his red target was flung backwards. Andy moved his hand two inches to the left and stared down the barrel with his right eye:

"Shoot!"

Ishbel caressed the trigger, and a second round smashed into its victim. Like reapers they worked their way along the hillside, cutting down all who appeared in Andy's sights. Steadily the firing from the northern slopes slackened, until at last the survivors broke, abandoning the hillside to the dead and dying.

Safe from the deadly crossfire, the defenders could now shelter behind the south-facing walls. Gradually the volley firing from that direction also died out.

Achnacon and his *bodachs* let out a stream of wild yells. Andy and Ishbel sat side by side, still holding the rifle between them. The soldier looked at the twisted figures littering the hillside and for a moment he thought he was going to be sick.

Not everyone rose to their feet as the firing died away. Here and there the silence was torn by groans and cries. Sam flopped over onto his back as he tried to allow Shawnee up.

"I been shot in the freakin ass! Are y'happy now? Is this enough adventure for yuh?"

Laughing and crying at the same time Shawnee did her best to tend to Sam's wound. A ricochet had caught him in the lower buttock, penetrating two or three inches. He grumbled bitterly as he was helped to the makeshift hospital, where he was joined by a dozen others.

Longholme returned to the east-facing stronghold. Some of the newly armed clansfolk joined him there. Others abandoned their muskets and went off to check on their kinfolk. Achnacon made sure his wife and younger daughter had come through unscathed before he and Ishbel helped Andy shuffle back to the storehouse. The soldier was shocked at the number of misshapen lead balls littering the ground.

Achnacon held his daughter's face in his hands as he spoke to her. Even before he'd finished she had thrown her arms around her father, burying her face in his whiskers.

"Since herself was a tiny babe she has pulled against the reins," he explained. "But Achnacon could not be more proud if she was his son. Herself has shown courage worthy of her husband to be."

Andy was barely listening, his attention focused on events elsewhere.

" 'Twill be a grand day for Glen Laragain when your vision comes to pass," Achnacon went on, his arm around Ishbel. " 'Twill mark the end of this terrible chapter in our lifes."

"Aye, Ah'm sure it will, right enough," Andy murmured. He could see movement amongst the troops to the west, but the red uniforms remained in position on the southern slopes. Nowhere could he see signs of the enemy preparing to withdraw.

"What are they up tae? Why aren't they getting the hell outtae here? Ye'd think they'd've had enough by now."

Achnacon's bliss would not be ruffled. "Och, themselfs will have lost the stomach for a fight after this latest drubbing. Trust me, young Andy, I haff crossed swords with the red soldiers before. They are stout enough when the day goes well, but they will run as swift as any once the day has turned."

Longholme, however, was also concerned by what he saw. He sought out the old Highlander.

"My former comrades show no sign of relinquishing their ground. I fear their bold leader is not done with us yet."

"They have many wounds to lick. They are chust drawing breath before leaving the field."

Longholme shook his head irritably. "No, sir. I understand the workings of this man's mind. Captain Scott has been drawn into a contest in which the stakes, to him, are worth the lives of every one of his men."

Ishbel was busy changing Andy's bloody dressings. There were fresh tears on her face, and Macmillan realised the old warrior had misread the emotions that welled from his daughter. His little spitfire was simply traumatised by what she'd done. She couldn't even look Andy in the face.

Longholme pointed directly at the young soldier. "You, sir, have become the prize of this bloody affair. You and that devilish weapon you possess."

Ishbel had bound the bandages so tightly Andy had difficulty speaking.

"What?"

"Our enemy, sir, has seen what all of us here have seen. A company of resolute men armed with such muskets could defeat an army. And an army, by God..." His eyes flashed wildly at the thought. "...An army so equipped would be invincible! You, sir, hold in your hands the staff of Moses; the means by which the very world may be conquered!"

The little blood that remained in Andy's face drained away. By a supreme irony, in helping to drive off the soldiers he'd only multiplied their resolve. But worse still was the fear that had gnawed at him since Shawnee planted the seed in his mind; the fear that he would in some way become death, the destroyer of worlds.

"If Ah gave maself up... maybe they'll leave..."

Longholme had developed an ear for Andy's outlandish accent.

"On the contrary, sir. If you surrender yourself you sign the death warrant of every one of us here. Make no mistake of it; all that stands between each of us and the bayonet is your quick-firing musket!"

The troops positioned on the southern slopes were now being reinforced from the main body to the west. Another detachment from the east had begun to take up position along the northern hillsides, five hundred feet above the corpse-ridden slopes below. As this scarlet noose was being tightened around them, Andy was about to discover that no matter how bad things become they can always get worse.

To the east, from behind the hillock littered with the bodies of the artillerymen, a plume of smoke suddenly appeared. Moments later a cannonball whistled overhead and ploughed into the burn, throwing up a fountain of water and steam.

Andy slumped against the wall. He realised now would not be a good time to tell them his quick-firing musket had barely twenty rounds left.

Chapter Twenty-Four

Mary held Alistair's cold hands against her breast, trying to bring warmth back to them. She could feel his heart still beating faintly, drawing little gasps of air into his lungs.

She had dragged him between the stacks of straw before the storm of musket fire crashed down on *Meall An Fhraoich*. Now the cannonade had begun again, the cannonade that *Alasdair Mhor* had given his life trying to halt. She could feel warm tears trickling down her face. Warm tears from a frozen heart. Perhaps her soul was grieving. His face looked calm and peaceful, death banishing all cares before claiming its final dues. Still he held on, drawing just enough air into his body to remain alive. Perhaps each heart is allotted so many beats; no more, no less.

Beyond the walls of the barn, people were rushing this way and that. She felt detached from events outside, waiting for life to leave this stranger who'd come from nowhere to touch her very soul. She didn't hear the rustling of straw in the far corner of the barn, nor did she see the squat shape that crept from the shadows, like a hunter stalking its prey. She only knew someone was there when a foul, sweating hand was held over her mouth, and she was dragged into the depths of the building.

She knew it was *him*, even before he'd thrust himself on top of her, tearing at her dress, his face alight with expectation. The redcoat forced himself between her legs and scrabbled to unbuckle his belt. Mary clawed at his face, drawing red furrows down each cheek, before he grabbed her arms and pinned them to the floor. She could feel him poised at her opening, relishing the moment before he entered her. She screamed, adding her voice to the bedlam outside. The soldier leaned over her and licked her face, like a connoisseur savouring a rare dish. Mary screamed again, her eyes wide with despair.

As if in a dream she saw the ghost of Alistair appear above her. She watched as the ghost clenched its hands together and fell upon her attacker. The impact pushed the redcoat onto Mary. He withdrew to throw off Alistair's dead weight, and for a moment Mary's right leg was free. She kicked out and connected with something soft and fleshy. The soldier grunted. Mary kicked again and again until he rolled away clutching his groin.

She had no idea where she found the strength to pull Alistair clear of the barn. The noise of the musket fire was deafening. Lead balls whistled around her, making cracking noises as they ricocheted off the walls. As Mary dragged Alistair beneath a nearby wall a red-hot cannonball, sparks trailing behind it, crashed through the thatch of the barn. The roof above the entrance collapsed in a cloud of smoke and sparks. Flames took hold, blocking any escape. This last explosion brought Alistair round. He opened his eyes and looked at Mary. Her screams had called him back from the brink, but the last of his strength had gone and he was failing fast now. He managed to summon a faint smile, a last poignant flicker of what might have been.

The smile faded as his eyes glazed over.

In that instant Mary felt as if the ice in her heart had shattered and turned to glass. She held Alistair in her arms, rocking him to and fro as though he had fallen asleep.

The two Americans had returned to the storehouse before the musketry had broken out again. Sam walked now with the proud limp of a wounded warrior.

Andy handed him the self-loading rifle. "Just one mag left," he grunted.

The American nodded. "I hoped after that last bloody nose they mighta hauled ass outta here..."

Andy nodded towards Longholme, who'd returned with Achnacon to his own strongpoint.

"Big guy reckons they've got the hots... for the rifle..."

Everybody ducked as another missile boomed out from the west. The cannonball flew lazily over the settlement and landed on the far side of the burn.

"Guess we didn't put 'em out of action completely," said Sam.

"...They're no' gunners... just redcoats... making a lottae noise..."

A volley of musket fire broke out from the southern slopes of the glen. This was followed by a rolling fusillade from the soldiers stationed eight hundred feet above them on the northern slopes. Some of the newly armed clansfolk sheltered in the passageways from this fresh crossfire. Others joined Longholme and added their fire to his. At the storehouse Andy and Sam dropped below the rampart and pulled Shawnee and Ishbel down with them.

Andy gave Ishbel a reassuring squeeze with his good arm. Her tears had dried and she'd recovered some of her colour, but she was unnaturally subdued. She curled up beside him and closed her eyes as if they were two lovers on their own once again.

"Didnae matter much... us being here," Andy gasped. "...All gonnae end the same way..."

The firefight continued for some time without either side inflicting much in the way of casualties. The cannon added its booming roar to the thunder of the musket fire. Most of the cannon balls fell short, or flew dramatically over the settlement. One crashed through a nearby roof. Soon the building was alight, sending another black pall into the smoke-filled sky.

With a squeal of alarm Shawnee leapt up. "Oh my God! That's where we left Alistair and Mary!"

Sam struggled to his feet and hobbled after Shawnee as she ran towards the barn. He spotted Mary and Alistair beneath one of the walls, and ran on, taking Shawnee into the nearby cottage that was set up as a hospital.

"You stay here!" he yelled above the clamour. "I'll bring them in." He ran out and pulled Mary to safety. The woman screamed and kicked, only calming down when she recognised Shawnee. Sam hobbled out again and dragged Alistair into the cottage. After he'd pulled him into a corner he caught Shawnee's eye and solemnly shook his head. Oblivious to everything else, Mary returned to Alistair's side.

As soon as they'd made their way back to the fortress, Sam raised his head above the parapet to make sure neither of the main bodies was on the move. With five rounds left for Alistair's rifle, and twenty for Andy's, it was agreed he would only fire as a last resort. At one point Andy too began to rise to his feet, but he was firmly held back by Ishbel, her eyes closed as if she were asleep.

On the far side of the burning barn something had begun to emerge from a small window. The redcoat had found another exit from the building, but like Andy before him had become stuck fast in the tiny gap. He levered his arms against the stone blocks on either side and heaved with all his strength, but only jammed his pelvis tighter into the narrow opening.

He could feel his boots beginning to melt around his feet, his breeches smouldering, as the flames licked around his lower torso. With the desperation of the damned he clawed at the stone blocks until the walls on either side of him were red with blood.

The fire consumed everything within the barn. Flames leapt from every opening in the building, except one. If anybody heard the soldier's screams above the pandemonium they paid no attention.

The cannon and musket fire continued until it seemed the walls must come crashing down soon. The smoke from the gunfire mixed with the black palls from the burning cottages to create a sickening smog.

Without warning the firing stopped.

Ishbel was first on her feet. She looked over to where her father stood, smoke rising from his musket. Achnacon shrugged his shoulders. The cries of the women and children fell away, fearful of attracting attention in the sudden silence. Andy clawed his way up the wall. Along both hillsides the Hanoverian troops had risen to their feet, the smoke from that last fusillade drifting above their heads.

Ishbel saw them first. Her eyes wide with alarm, she pointed towards the southern ridge. Along the skyline, a thousand feet above the glen, a long line of figures had come into view. They were dark and featureless against the bright sky, but the precision with which they'd appeared made it obvious they were trained soldiers.

"Aw naw," Andy groaned. "Give us a break…"

Sam put his arms around Shawnee. "Bastards," he snarled at the distant shapes. "Bastards…"

On the opposite side of the glen a second line of soldiers appeared, silhouetted against the northern sky. Ishbel found her way under Andy's good arm. He could feel her shivering against him.

Behind them the soldiers on the northern slopes were on the move, running downhill towards the clachan. Moments later their comrades on the opposite slopes were careering down the hillside. To the east the troops had also broken into the charge, completing a three pronged advance on the village. A ragged volley crashed out from Longholme's position. Sam picked up Andy's S.L.R. and jammed the butt into his shoulder. He could hear his friend yelling at him, but he had already begun firing. Suddenly the barrel of the weapon was pushed skywards, and Andy was shouting into his face:

"They're no' charging... they're scattering!"

Beside him Ishbel and Shawnee were jumping up and down in each other's arms. At the other stronghold, redcoats and clansmen, men and women, were hugging each other, their muskets raised in triumph. Only then did Sam realise that attacking *Meall An Fhraoich* was the last thing on the redcoats' minds. Those running from the east were racing past the barricades, without even glancing at the defenders. The soldiers on the hillsides had veered to the west as they ran downhill. Already the column that had plodded into the glen from the west had disappeared over the horizon, fleeing towards the safety of far away Loch Eil. From the ridges high above Glen Laragain the new arrivals were pouring down the hillsides. A chorus of blood-chilling roars rang out from both sides of the glen.

"Who the hell are they?" Sam shouted.

"*Camshron! Clann Camshron!*" screamed Ishbel.

"What did she say?"

"Think she said Camerons," Andy yelled back. Then he realised what he'd said. "...Camerons...?"

The vanguard had already reached the floor of the glen. They were no longer featureless figures, but a band of ragged warriors, their loins and torsos barely covered in threadbare tartan, their broadswords held high in the air. Some had already caught up with the tail enders. Swords gleamed like butchers' cleavers in the pale sunshine. An overweight soldier was brought to earth by the slash of a blade. A screaming flurry of blows followed; the clansman moved on, his sword red to the hilt.

One after another, fleeing soldiers were hacked to the ground. One body of redcoats dropped their weapons and threw their arms in the air. The screaming swordsmen ran past, hunting down escapees. A second group threw down their weapons and were also bypassed. Others fled westwards, pursued by swarms of red broadswords. Within minutes hunters and hunted had disappeared beyond the horizon.

Andy, Shawnee and Sam looked at each other as though they'd glimpsed the hounds of hell. Sam was clutching the rifle so tightly his knuckles had turned white.

"Who did y'say those guys were?"

"Camerons," Andy breathed.

Women and children began to emerge from the cottages, blinking in the afternoon light, their faces grimy and tear stained. As soon as Ishbel's mother and sister appeared she ran over to them. Breathlessly she told her family what had happened. The news spread like wildfire. Some people dropped to their knees, others held each other and wept.

Sam scratched the back of his head. "Aren't the Camerons supposed to be somewhere else fighting this bad-assed Cumberland guy?"

"Culloden," Shawnee put in. Her euphoria had subsided as soon as she'd seen the first redcoat being hacked to pieces. "The Camerons shoulda been at Culloden today with the rest of Prince Charlie's army."

"Y'don't suppose them being here's got something to do with us, do yuh?" asked Sam.

"Duh," she replied, her face pale and mocking.

A small body of Highlanders approached the fortified village. While they were still some distance away Achnacon scrambled over the wall and ran to meet them. He knelt before one of the men.

"Y'don't suppose one of those guys is Bonnie Prince Charlie?" Shawnee wondered, unconsciously touching her hair.

Sam was still trying to make sense of what had happened. "D'y'suppose Jamie and the others reached Culloden before the battle and brought these guys back?"

Andy shook his head. "No' enough time... tae reach there and back..."

Achnacon brought the new arrivals to Longholme's fortress. The clansfolk bowed and curtsied. Even Longholme lowered his head sharply.

Shawnee was straining at the leash. "It'd be rude not to go over there and introduce ourselves, don't y'think?"

Now that the crisis was over Andy needed all his strength to remain on his feet. "You two go on over... Ah'll bide here a wee while..."

Shawnee looked at the soldier and smiled that little secret smile of hers. She caressed his lifeless right arm. "On second thoughts, I think Sam and I will just bide here a wee while with you."

Two of the Highlanders broke away from the crowd and made their way along the battered passageway to the smaller fortress. They were indistinguishable from the ragged warriors who'd roared down the hillsides only minutes before. They were only a few yards away when Macmillan recognised the red hair and ginger stubble of the foremost clansman.

"Jamie…"

"How's it goin', Corp?" said Macsorley, grinning. He was about to embrace his N.C.O. when he saw the bandages around his chest. "Ah see you guys've been through the wars."

"Yeah, tell me about it," grumbled Sam.

"It's good to see yourselves again," said the other clansman.

"Colin?" Shawnee put in. "My God, is that you under there?"

The young Highlander had acquired a phillamhor since he'd left Glen Laragain three days earlier. As Shawnee threw her arms around him a pink glow appeared through the grime on his face.

"Oh Colin, I don't know how to tell y'this… I'm so sorry…"

Gently he pulled himself free. "It's all right, I know about himself. If you could tell me where he is."

Shawnee looked towards the cottage that had become a front-line hospital. "Mary was with him right 'til the end. She's still there now. We'll come along with you if y'like."

Colin shook his head. "That's all right. I'll be fine, thank you."

He seemed oddly composed as he made his way towards the cottage.

"How'd he know about Alistair?" Sam asked.

Jamie shook his head in wonder. "It was the weirdest thing. Last night it was, he woke up… we've been sleeping rough, like… and he was in tears. Ah mean great big tears rolling down his face. He told me that Alistair had come tae him and told him… get this now… he'd told him that he was tae be the last one laid tae rest, that he'd be proud tae stand his watch over the others."

"What the hell is that supposed to mean?"

Jamie shrugged his shoulders. "No idea, but the wee guy knew his brother wasnae gonnae make it."

Shawnee sniffled softly. "D'you think maybe we should go and see if he's all right?"

"He'll be fine," said Jamie. "He's grown up quite a bit these past couple of days."

"Not too much, I hope," she murmured.

"Who's the guy everybody's bowing to?" Sam asked.

"That's Locheil; chief of the Camerons."

"Cameron of Locheil," Shawnee whispered. "My God…"

Andy nodded towards the eastern entrance to the glen. "…Where's Laurel and Hardy?"

Jamie shook his head in disgust. "Half a day's march away. They couldnae keep up, so they were left behind. With any luck they'll wander intae a redcoat patrol. Probably the best thing that could happen tae the Jacobite cause."

"Not if they've still got the jimpy…"

Jamie shrugged his shoulders.

"So where did y'meet those other guys anyhow?" asked Sam.

"Locheil's and Keppoch's men? They're something else, aren't they? We met them yesterday morning at Invergarry. It's as well Rhona was there, they were all for taking no chances and slitting our throats."

"…What were they doing at Invergarry yesterday? Forty miles from Inverness… They shouldae been at Culloden…"

Jamie smiled knowingly. "D'ye remember the wee laddies Achnacon sent tae Inverness? It seems by the time they reached the Jacobite camp their story had become a wee bit garbled."

"Y'mean like Chinese whispers?"

"Aye, something like that. The story they got was; the redcoats were gonnae put the whole of Lochaber tae the sword… Camerons, MacDonnells, Stewarts… Waste the whole country, ye know? So the local boys decided that wasnae gonnae happen, and they just upped and came home again."

"Leaving their buddies to be slaughtered at Culloden?"

The young soldier scratched the back of his head. "Well, no, not exactly. Ye see, there's been messengers galloping between us and the main force. It seems Lord George Murray convinced Charlie not tae risk a battle, but instead tae follow the Lochaber clans towards the west coast."

Andy groaned. "Ye mean the Jacobite army's on its way here; tae Lochaber?"

"Who's Lord George Murray?" asked Sam.

Shawnee clapped her hands with excitement. "We've done it! We've done it. *Oh my God!*"

"Who the hell is Lord George Murray?"

"He's the equivalent to these guys of Robert E. Lee." Shawnee's eyes were wide with wonder. "To these people, it's like we've prevented Gettysburg."

Ishbel had returned to Andy's side, attracted by the rising excitement. Her intended, however, remained stubbornly unaffected by it all.

"If the Jacobite army's heading west... towards Lochaber... then where's Cumberland...?"

The expression on Jamie's face was answer enough. Andy groaned again. "Aw Gawd Almighty... if Charlie's on his way here... they'll no' be far behind..."

"Bonnie Prince Charlie's on his way here?" Shawnee's eyes sparkled at the thought. Ishbel looked to Jamie for a translation. Her eyes nearly popped from her head at what she was told.

"What Ah don't understand," Andy persisted, "is why the rest o' the army... followed the Lochaber clans west."

Jamie was caught between the ladies' excitement and his N.C.O.'s relentless interrogation.

"It's that Chinese whispers thing again," he replied, smiling at Shawnee and Ishbel.

"What d'ye mean?"

"Well, it's like, they were led tae believe that fresh forces had landed on the west coast, with amazing new weapons and everything."

Sam nodded his head. "That's why they've moved to the west. To link up with the troops they think've landed here... Boy, are they gonna be sore when they find out."

"That's what Ah thought," said Jamie, "so Ah had tae tell them there was only a handful of us, like. They didnae seem all that bothered. They were more interested in these weapons of ours."

"How the hell did y'explain them?"

Jamie glanced apprehensively at his N.C.O. "Well, obviously Ah had tae tell them about you, like."

"What did ye have tae tell them about me?" said Andy uneasily.

Jamie squirmed. "Ye know? About yer visions and that... Ah mean, if Ah couldnae get through tae Achnacon Ah was hardly gonnae get through tae that lot. Oh, and by the way, if anybody asks, you're a Captain. Ah didnae think they'd be impressed by a buckshee corporal."

Andy groaned horribly. "Why d'ye keep doing this tae me?"

"We haven't really changed anything then, have we?" Sam put in quietly. "I mean, if this bad-ass duke is on his way here with his whole Limey army then what the hell have we achieved?"

"Are you for real?" said Shawnee. "Why don't you ask these people what they think we've achieved today."

"Ah can think of a couple of thousand empty graves on Culloden Moor," said Jamie.

"Yeah, for now."

"They're alive Sam, and so are we. For now that's gotta be enough."

"…And tomorrow?"

"Tomorrow we do what it takes. It's all any of us can do."

"But what if it's not enough? What if no matter what we do it all turns into the same rotten crap heap? The same mistakes… The same red sky over this goddamn glen?"

"All we can do is flap our wings," said Shawnee. "If we can beat up a big enough storm, then who knows. As long as we're alive anything's possible."

Before the end of the day some of the younger children began to make a game of the fear they'd so recently felt. They collected some of the misshapen musket balls that littered the ground, as if they were gathering hazelnuts. They ran between the walls, throwing the lead bullets at each other, making little popping noises with their mouths.

The game came to an untidy end as one after another the children came to a halt at the rear of the burnt-out barn. Something was protruding from the tiny window. Something that looked and smelt like the front portion of a barbecued calf, but also had the shape of a man.

None of the children could say for certain what it was, but it made a grand target for their musket balls.

Epilogue

He awoke with a start, knowing instantly that something was wrong. The air was so quiet that nature itself seemed to be holding its breath. Clutching his rifle he peered over the lip of the trenchworks into the valley below. He could see fresh fields of green and gold, bordered by tangled hedgerows. He had no recollection of arriving in an untouched sector of the front. Seeing an area so pure and unsullied had always delighted and then saddened him, knowing it would soon be poisoned forever.

The landscape was familiar to him. He knew every hillock and hollow, but in his mind's eye he could see it, not draped in a living carpet of yellow and green, but lifeless and shell-cratered, like the surface of the moon. As he tried to draw the memory from his mind the image faded as though it had been no more than imagination.

The sky was a perfect shade of blue, in which clouds drifted by like ancient galleons. It reminded him of spring days spent fishing the hill lochs of home, robbing the azure waters of their golden treasure.

Everything was eerily quiet. The usual intermittent firing had died away. Even the rumble of guns to the east had fallen silent. He scanned the earthworks about him, and for the first time realised he was on his own. To left and right there was no sign of friend or foe. He also noticed the earthworks were curiously overgrown, as if they hadn't known shot, or shell, or clambering boots in a very long time. He felt no sense of anxiety or alarm. Something had happened which he couldn't bring to mind, as if he was trying to recollect a brain injury with that part of the brain that had been injured.

There were figures by the hedgerow a hundred yards to the east. Odd he hadn't noticed them before. There were a dozen or so, each of them familiar in some way. As he looked closer he realised the figures were entangled in the thorns, as though they were caught in a line of barbed wire. They writhed and twisted, trying to free themselves, but only succeeded in ensnaring themselves further. The image stirred a dark impression in his mind; a sense that something terrible had taken place here, something that remained unfinished.

He scrambled out of the earthworks with the assuredness of one acting out a dream. As he rose to his feet he realised he hadn't been lying behind earthworks at all, but in a natural hollow, on the edge of a wood. What he'd thought was a rifle was no more than a walking stick. His khaki uniform the simple tweed of home.

He could feel the warm sun on his face as he strode across the fields. Around him insects buzzed and birds sang. In the distance he could hear a child shouting excitedly in French. A dog barked in reply.

It didn't take him long to reach the hedgerow. He could see only one figure there now, tangled in the thorns like a soldier caught in a barbed mesh. The figure was perfectly still, as though he knew he was about to be released.

Alistair was not in the least surprised to find he was looking at his own lifeless face. Nor was he surprised at the expression of peace he saw there. These green French fields, where corn could now be harvested instead of men, these fields could at last be left unguarded.

Alistair would stand his watch amongst the hills of home.

About this Story

The Last Sunset was conceived amongst the empty glens and ruined townships of Lochaber. The events of the eighteenth and nineteenth centuries still scar this land, and indeed continue to scar the psyche of many of the older inhabitants.

There are glens within ten miles of Fort William where you can walk all day without seeing another living soul. Once heavily populated, these places have long been left to the wind and heather.

The past hangs heavy here, and occasionally - just occasionally - you can sense moments from those days. A brief scent of peat smoke in a ruined settlement. The tang of manure amidst the green swathes of a shieling that haven't seen cattle in two hundred years.

Indeed, Sam's tale from Gettysburg is closely based on the story told to me by a rational, well-educated woman who watched the spectres of two ragged clansmen materialise around her campfire by the shores of a remote loch some years ago.

The world is dotted with places around which the wheel of history briefly turned: Stalingrad. Waterloo. Gettysburg. The skies above England in 1940. Likewise for a few months in 1745/46, the Highlands occupied one of those crossroads of history.

Who knows what kind of world we would inhabit had events transpired differently here?

And on some other shore perhaps lies Tir Nan Og
The land of the Gael.
Where Highland hills no longer mourn their brood
Of empty ruined glens.
Where bleating sheep no longer rule where Highland hearts
Have tried and failed.
And where at last Culloden's graves
Are empty of their Highland dead.

— Bob Atkinson, Fort William, May 2012

About the Author

I was born and raised in the district of Lochaber, in the Western Highlands of Scotland. At the age of seventeen the age old curse of the Highlands, lack of work and opportunity, forced me to take the same military path taken by many of my forebears.

While serving with the army in Northern Ireland I met my future wife; the lovely and diminutive Ruby, inspiration for at least one of the female characters in *The Last Sunset*.

After leaving the army I moved to Belfast where together Ruby and I lived through many of the worst years of the Troubles.

Eventually, very much the worse for wear, we brought our young family of three home to the Highlands.

Here I worked for many years in the civil service, retaining some sanity by fleeing into the wilderness as often as possible. Eventually I was rescued by early retirement.

The lochs, hills and glens of Lochaber are like balm to the soul, and have inspired storytellers for as long as people have lived in these glens.

The Last Sunset is simply the latest in a long line of tales inspired by this ancient land.

Influences and Recommendations

I will never forget, as a young child, being scared witless by *Quatermass and the Pit* on my parents' spluttering black and white TV set. Kids who are used to shoot-em-up computer games, or the visceral delights of films such as *Saw*, would find *Quatermass* as frightening as an episode of the *Teletubbies*. But to my generation this was ground-breaking science fiction.

Then came *Doctor Who*, with its cardboard sets and tinfoil aliens - light years away from the subtle story lines and clever nuances of the current *Doctor* series.

Star Trek. The Twilight Zone. The Outer Limits. Programmes became more sophisticated, ideas more original and thought provoking.

Each new concept nourished our imagination and broadened our young minds. As I grew older I read Isaac Asimov and Robert Heinlein, Arthur C Clarke and the beautifully expressive Ray Bradbury. The wonderfully quirky Douglas Adams. Giants in their field.

Over the years there have been so many great books. So many amazing films. Yet still, in the dead of night, when I think of that creaky, black and white alien craft buried deep in that pit in London the covers become pulled around me just that little bit tighter.

Anyone interested in exploring the history of the Highlands will find John Prebble's trilogy *Glencoe, Culloden and The Highland Clearances* an excellent place to start. For the more classically minded Robert Louis Stevenson's *Kidnapped* retains a power and freshness that is extraordinary for a book written in the nineteenth century.

Gaelic words and phrases feature prominently in *The Last Sunset*. My publisher, Tim Taylor, and I were conscious that too many obscure and unreadable words might discourage readers unfamiliar with the language. However this was the language spoken throughout the Highlands during this period, and although Gaelic has suffered a long and steady decline the last few decades have seen something of a resurgence. This is thanks in no small measure to musical groups such as Capercaillie and Runrig.

Anyone interested in what a fusion of modern rock and roll and traditional Gaelic music would sound like should go to YouTube and listen to some of Runrig's unique music. *Abhainn An T-Sluaigh* or *Air A'Chuan* would be a good introduction to this underrated band.

In the end, I suppose, this fusion of influences; the past and the present, ancient and modern, which helped to create the music of Runrig, also found form in its own small way in *The Last Sunset*.

Also from Greyhart Press

The Legends of Light by Gill Shutt

A high fantasy saga told in six poems

"... very refreshing, a completely different style and format."—SF Book Reviews

"... a cross between Beowulf and Lord of the Rings."— amazon.com review

Available now as an eBook RRP $2.99/ £2.00 (Kindle, Nook, iTunes, Kobo, Sony Reader), and paperback from Amazon $5.99 / £4.50

The Reality War by Tim C. Taylor

In 1992, Radlan Saravanan runs a small business out of a Tudor cottage in the sleepy English village of Elstow. But Radlan was born in 2951, and when he falls in love with a local girl, he has to choose between running from his own people and condemning his lover to die.

He makes *the wrong choice.*

"The concept of time-travel, paradox and alternate reality has always been mind-blowing and now a mind-blowing novel to live up to it. Hollywood check this out!"—Bookish Things

Book1 available now as a Kindle eBook RRP $0.99/ £0.77, and paperback from Amazon $9.99 / £7.99. Book 2 out now!

About Greyhart Press

Talk to us on Twitter (@GreyhartPress) or email
(editors@greyhartpress.com)

www.greyhartpress.com

Greyhart Press is an indie publisher of quality genre fiction: fantasy, science fiction, horror, and some stories that defy description.

We publish eBooks through online retailers. That's great for us and for you, because we don't have to worry about all that costly hassle of printing and distribution. Instead we can concentrate on finding great stories AND giving some away for free! Visit our free story promotion page for no-strings-attached free downloads.

But we love print too, so we're bringing our stories to paperback, starting spring 2012.

Our motto is *Real Stories for Real People!* What's that about, then? It's about the Real Story Manifesto (credit where it's due: this is inspired by the Agile Software Development Manifesto).

We seek to tell great stories by writing them and helping others to find them.

Through this (highly enjoyable work) we have come to value:

Writing clarity over writing style.

Plots that move over plots that are clever.

Characters who make hard choices over characters who observe interesting events.

A reader left satisfied over a critic left impressed.

That is, while there is value in the items on

the right, we value the items on the left more.

Do You want free eBooks?

If so, our READ... REVIEW... REPEAT... promotion is for you. Follow @GreyhartPress or see our website for more details, even if you aren't on Twitter. You could qualify to read all our eBooks for free!

If you enjoyed this book, please consider leaving an online review at Amazon or elsewhere (you don't need to have purchased this book from Amazon to write a review there, but you do need an Amazon account). Even if it's only a line or two, it would be very helpful and would be very much appreciated.

Thank you.

Printed in Great Britain
by Amazon.co.uk, Ltd.,
Marston Gate.